image comics presents

THE WALKING DEAD™

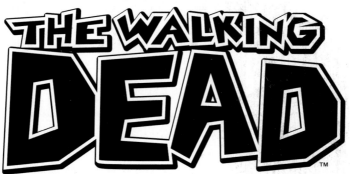

ROBERT KIRKMAN
CREATOR, WRITER

CHARLIE ADLARD
PENCILER, INKER

CLIFF RATHBURN
GRAY TONES

RUS WOOTON
LETTERER

CHARLIE ADLARD
&
CLIFF RATHBURN
COVER

IMAGE COMICS, INC.

Robert Kirkman - Chief Operating Officer
Erik Larsen - Chief Financial Officer
Todd McFarlane - President
Marc Silvestri - Chief Executive Officer
Jim Valentino - Vice-President

ericstephenson - Publisher
Joe Keatinge - PR & Marketing Coordinator
Branwyn Bigglestone - Accounts Manger
Sarah deLaine - Administrative Assistant
Tyler Shainline - Production Manager
Drew Gill - Art Director
Jonathan Chan - Production Artist
Monica Howard - Production Artist
Vincent Kukua - Production Artist

www.imagecomics.com

THE WALKING DEAD, VOL. 11: FEAR THE HUNTERS. First Printing. Published by Image Comics, Inc. Office of publication: 2134 Allston Way, 2nd Floor, Berkeley, California 94704.

PRINTED IN CHINA

ISBN: 978-1-60706-181-6

International Rights Representative: Christine Jensen (christine@gfloystudio.com)

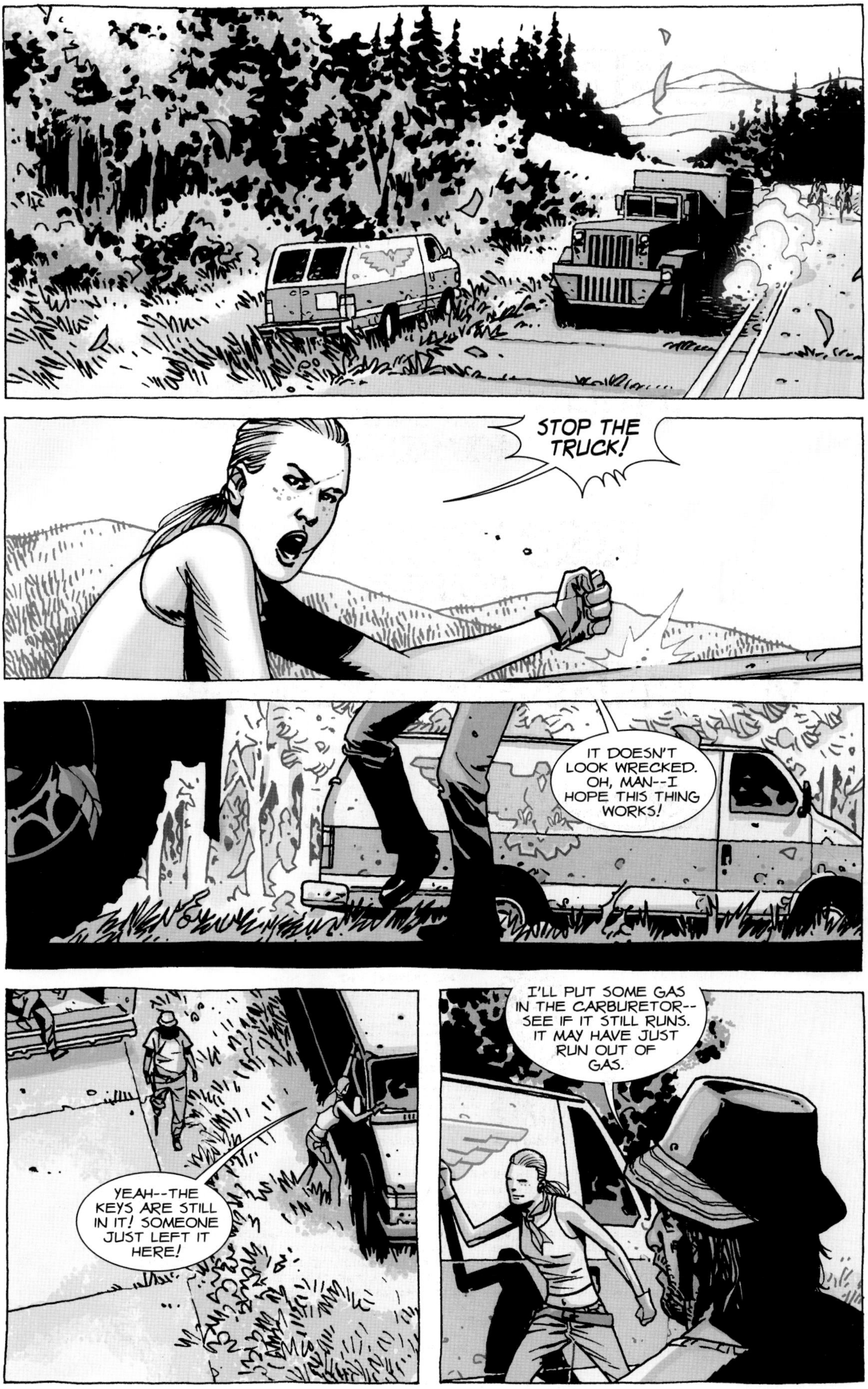
STOP THE TRUCK!
IT DOESN'T LOOK WRECKED. OH, MAN--I HOPE THIS THING WORKS!
YEAH--THE KEYS ARE STILL IN IT! SOMEONE JUST LEFT IT HERE!
I'LL PUT SOME GAS IN THE CARBURETOR--SEE IF IT STILL RUNS. IT MAY HAVE JUST RUN OUT OF GAS.

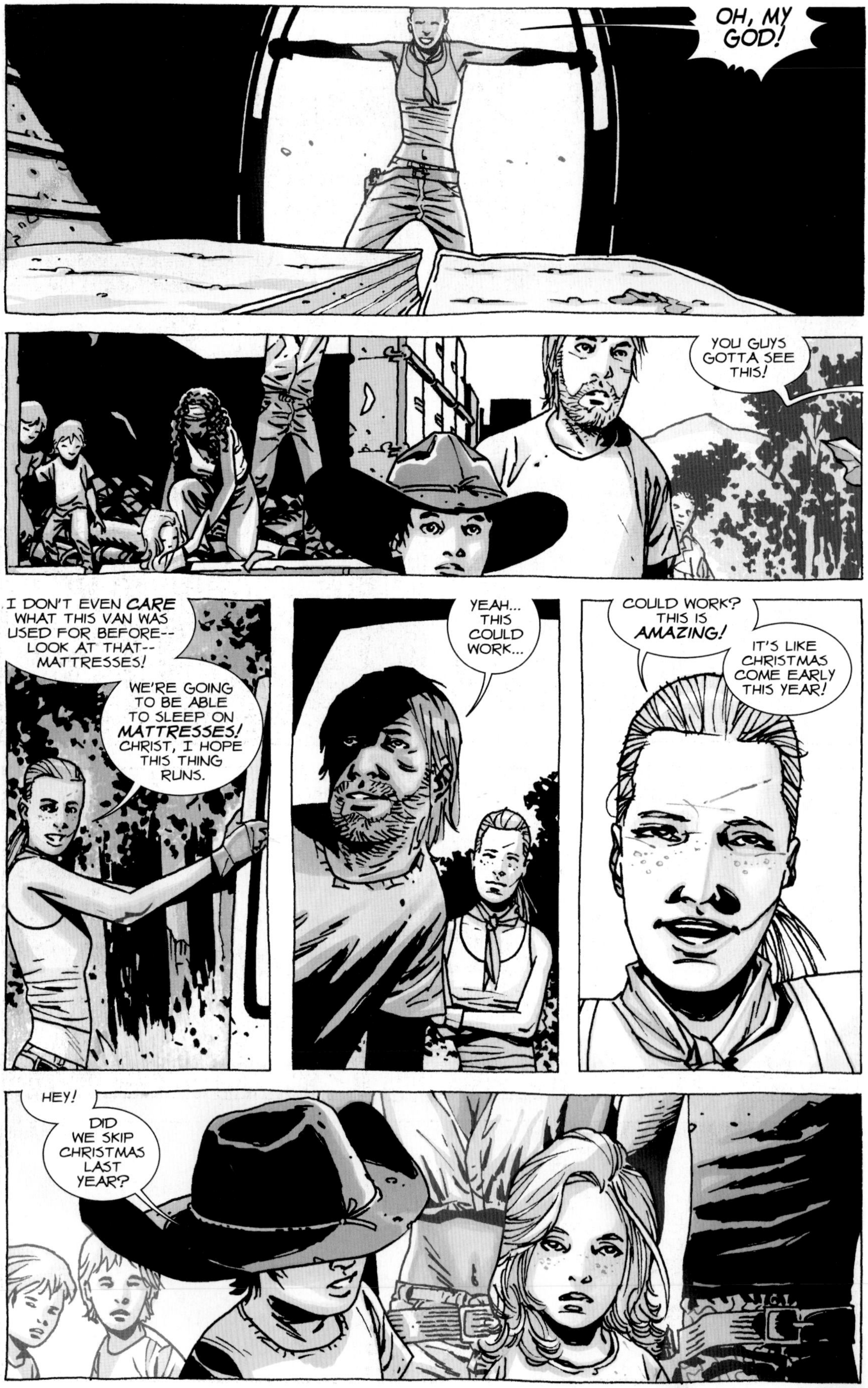
OH, MY GOD!
YOU GUYS GOTTA SEE THIS!
I DON'T EVEN CARE WHAT THIS VAN WAS USED FOR BEFORE-- LOOK AT THAT-- MATTRESSES!
WE'RE GOING TO BE ABLE TO SLEEP ON MATTRESSES! CHRIST, I HOPE THIS THING RUNS.
YEAH... THIS COULD WORK...
COULD WORK? THIS IS AMAZING!
IT'S LIKE CHRISTMAS COME EARLY THIS YEAR!
HEY!
DID WE SKIP CHRISTMAS LAST YEAR?

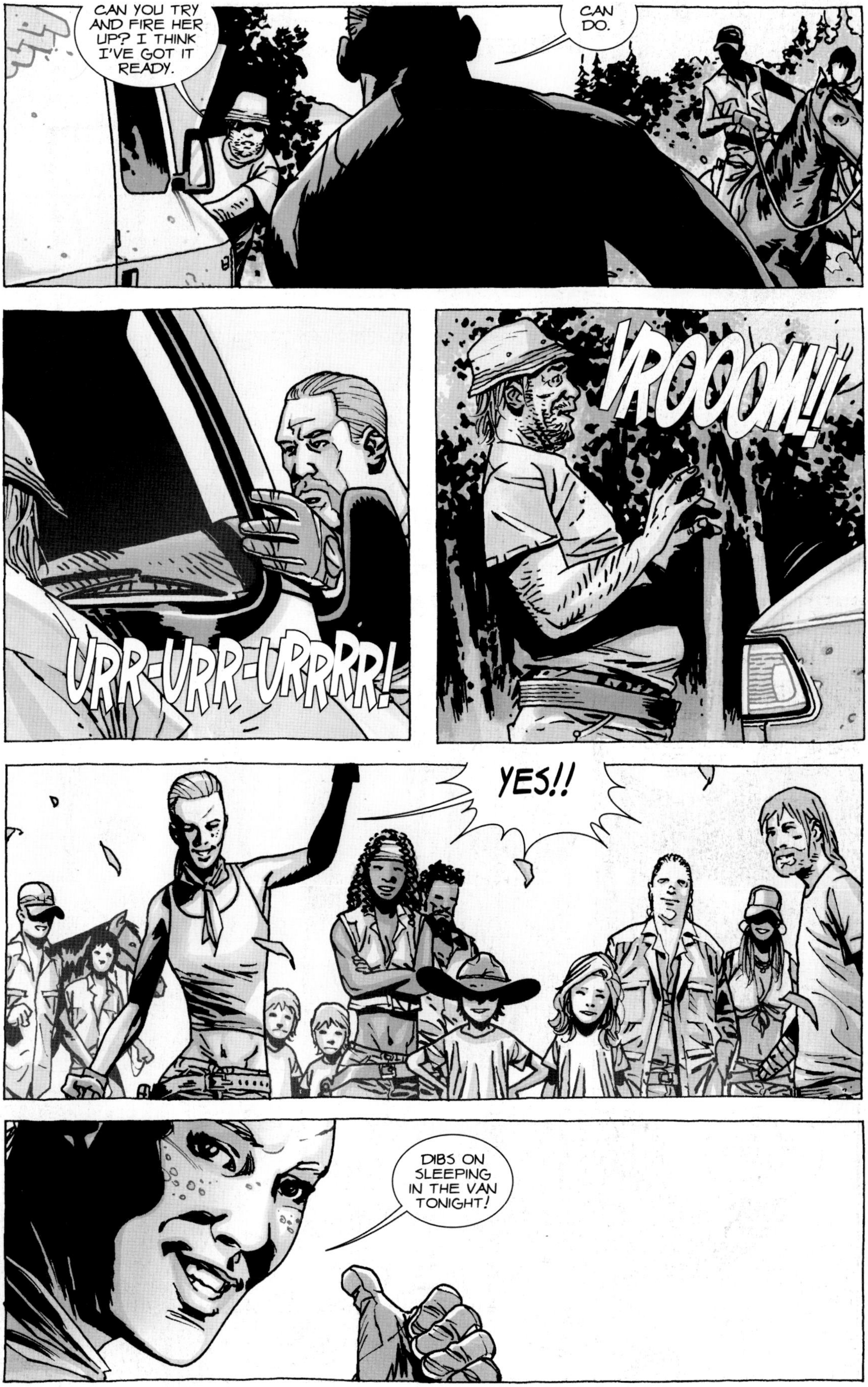

CAN YOU TRY AND FIRE HER UP? I THINK I'VE GOT IT READY.
CAN DO.
URR-URR-URRRR!
VROOOM!!
YES!!
DIBS ON SLEEPING IN THE VAN TONIGHT!

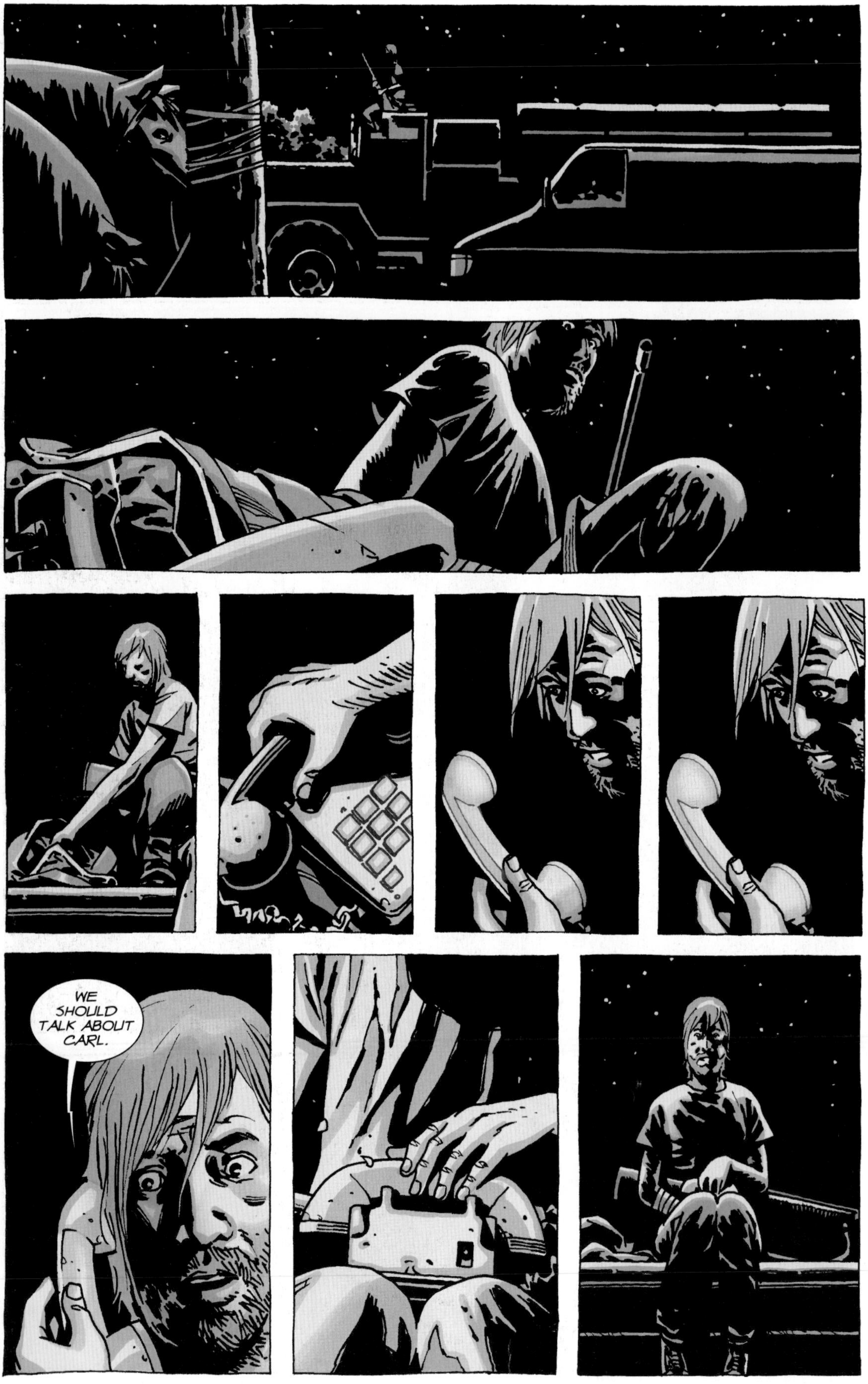
WE SHOULD TALK ABOUT CARL.

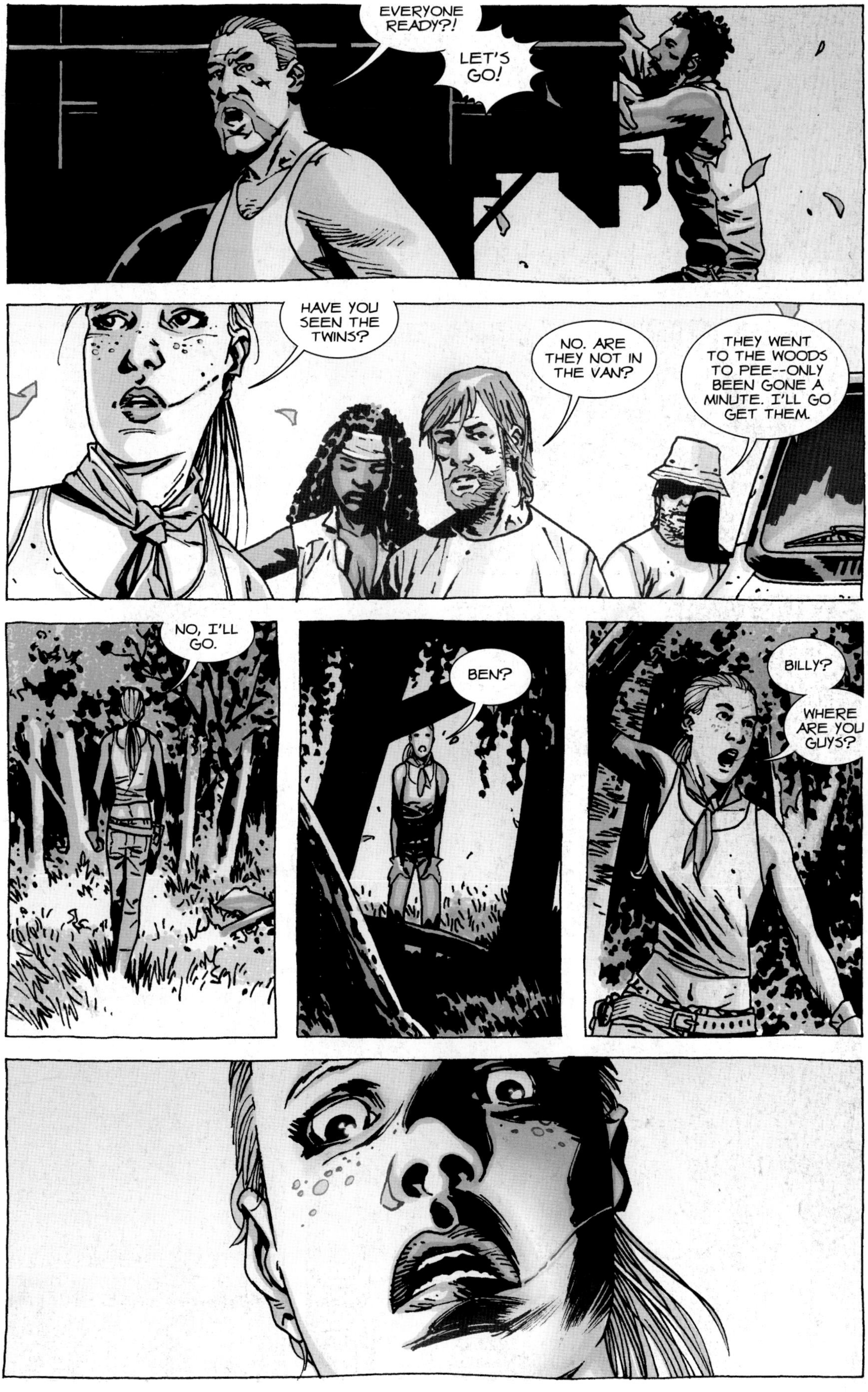
EVERYONE READY?!
LET'S GO!
HAVE YOU SEEN THE TWINS?
NO. ARE THEY NOT IN THE VAN?
THEY WENT TO THE WOODS TO PEE--ONLY BEEN GONE A MINUTE. I'LL GO GET THEM.
NO, I'LL GO.
BEN?
BILLY?
WHERE ARE YOU GUYS?

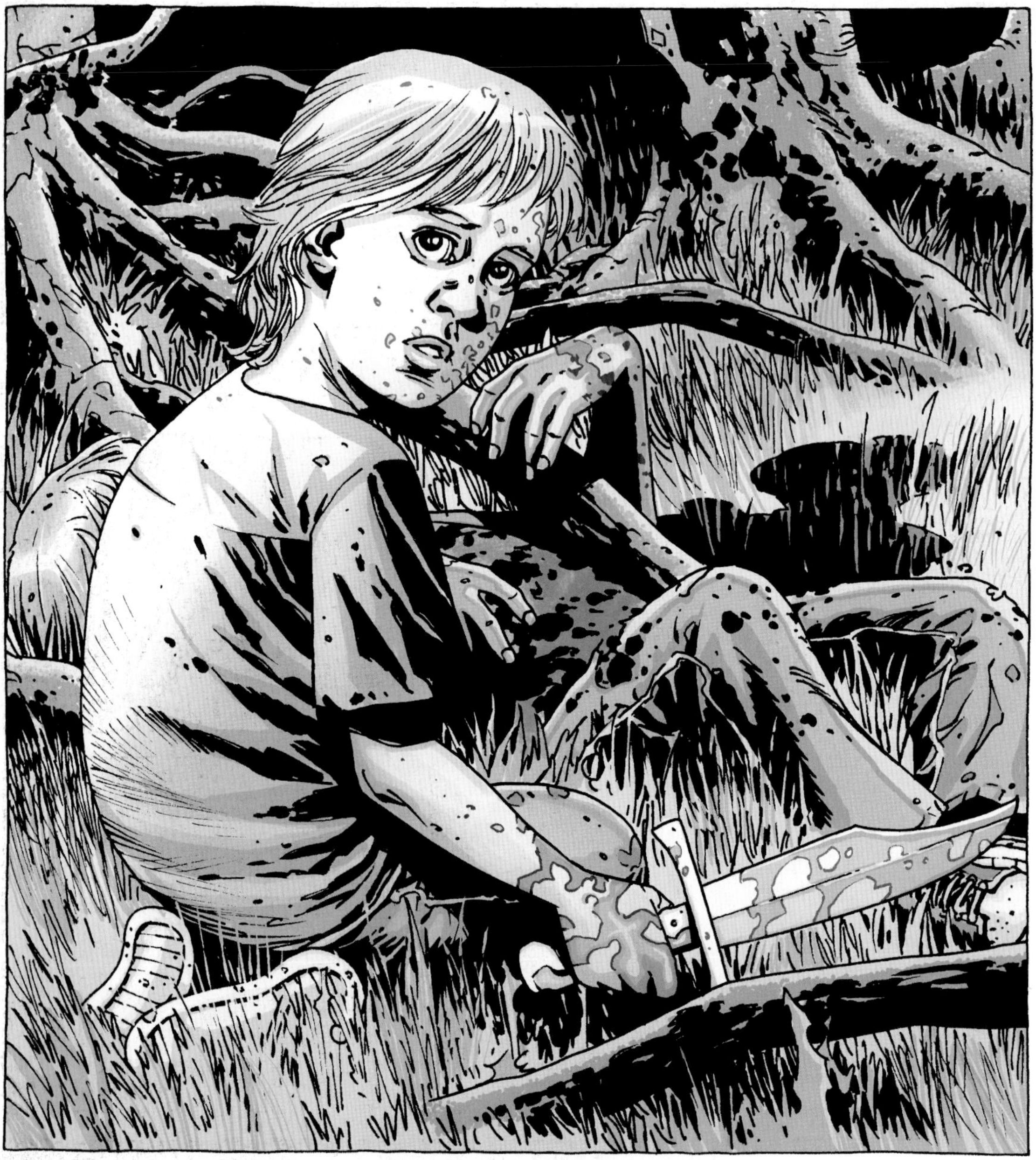

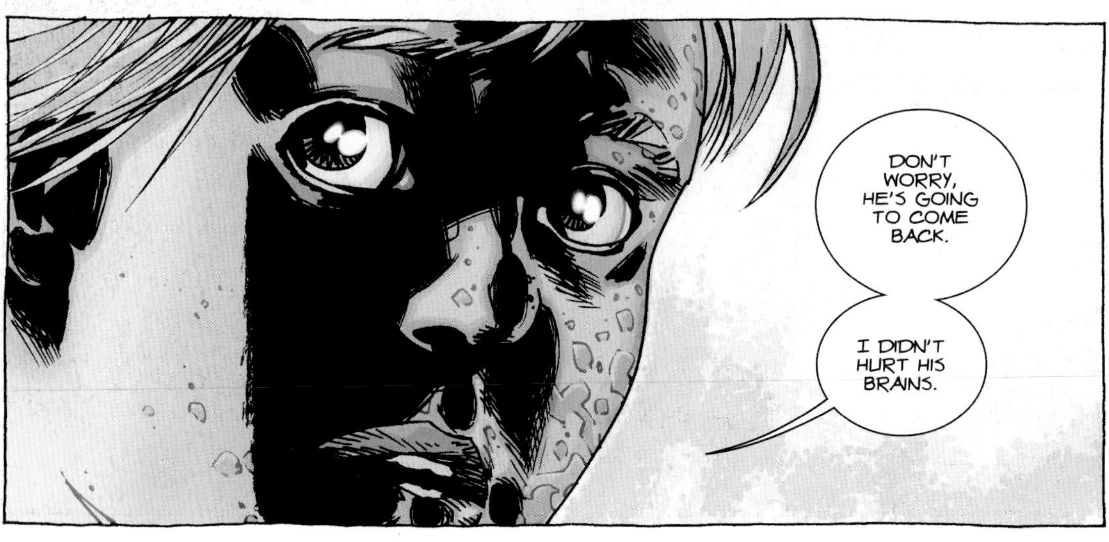
DON'T WORRY, HE'S GOING TO COME BACK.
I DIDN'T HURT HIS BRAINS.

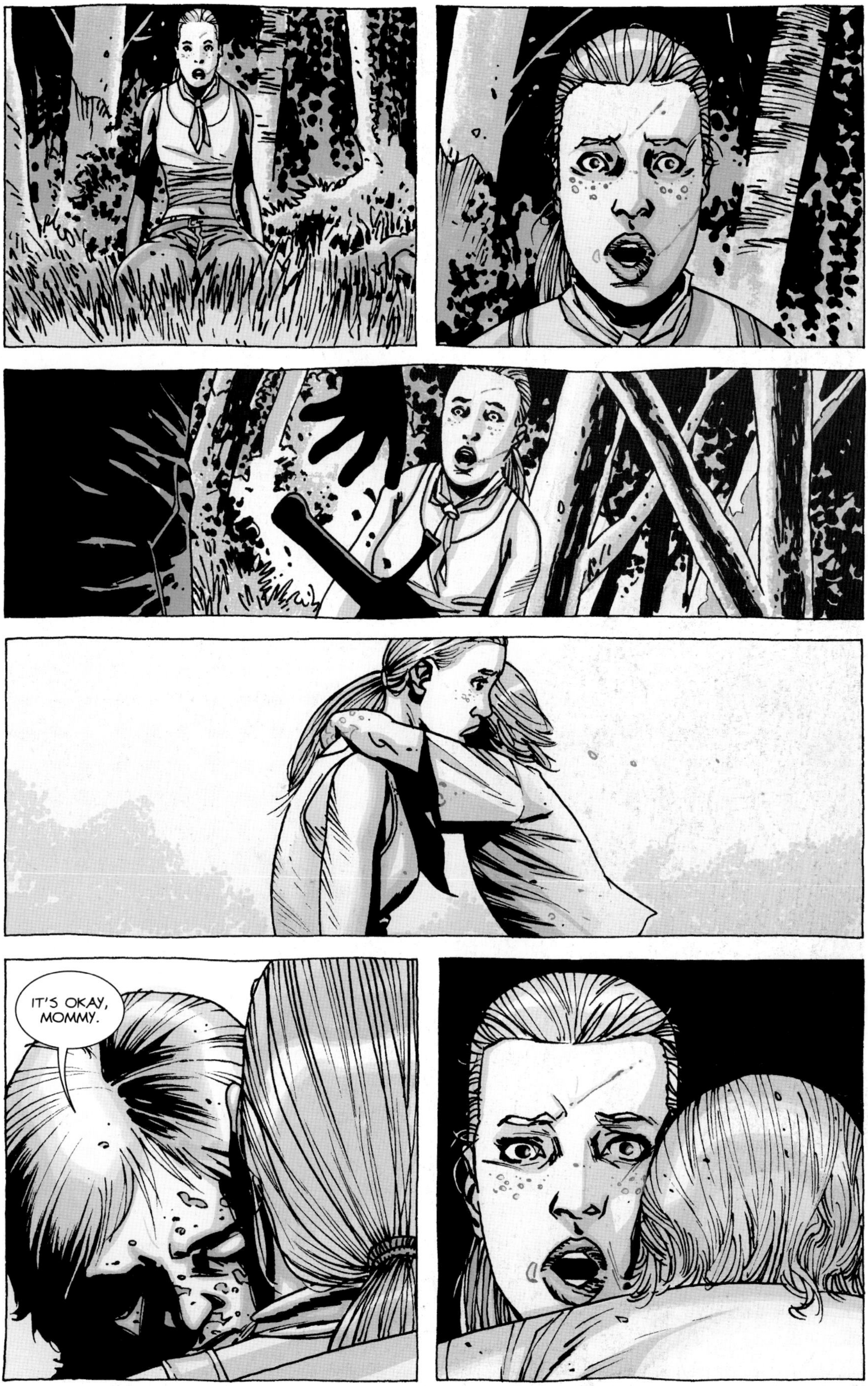
IT'S OKAY, MOMMY.

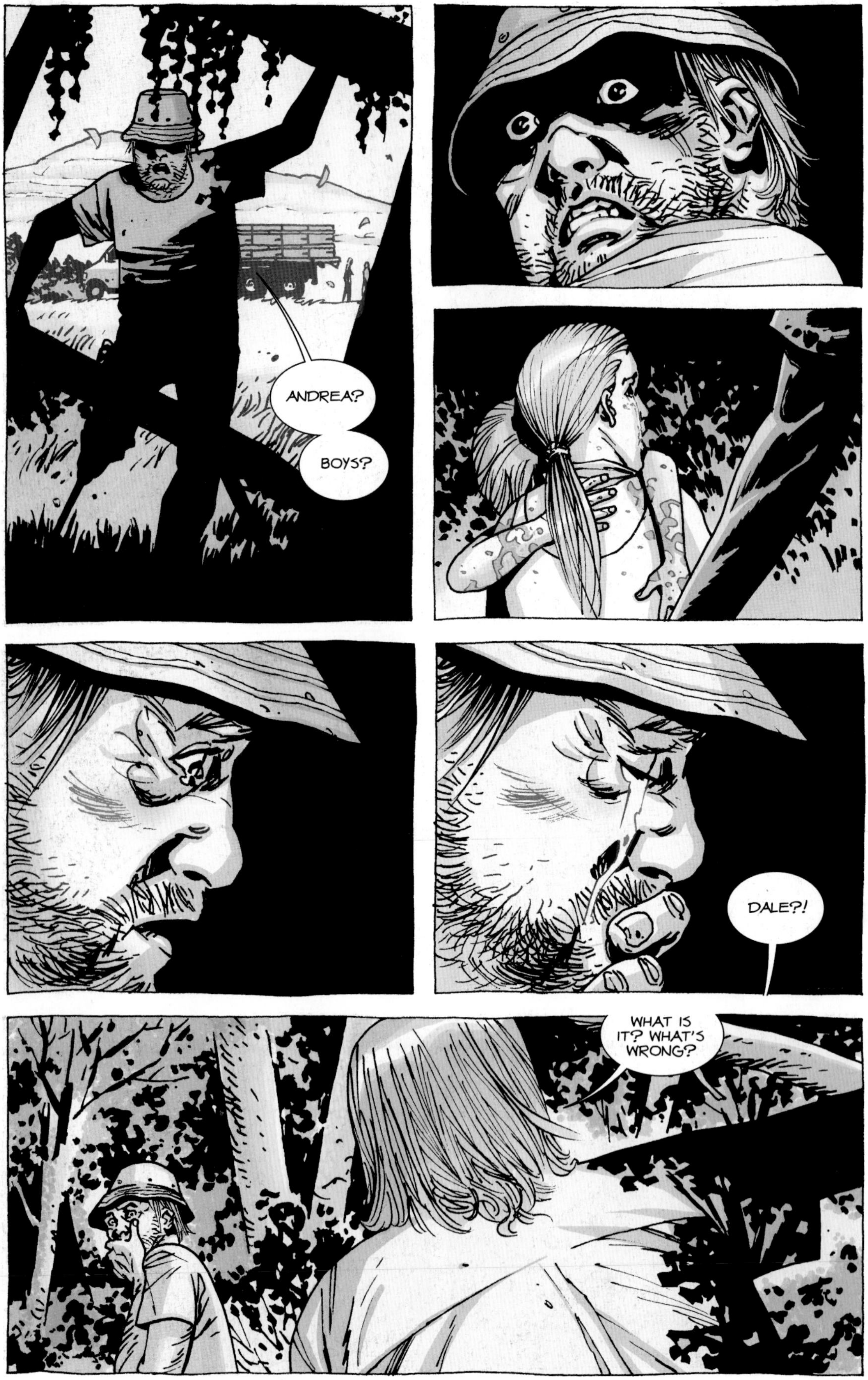
ANDREA?
BOYS?
DALE?!
WHAT IS IT? WHAT'S WRONG?

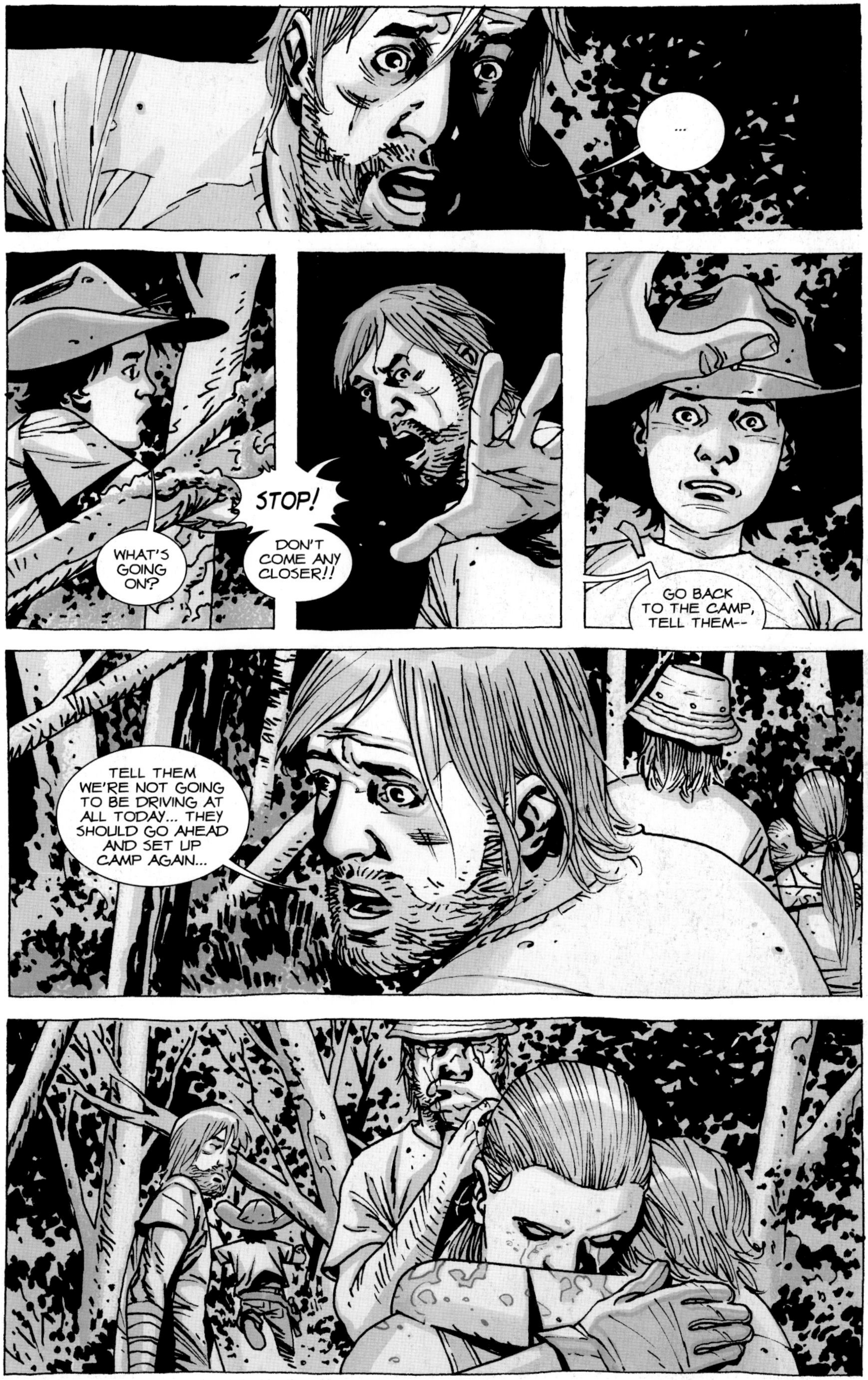
...
WHAT'S GOING ON?
STOP!
DON'T COME ANY CLOSER!!
GO BACK TO THE CAMP, TELL THEM--
TELL THEM WE'RE NOT GOING TO BE DRIVING AT ALL TODAY... THEY SHOULD GO AHEAD AND SET UP CAMP AGAIN...

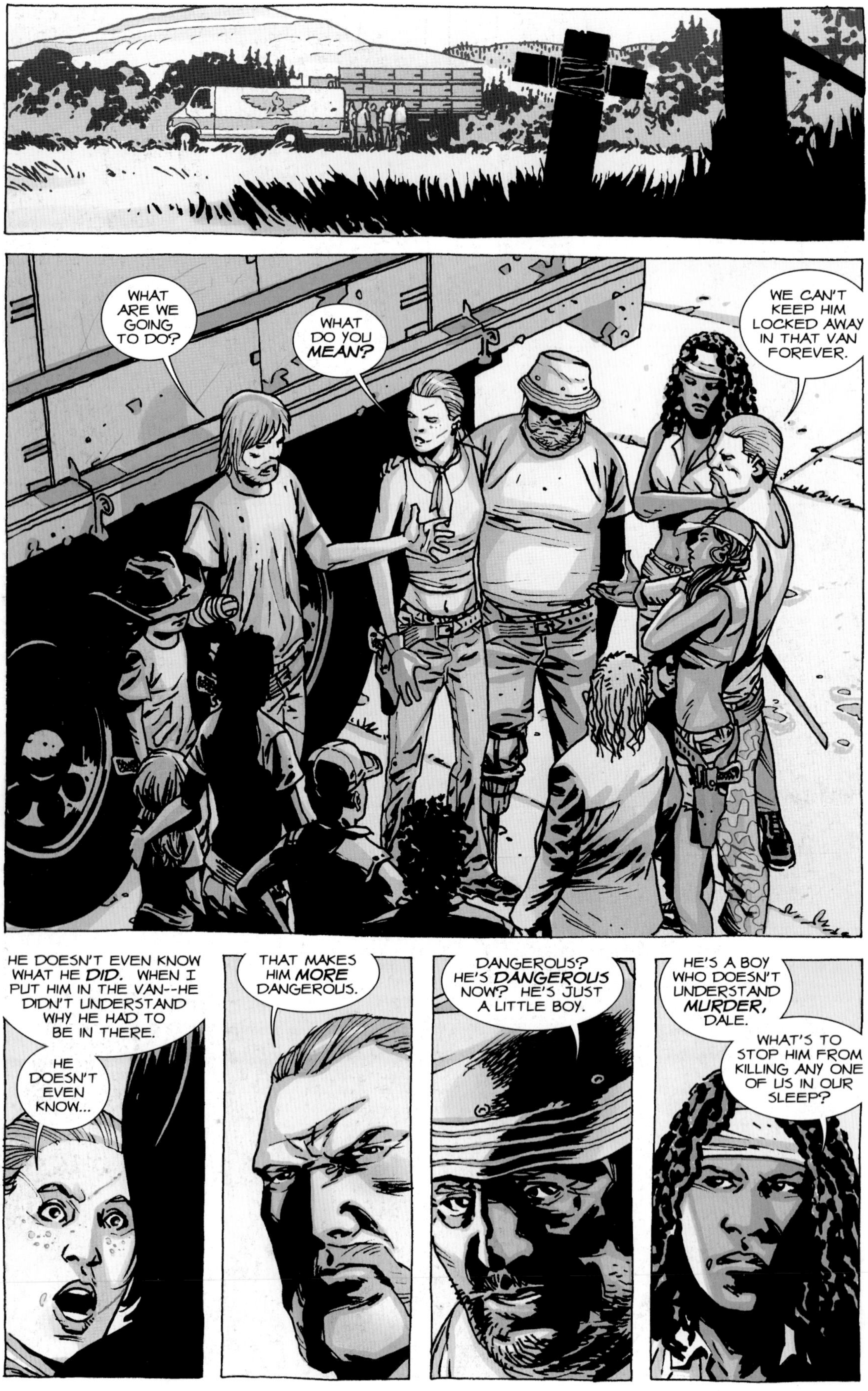
WHAT ARE WE GOING TO DO?
WHAT DO YOU MEAN?
WE CAN'T KEEP HIM LOCKED AWAY IN THAT VAN FOREVER.
HE DOESN'T EVEN KNOW WHAT HE DID. WHEN I PUT HIM IN THE VAN--HE DIDN'T UNDERSTAND WHY HE HAD TO BE IN THERE.
HE DOESN'T EVEN KNOW...
THAT MAKES HIM MORE DANGEROUS.
DANGEROUS? HE'S DANGEROUS NOW? HE'S JUST A LITTLE BOY.
HE'S A BOY WHO DOESN'T UNDERSTAND MURDER, DALE.
WHAT'S TO STOP HIM FROM KILLING ANY ONE OF US IN OUR SLEEP?

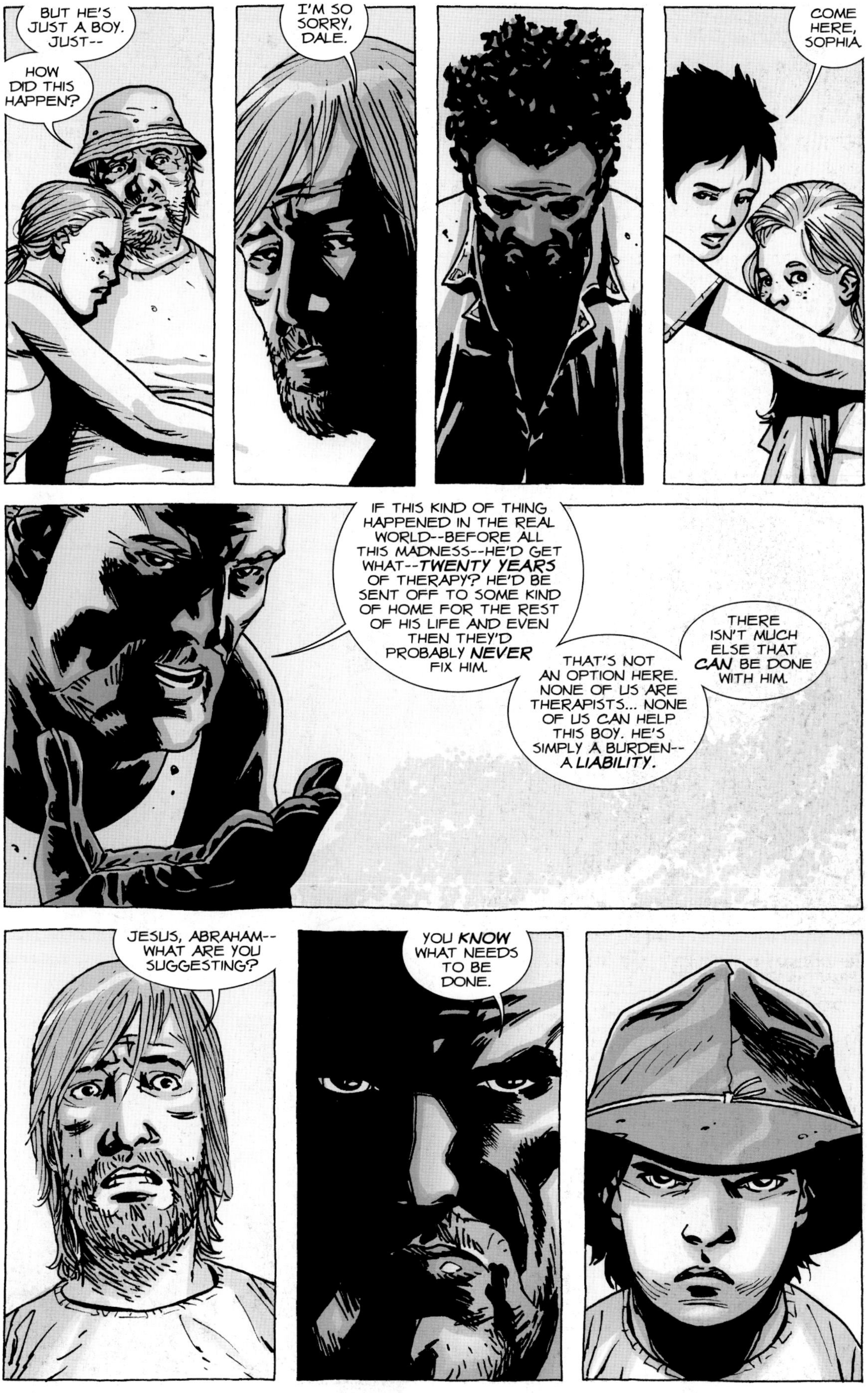
BUT HE'S JUST A BOY. JUST--
HOW DID THIS HAPPEN?
I'M SO SORRY, DALE.
COME HERE, SOPHIA.
IF THIS KIND OF THING HAPPENED IN THE REAL WORLD--BEFORE ALL THIS MADNESS--HE'D GET WHAT--TWENTY YEARS OF THERAPY? HE'D BE SENT OFF TO SOME KIND OF HOME FOR THE REST OF HIS LIFE AND EVEN THEN THEY'D PROBABLY NEVER FIX HIM.
THAT'S NOT AN OPTION HERE. NONE OF US ARE THERAPISTS... NONE OF US CAN HELP THIS BOY. HE'S SIMPLY A BURDEN-- A LIABILITY.
THERE ISN'T MUCH ELSE THAT CAN BE DONE WITH HIM.
JESUS, ABRAHAM-- WHAT ARE YOU SUGGESTING?
YOU KNOW WHAT NEEDS TO BE DONE.

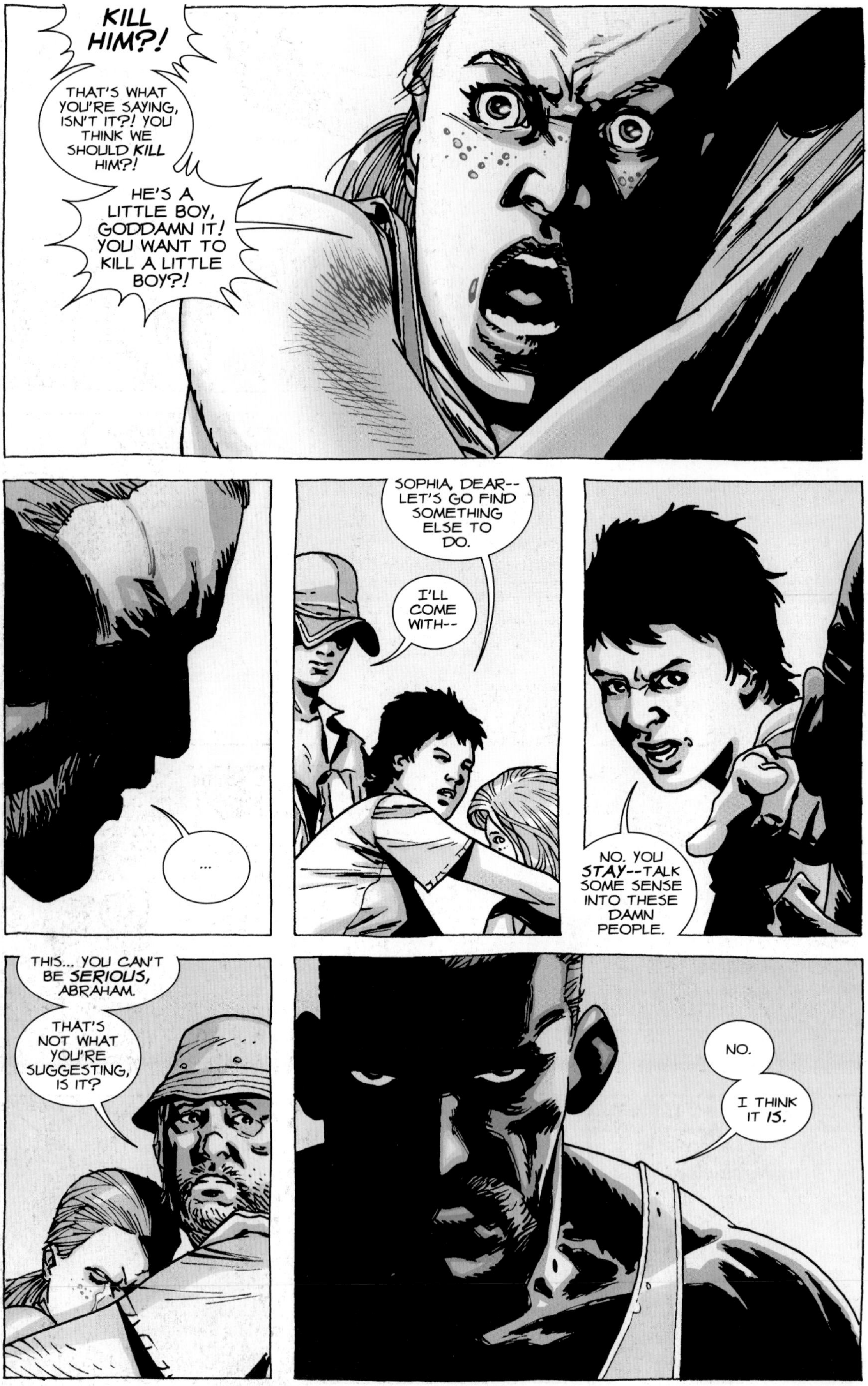
KILL HIM?!
THAT'S WHAT YOU'RE SAYING, ISN'T IT?! YOU THINK WE SHOULD KILL HIM?!
HE'S A LITTLE BOY, GODDAMN IT! YOU WANT TO KILL A LITTLE BOY?!
...
SOPHIA, DEAR-- LET'S GO FIND SOMETHING ELSE TO DO.
I'LL COME WITH--
NO. YOU STAY--TALK SOME SENSE INTO THESE DAMN PEOPLE.
THIS... YOU CAN'T BE SERIOUS, ABRAHAM.
THAT'S NOT WHAT YOU'RE SUGGESTING, IS IT?
NO.
I THINK IT IS.

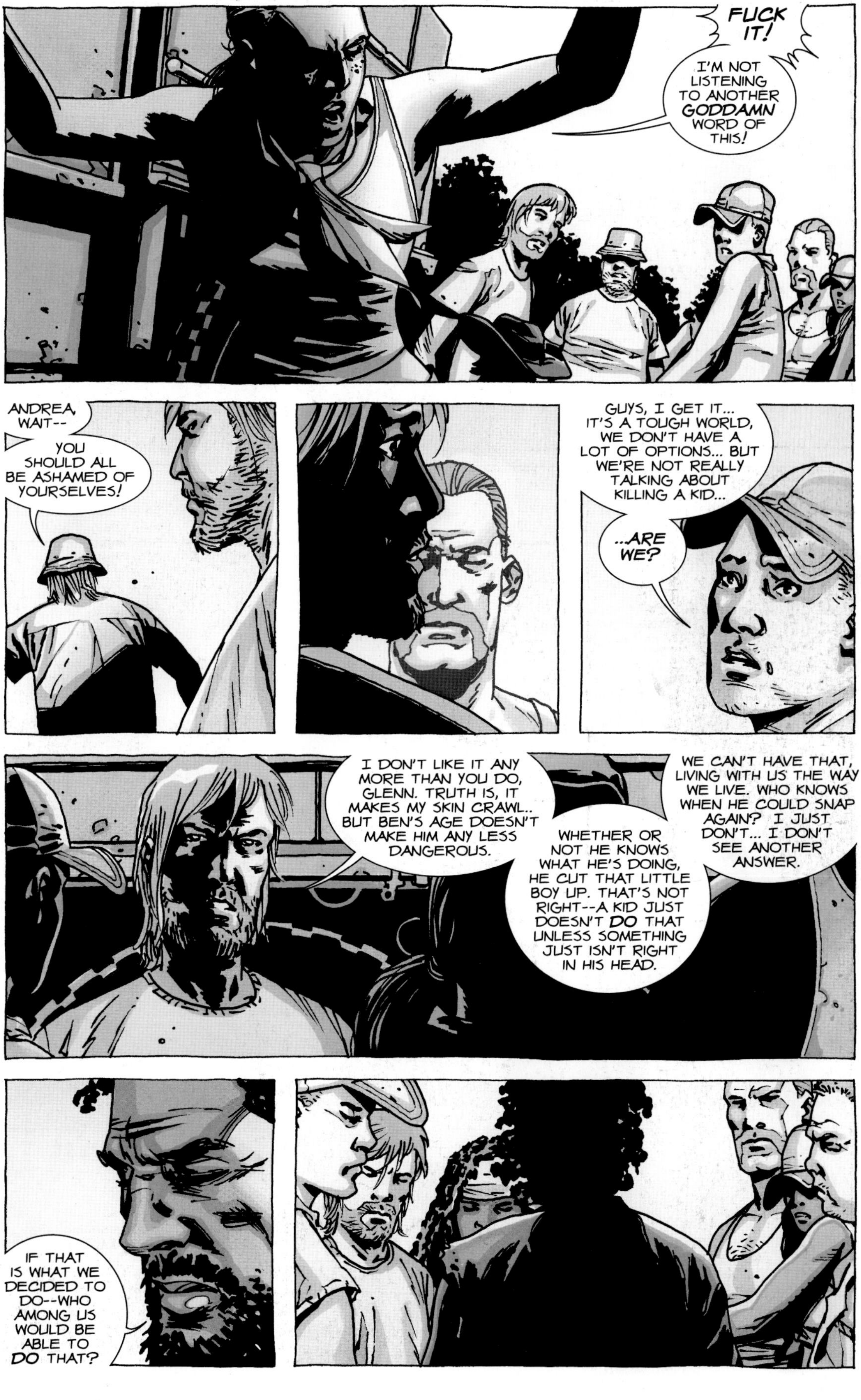
FUCK IT!
I'M NOT LISTENING TO ANOTHER GODDAMN WORD OF THIS!
ANDREA, WAIT--
YOU SHOULD ALL BE ASHAMED OF YOURSELVES!
GUYS, I GET IT... IT'S A TOUGH WORLD, WE DON'T HAVE A LOT OF OPTIONS... BUT WE'RE NOT REALLY TALKING ABOUT KILLING A KID...
...ARE WE?
I DON'T LIKE IT ANY MORE THAN YOU DO, GLENN. TRUTH IS, IT MAKES MY SKIN CRAWL.. BUT BEN'S AGE DOESN'T MAKE HIM ANY LESS DANGEROUS.
WHETHER OR NOT HE KNOWS WHAT HE'S DOING, HE CUT THAT LITTLE BOY UP. THAT'S NOT RIGHT--A KID JUST DOESN'T DO THAT UNLESS SOMETHING JUST ISN'T RIGHT IN HIS HEAD.
WE CAN'T HAVE THAT, LIVING WITH US THE WAY WE LIVE. WHO KNOWS WHEN HE COULD SNAP AGAIN? I JUST DON'T... I DON'T SEE ANOTHER ANSWER.
IF THAT IS WHAT WE DECIDED TO DO--WHO AMONG US WOULD BE ABLE TO DO THAT?

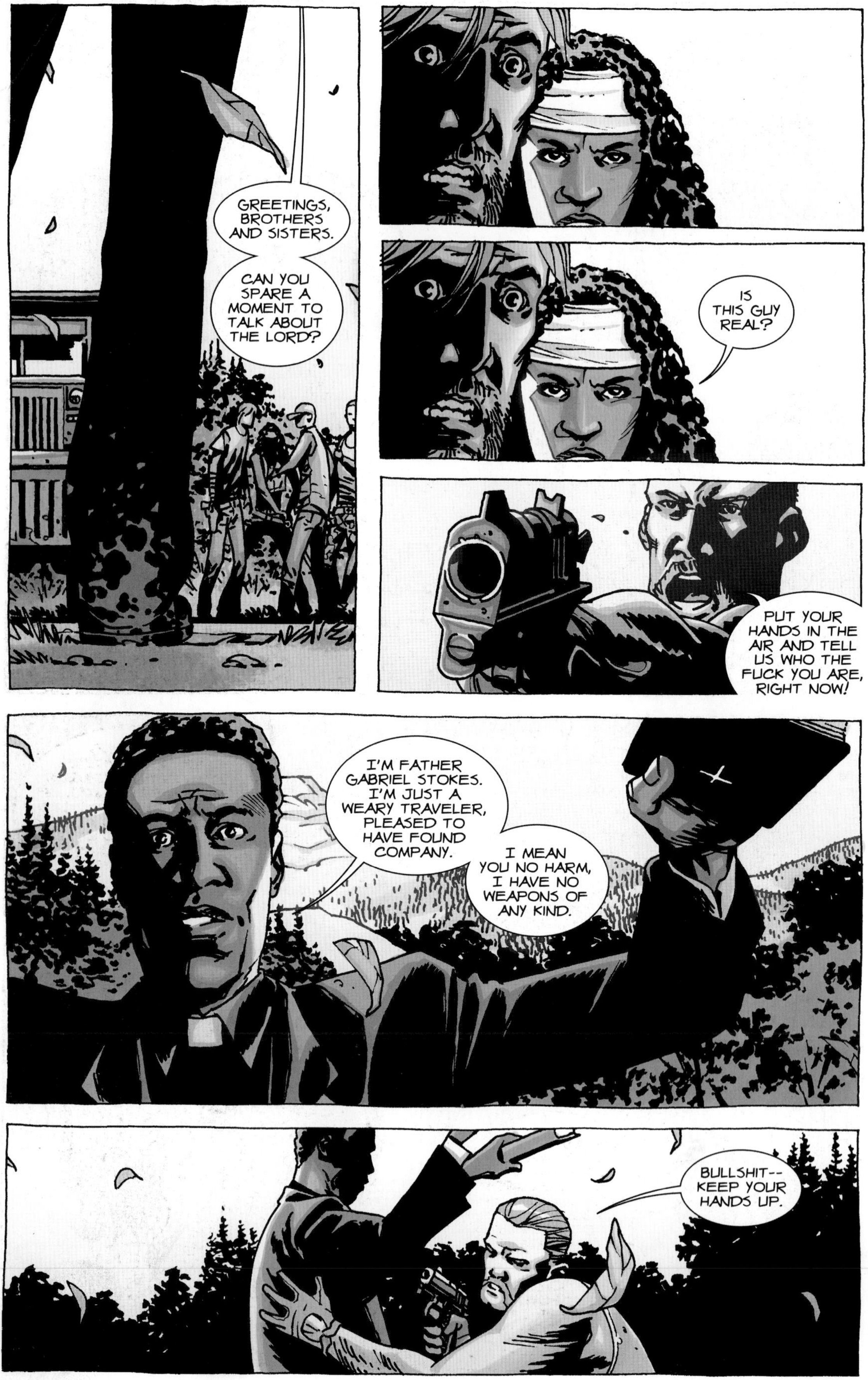

GREETINGS, BROTHERS AND SISTERS.
CAN YOU SPARE A MOMENT TO TALK ABOUT THE LORD?
IS THIS GUY REAL?
PUT YOUR HANDS IN THE AIR AND TELL US WHO THE FUCK YOU ARE, RIGHT NOW!
I'M FATHER GABRIEL STOKES. I'M JUST A WEARY TRAVELER, PLEASED TO HAVE FOUND COMPANY.
I MEAN YOU NO HARM, I HAVE NO WEAPONS OF ANY KIND.
BULLSHIT-- KEEP YOUR HANDS UP.

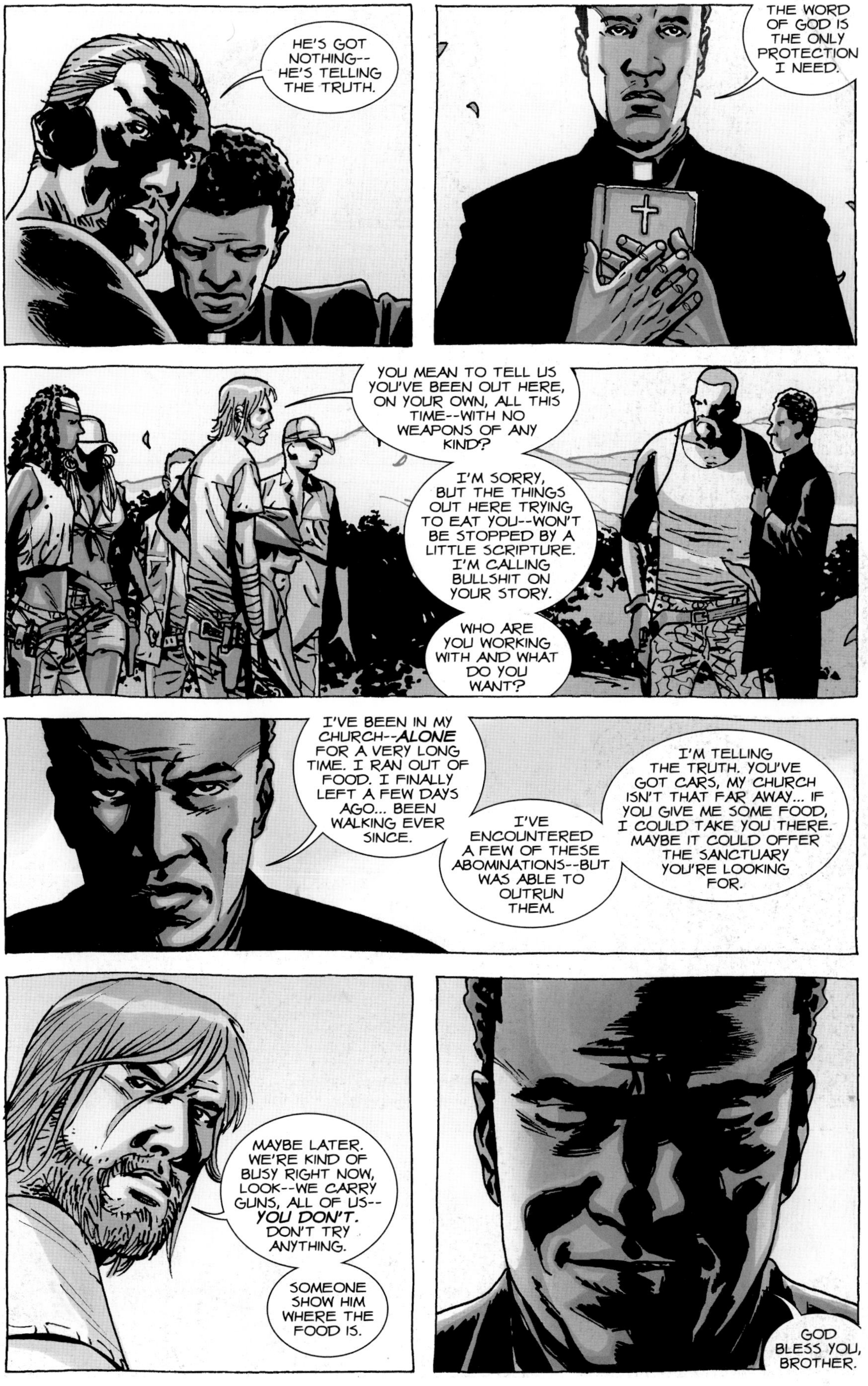
HE'S GOT NOTHING-- HE'S TELLING THE TRUTH.
THE WORD OF GOD IS THE ONLY PROTECTION I NEED.
YOU MEAN TO TELL US YOU'VE BEEN OUT HERE, ON YOUR OWN, ALL THIS TIME--WITH NO WEAPONS OF ANY KIND?
I'M SORRY, BUT THE THINGS OUT HERE TRYING TO EAT YOU--WON'T BE STOPPED BY A LITTLE SCRIPTURE. I'M CALLING BULLSHIT ON YOUR STORY.
WHO ARE YOU WORKING WITH AND WHAT DO YOU WANT?
I'VE BEEN IN MY CHURCH--*ALONE* FOR A VERY LONG TIME. I RAN OUT OF FOOD. I FINALLY LEFT A FEW DAYS AGO... BEEN WALKING EVER SINCE.
I'VE ENCOUNTERED A FEW OF THESE ABOMINATIONS--BUT WAS ABLE TO OUTRUN THEM.
I'M TELLING THE TRUTH. YOU'VE GOT CARS, MY CHURCH ISN'T THAT FAR AWAY... IF YOU GIVE ME SOME FOOD, I COULD TAKE YOU THERE. MAYBE IT COULD OFFER THE SANCTUARY YOU'RE LOOKING FOR.
MAYBE LATER. WE'RE KIND OF BUSY RIGHT NOW, LOOK--WE CARRY GUNS, ALL OF US-- *YOU DON'T.* DON'T TRY ANYTHING.
SOMEONE SHOW HIM WHERE THE FOOD IS.
GOD BLESS YOU, BROTHER.

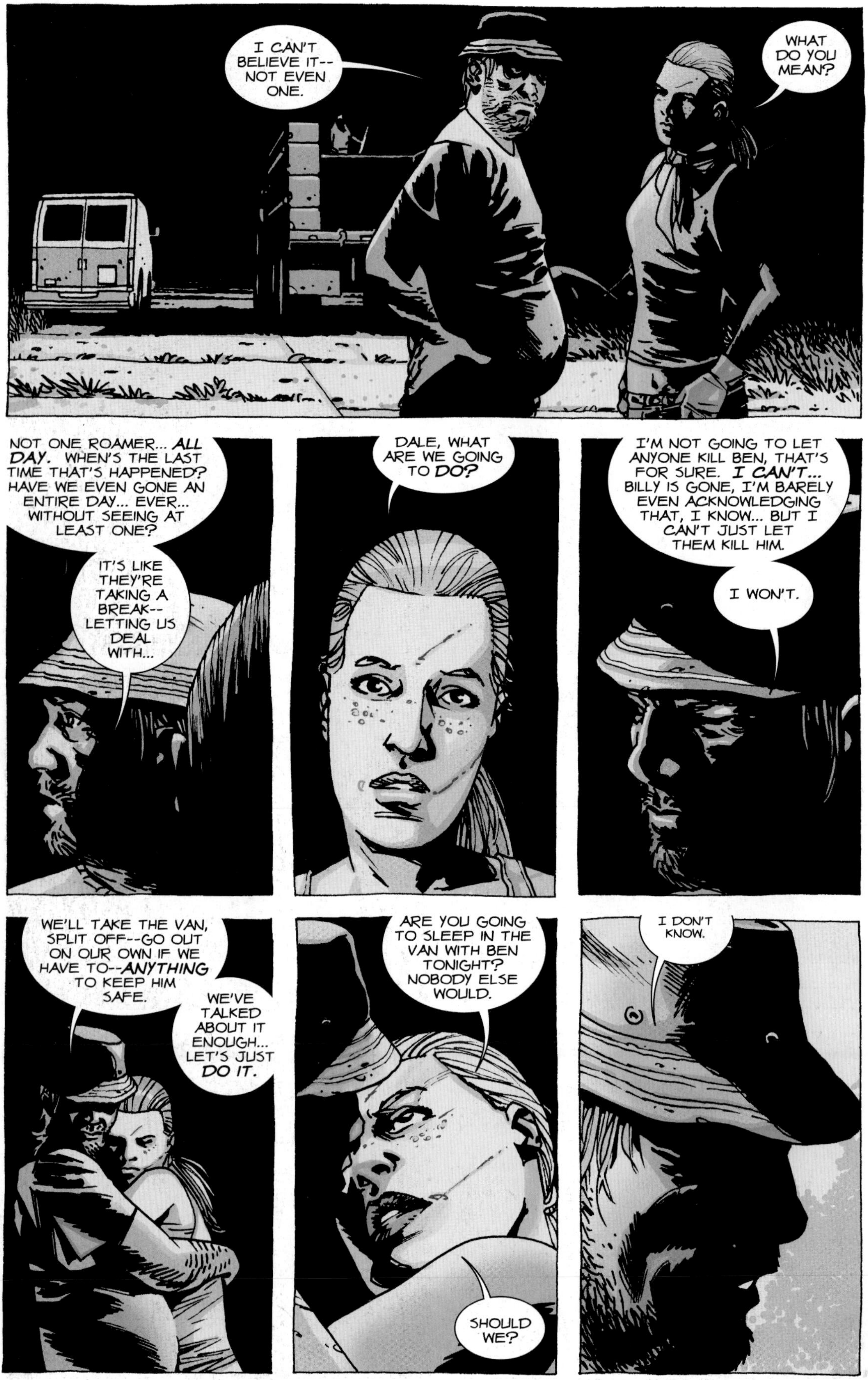
I CAN'T BELIEVE IT-- NOT EVEN ONE.
WHAT DO YOU MEAN?
NOT ONE ROAMER... ALL DAY. WHEN'S THE LAST TIME THAT'S HAPPENED? HAVE WE EVEN GONE AN ENTIRE DAY... EVER... WITHOUT SEEING AT LEAST ONE?
IT'S LIKE THEY'RE TAKING A BREAK-- LETTING US DEAL WITH...
DALE, WHAT ARE WE GOING TO DO?
I'M NOT GOING TO LET ANYONE KILL BEN, THAT'S FOR SURE. I CAN'T... BILLY IS GONE, I'M BARELY EVEN ACKNOWLEDGING THAT, I KNOW... BUT I CAN'T JUST LET THEM KILL HIM.
I WON'T.
WE'LL TAKE THE VAN, SPLIT OFF--GO OUT ON OUR OWN IF WE HAVE TO--ANYTHING TO KEEP HIM SAFE.
WE'VE TALKED ABOUT IT ENOUGH... LET'S JUST DO IT.
ARE YOU GOING TO SLEEP IN THE VAN WITH BEN TONIGHT? NOBODY ELSE WOULD.
SHOULD WE?
I DON'T KNOW.

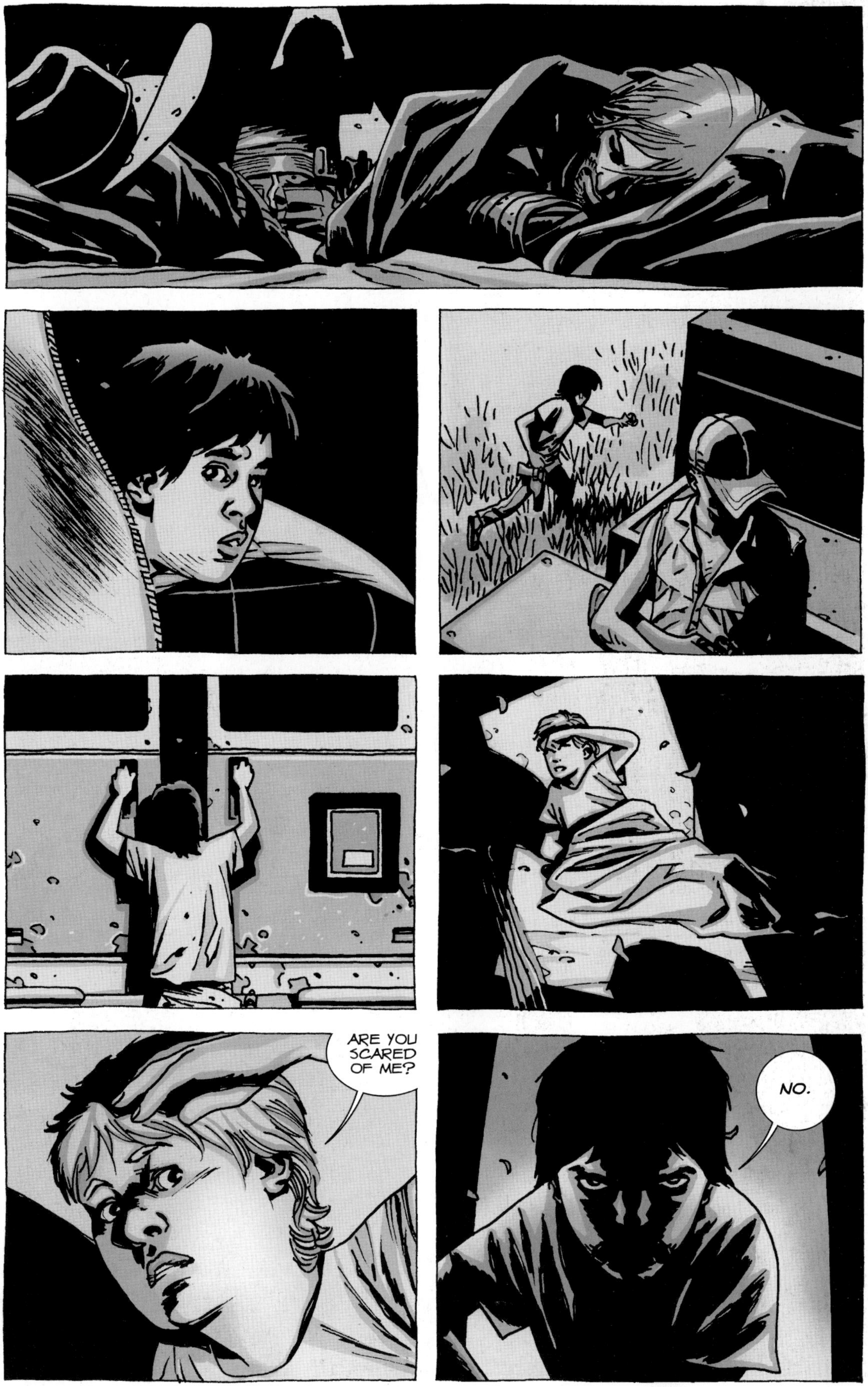
ARE YOU SCARED OF ME?
NO.

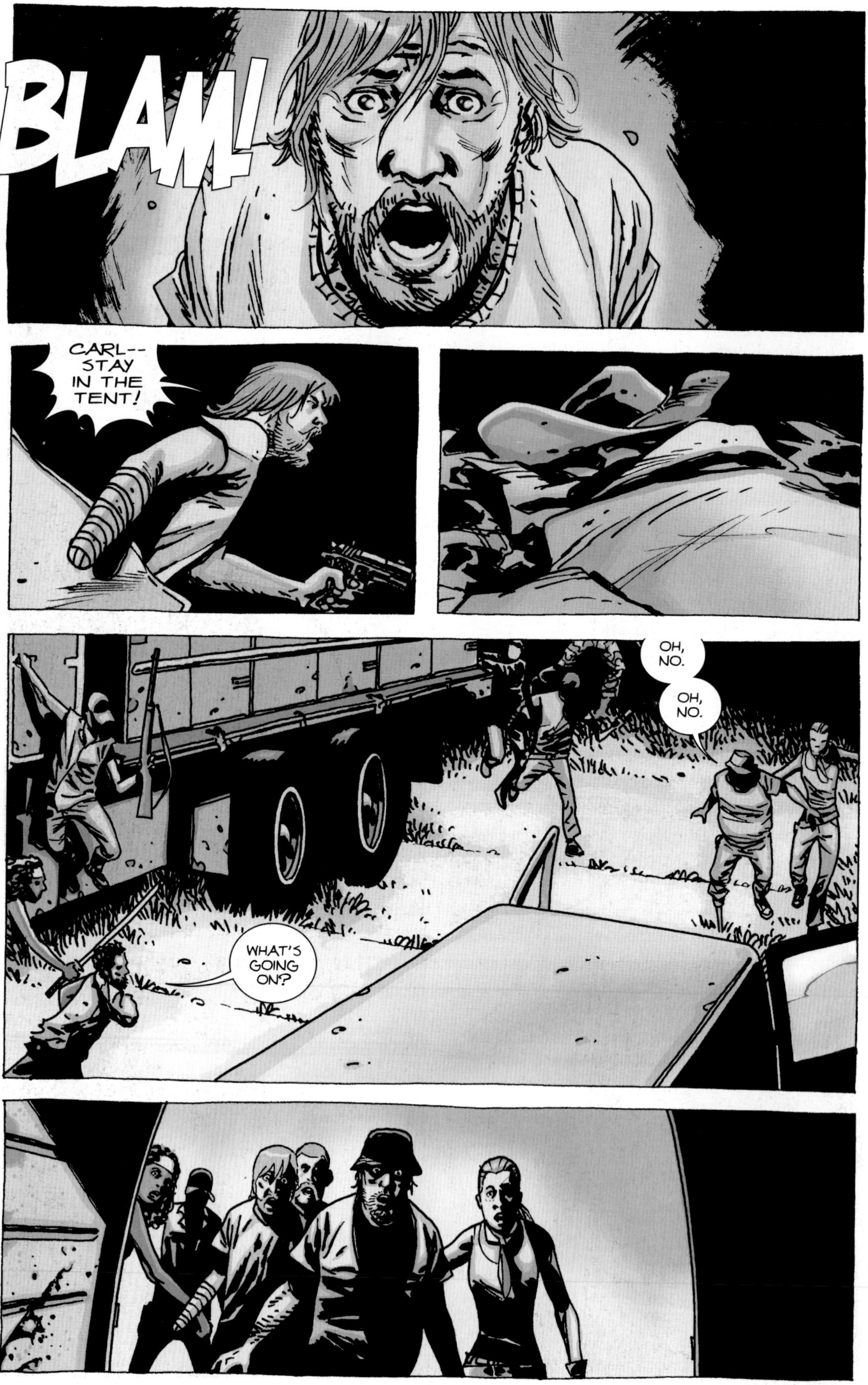
BLAM!
CARL-- STAY IN THE TENT!
OH, NO.
OH, NO.
WHAT'S GOING ON?

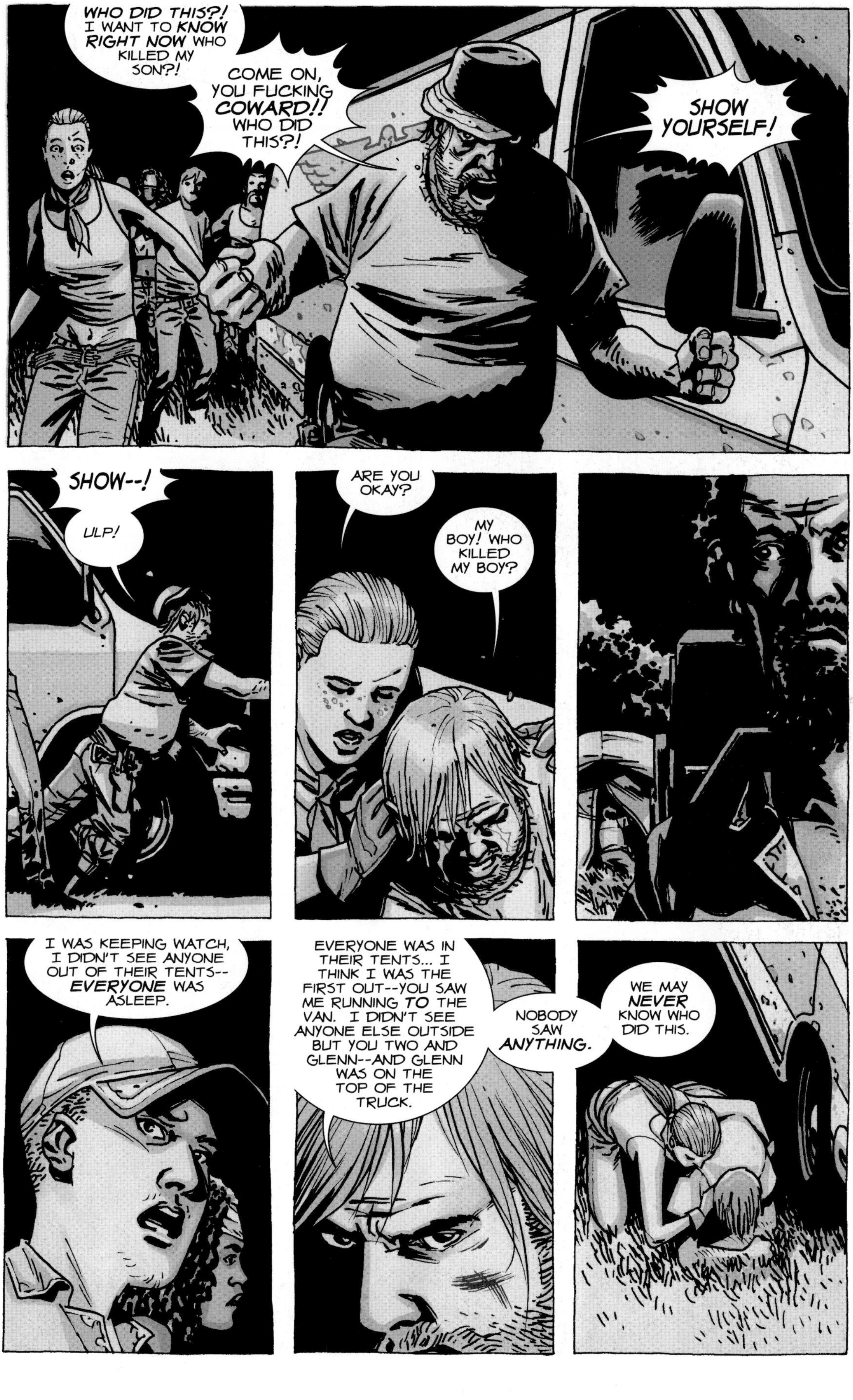
WHO DID THIS?! I WANT TO KNOW RIGHT NOW WHO KILLED MY SON?!
COME ON, YOU FUCKING COWARD!! WHO DID THIS?!
SHOW YOURSELF!
SHOW--!
ULP!
ARE YOU OKAY?
MY BOY! WHO KILLED MY BOY?
I WAS KEEPING WATCH, I DIDN'T SEE ANYONE OUT OF THEIR TENTS-- EVERYONE WAS ASLEEP.
EVERYONE WAS IN THEIR TENTS... I THINK I WAS THE FIRST OUT--YOU SAW ME RUNNING TO THE VAN. I DIDN'T SEE ANYONE ELSE OUTSIDE BUT YOU TWO AND GLENN--AND GLENN WAS ON THE TOP OF THE TRUCK.
NOBODY SAW ANYTHING.
WE MAY NEVER KNOW WHO DID THIS.

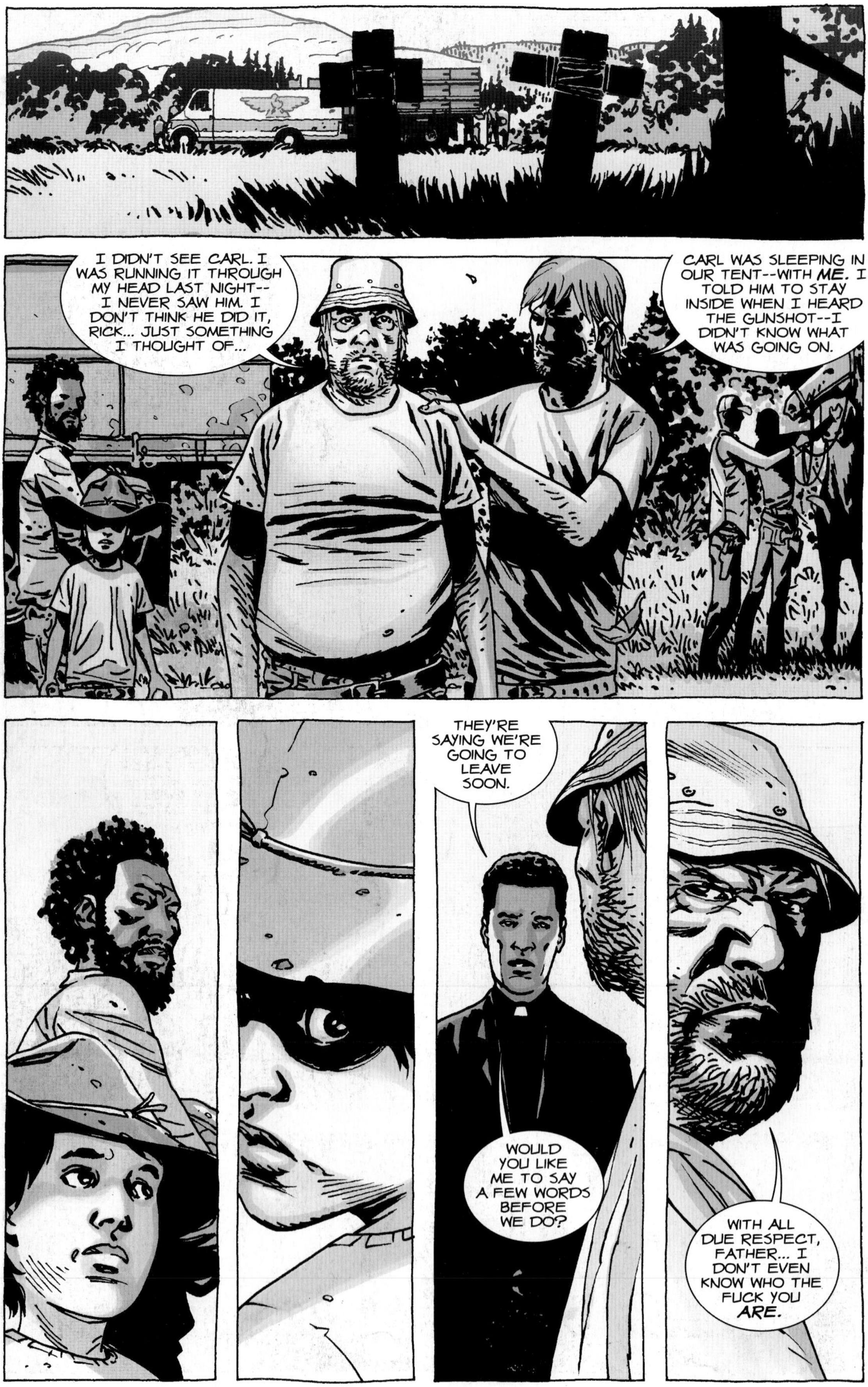

I DIDN'T SEE CARL. I WAS RUNNING IT THROUGH MY HEAD LAST NIGHT-- I NEVER SAW HIM. I DON'T THINK HE DID IT, RICK... JUST SOMETHING I THOUGHT OF...
CARL WAS SLEEPING IN OUR TENT--WITH ME. I TOLD HIM TO STAY INSIDE WHEN I HEARD THE GUNSHOT--I DIDN'T KNOW WHAT WAS GOING ON.
THEY'RE SAYING WE'RE GOING TO LEAVE SOON.
WOULD YOU LIKE ME TO SAY A FEW WORDS BEFORE WE DO?
WITH ALL DUE RESPECT, FATHER... I DON'T EVEN KNOW WHO THE FUCK YOU ARE.

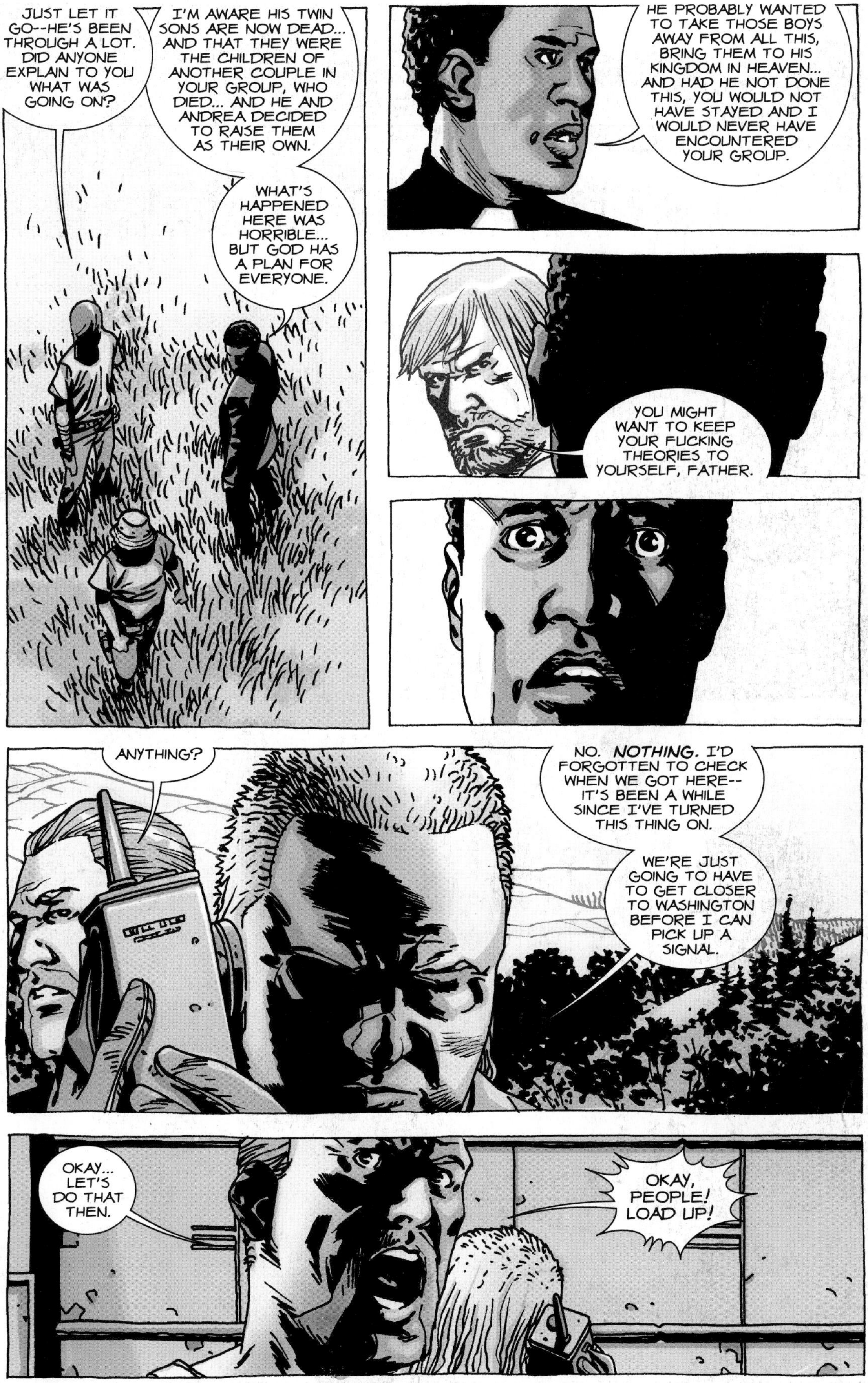

JUST LET IT GO--HE'S BEEN THROUGH A LOT. DID ANYONE EXPLAIN TO YOU WHAT WAS GOING ON?
I'M AWARE HIS TWIN SONS ARE NOW DEAD... AND THAT THEY WERE THE CHILDREN OF ANOTHER COUPLE IN YOUR GROUP, WHO DIED... AND HE AND ANDREA DECIDED TO RAISE THEM AS THEIR OWN.
WHAT'S HAPPENED HERE WAS HORRIBLE... BUT GOD HAS A PLAN FOR EVERYONE.
HE PROBABLY WANTED TO TAKE THOSE BOYS AWAY FROM ALL THIS, BRING THEM TO HIS KINGDOM IN HEAVEN... AND HAD HE NOT DONE THIS, YOU WOULD NOT HAVE STAYED AND I WOULD NEVER HAVE ENCOUNTERED YOUR GROUP.
YOU MIGHT WANT TO KEEP YOUR FUCKING THEORIES TO YOURSELF, FATHER.
ANYTHING?
NO. NOTHING. I'D FORGOTTEN TO CHECK WHEN WE GOT HERE-- IT'S BEEN A WHILE SINCE I'VE TURNED THIS THING ON.
WE'RE JUST GOING TO HAVE TO GET CLOSER TO WASHINGTON BEFORE I CAN PICK UP A SIGNAL.
OKAY... LET'S DO THAT THEN.
OKAY, PEOPLE! LOAD UP!

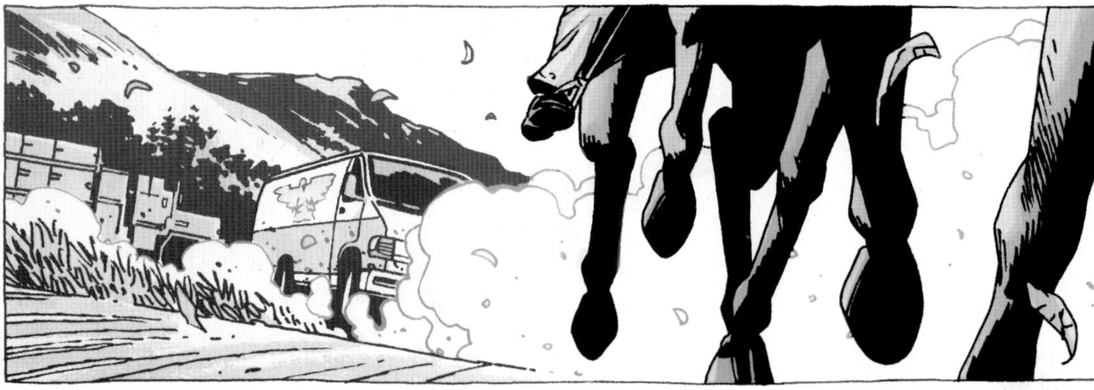

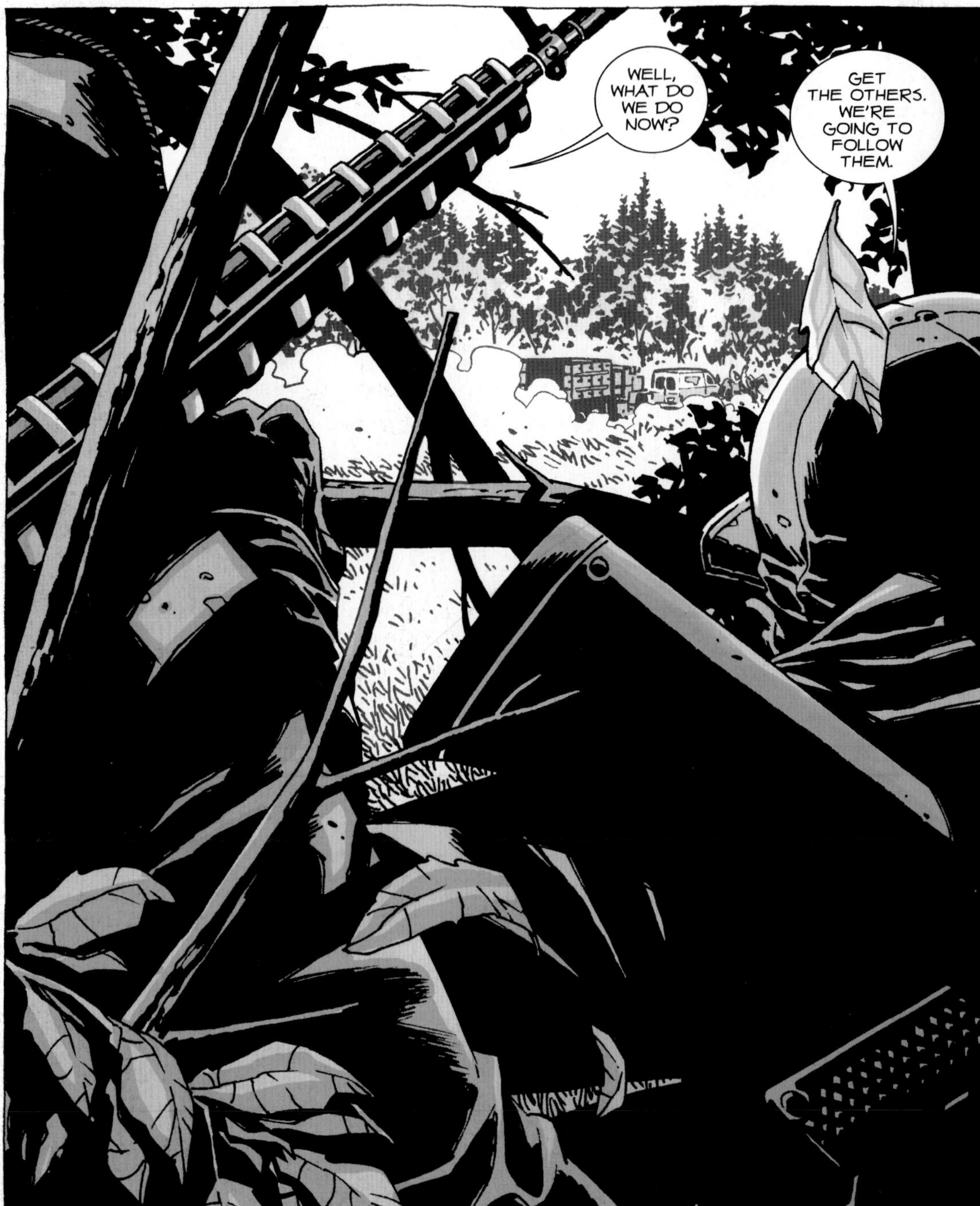
WELL, WHAT DO WE DO NOW?
GET THE OTHERS. WE'RE GOING TO FOLLOW THEM.

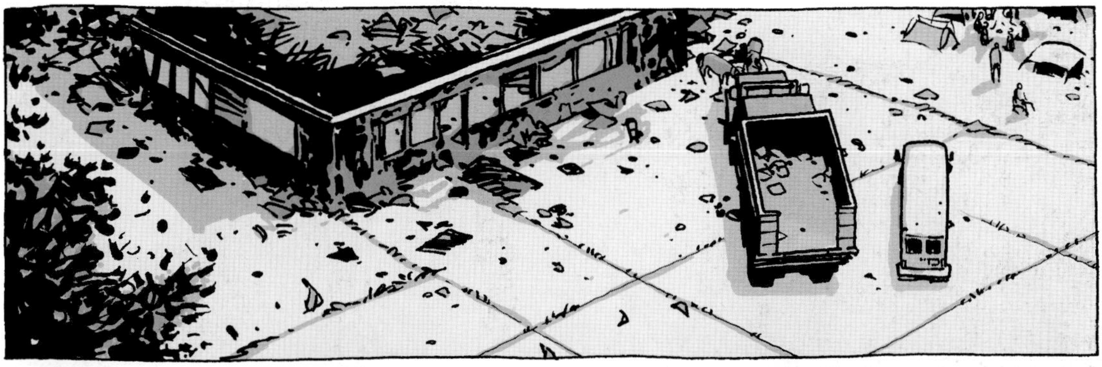

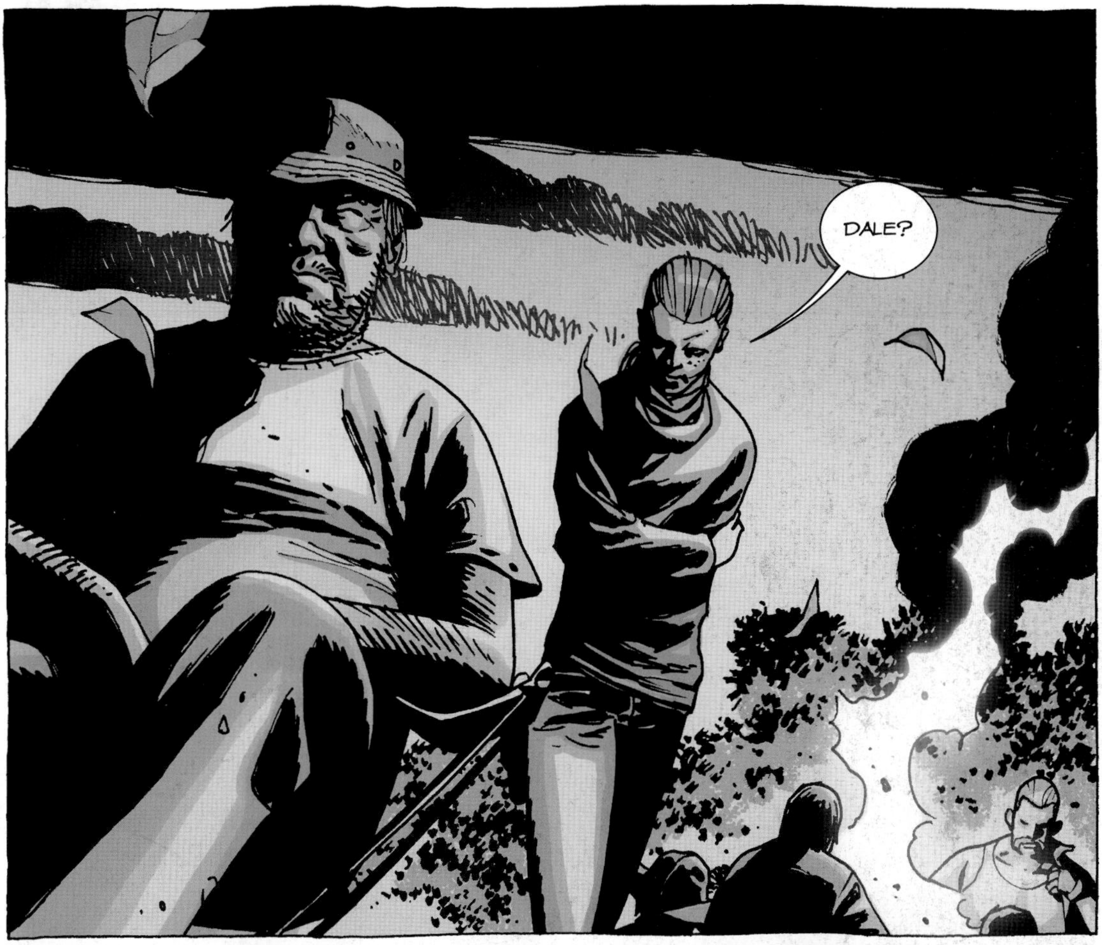
DALE?

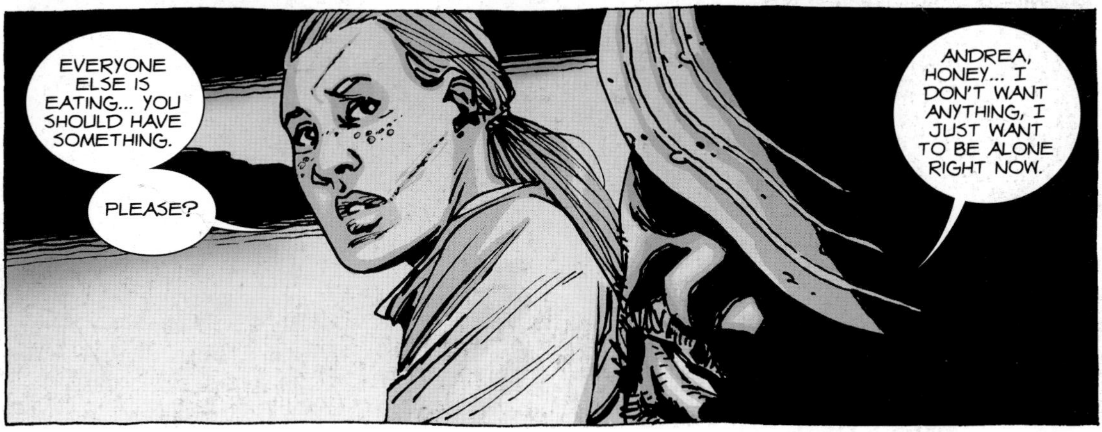
EVERYONE ELSE IS EATING... YOU SHOULD HAVE SOMETHING.
PLEASE?
ANDREA, HONEY... I DON'T WANT ANYTHING, I JUST WANT TO BE ALONE RIGHT NOW.

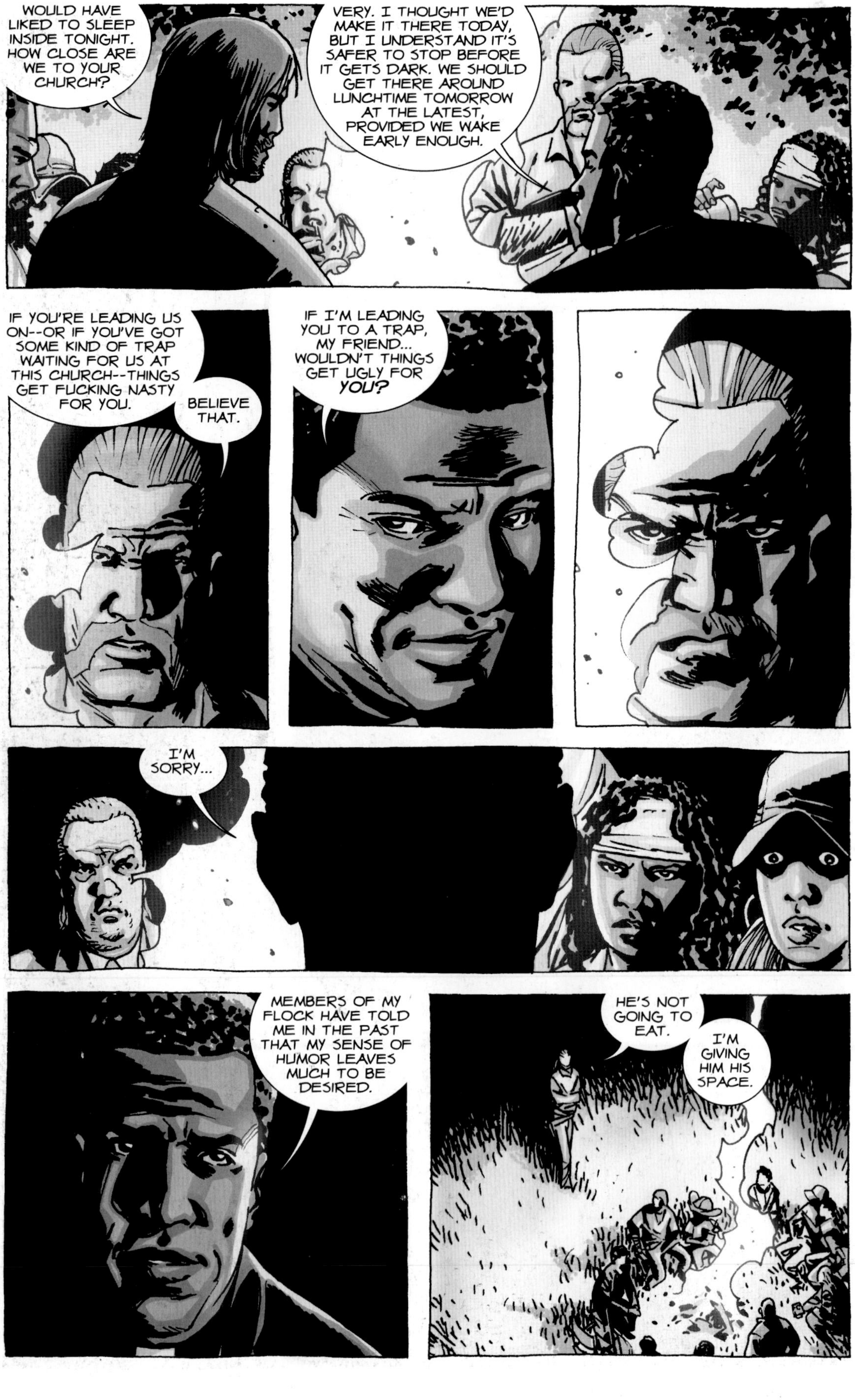
WOULD HAVE LIKED TO SLEEP INSIDE TONIGHT. HOW CLOSE ARE WE TO YOUR CHURCH?
VERY. I THOUGHT WE'D MAKE IT THERE TODAY, BUT I UNDERSTAND IT'S SAFER TO STOP BEFORE IT GETS DARK. WE SHOULD GET THERE AROUND LUNCHTIME TOMORROW AT THE LATEST, PROVIDED WE WAKE EARLY ENOUGH.
IF YOU'RE LEADING US ON--OR IF YOU'VE GOT SOME KIND OF TRAP WAITING FOR US AT THIS CHURCH--THINGS GET FUCKING NASTY FOR YOU.
BELIEVE THAT.
IF I'M LEADING YOU TO A TRAP, MY FRIEND... WOULDN'T THINGS GET UGLY FOR *YOU?*
I'M SORRY...
MEMBERS OF MY FLOCK HAVE TOLD ME IN THE PAST THAT MY SENSE OF HUMOR LEAVES MUCH TO BE DESIRED.
HE'S NOT GOING TO EAT.
I'M GIVING HIM HIS SPACE.

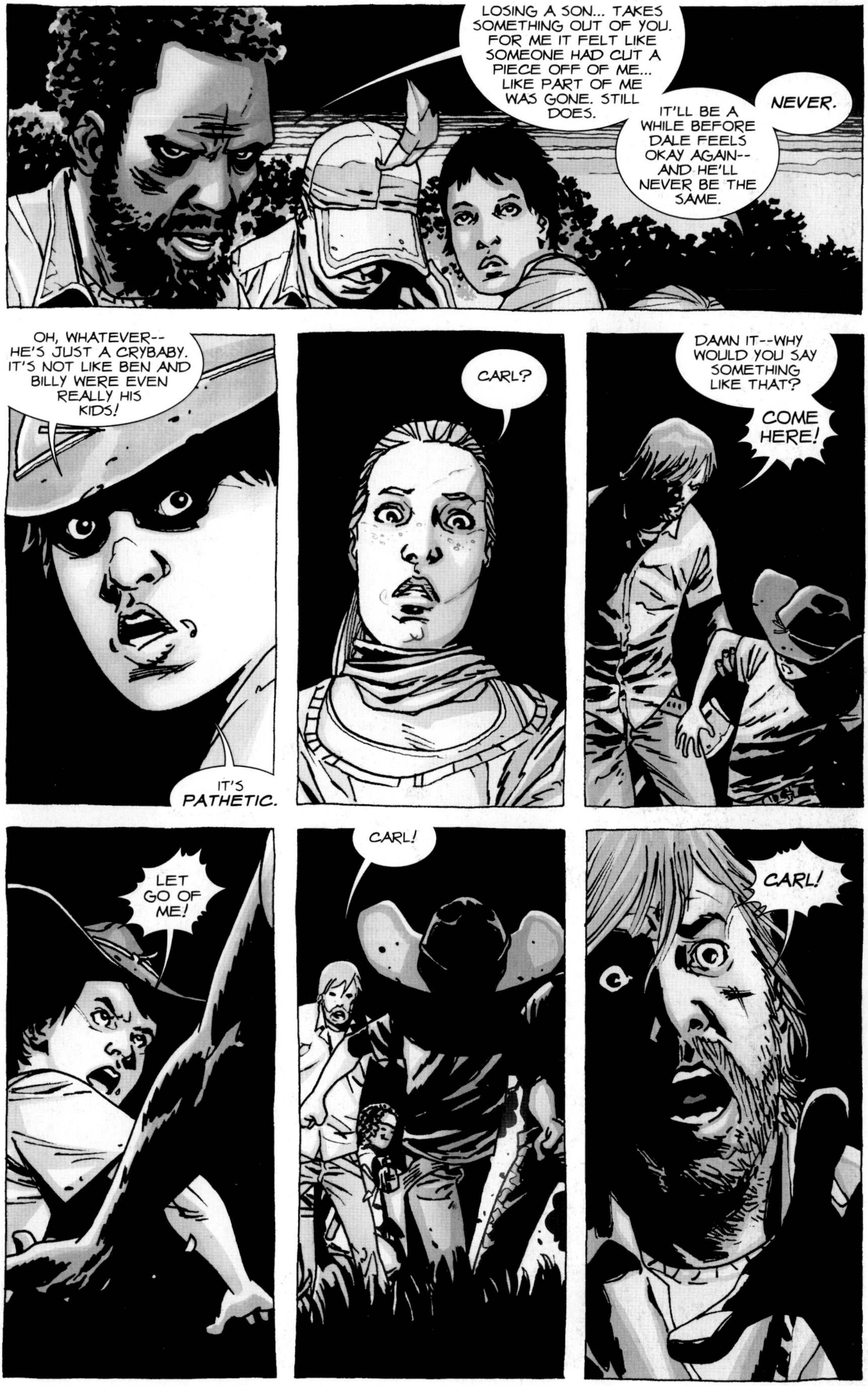
LOSING A SON... TAKES SOMETHING OUT OF YOU. FOR ME IT FELT LIKE SOMEONE HAD CUT A PIECE OFF OF ME... LIKE PART OF ME WAS GONE. STILL DOES.
IT'LL BE A WHILE BEFORE DALE FEELS OKAY AGAIN-- AND HE'LL NEVER BE THE SAME.
NEVER.
OH, WHATEVER-- HE'S JUST A CRYBABY. IT'S NOT LIKE BEN AND BILLY WERE EVEN REALLY HIS KIDS!
IT'S PATHETIC.
CARL?
DAMN IT--WHY WOULD YOU SAY SOMETHING LIKE THAT?
COME HERE!
LET GO OF ME!
CARL!
CARL!

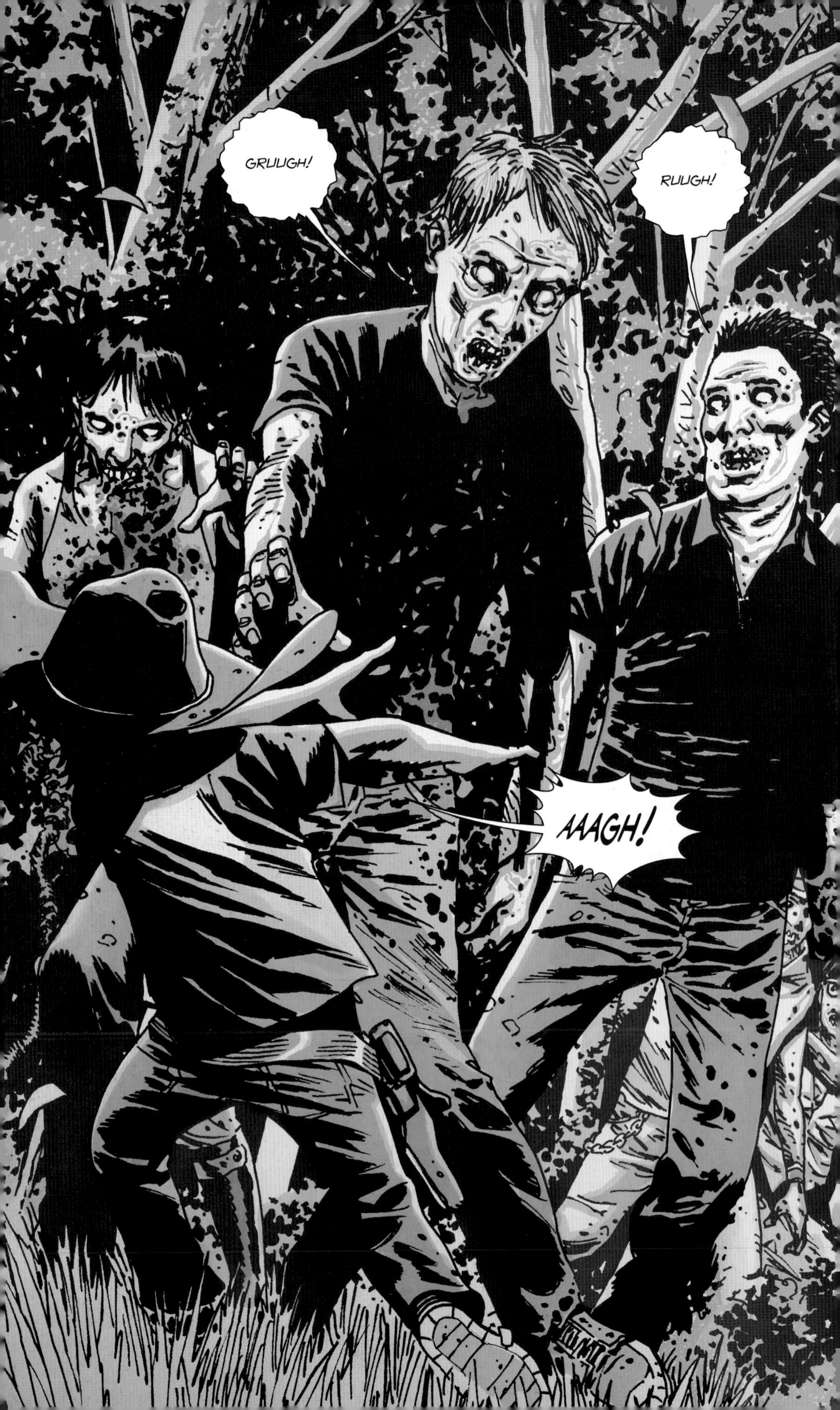
GRUUGH!
RUUGH!
AAAGH!

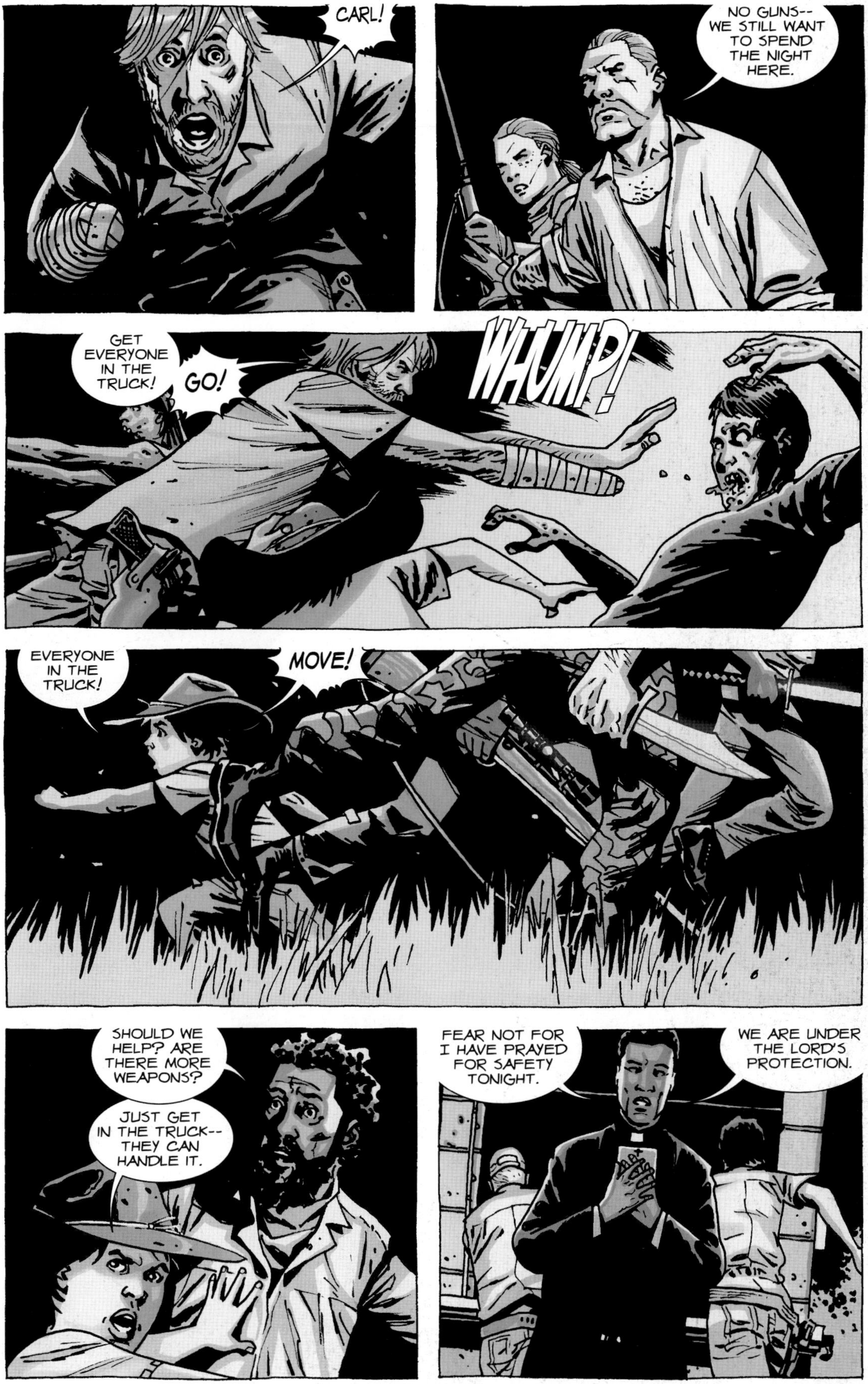
CARL!
NO GUNS-- WE STILL WANT TO SPEND THE NIGHT HERE.
GET EVERYONE IN THE TRUCK!
GO!
WHUMP!
EVERYONE IN THE TRUCK!
MOVE!
SHOULD WE HELP? ARE THERE MORE WEAPONS?
JUST GET IN THE TRUCK-- THEY CAN HANDLE IT.
FEAR NOT FOR I HAVE PRAYED FOR SAFETY TONIGHT.
WE ARE UNDER THE LORD'S PROTECTION.

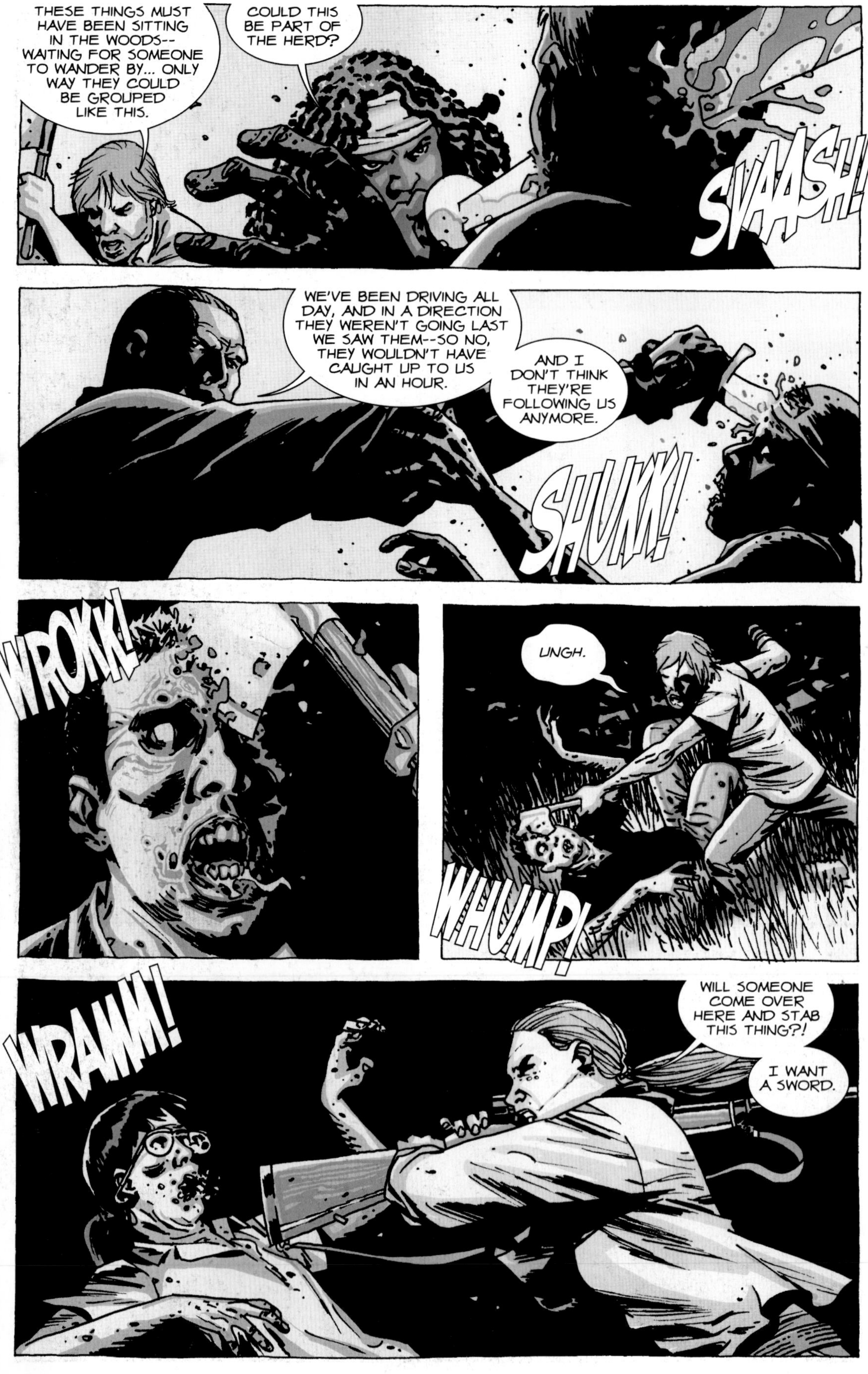
THESE THINGS MUST HAVE BEEN SITTING IN THE WOODS-- WAITING FOR SOMEONE TO WANDER BY... ONLY WAY THEY COULD BE GROUPED LIKE THIS.
COULD THIS BE PART OF THE HERD?
SVAASH!
WE'VE BEEN DRIVING ALL DAY, AND IN A DIRECTION THEY WEREN'T GOING LAST WE SAW THEM--SO NO, THEY WOULDN'T HAVE CAUGHT UP TO US IN AN HOUR.
AND I DON'T THINK THEY'RE FOLLOWING US ANYMORE.
SHUKK!
WROKK!
UNGH.
WHUMP!
WRAMM!
WILL SOMEONE COME OVER HERE AND STAB THIS THING?!
I WANT A SWORD.

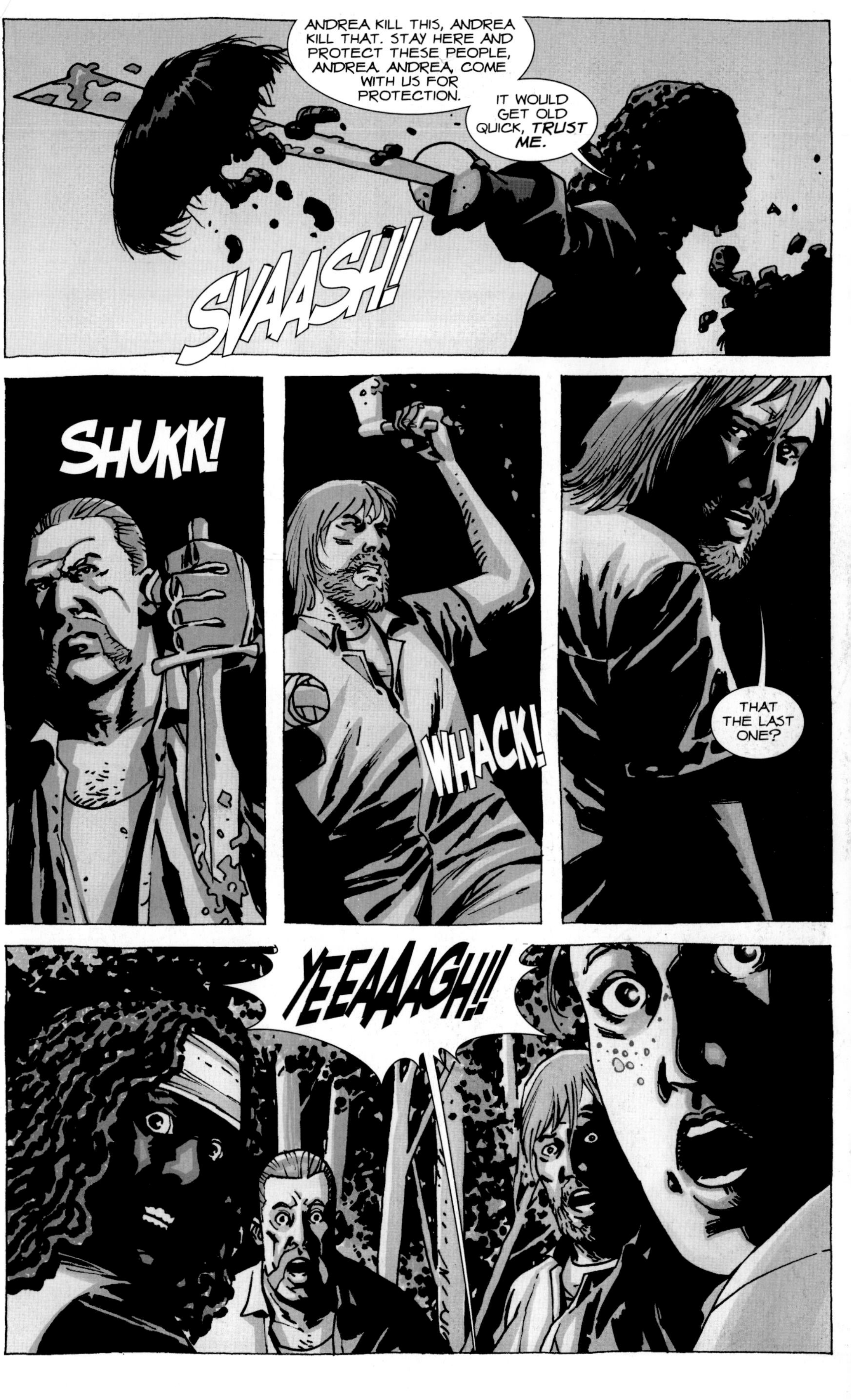
ANDREA KILL THIS, ANDREA KILL THAT. STAY HERE AND PROTECT THESE PEOPLE, ANDREA. ANDREA, COME WITH US FOR PROTECTION.
IT WOULD GET OLD QUICK, TRUST ME.
SVAASH!
SHUKK!
WHACK!
THAT THE LAST ONE?
YEEAAAGH!!

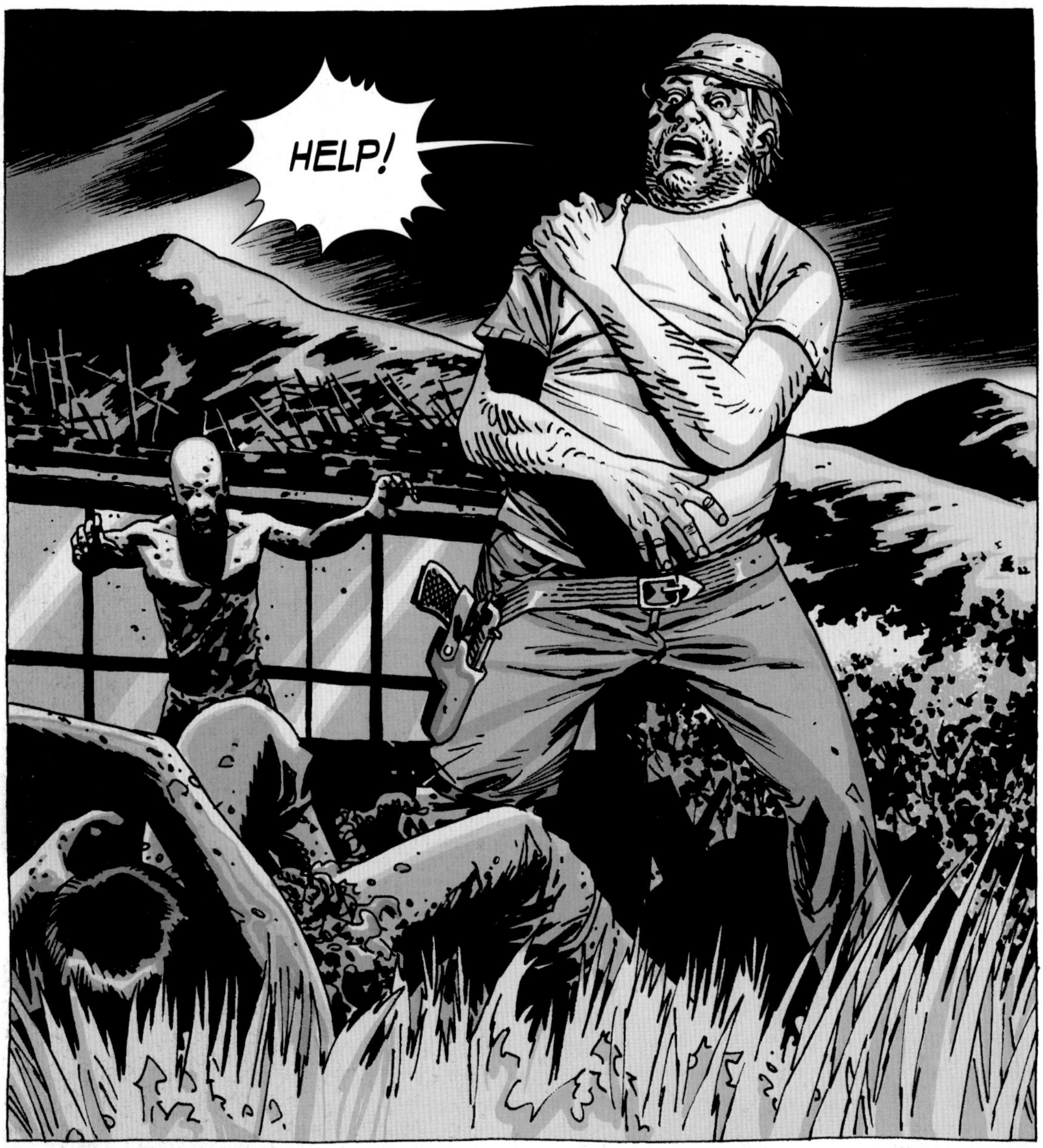
HELP!

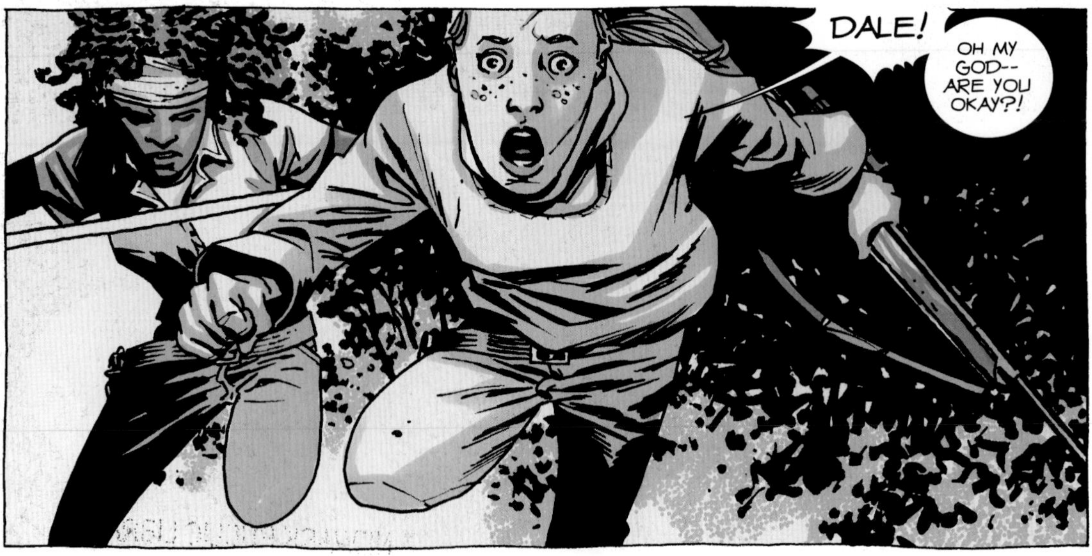
DALE!
OH MY GOD-- ARE YOU OKAY?!

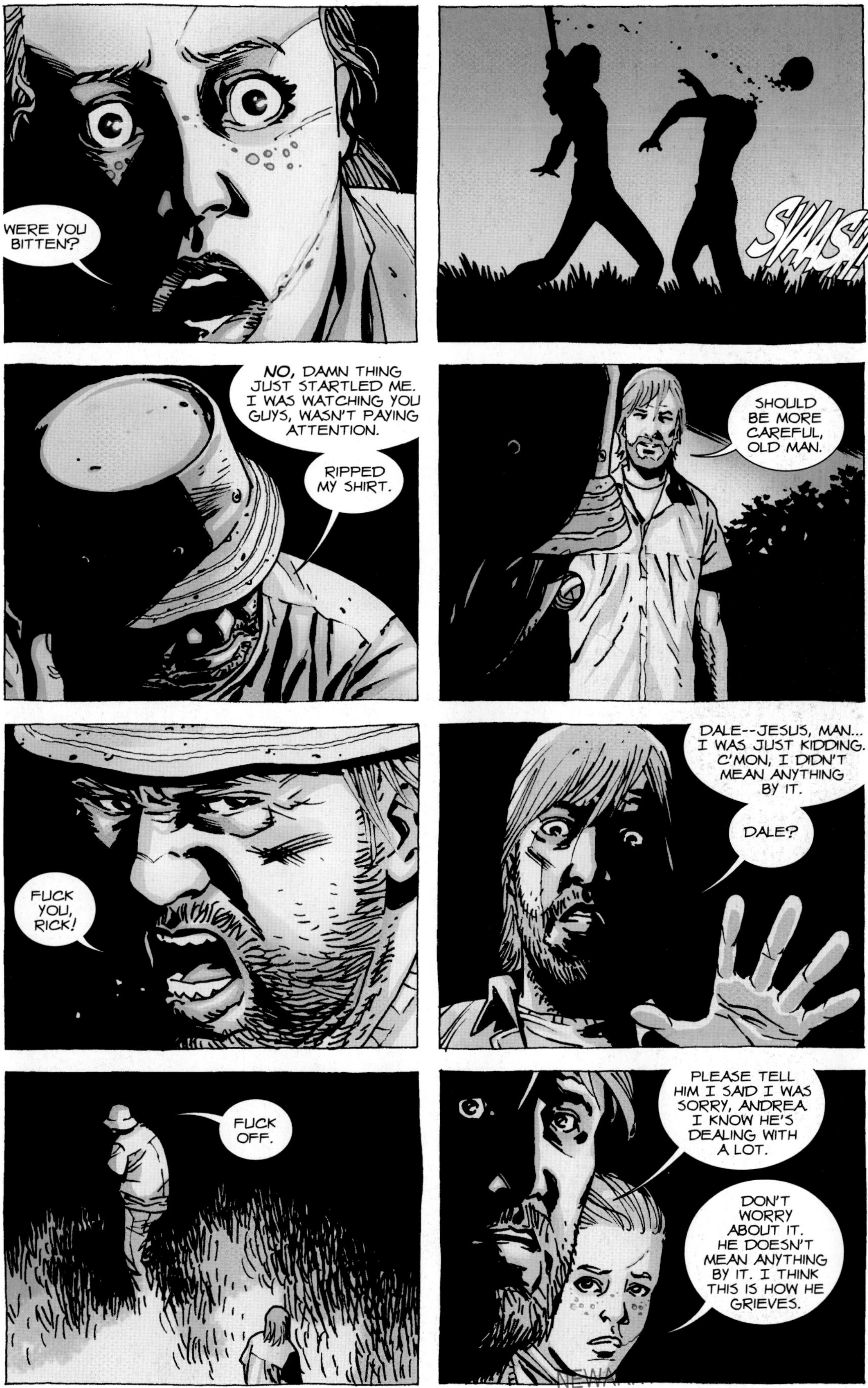
WERE YOU BITTEN?
NO, DAMN THING JUST STARTLED ME. I WAS WATCHING YOU GUYS, WASN'T PAYING ATTENTION.
RIPPED MY SHIRT.
SHOULD BE MORE CAREFUL, OLD MAN.
FUCK YOU, RICK!
DALE--JESUS, MAN... I WAS JUST KIDDING. C'MON, I DIDN'T MEAN ANYTHING BY IT.
DALE?
FUCK OFF.
PLEASE TELL HIM I SAID I WAS SORRY, ANDREA. I KNOW HE'S DEALING WITH A LOT.
DON'T WORRY ABOUT IT. HE DOESN'T MEAN ANYTHING BY IT. I THINK THIS IS HOW HE GRIEVES.

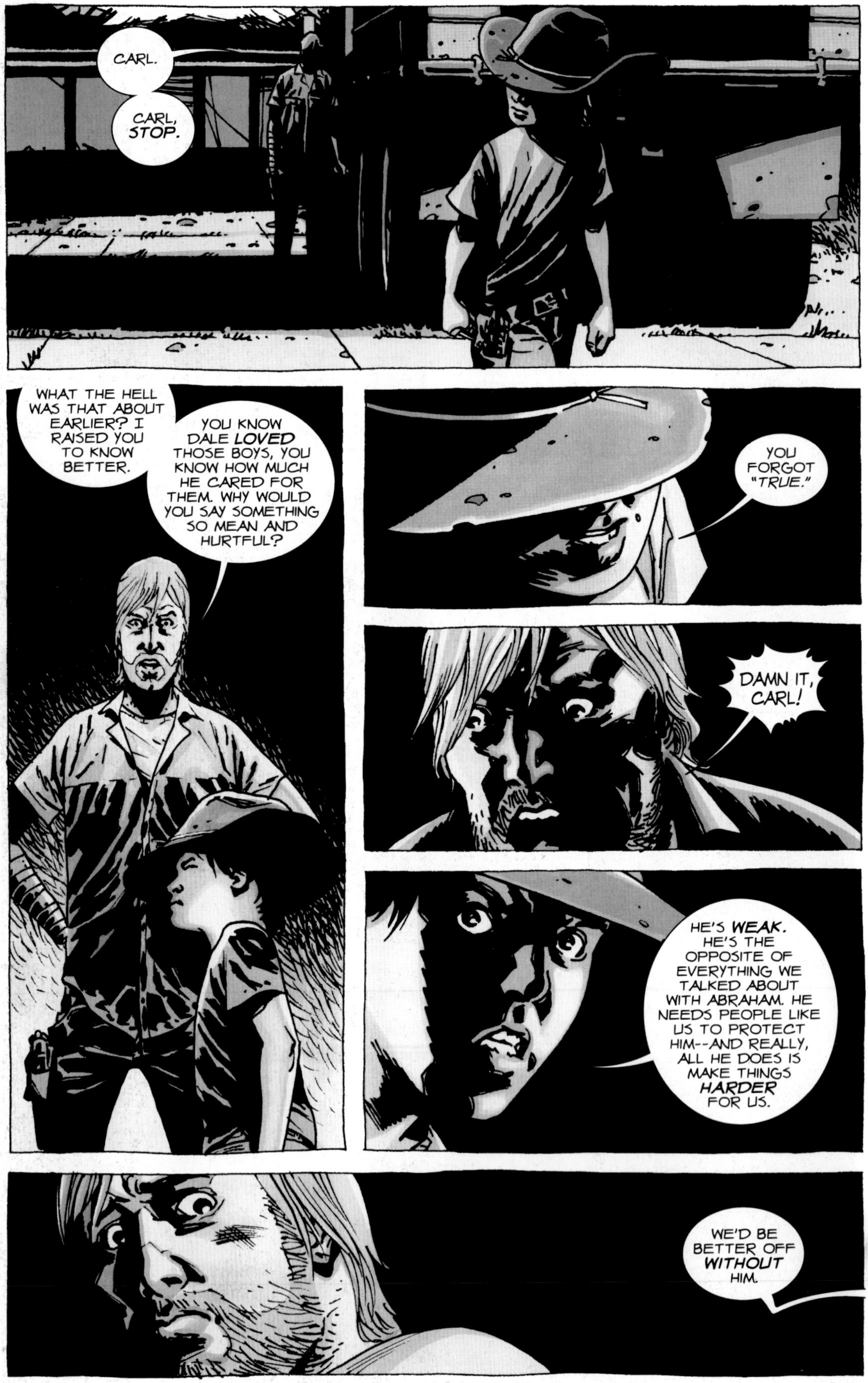
CARL.
CARL, STOP.
WHAT THE HELL WAS THAT ABOUT EARLIER? I RAISED YOU TO KNOW BETTER.
YOU KNOW DALE LOVED THOSE BOYS, YOU KNOW HOW MUCH HE CARED FOR THEM. WHY WOULD YOU SAY SOMETHING SO MEAN AND HURTFUL?
YOU FORGOT "TRUE."
DAMN IT, CARL!
HE'S WEAK. HE'S THE OPPOSITE OF EVERYTHING WE TALKED ABOUT WITH ABRAHAM. HE NEEDS PEOPLE LIKE US TO PROTECT HIM--AND REALLY, ALL HE DOES IS MAKE THINGS HARDER FOR US.
WE'D BE BETTER OFF WITHOUT HIM.

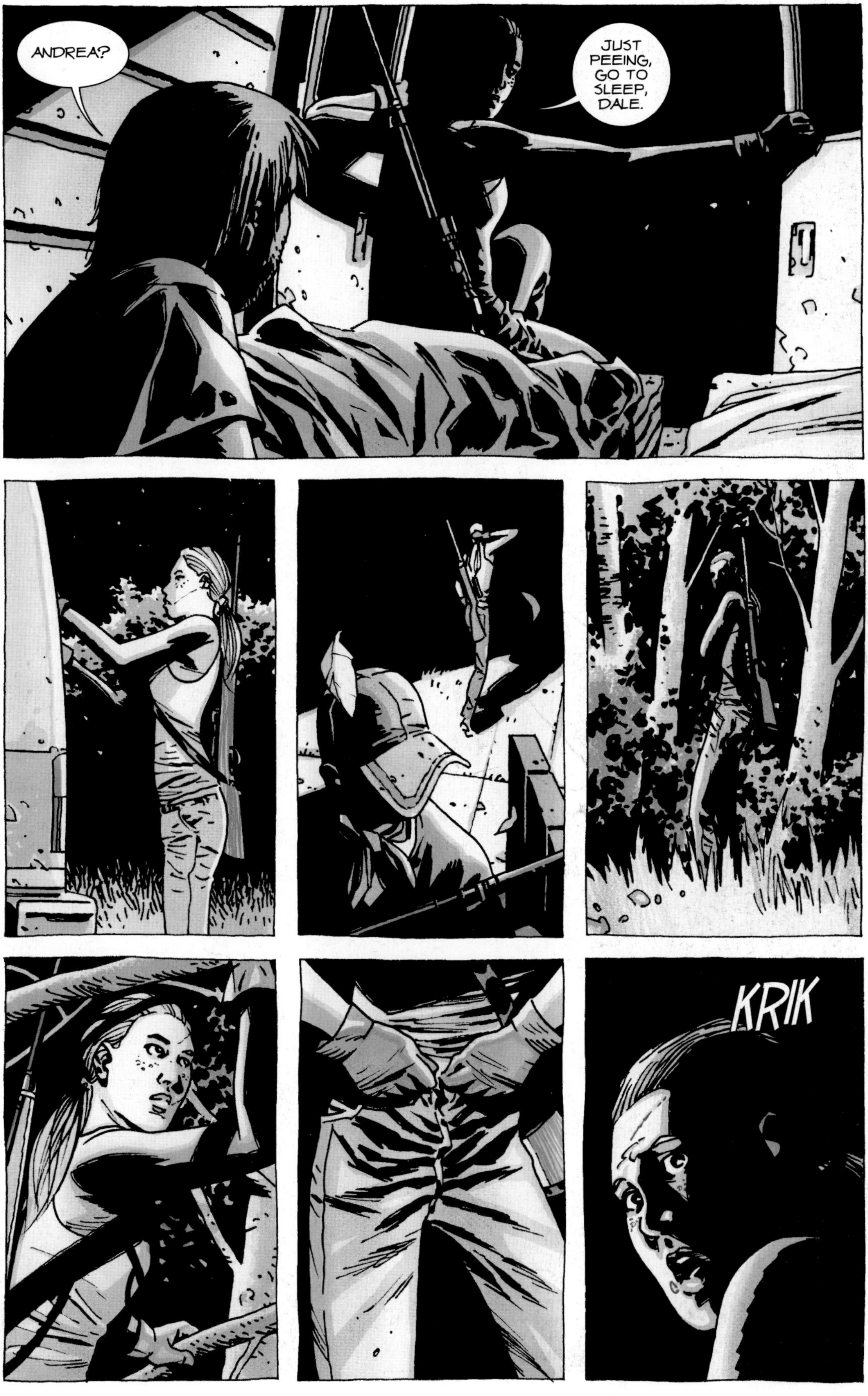
ANDREA?
JUST PEEING, GO TO SLEEP, DALE.
KRIK

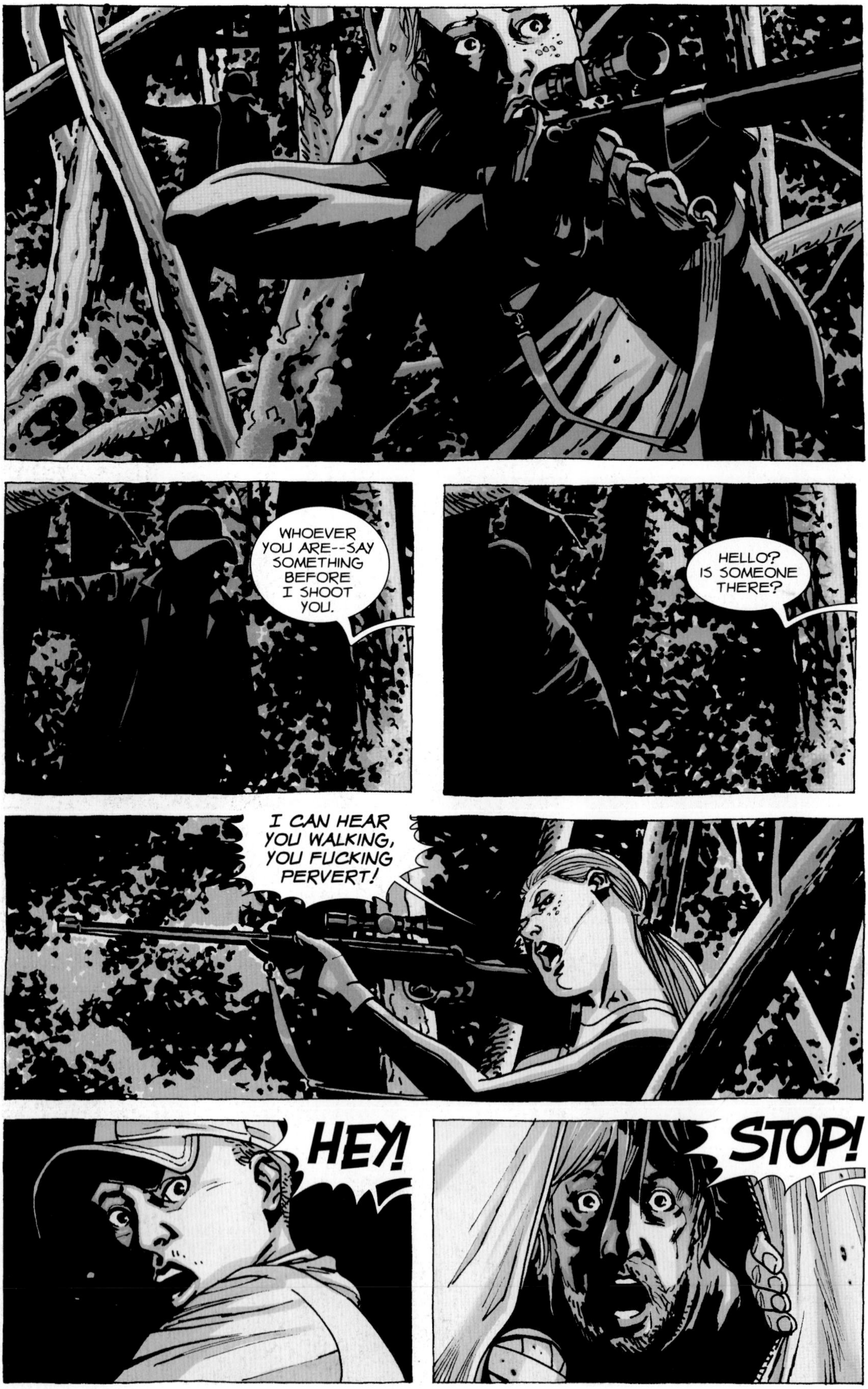
WHOEVER YOU ARE--SAY SOMETHING BEFORE I SHOOT YOU.
HELLO? IS SOMEONE THERE?
I CAN HEAR YOU WALKING, YOU FUCKING PERVERT!
HEY!
STOP!

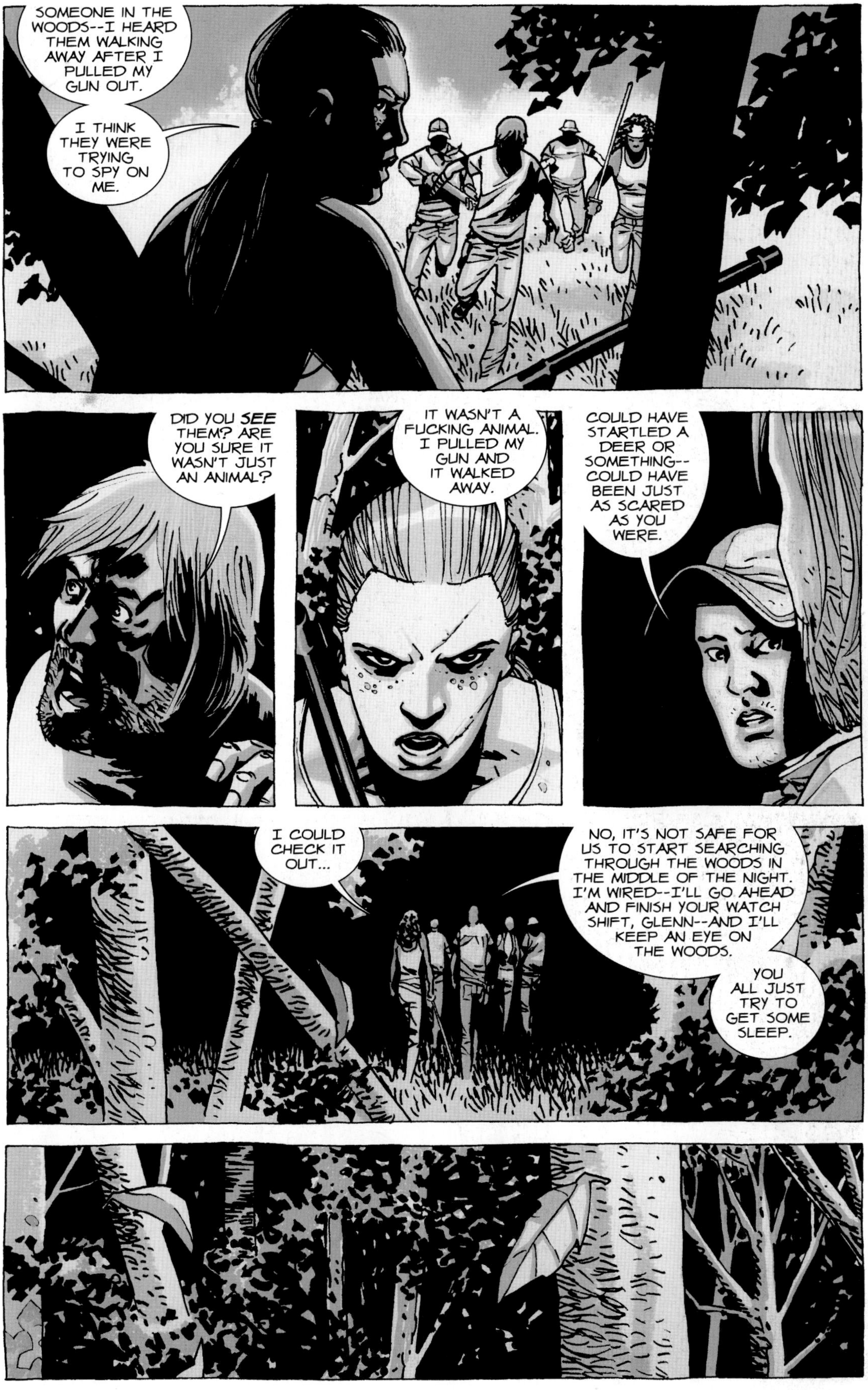
SOMEONE IN THE WOODS--I HEARD THEM WALKING AWAY AFTER I PULLED MY GUN OUT.
I THINK THEY WERE TRYING TO SPY ON ME.
DID YOU **SEE** THEM? ARE YOU SURE IT WASN'T JUST AN ANIMAL?
IT WASN'T A FUCKING ANIMAL. I PULLED MY GUN AND IT WALKED AWAY.
COULD HAVE STARTLED A DEER OR SOMETHING--COULD HAVE BEEN JUST AS SCARED AS YOU WERE.
I COULD CHECK IT OUT...
NO, IT'S NOT SAFE FOR US TO START SEARCHING THROUGH THE WOODS IN THE MIDDLE OF THE NIGHT. I'M WIRED--I'LL GO AHEAD AND FINISH YOUR WATCH SHIFT, GLENN--AND I'LL KEEP AN EYE ON THE WOODS.
YOU ALL JUST TRY TO GET SOME SLEEP.

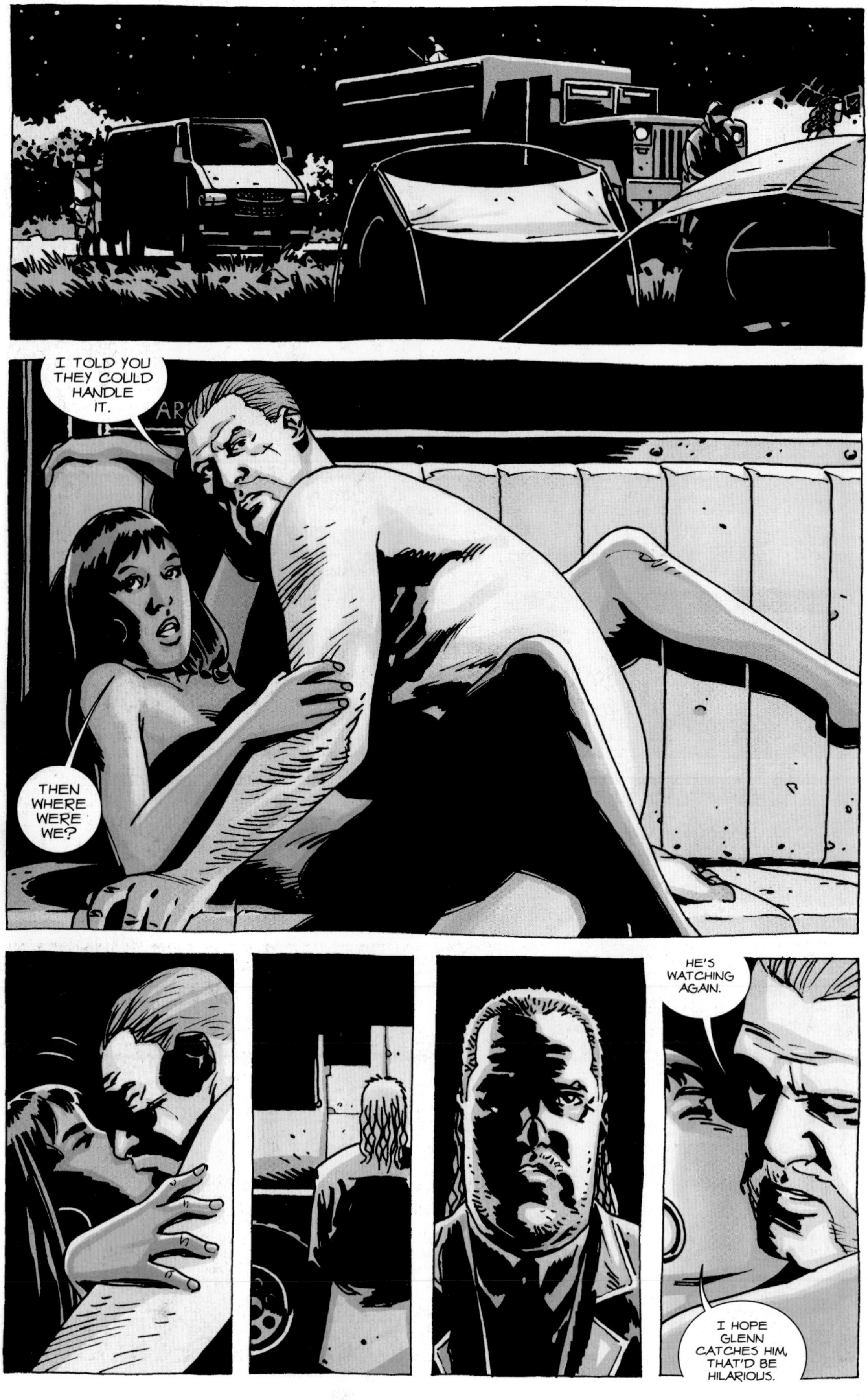
I TOLD YOU THEY COULD HANDLE IT.
THEN WHERE WERE WE?
HE'S WATCHING AGAIN.
I HOPE GLENN CATCHES HIM, THAT'D BE HILARIOUS.

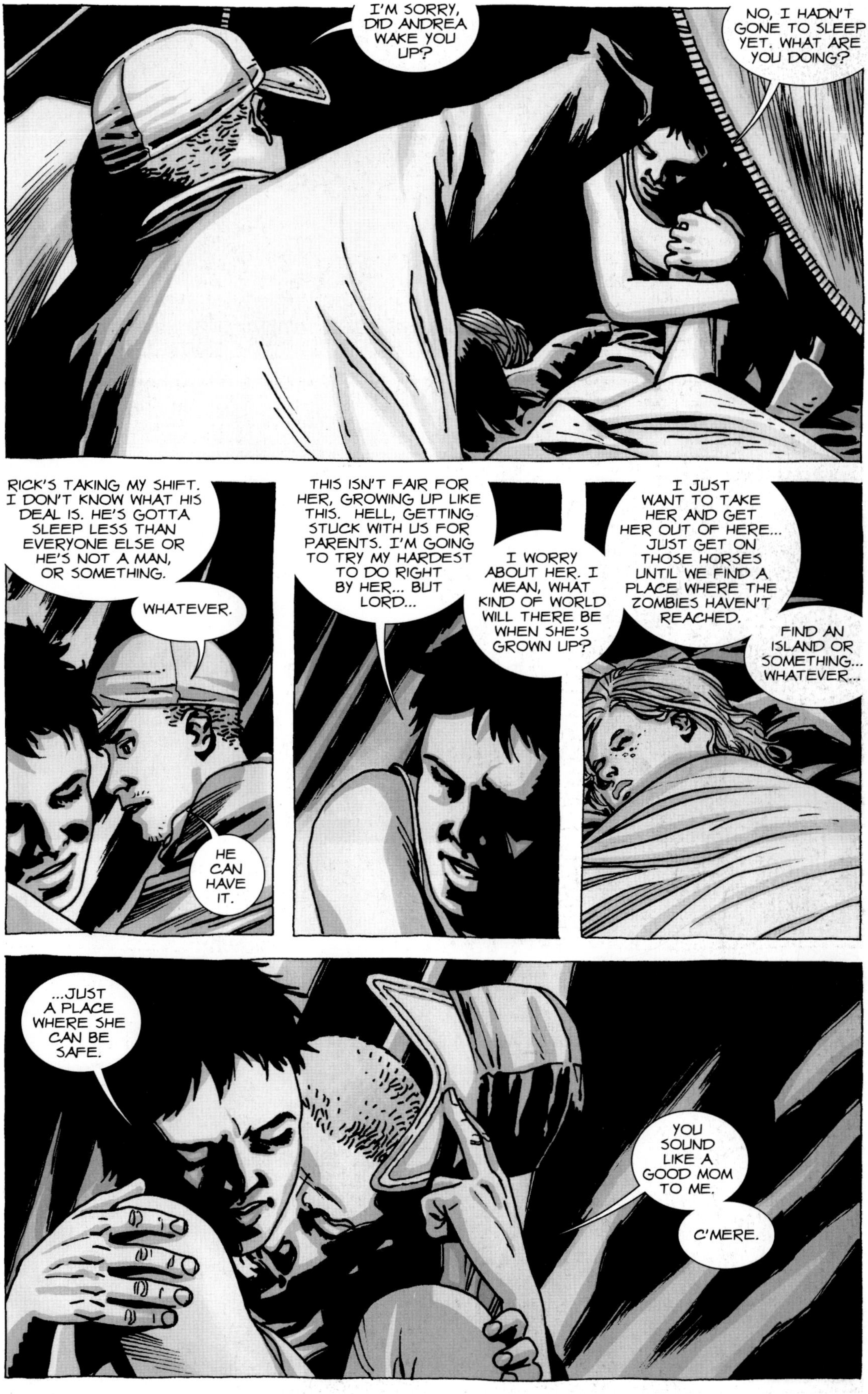
I'M SORRY, DID ANDREA WAKE YOU UP?
NO, I HADN'T GONE TO SLEEP YET. WHAT ARE YOU DOING?
RICK'S TAKING MY SHIFT. I DON'T KNOW WHAT HIS DEAL IS. HE'S GOTTA SLEEP LESS THAN EVERYONE ELSE OR HE'S NOT A MAN, OR SOMETHING.
WHATEVER.
HE CAN HAVE IT.
THIS ISN'T FAIR FOR HER, GROWING UP LIKE THIS. HELL, GETTING STUCK WITH US FOR PARENTS. I'M GOING TO TRY MY HARDEST TO DO RIGHT BY HER... BUT LORD...
I WORRY ABOUT HER. I MEAN, WHAT KIND OF WORLD WILL THERE BE WHEN SHE'S GROWN UP?
I JUST WANT TO TAKE HER AND GET HER OUT OF HERE... JUST GET ON THOSE HORSES UNTIL WE FIND A PLACE WHERE THE ZOMBIES HAVEN'T REACHED.
FIND AN ISLAND OR SOMETHING... WHATEVER...
...JUST A PLACE WHERE SHE CAN BE SAFE.
YOU SOUND LIKE A GOOD MOM TO ME.
C'MERE.

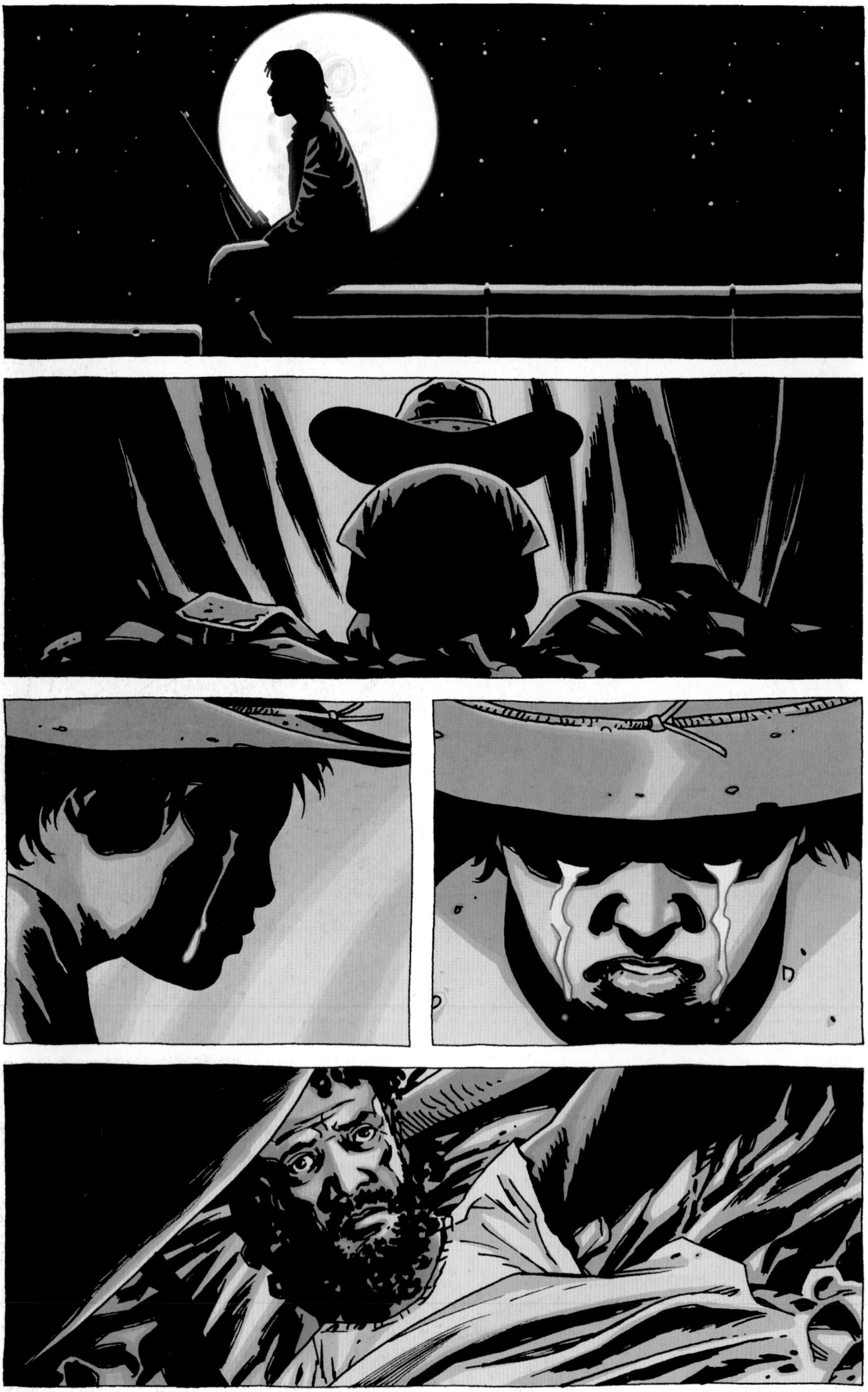

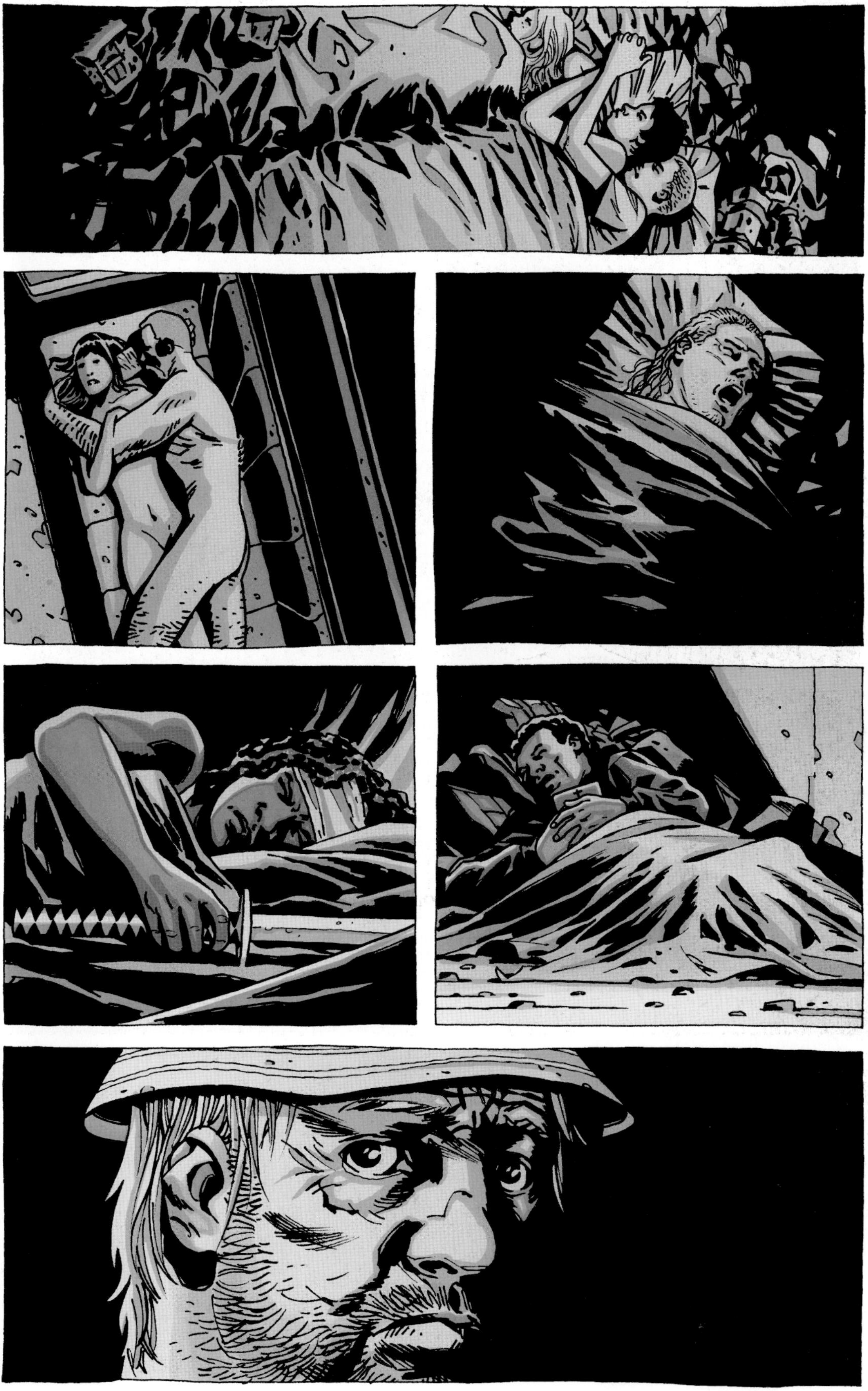

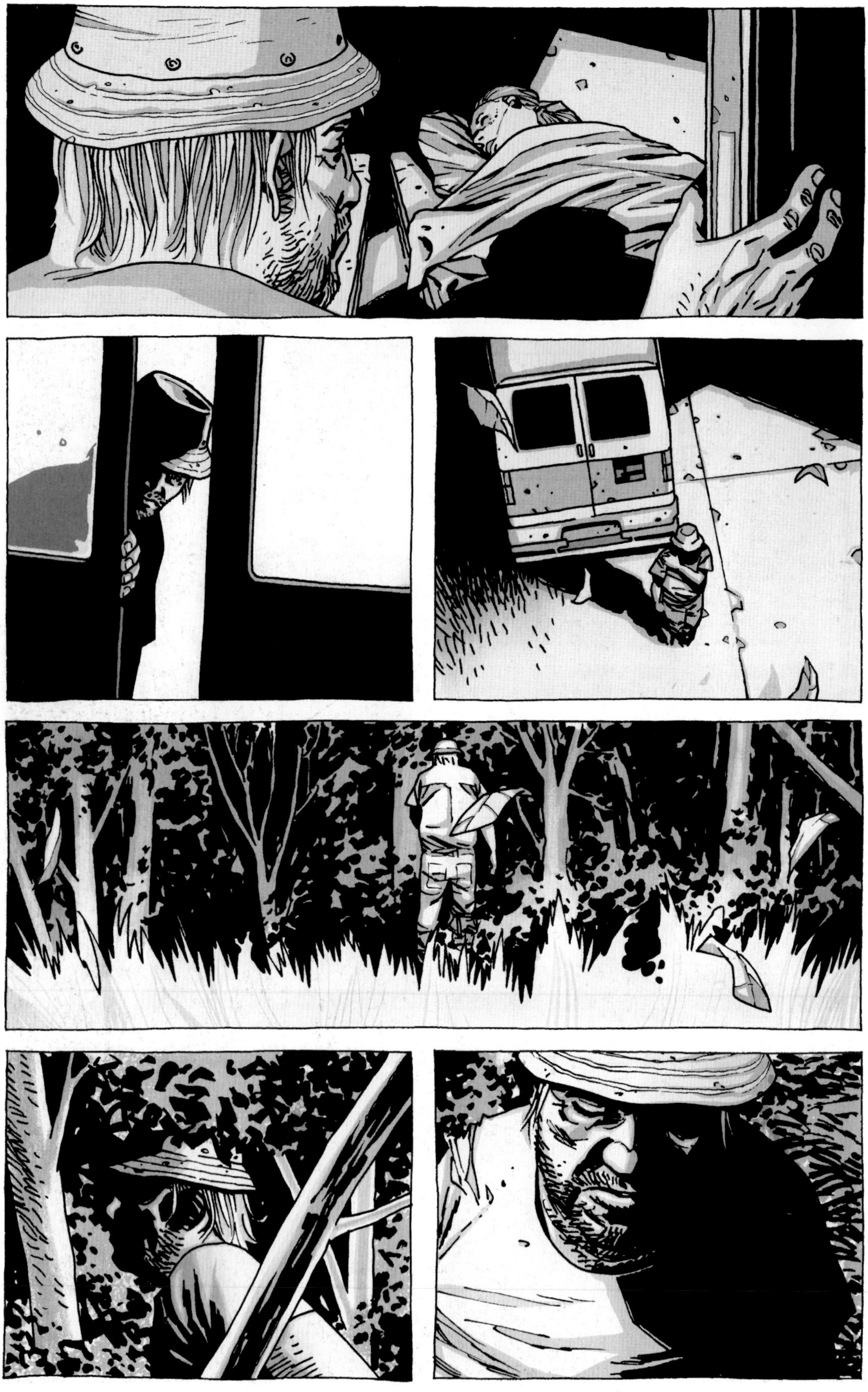

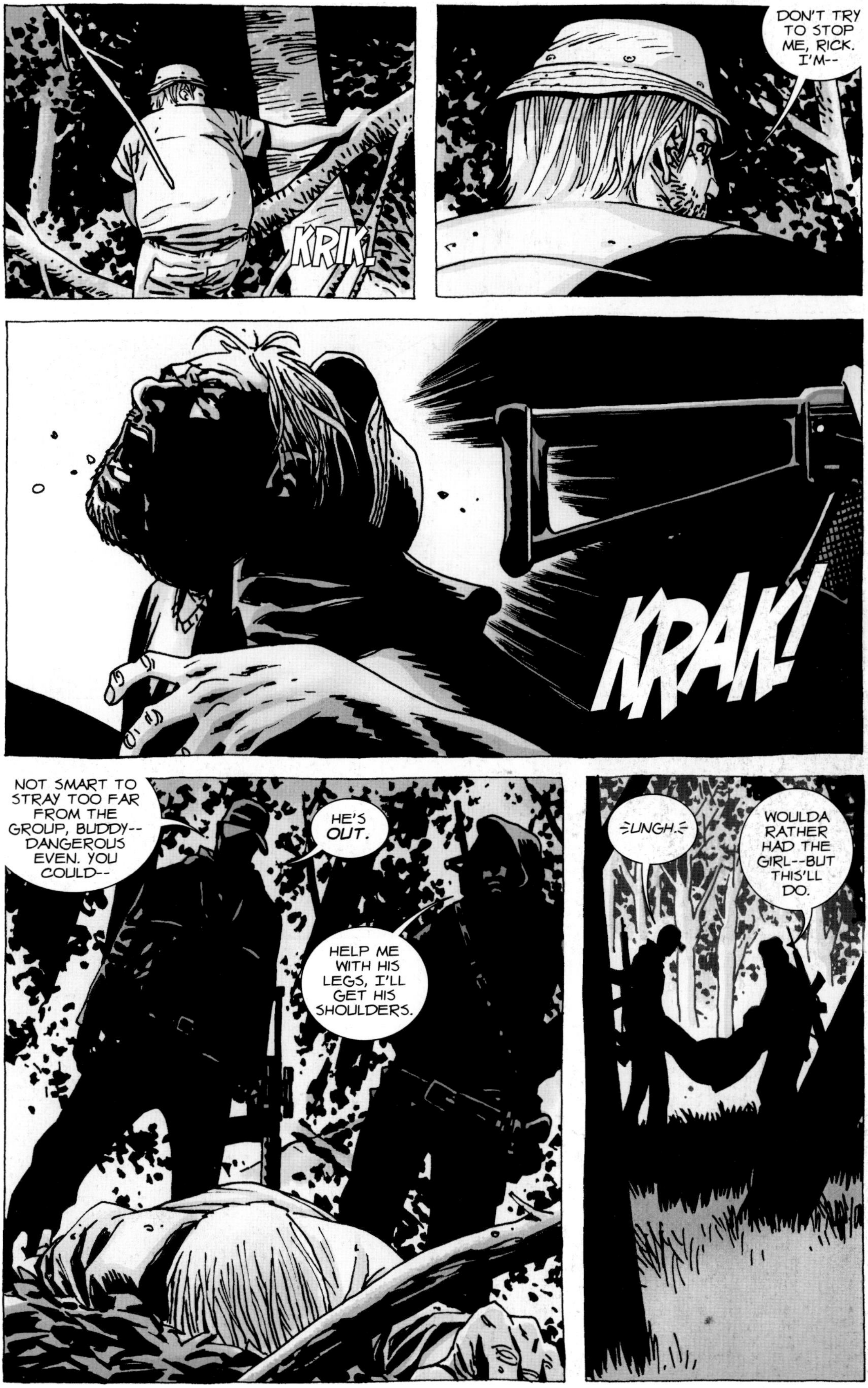
KRIK!
DON'T TRY TO STOP ME, RICK. I'M--
KRAK!
NOT SMART TO STRAY TOO FAR FROM THE GROUP, BUDDY-- DANGEROUS EVEN. YOU COULD--
HE'S OUT.
HELP ME WITH HIS LEGS, I'LL GET HIS SHOULDERS.
UNGH.
WOULDA RATHER HAD THE GIRL--BUT THIS'LL DO.

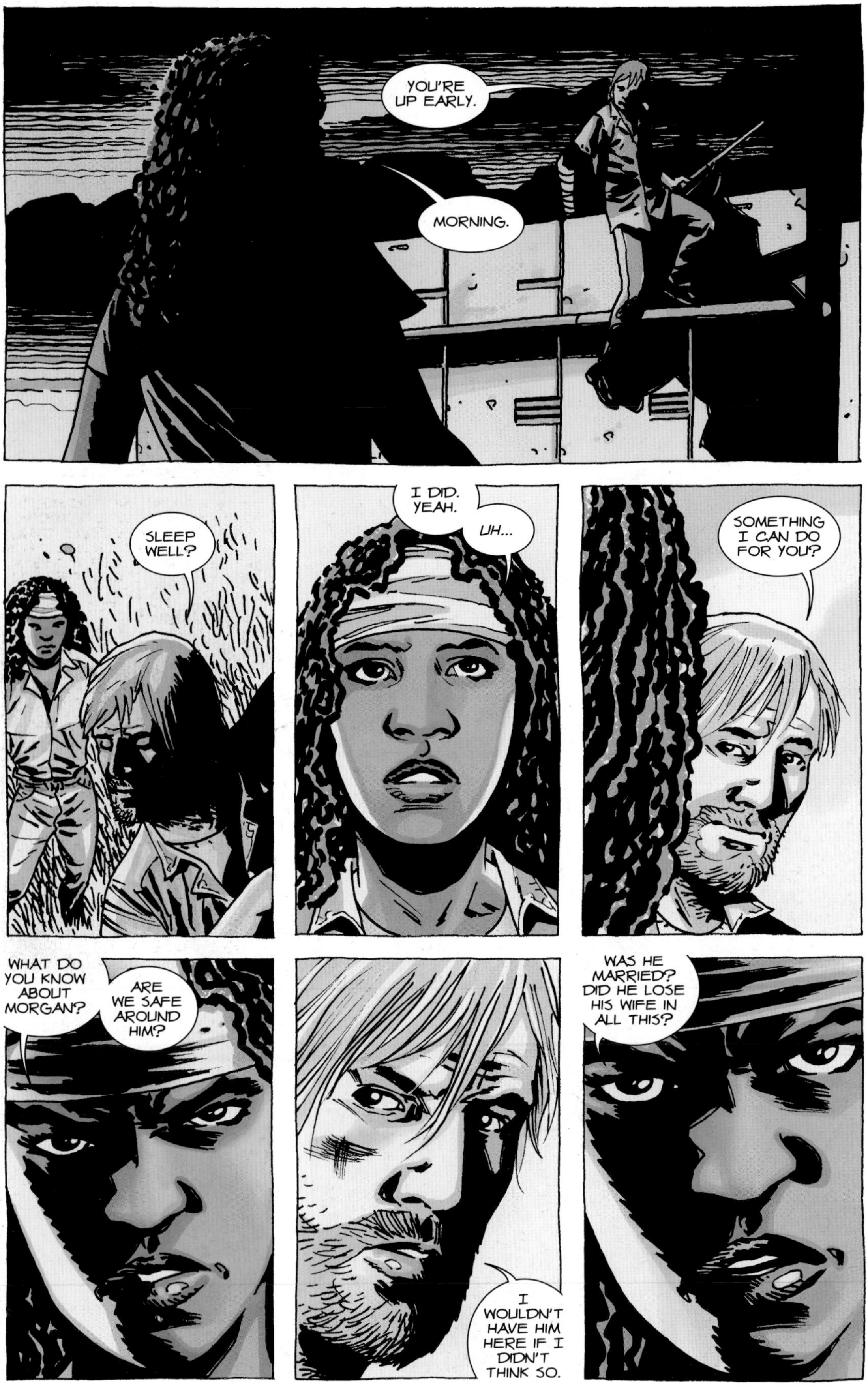
YOU'RE UP EARLY.
MORNING.
SLEEP WELL?
I DID. YEAH.
UH...
SOMETHING I CAN DO FOR YOU?
WHAT DO YOU KNOW ABOUT MORGAN?
ARE WE SAFE AROUND HIM?
I WOULDN'T HAVE HIM HERE IF I DIDN'T THINK SO.
WAS HE MARRIED? DID HE LOSE HIS WIFE IN ALL THIS?

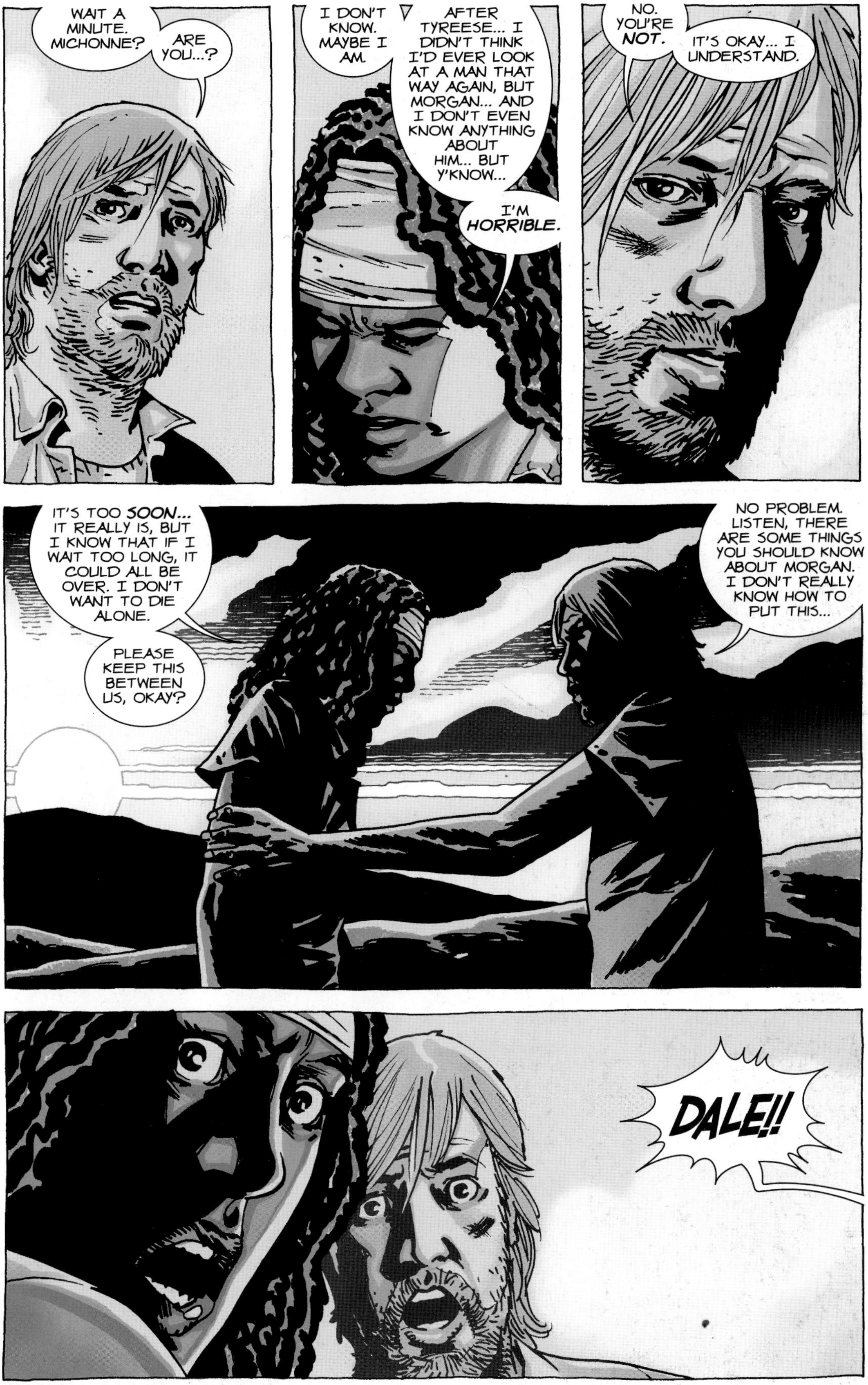
WAIT A MINUTE. MICHONNE?
ARE YOU...?
I DON'T KNOW. MAYBE I AM.
AFTER TYREESE... I DIDN'T THINK I'D EVER LOOK AT A MAN THAT WAY AGAIN, BUT MORGAN... AND I DON'T EVEN KNOW ANYTHING ABOUT HIM... BUT Y'KNOW...
I'M HORRIBLE.
NO. YOU'RE NOT.
IT'S OKAY... I UNDERSTAND.
IT'S TOO SOON... IT REALLY IS, BUT I KNOW THAT IF I WAIT TOO LONG, IT COULD ALL BE OVER. I DON'T WANT TO DIE ALONE.
PLEASE KEEP THIS BETWEEN US, OKAY?
NO PROBLEM. LISTEN, THERE ARE SOME THINGS YOU SHOULD KNOW ABOUT MORGAN. I DON'T REALLY KNOW HOW TO PUT THIS...
DALE!!

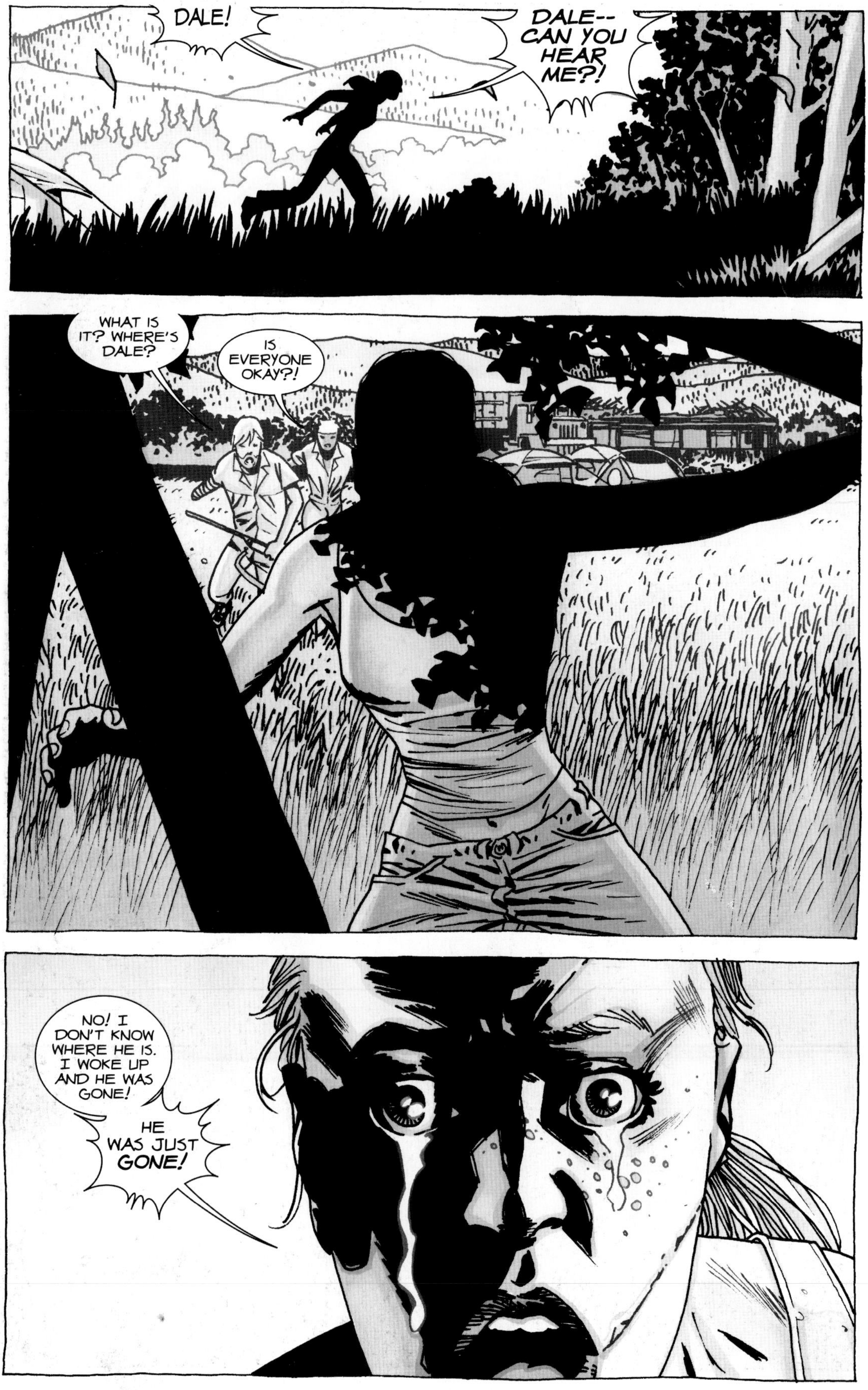
DALE!
DALE-- CAN YOU HEAR ME?!
WHAT IS IT? WHERE'S DALE?
IS EVERYONE OKAY?!
NO! I DON'T KNOW WHERE HE IS. I WOKE UP AND HE WAS GONE!
HE WAS JUST GONE!

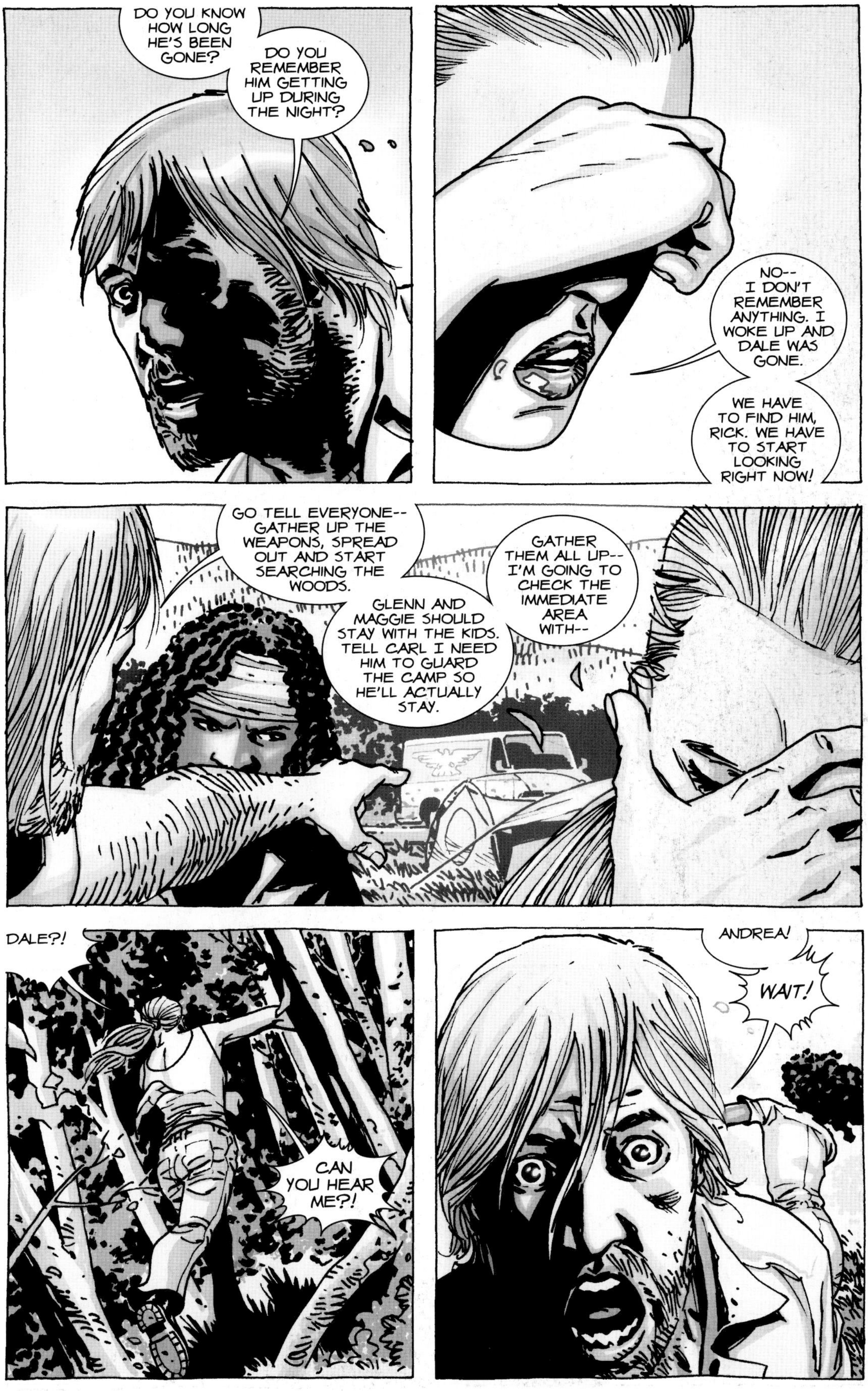
DO YOU KNOW HOW LONG HE'S BEEN GONE?
DO YOU REMEMBER HIM GETTING UP DURING THE NIGHT?
NO-- I DON'T REMEMBER ANYTHING. I WOKE UP AND DALE WAS GONE.
WE HAVE TO FIND HIM, RICK. WE HAVE TO START LOOKING RIGHT NOW!
GO TELL EVERYONE-- GATHER UP THE WEAPONS, SPREAD OUT AND START SEARCHING THE WOODS.
GLENN AND MAGGIE SHOULD STAY WITH THE KIDS. TELL CARL I NEED HIM TO GUARD THE CAMP SO HE'LL ACTUALLY STAY.
GATHER THEM ALL UP-- I'M GOING TO CHECK THE IMMEDIATE AREA WITH--
DALE?!
CAN YOU HEAR ME?!
ANDREA!
WAIT!

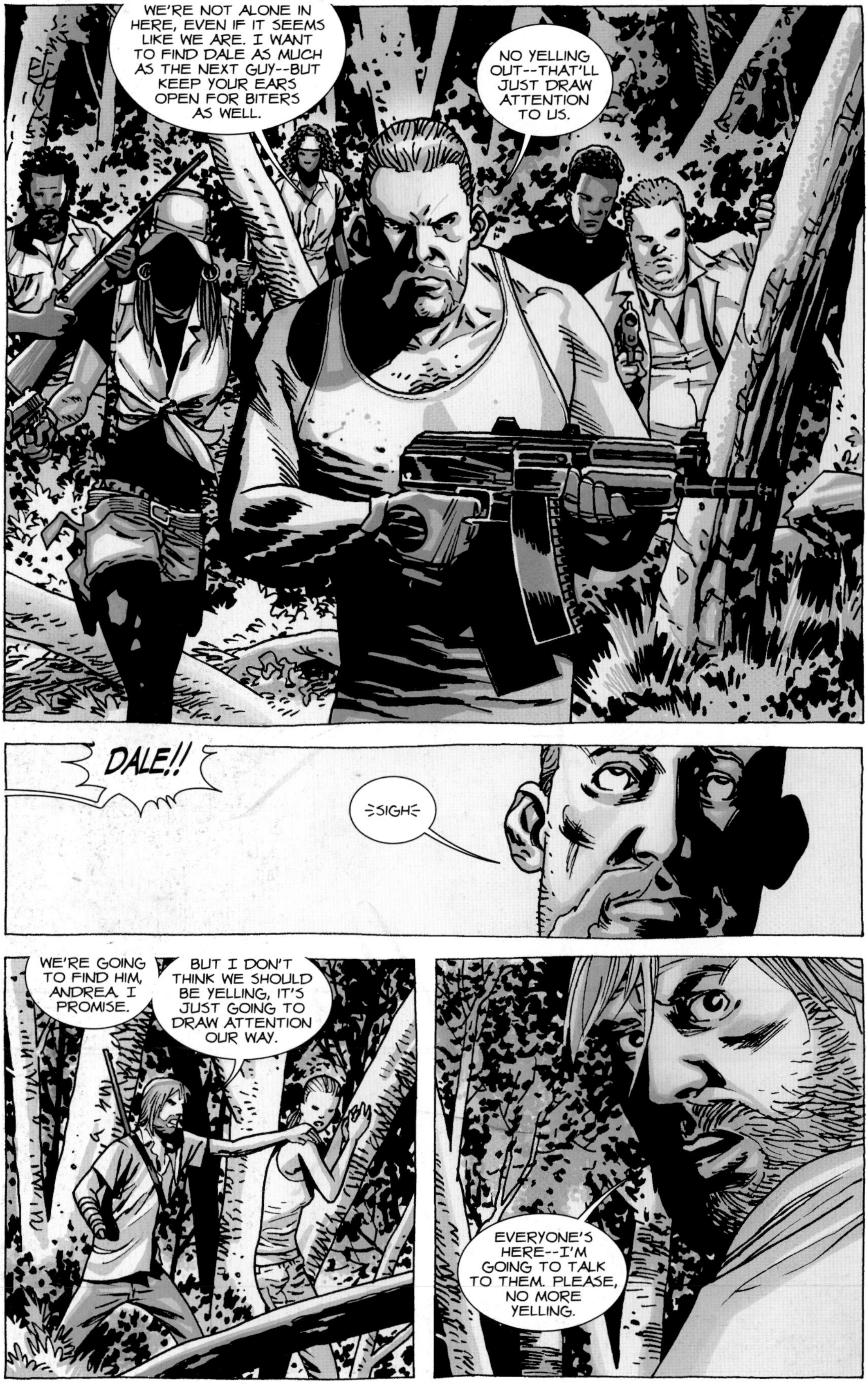
WE'RE NOT ALONE IN HERE, EVEN IF IT SEEMS LIKE WE ARE. I WANT TO FIND DALE AS MUCH AS THE NEXT GUY--BUT KEEP YOUR EARS OPEN FOR BITERS AS WELL.
NO YELLING OUT--THAT'LL JUST DRAW ATTENTION TO US.
DALE!!
SIGH
WE'RE GOING TO FIND HIM, ANDREA. I PROMISE.
BUT I DON'T THINK WE SHOULD BE YELLING, IT'S JUST GOING TO DRAW ATTENTION OUR WAY.
EVERYONE'S HERE--I'M GOING TO TALK TO THEM. PLEASE, NO MORE YELLING.

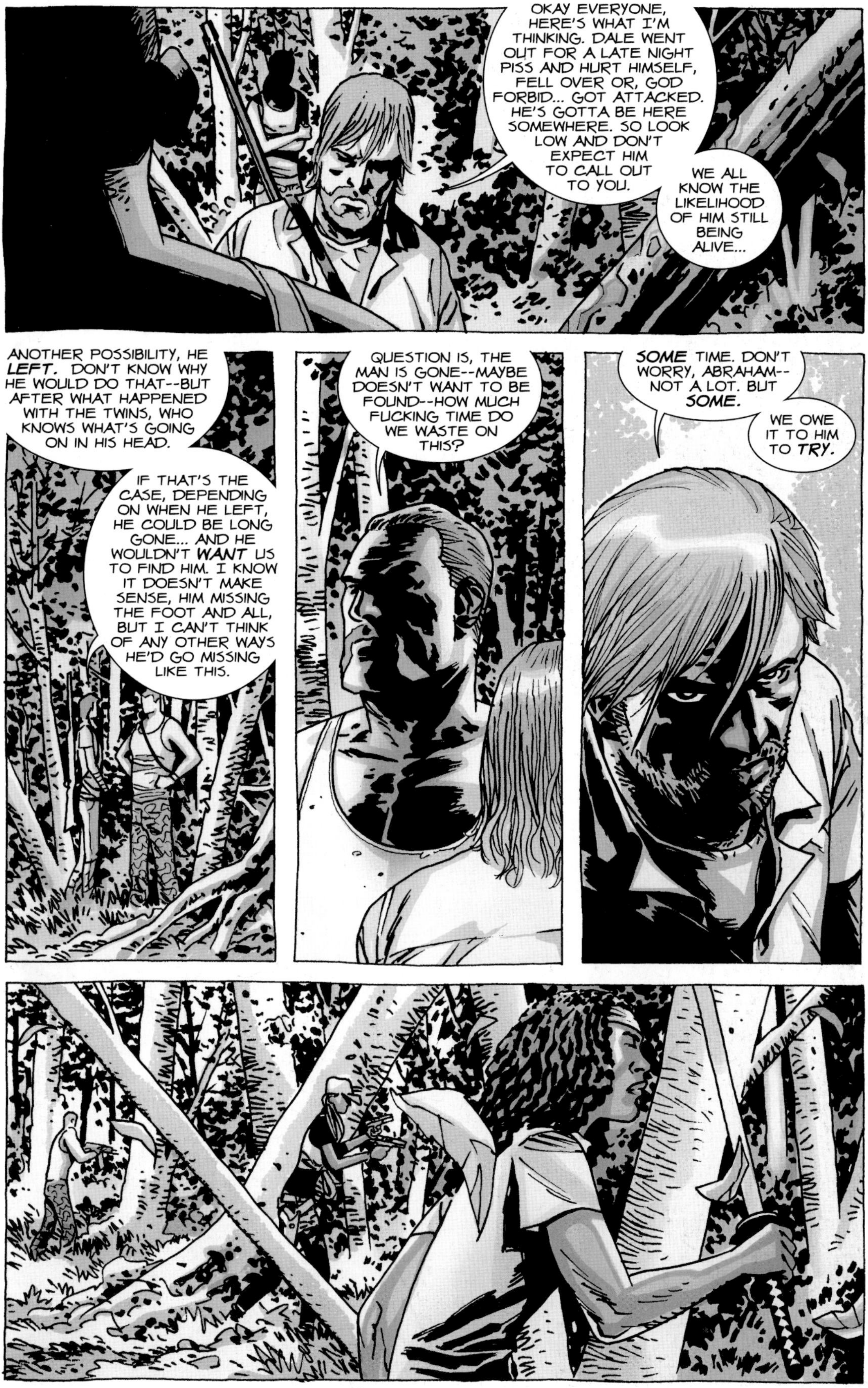
OKAY EVERYONE, HERE'S WHAT I'M THINKING. DALE WENT OUT FOR A LATE NIGHT PISS AND HURT HIMSELF, FELL OVER OR, GOD FORBID... GOT ATTACKED. HE'S GOTTA BE HERE SOMEWHERE. SO LOOK LOW AND DON'T EXPECT HIM TO CALL OUT TO YOU.
WE ALL KNOW THE LIKELIHOOD OF HIM STILL BEING ALIVE...
ANOTHER POSSIBILITY, HE *LEFT.* DON'T KNOW WHY HE WOULD DO THAT--BUT AFTER WHAT HAPPENED WITH THE TWINS, WHO KNOWS WHAT'S GOING ON IN HIS HEAD.
IF THAT'S THE CASE, DEPENDING ON WHEN HE LEFT, HE COULD BE LONG GONE... AND HE WOULDN'T *WANT* US TO FIND HIM. I KNOW IT DOESN'T MAKE SENSE, HIM MISSING THE FOOT AND ALL, BUT I CAN'T THINK OF ANY OTHER WAYS HE'D GO MISSING LIKE THIS.
QUESTION IS, THE MAN IS GONE--MAYBE DOESN'T WANT TO BE FOUND--HOW MUCH FUCKING TIME DO WE WASTE ON THIS?
SOME TIME. DON'T WORRY, ABRAHAM--NOT A LOT. BUT *SOME.*
WE OWE IT TO HIM TO *TRY.*

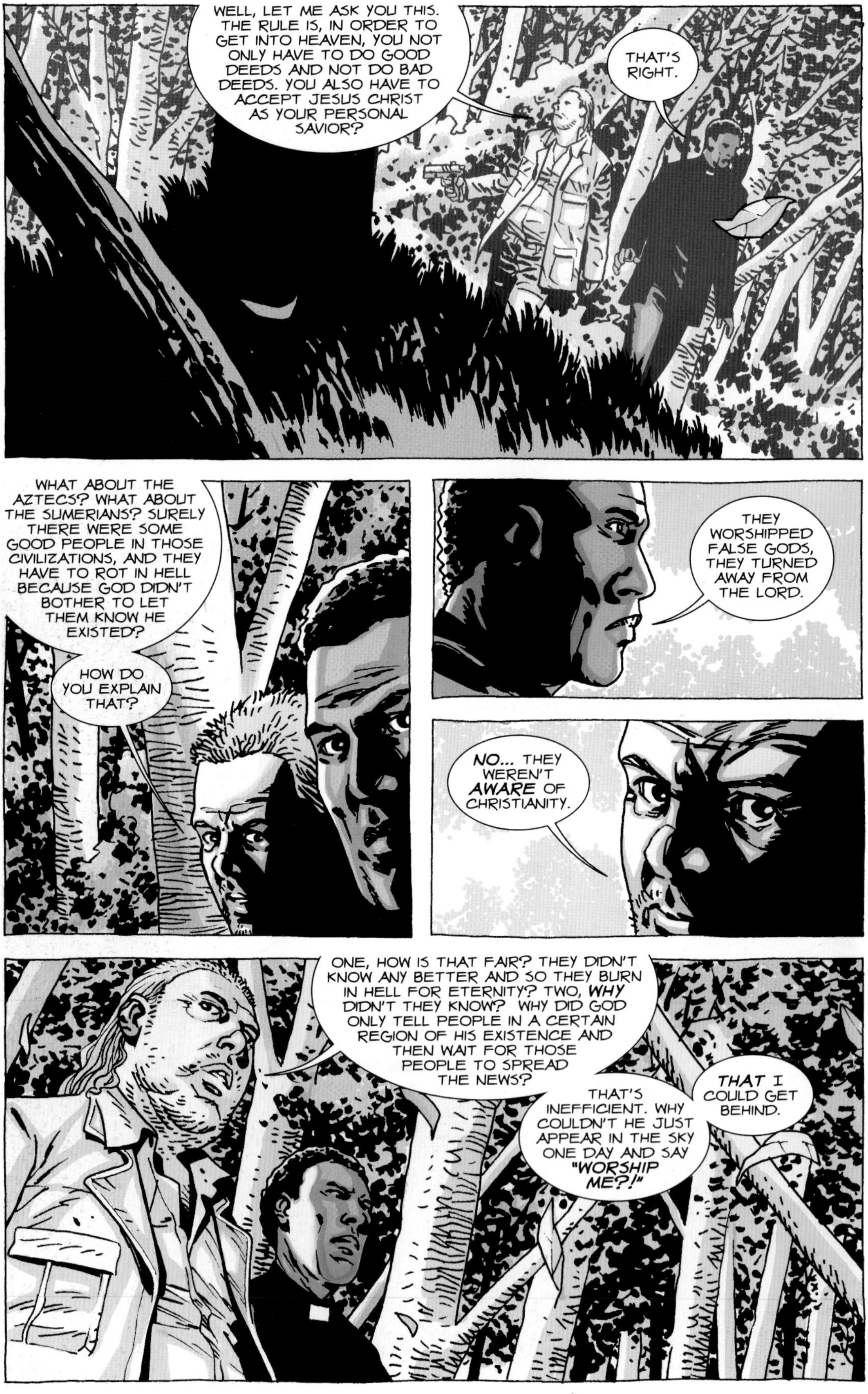
WELL, LET ME ASK YOU THIS. THE RULE IS, IN ORDER TO GET INTO HEAVEN, YOU NOT ONLY HAVE TO DO GOOD DEEDS AND NOT DO BAD DEEDS. YOU ALSO HAVE TO ACCEPT JESUS CHRIST AS YOUR PERSONAL SAVIOR?
THAT'S RIGHT.
WHAT ABOUT THE AZTECS? WHAT ABOUT THE SUMERIANS? SURELY THERE WERE SOME GOOD PEOPLE IN THOSE CIVILIZATIONS, AND THEY HAVE TO ROT IN HELL BECAUSE GOD DIDN'T BOTHER TO LET THEM KNOW HE EXISTED?
HOW DO YOU EXPLAIN THAT?
THEY WORSHIPPED FALSE GODS, THEY TURNED AWAY FROM THE LORD.
NO... THEY WEREN'T AWARE OF CHRISTIANITY.
ONE, HOW IS THAT FAIR? THEY DIDN'T KNOW ANY BETTER AND SO THEY BURN IN HELL FOR ETERNITY? TWO, WHY DIDN'T THEY KNOW? WHY DID GOD ONLY TELL PEOPLE IN A CERTAIN REGION OF HIS EXISTENCE AND THEN WAIT FOR THOSE PEOPLE TO SPREAD THE NEWS?
THAT'S INEFFICIENT. WHY COULDN'T HE JUST APPEAR IN THE SKY ONE DAY AND SAY "WORSHIP ME?!"
THAT I COULD GET BEHIND.

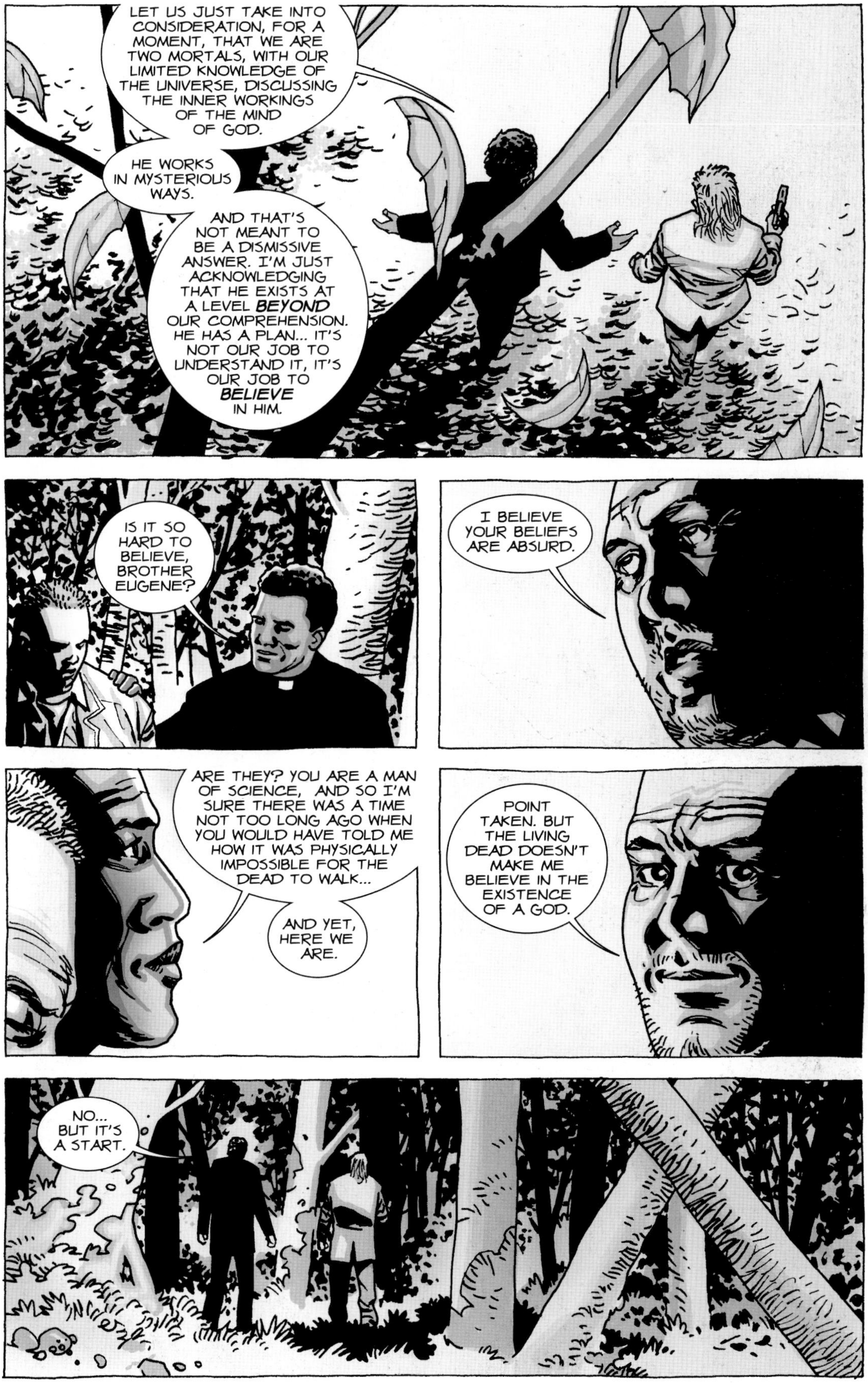
LET US JUST TAKE INTO CONSIDERATION, FOR A MOMENT, THAT WE ARE TWO MORTALS, WITH OUR LIMITED KNOWLEDGE OF THE UNIVERSE, DISCUSSING THE INNER WORKINGS OF THE MIND OF GOD.
HE WORKS IN MYSTERIOUS WAYS.
AND THAT'S NOT MEANT TO BE A DISMISSIVE ANSWER. I'M JUST ACKNOWLEDGING THAT HE EXISTS AT A LEVEL BEYOND OUR COMPREHENSION. HE HAS A PLAN... IT'S NOT OUR JOB TO UNDERSTAND IT, IT'S OUR JOB TO BELIEVE IN HIM.
IS IT SO HARD TO BELIEVE, BROTHER EUGENE?
I BELIEVE YOUR BELIEFS ARE ABSURD.
ARE THEY? YOU ARE A MAN OF SCIENCE, AND SO I'M SURE THERE WAS A TIME NOT TOO LONG AGO WHEN YOU WOULD HAVE TOLD ME HOW IT WAS PHYSICALLY IMPOSSIBLE FOR THE DEAD TO WALK...
AND YET, HERE WE ARE.
POINT TAKEN. BUT THE LIVING DEAD DOESN'T MAKE ME BELIEVE IN THE EXISTENCE OF A GOD.
NO... BUT IT'S A START.

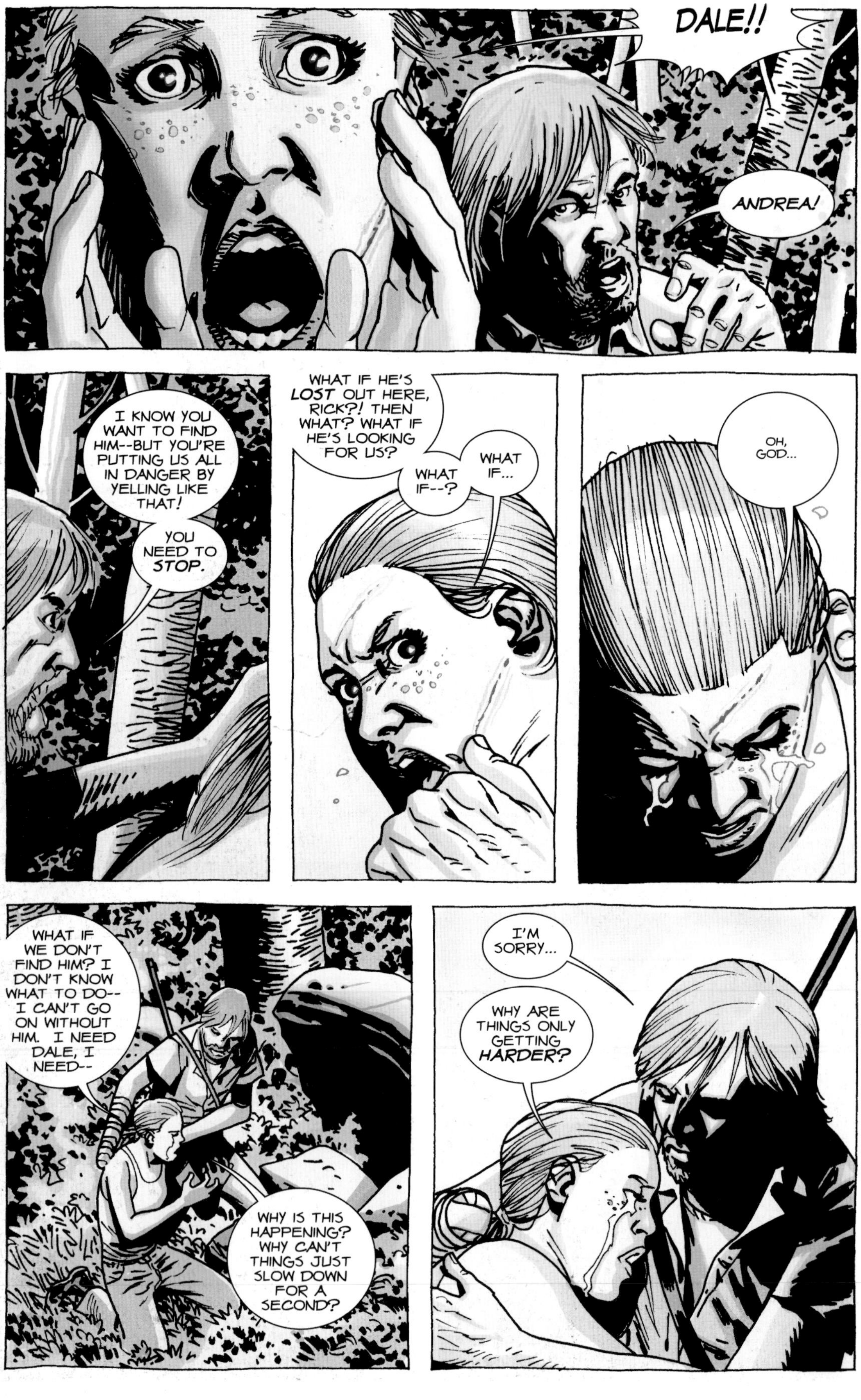
DALE!!
ANDREA!
I KNOW YOU WANT TO FIND HIM--BUT YOU'RE PUTTING US ALL IN DANGER BY YELLING LIKE THAT!
YOU NEED TO STOP.
WHAT IF HE'S LOST OUT HERE, RICK?! THEN WHAT? WHAT IF HE'S LOOKING FOR US?
WHAT IF--?
WHAT IF...
OH, GOD...
WHAT IF WE DON'T FIND HIM? I DON'T KNOW WHAT TO DO-- I CAN'T GO ON WITHOUT HIM. I NEED DALE, I NEED--
WHY IS THIS HAPPENING? WHY CAN'T THINGS JUST SLOW DOWN FOR A SECOND?
I'M SORRY...
WHY ARE THINGS ONLY GETTING HARDER?

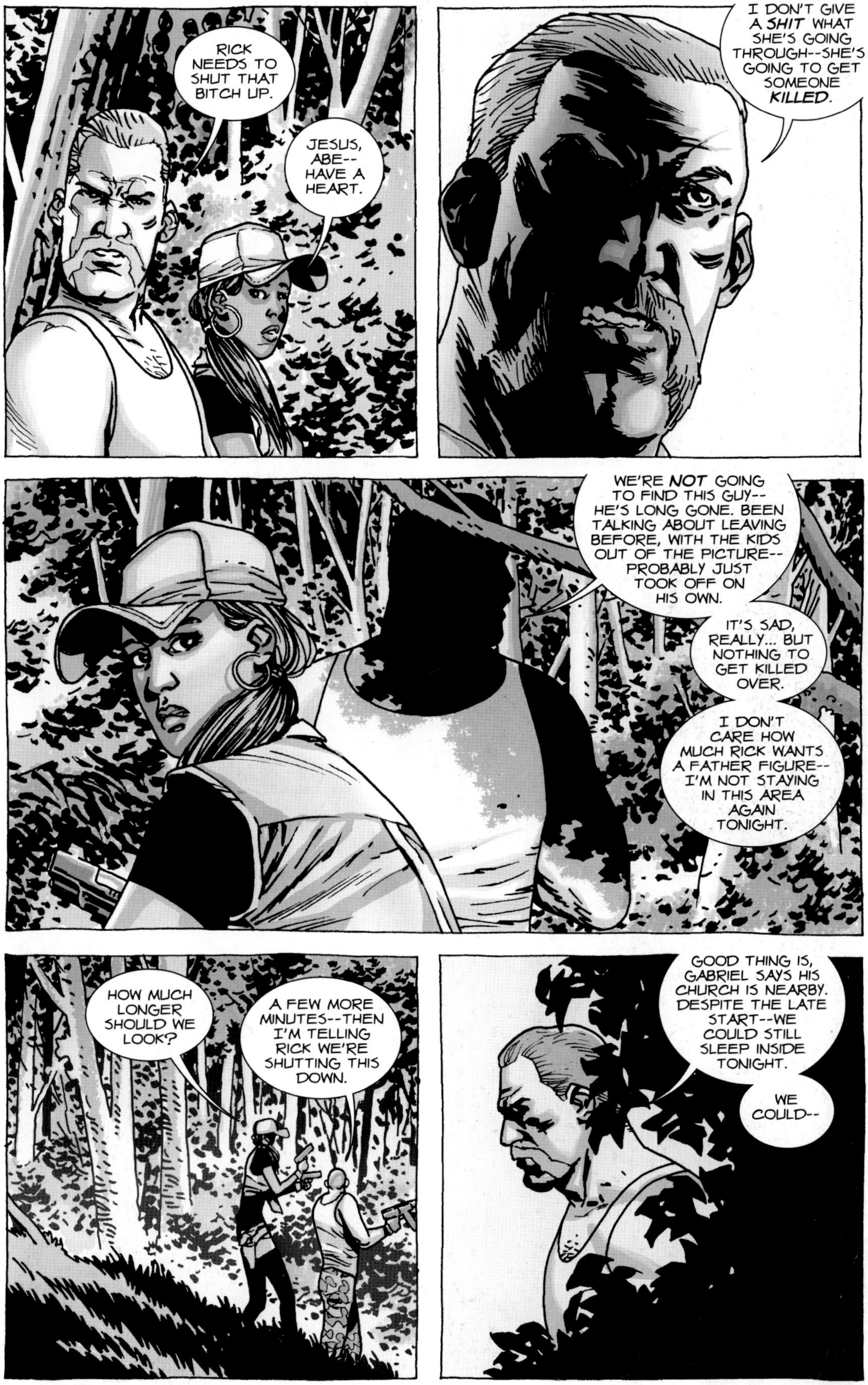

RICK NEEDS TO SHUT THAT BITCH UP.
JESUS, ABE-- HAVE A HEART.
I DON'T GIVE A ***SHIT*** WHAT SHE'S GOING THROUGH--SHE'S GOING TO GET SOMEONE ***KILLED***.
WE'RE ***NOT*** GOING TO FIND THIS GUY-- HE'S LONG GONE. BEEN TALKING ABOUT LEAVING BEFORE, WITH THE KIDS OUT OF THE PICTURE-- PROBABLY JUST TOOK OFF ON HIS OWN.
IT'S SAD, REALLY... BUT NOTHING TO GET KILLED OVER.
I DON'T CARE HOW MUCH RICK WANTS A FATHER FIGURE-- I'M NOT STAYING IN THIS AREA AGAIN TONIGHT.
HOW MUCH LONGER SHOULD WE LOOK?
A FEW MORE MINUTES--THEN I'M TELLING RICK WE'RE SHUTTING THIS DOWN.
GOOD THING IS, GABRIEL SAYS HIS CHURCH IS NEARBY. DESPITE THE LATE START--WE COULD STILL SLEEP INSIDE TONIGHT.
WE COULD--

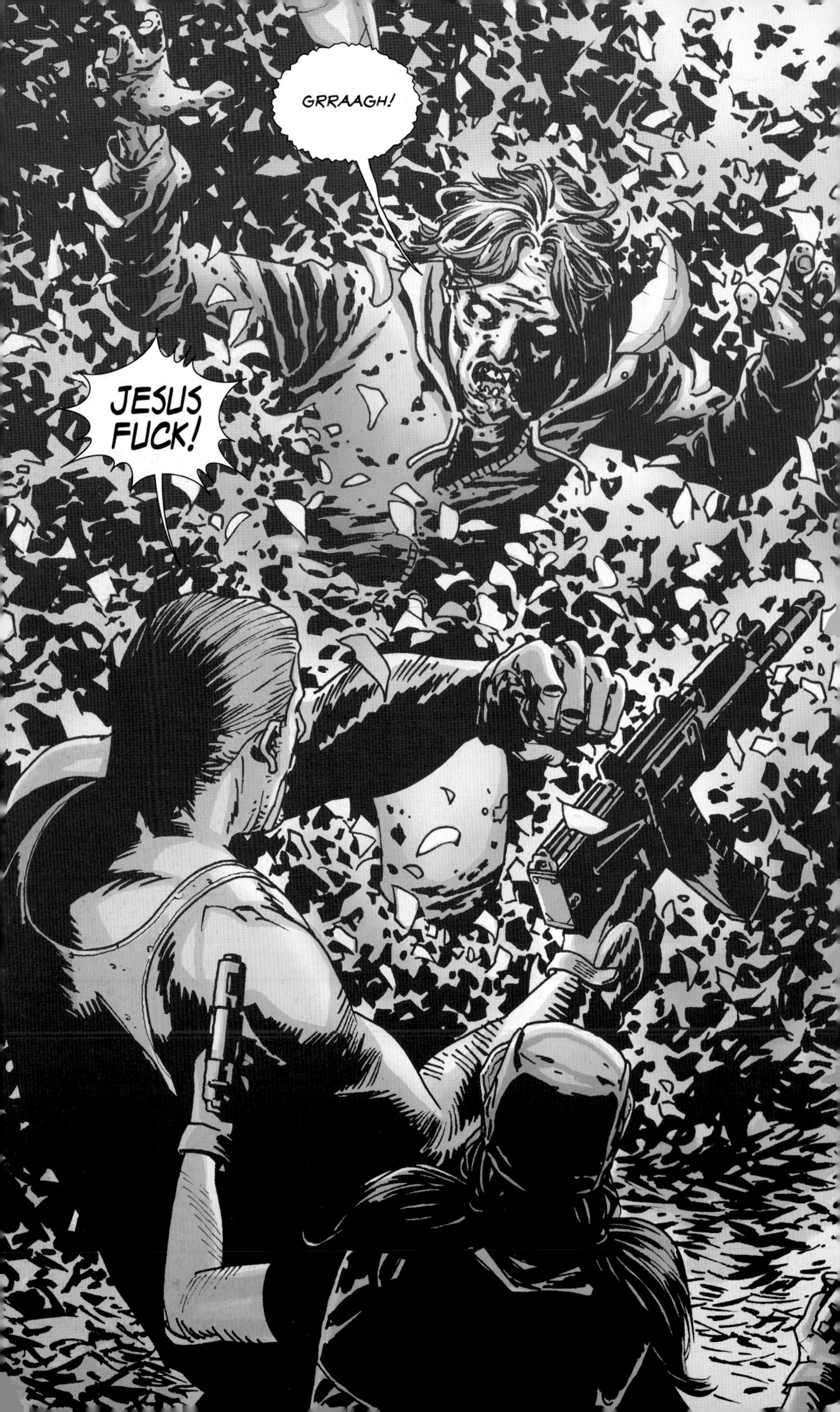
GRRAAGH!
JESUS FUCK!

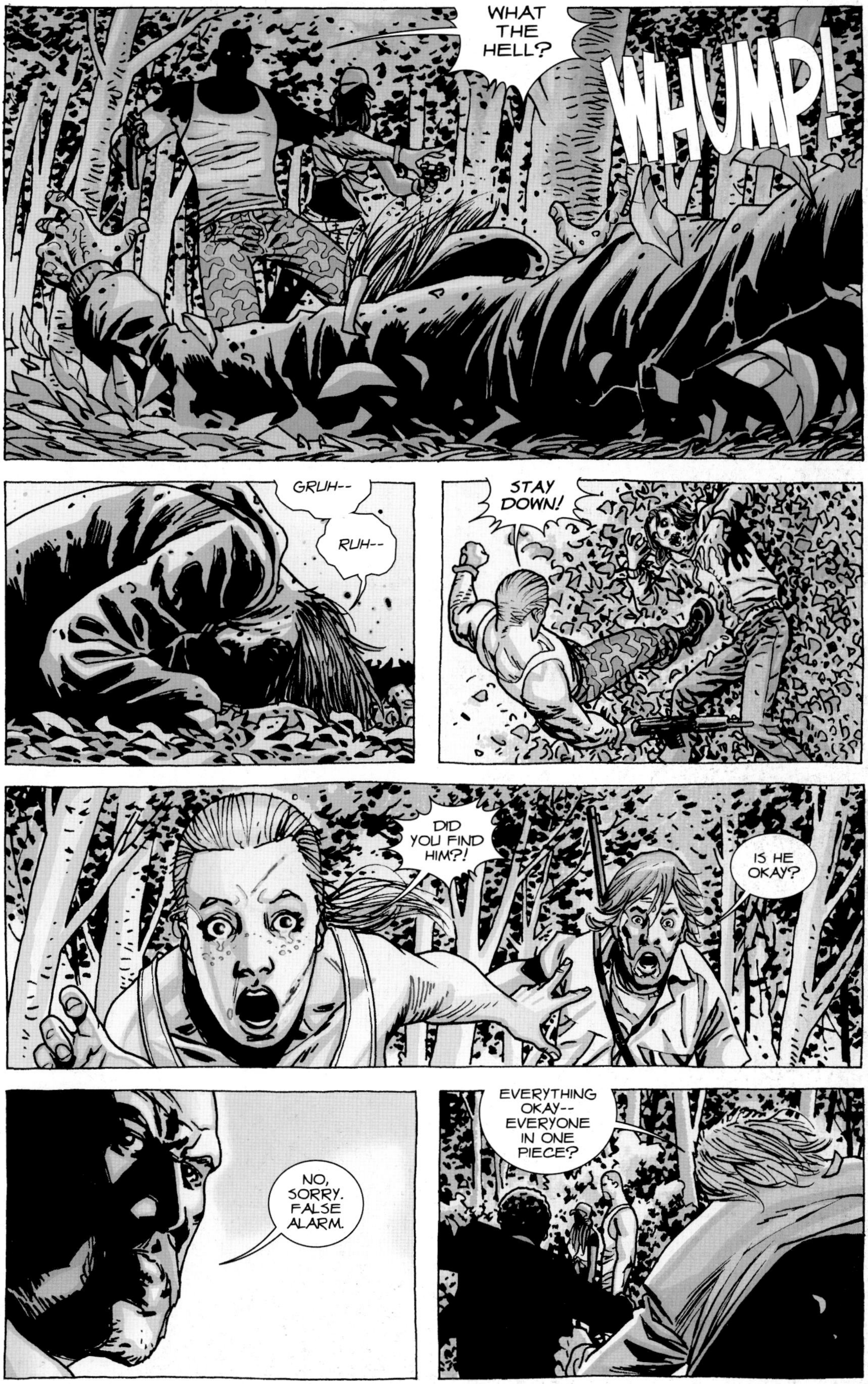
WHAT THE HELL?
WHUMP!
GRUH--
RUH--
STAY DOWN!
DID YOU FIND HIM?!
IS HE OKAY?
NO, SORRY. FALSE ALARM.
EVERYTHING OKAY-- EVERYONE IN ONE PIECE?

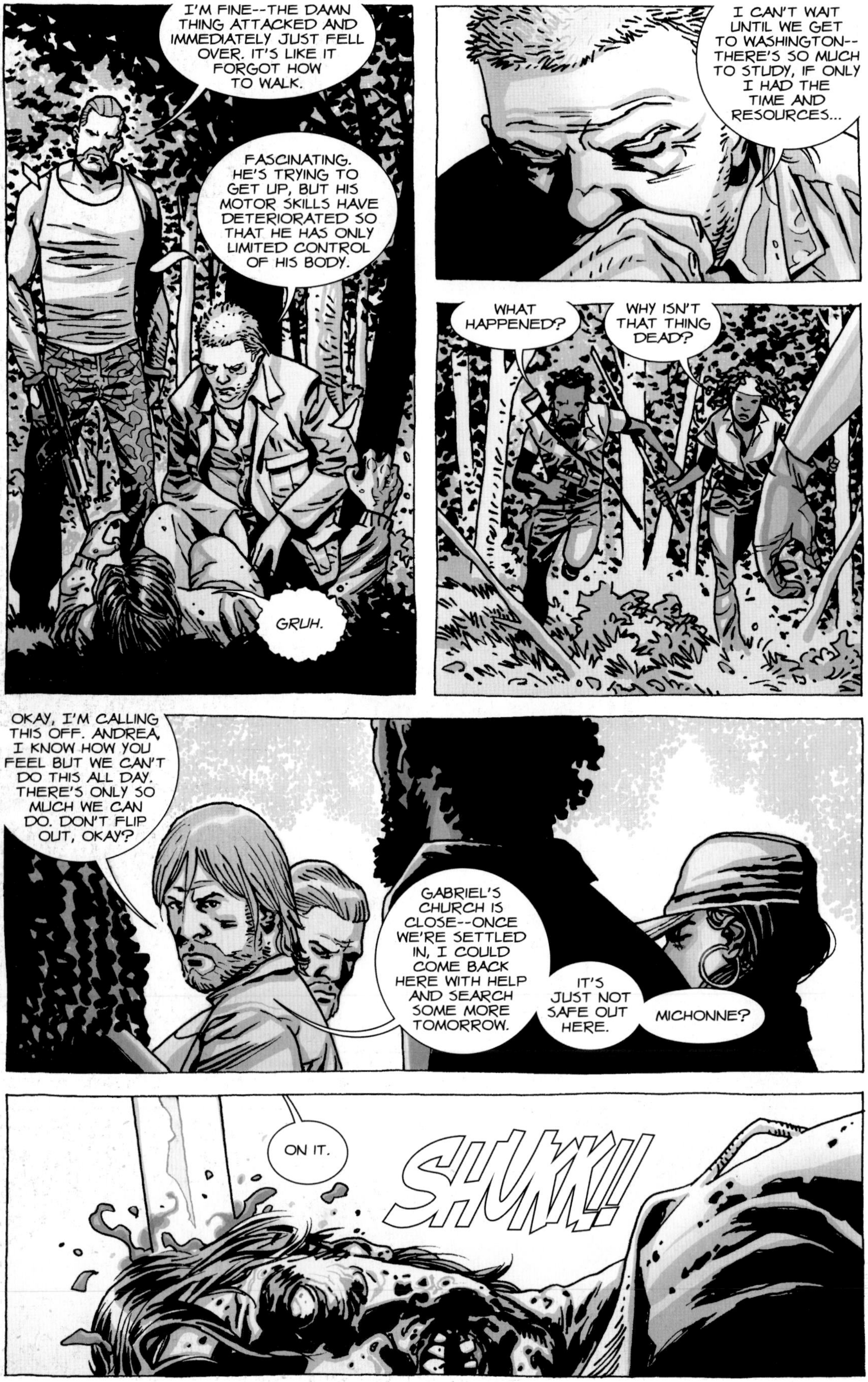
I'M FINE--THE DAMN THING ATTACKED AND IMMEDIATELY JUST FELL OVER. IT'S LIKE IT FORGOT HOW TO WALK.
FASCINATING. HE'S TRYING TO GET UP, BUT HIS MOTOR SKILLS HAVE DETERIORATED SO THAT HE HAS ONLY LIMITED CONTROL OF HIS BODY.
GRUH.
I CAN'T WAIT UNTIL WE GET TO WASHINGTON--THERE'S SO MUCH TO STUDY, IF ONLY I HAD THE TIME AND RESOURCES...
WHAT HAPPENED?
WHY ISN'T THAT THING DEAD?
OKAY, I'M CALLING THIS OFF. ANDREA, I KNOW HOW YOU FEEL BUT WE CAN'T DO THIS ALL DAY. THERE'S ONLY SO MUCH WE CAN DO. DON'T FLIP OUT, OKAY?
GABRIEL'S CHURCH IS CLOSE--ONCE WE'RE SETTLED IN, I COULD COME BACK HERE WITH HELP AND SEARCH SOME MORE TOMORROW.
IT'S JUST NOT SAFE OUT HERE.
MICHONNE?
ON IT.
SHUNK!!

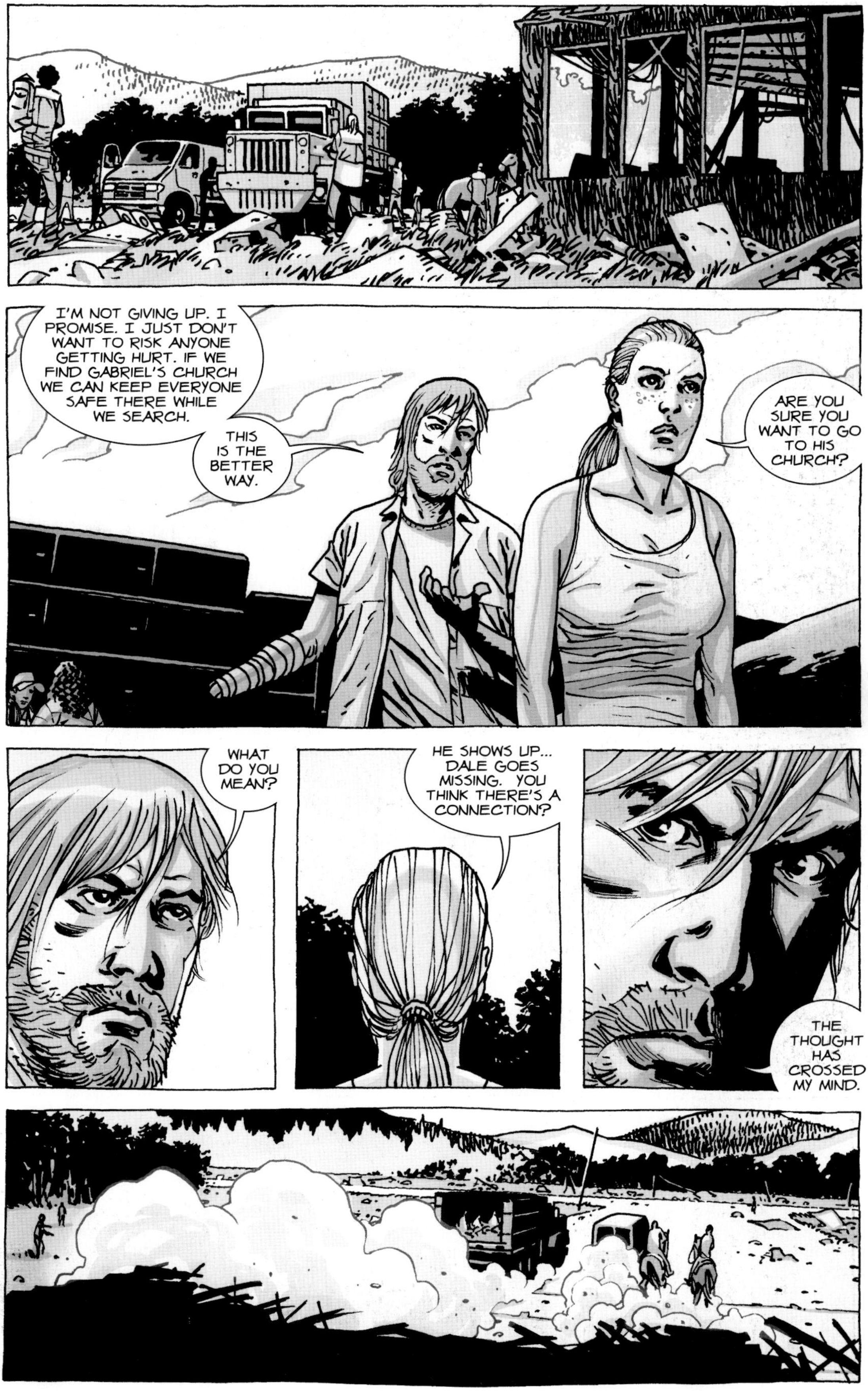
I'M NOT GIVING UP. I PROMISE. I JUST DON'T WANT TO RISK ANYONE GETTING HURT. IF WE FIND GABRIEL'S CHURCH WE CAN KEEP EVERYONE SAFE THERE WHILE WE SEARCH.
THIS IS THE BETTER WAY.
ARE YOU SURE YOU WANT TO GO TO HIS CHURCH?
WHAT DO YOU MEAN?
HE SHOWS UP... DALE GOES MISSING. YOU THINK THERE'S A CONNECTION?
THE THOUGHT HAS CROSSED MY MIND.

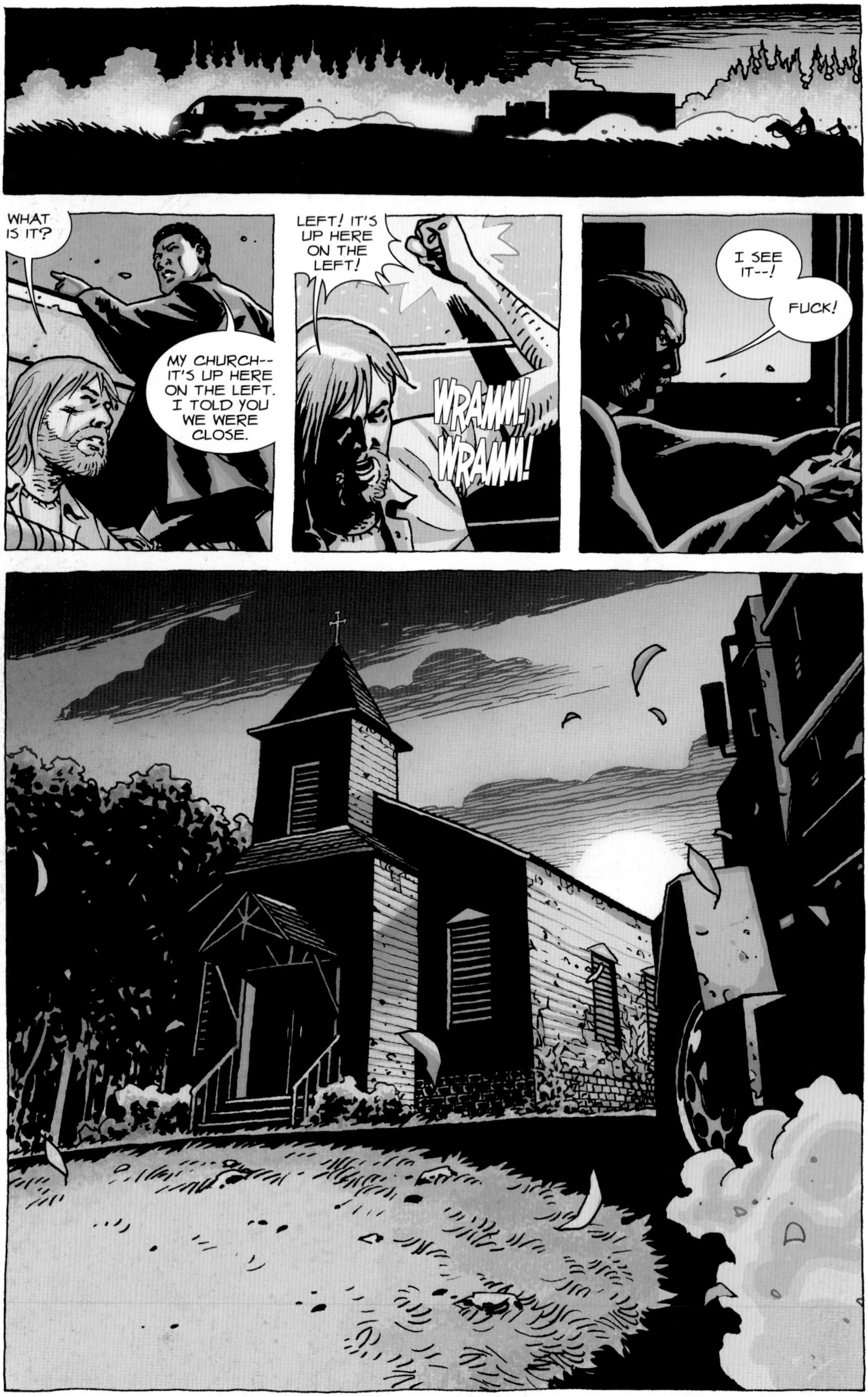
WHAT IS IT?
MY CHURCH-- IT'S UP HERE ON THE LEFT. I TOLD YOU WE WERE CLOSE.
LEFT! IT'S UP HERE ON THE LEFT!
WRAMM! WRAMM!
I SEE IT--!
FUCK!

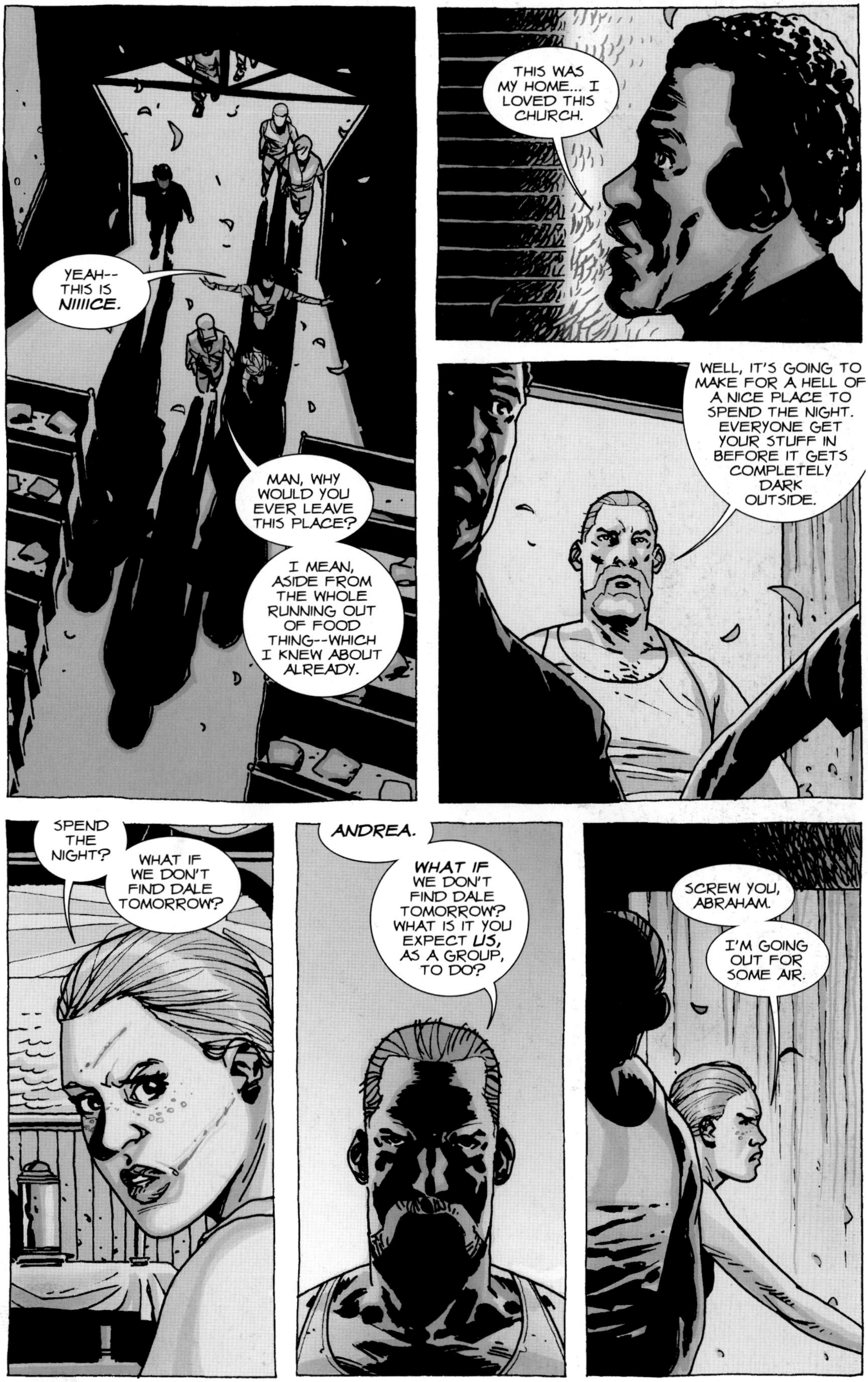
YEAH-- THIS IS NIIIICE.
MAN, WHY WOULD YOU EVER LEAVE THIS PLACE?
I MEAN, ASIDE FROM THE WHOLE RUNNING OUT OF FOOD THING--WHICH I KNEW ABOUT ALREADY.
THIS WAS MY HOME... I LOVED THIS CHURCH.
WELL, IT'S GOING TO MAKE FOR A HELL OF A NICE PLACE TO SPEND THE NIGHT. EVERYONE GET YOUR STUFF IN BEFORE IT GETS COMPLETELY DARK OUTSIDE.
SPEND THE NIGHT?
WHAT IF WE DON'T FIND DALE TOMORROW?
ANDREA.
WHAT IF WE DON'T FIND DALE TOMORROW? WHAT IS IT YOU EXPECT US, AS A GROUP, TO DO?
SCREW YOU, ABRAHAM.
I'M GOING OUT FOR SOME AIR.

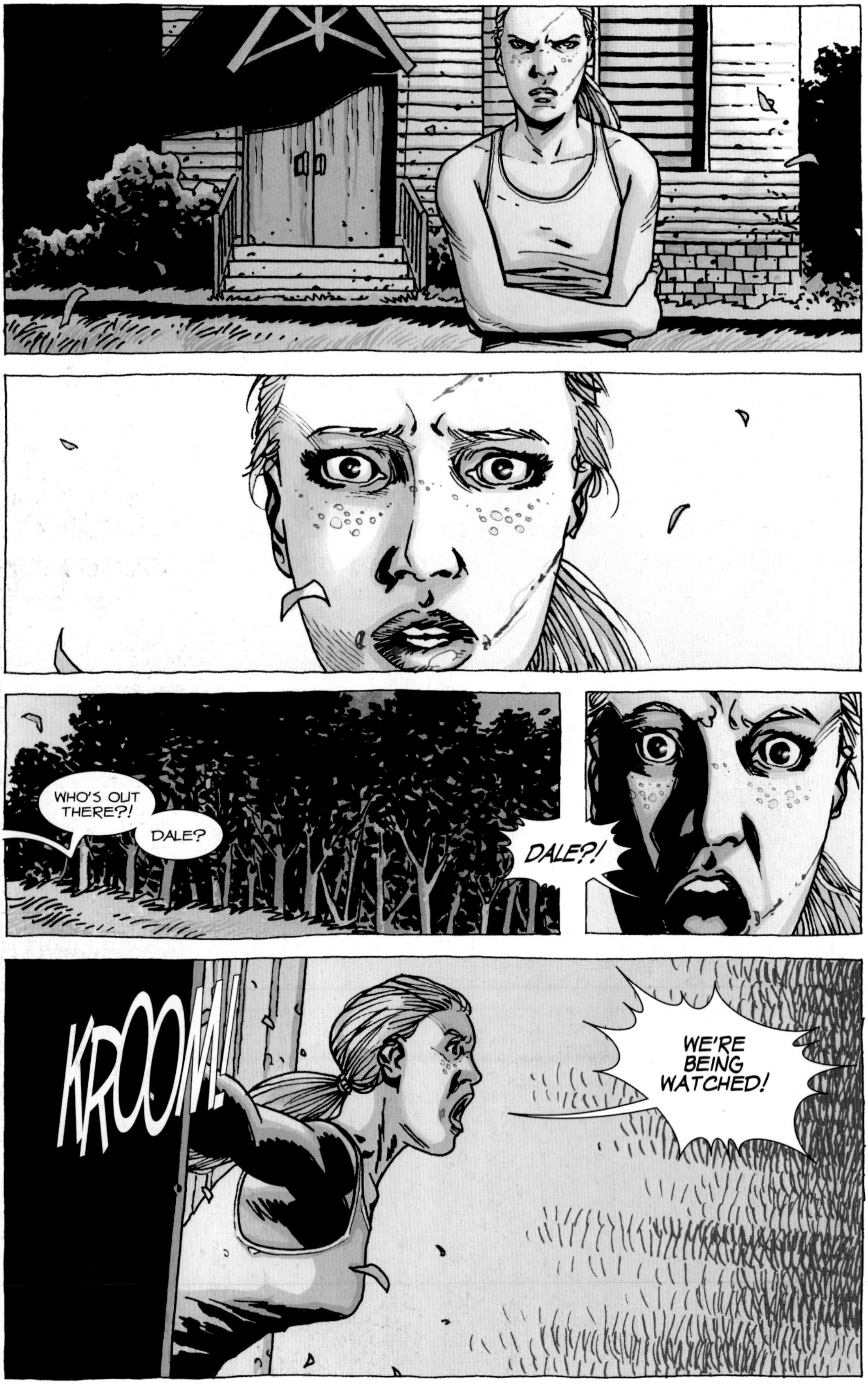
WHO'S OUT THERE?!
DALE?
DALE?!
KROOM!
WE'RE BEING WATCHED!

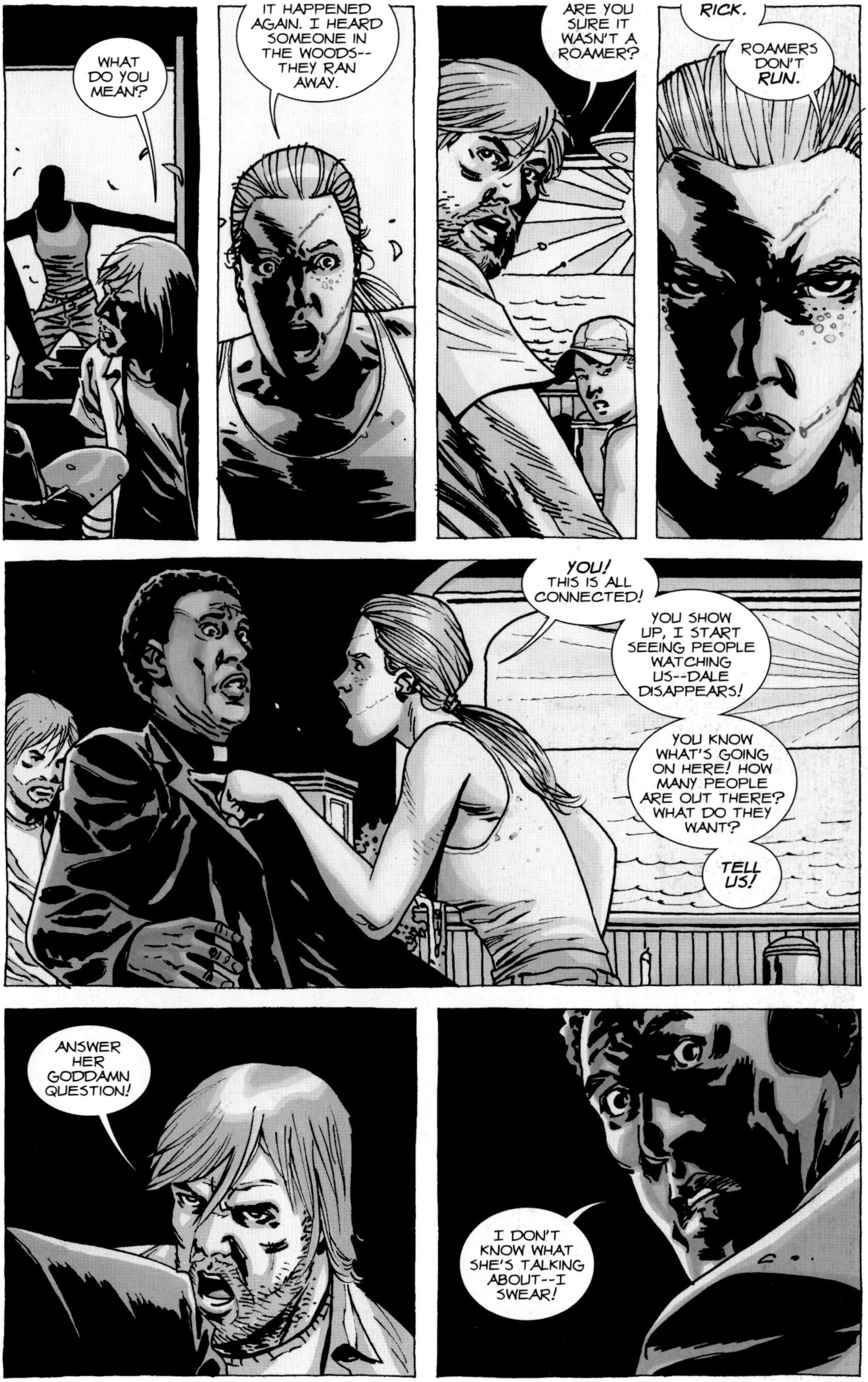
WHAT DO YOU MEAN?
IT HAPPENED AGAIN. I HEARD SOMEONE IN THE WOODS-- THEY RAN AWAY.
ARE YOU SURE IT WASN'T A ROAMER?
RICK.
ROAMERS DON'T RUN.
YOU! THIS IS ALL CONNECTED!
YOU SHOW UP, I START SEEING PEOPLE WATCHING US--DALE DISAPPEARS!
YOU KNOW WHAT'S GOING ON HERE! HOW MANY PEOPLE ARE OUT THERE? WHAT DO THEY WANT?
TELL US!
ANSWER HER GODDAMN QUESTION!
I DON'T KNOW WHAT SHE'S TALKING ABOUT--I SWEAR!

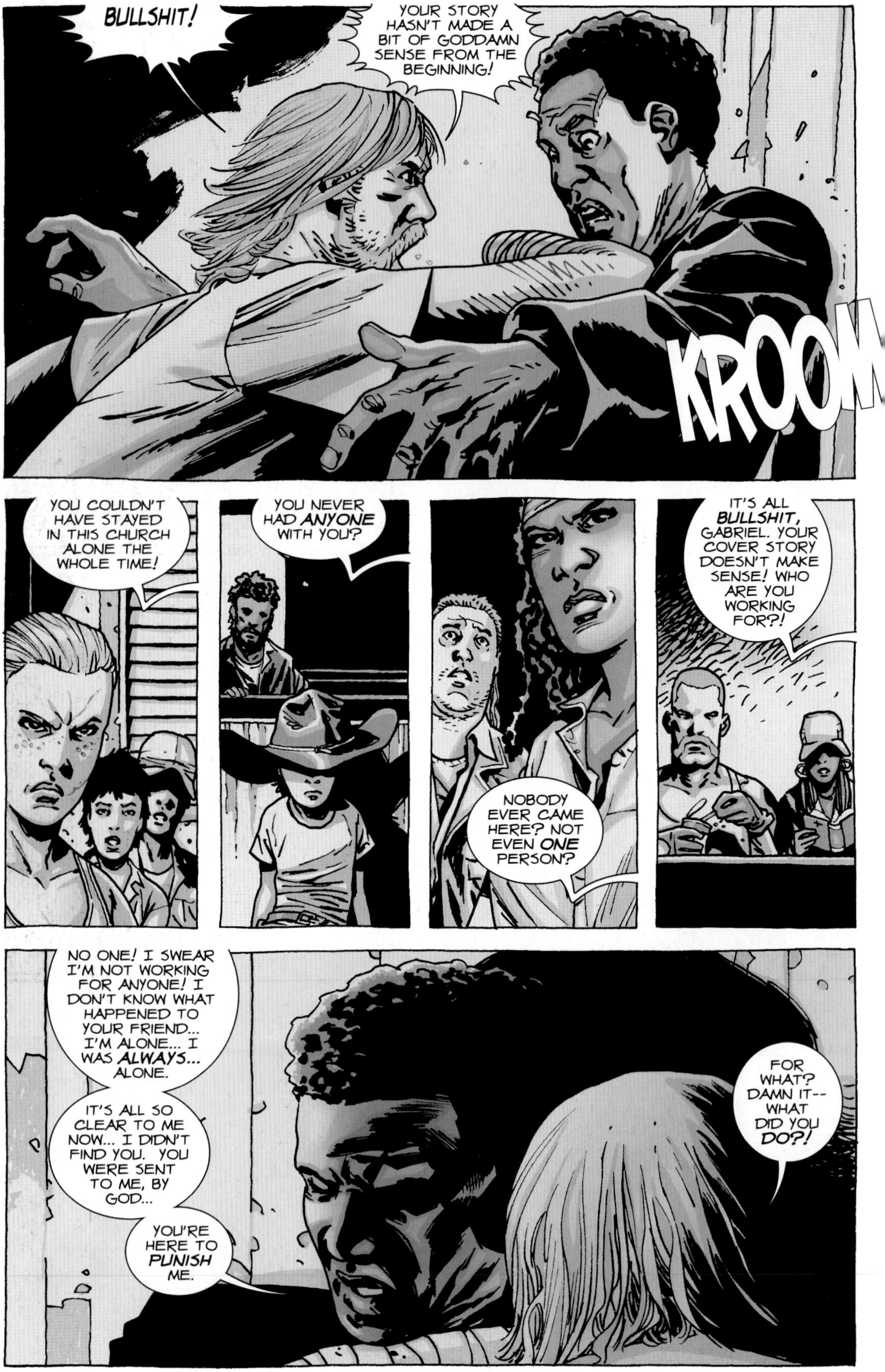
BULLSHIT!
YOUR STORY HASN'T MADE A BIT OF GODDAMN SENSE FROM THE BEGINNING!
KROOM
YOU COULDN'T HAVE STAYED IN THIS CHURCH ALONE THE WHOLE TIME!
YOU NEVER HAD ANYONE WITH YOU?
NOBODY EVER CAME HERE? NOT EVEN ONE PERSON?
IT'S ALL BULLSHIT, GABRIEL. YOUR COVER STORY DOESN'T MAKE SENSE! WHO ARE YOU WORKING FOR?!
NO ONE! I SWEAR I'M NOT WORKING FOR ANYONE! I DON'T KNOW WHAT HAPPENED TO YOUR FRIEND... I'M ALONE... I WAS ALWAYS... ALONE.
IT'S ALL SO CLEAR TO ME NOW... I DIDN'T FIND YOU. YOU WERE SENT TO ME, BY GOD...
YOU'RE HERE TO PUNISH ME.
FOR WHAT? DAMN IT-- WHAT DID YOU DO?!

WHEN IT ALL STARTED, I WAS *HERE*--ALONE. IT WAS LATE AT NIGHT WHEN I FIRST HEARD ABOUT EVERYTHING. I GOT SCARED--I LOCKED UP--JUST TO BE SAFE.

THE NEXT MORNING... THEY STARTED COMING.

NEIGHBORS, FRIENDS... MEMBERS OF MY CONGREGATION... NOT MANY AT FIRST, THEN MORE AS THE DAYS WENT ON. THEY WANTED A SAFE PLACE TO STAY--A SANCTUARY.

I TURNED THEM ALL AWAY...

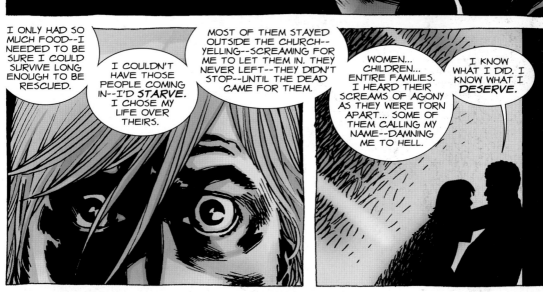

I ONLY HAD SO MUCH FOOD--I NEEDED TO BE SURE I COULD SURVIVE LONG ENOUGH TO BE RESCUED.

I COULDN'T HAVE THOSE PEOPLE COMING IN--I'D *STARVE*. I CHOSE MY LIFE OVER THEIRS.

MOST OF THEM STAYED OUTSIDE THE CHURCH--YELLING--SCREAMING FOR ME TO LET THEM IN. THEY NEVER LEFT--THEY DIDN'T STOP--UNTIL THE DEAD CAME FOR THEM.

WOMEN... CHILDREN... ENTIRE FAMILIES. I HEARD THEIR SCREAMS OF AGONY AS THEY WERE TORN APART... SOME OF THEM CALLING MY NAME--DAMNING ME TO HELL.

I KNOW WHAT I DID. I KNOW WHAT I *DESERVE*.

KILL ME. PLEASE, I'VE SUFFERED ENOUGH--I *WANT* YOU TO DO IT.

I FORGIVE YOU. KILL ME AND I FORGIVE YOU. YOU ARE ONLY CARRYING OUT GOD'S WILL.

THEY DIED--THEY *ALL* DIED BECAUSE OF ME.

YOU HAVE TO MAKE THIS RIGHT.

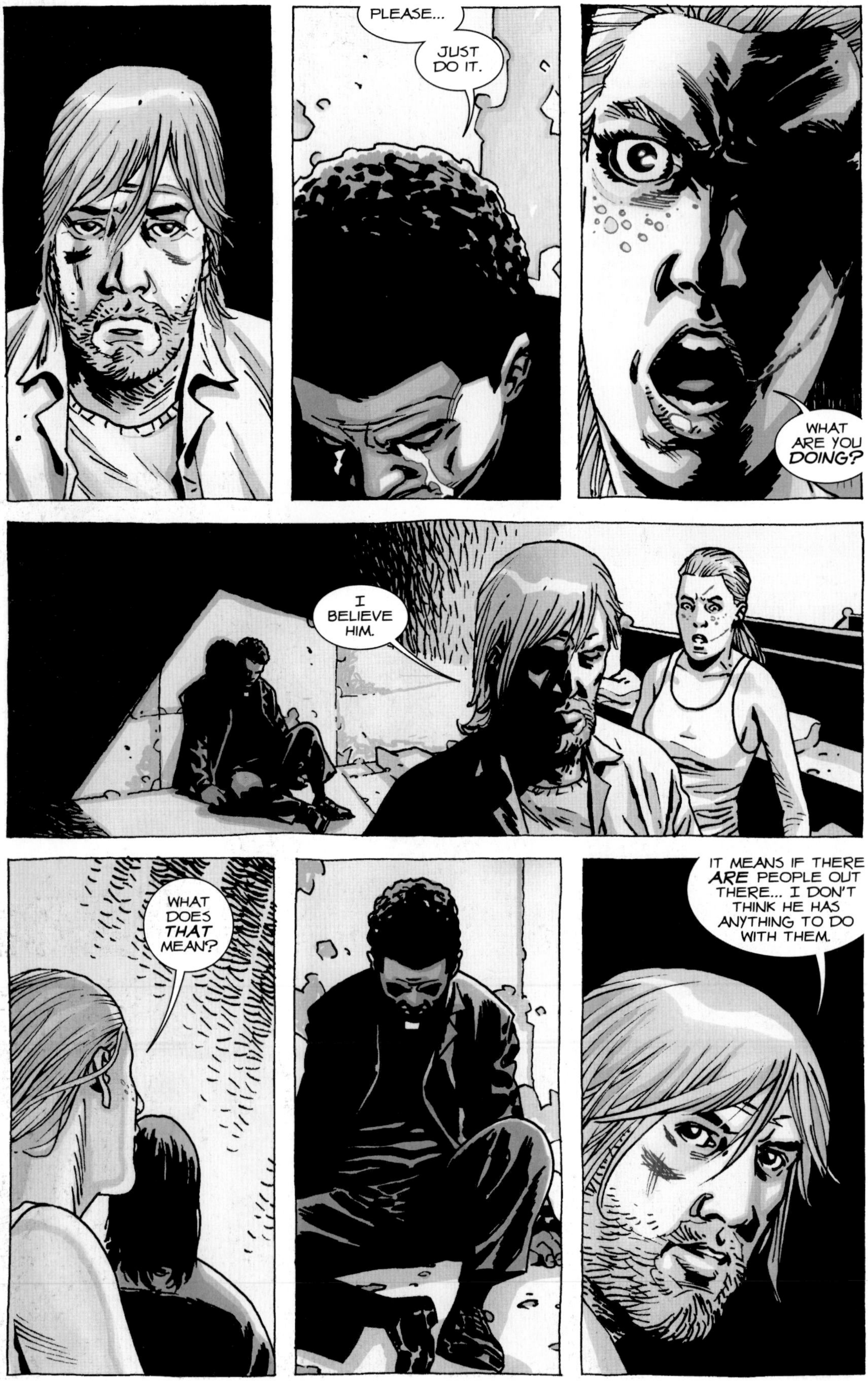
PLEASE...
JUST DO IT.
WHAT ARE YOU DOING?
I BELIEVE HIM.
WHAT DOES THAT MEAN?
IT MEANS IF THERE ARE PEOPLE OUT THERE... I DON'T THINK HE HAS ANYTHING TO DO WITH THEM.

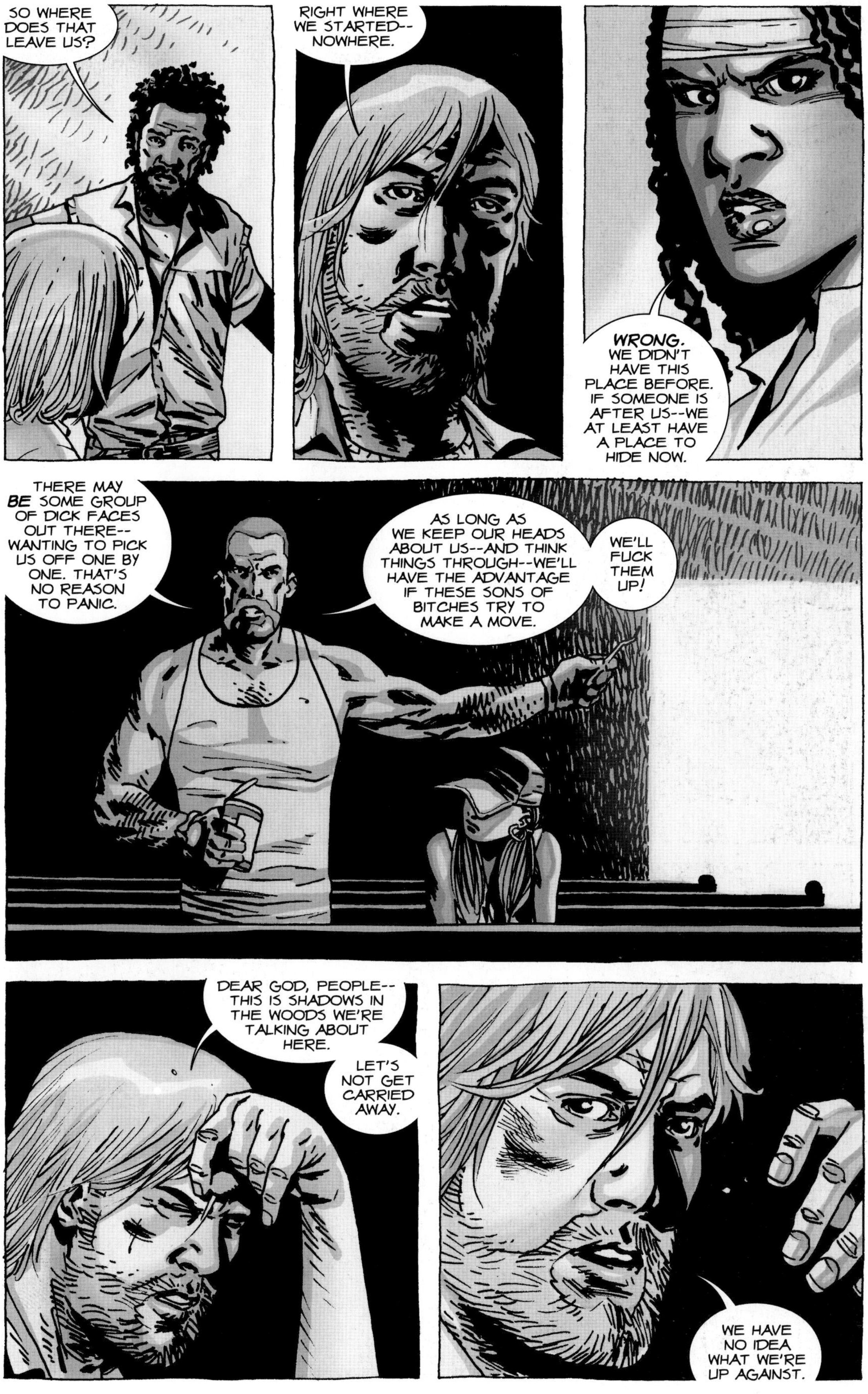
SO WHERE DOES THAT LEAVE US?
RIGHT WHERE WE STARTED-- NOWHERE.
WRONG. WE DIDN'T HAVE THIS PLACE BEFORE. IF SOMEONE IS AFTER US--WE AT LEAST HAVE A PLACE TO HIDE NOW.
THERE MAY BE SOME GROUP OF DICK FACES OUT THERE-- WANTING TO PICK US OFF ONE BY ONE. THAT'S NO REASON TO PANIC.
AS LONG AS WE KEEP OUR HEADS ABOUT US--AND THINK THINGS THROUGH--WE'LL HAVE THE ADVANTAGE IF THESE SONS OF BITCHES TRY TO MAKE A MOVE.
WE'LL FUCK THEM UP!
DEAR GOD, PEOPLE-- THIS IS SHADOWS IN THE WOODS WE'RE TALKING ABOUT HERE.
LET'S NOT GET CARRIED AWAY.
WE HAVE NO IDEA WHAT WE'RE UP AGAINST.

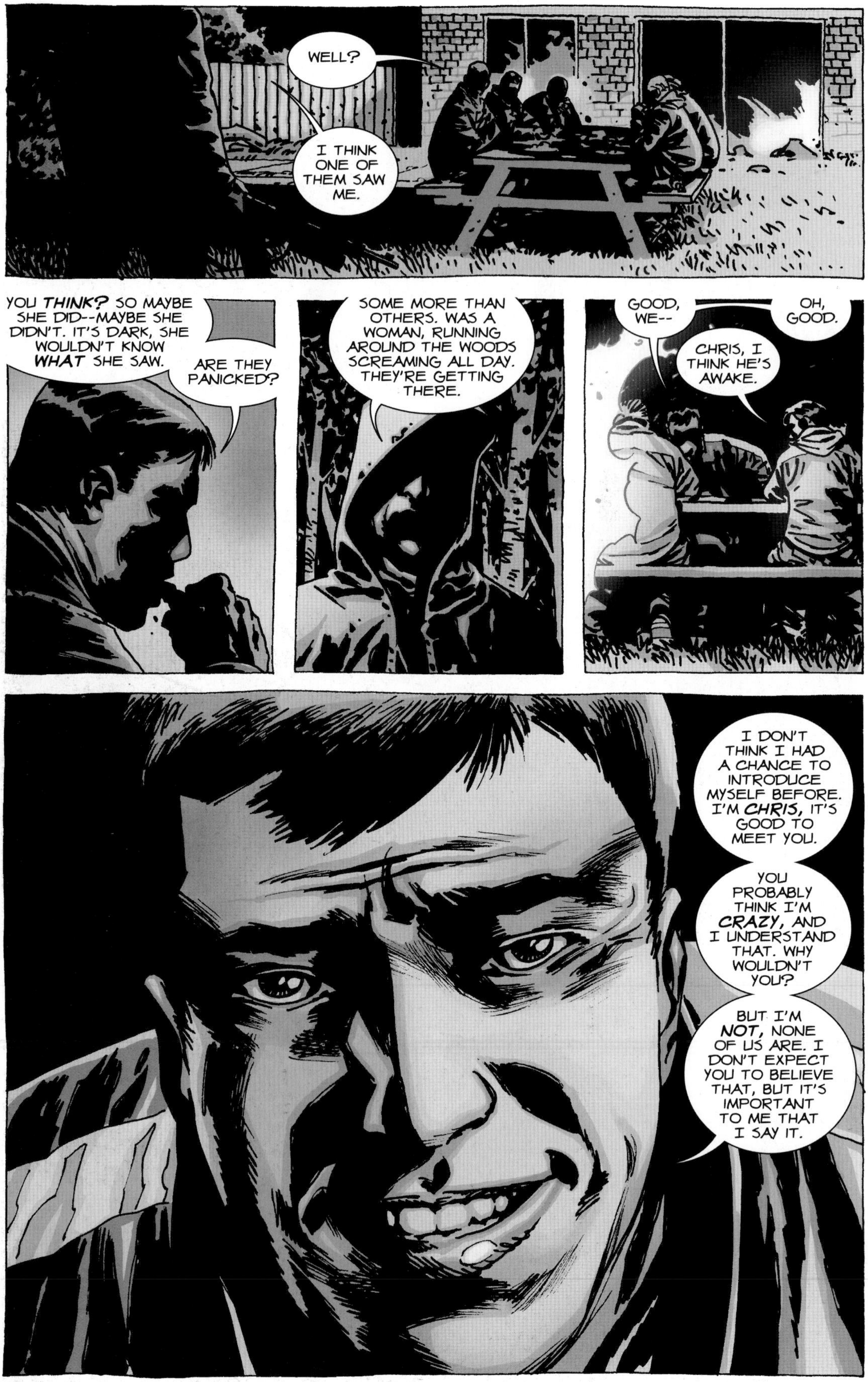
WELL?
I THINK ONE OF THEM SAW ME.
YOU *THINK?* SO MAYBE SHE DID--MAYBE SHE DIDN'T. IT'S DARK, SHE WOULDN'T KNOW *WHAT* SHE SAW.
ARE THEY PANICKED?
SOME MORE THAN OTHERS. WAS A WOMAN, RUNNING AROUND THE WOODS SCREAMING ALL DAY. THEY'RE GETTING THERE.
GOOD, WE--
OH, GOOD.
CHRIS, I THINK HE'S AWAKE.
I DON'T THINK I HAD A CHANCE TO INTRODUCE MYSELF BEFORE. I'M *CHRIS,* IT'S GOOD TO MEET YOU.
YOU PROBABLY THINK I'M *CRAZY,* AND I UNDERSTAND THAT. WHY WOULDN'T YOU?
BUT I'M *NOT,* NONE OF US ARE. I DON'T EXPECT YOU TO BELIEVE THAT, BUT IT'S IMPORTANT TO ME THAT I SAY IT.

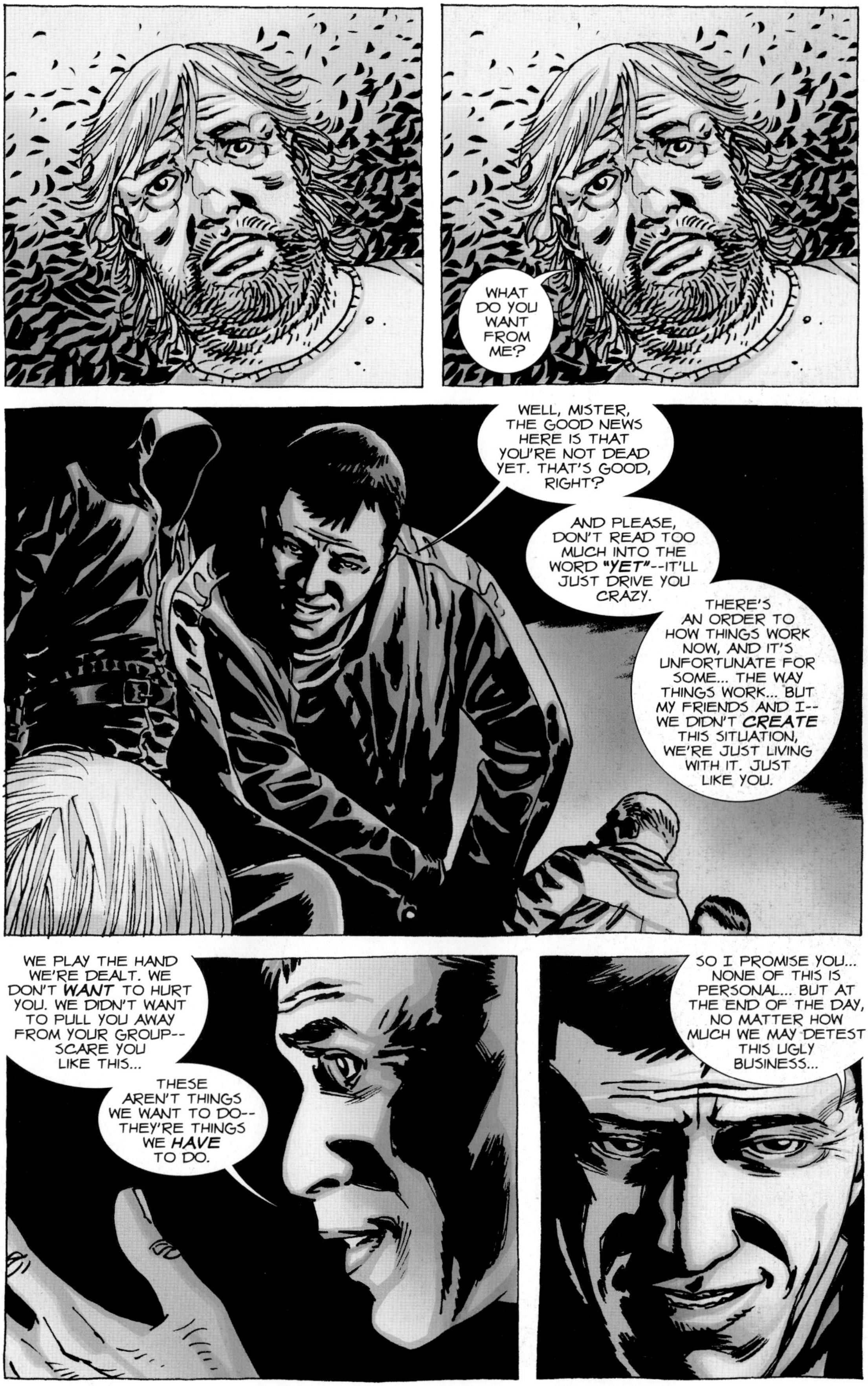
WHAT DO YOU WANT FROM ME?
WELL, MISTER, THE GOOD NEWS HERE IS THAT YOU'RE NOT DEAD YET. THAT'S GOOD, RIGHT?
AND PLEASE, DON'T READ TOO MUCH INTO THE WORD "YET"--IT'LL JUST DRIVE YOU CRAZY.
THERE'S AN ORDER TO HOW THINGS WORK NOW, AND IT'S UNFORTUNATE FOR SOME... THE WAY THINGS WORK... BUT MY FRIENDS AND I-- WE DIDN'T CREATE THIS SITUATION, WE'RE JUST LIVING WITH IT. JUST LIKE YOU.
WE PLAY THE HAND WE'RE DEALT. WE DON'T WANT TO HURT YOU. WE DIDN'T WANT TO PULL YOU AWAY FROM YOUR GROUP-- SCARE YOU LIKE THIS...
THESE AREN'T THINGS WE WANT TO DO-- THEY'RE THINGS WE HAVE TO DO.
SO I PROMISE YOU... NONE OF THIS IS PERSONAL... BUT AT THE END OF THE DAY, NO MATTER HOW MUCH WE MAY DETEST THIS UGLY BUSINESS...

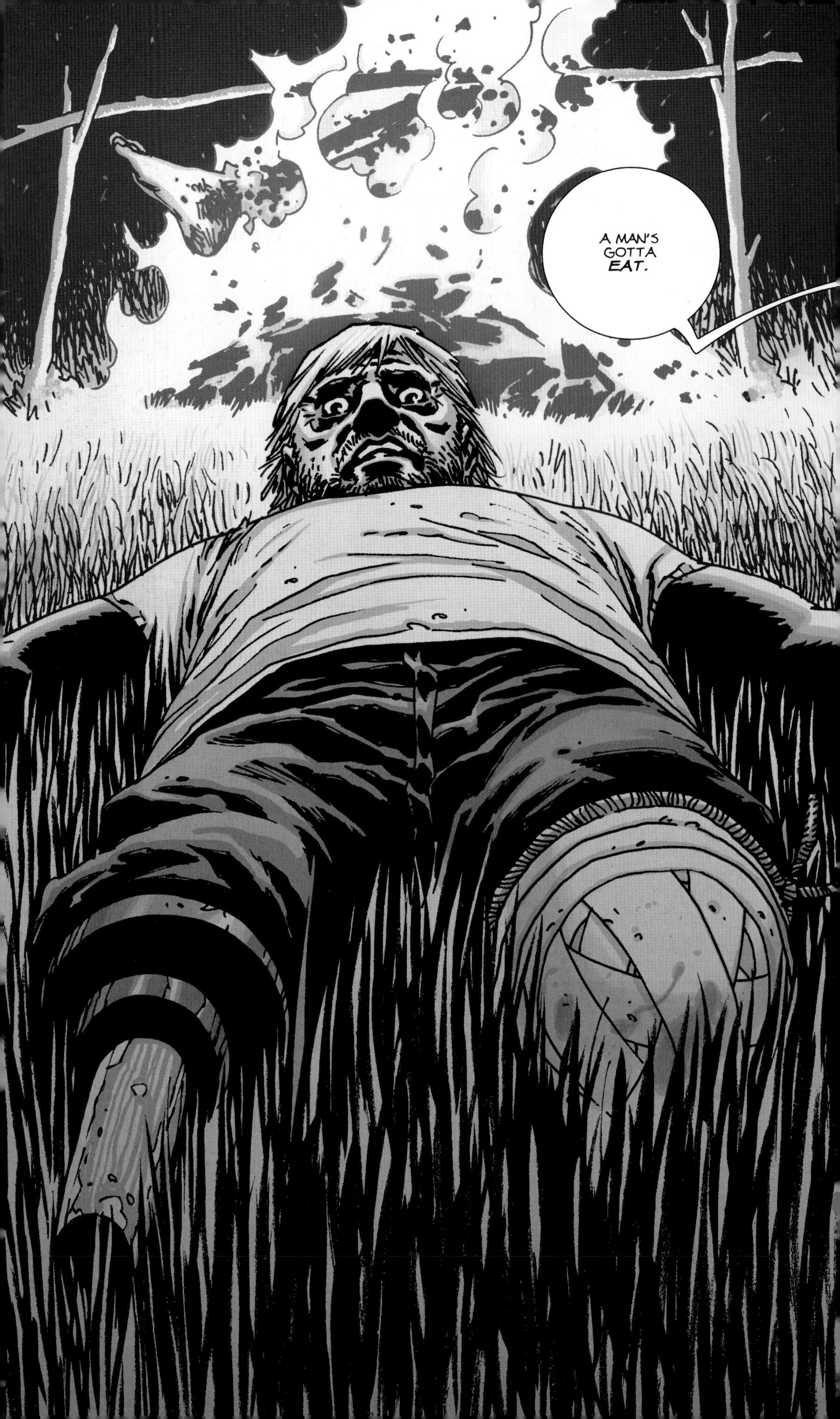
A MAN'S GOTTA *EAT.*

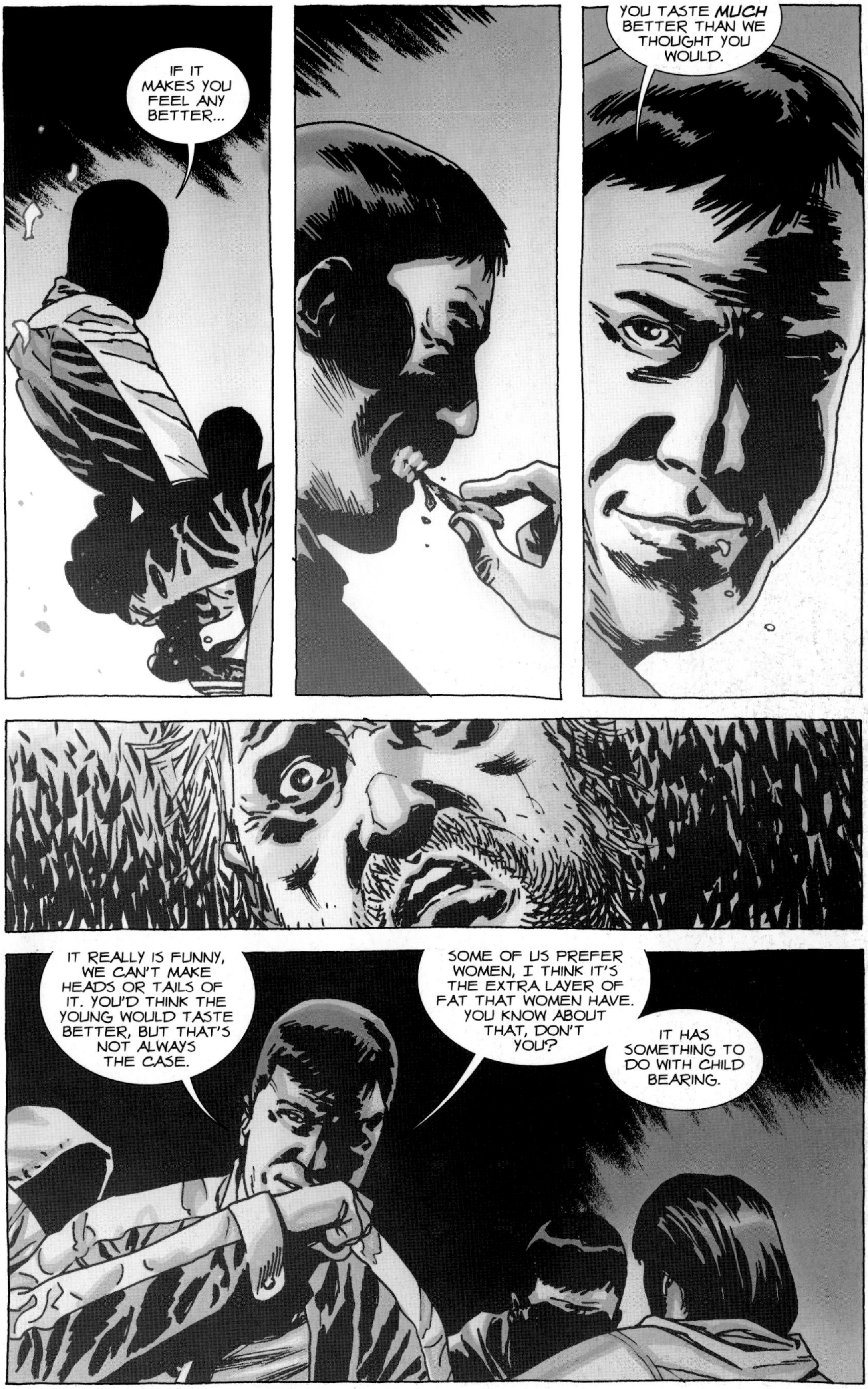
IF IT MAKES YOU FEEL ANY BETTER...
YOU TASTE MUCH BETTER THAN WE THOUGHT YOU WOULD.
IT REALLY IS FUNNY, WE CAN'T MAKE HEADS OR TAILS OF IT. YOU'D THINK THE YOUNG WOULD TASTE BETTER, BUT THAT'S NOT ALWAYS THE CASE.
SOME OF US PREFER WOMEN, I THINK IT'S THE EXTRA LAYER OF FAT THAT WOMEN HAVE. YOU KNOW ABOUT THAT, DON'T YOU?
IT HAS SOMETHING TO DO WITH CHILD BEARING.

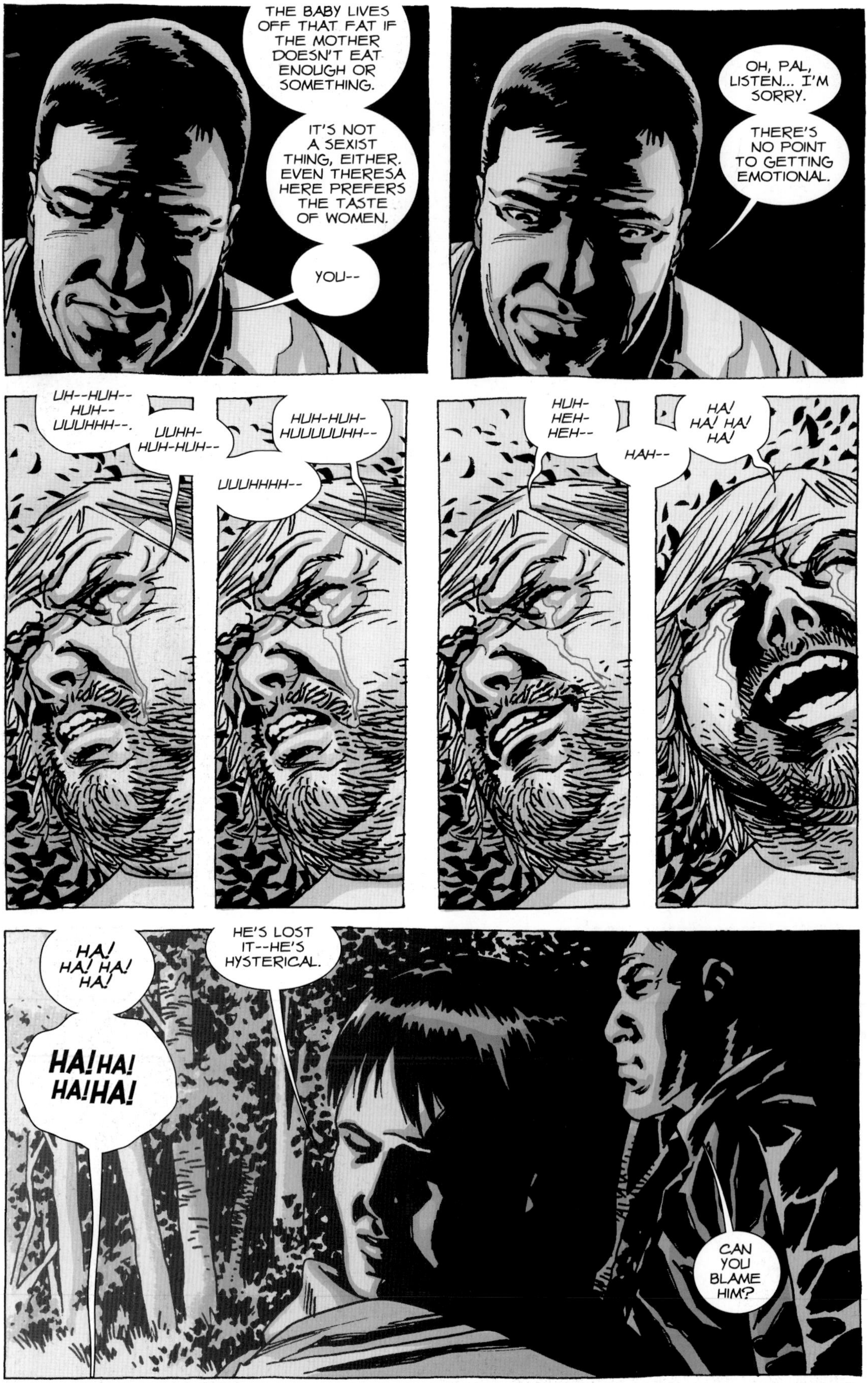

THE BABY LIVES OFF THAT FAT IF THE MOTHER DOESN'T EAT ENOUGH OR SOMETHING.
IT'S NOT A SEXIST THING, EITHER. EVEN THERESA HERE PREFERS THE TASTE OF WOMEN.
YOU--
OH, PAL, LISTEN... I'M SORRY.
THERE'S NO POINT TO GETTING EMOTIONAL.
UH--HUH--HUH--UUUHHH--.
UUHH-HUH-HUH--
HUH-HUH-HUUUUUHH--
UUUHHHH--
HUH-HEH-HEH--
HAH--
HA! HA! HA! HA!
HA! HA! HA! HA!
HE'S LOST IT--HE'S HYSTERICAL.
HA!HA! HA!HA!
CAN YOU BLAME HIM?

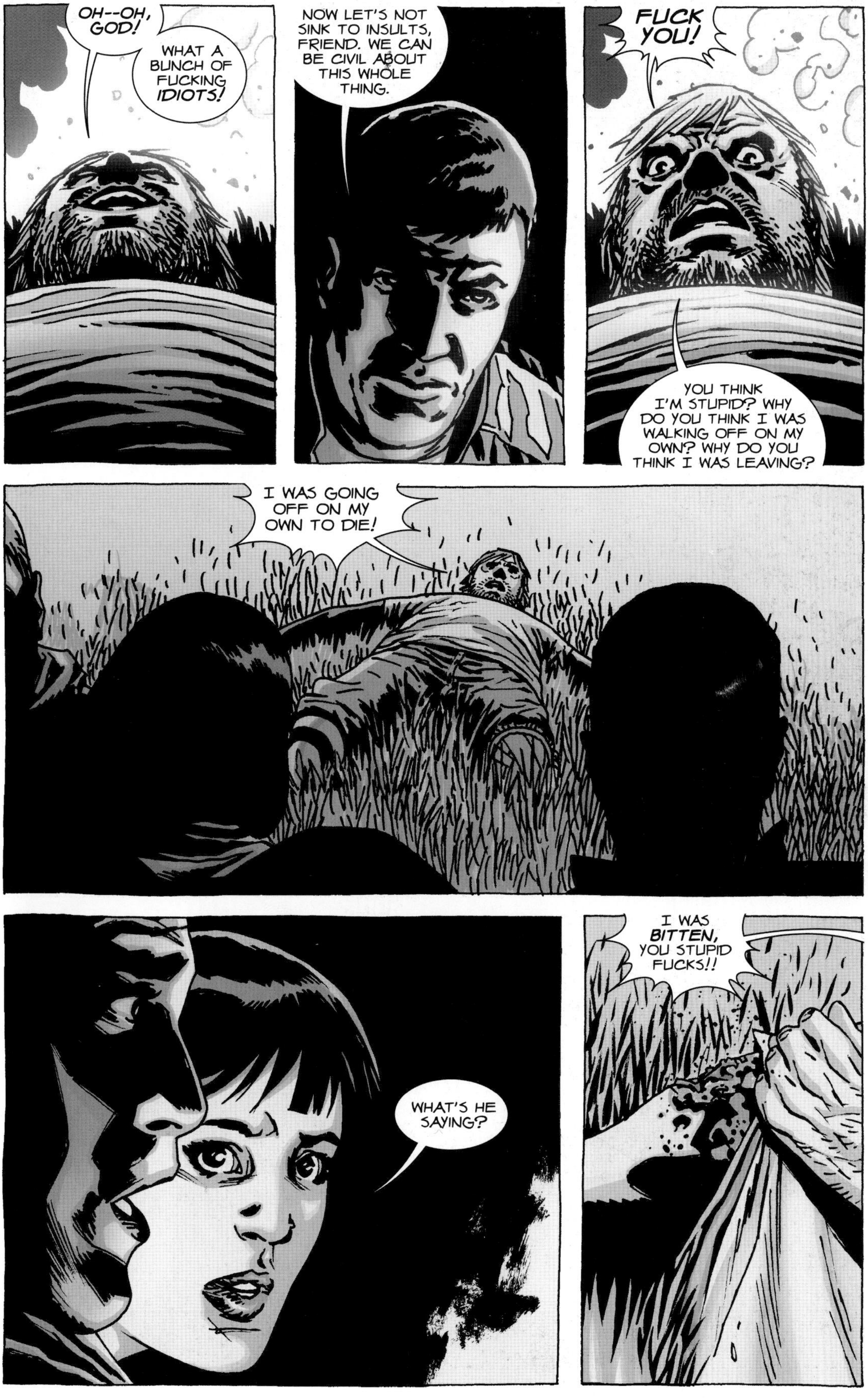
OH--OH, GOD!
WHAT A BUNCH OF FUCKING IDIOTS!
NOW LET'S NOT SINK TO INSULTS, FRIEND. WE CAN BE CIVIL ABOUT THIS WHOLE THING.
FUCK YOU!
YOU THINK I'M STUPID? WHY DO YOU THINK I WAS WALKING OFF ON MY OWN? WHY DO YOU THINK I WAS LEAVING?
I WAS GOING OFF ON MY OWN TO DIE!
WHAT'S HE SAYING?
I WAS BITTEN, YOU STUPID FUCKS!!

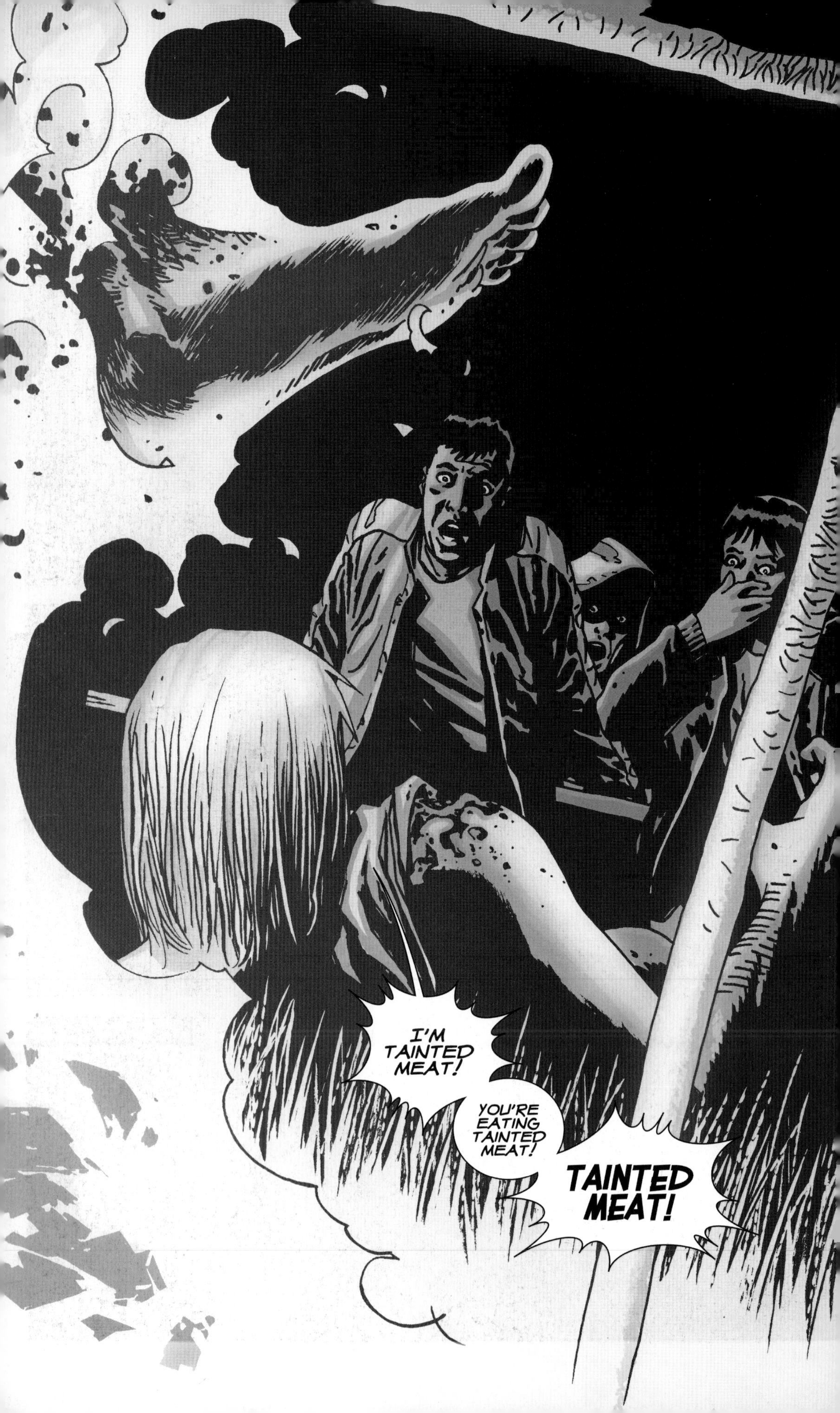
I'M TAINTED MEAT!
YOU'RE EATING TAINTED MEAT!
TAINTED MEAT!

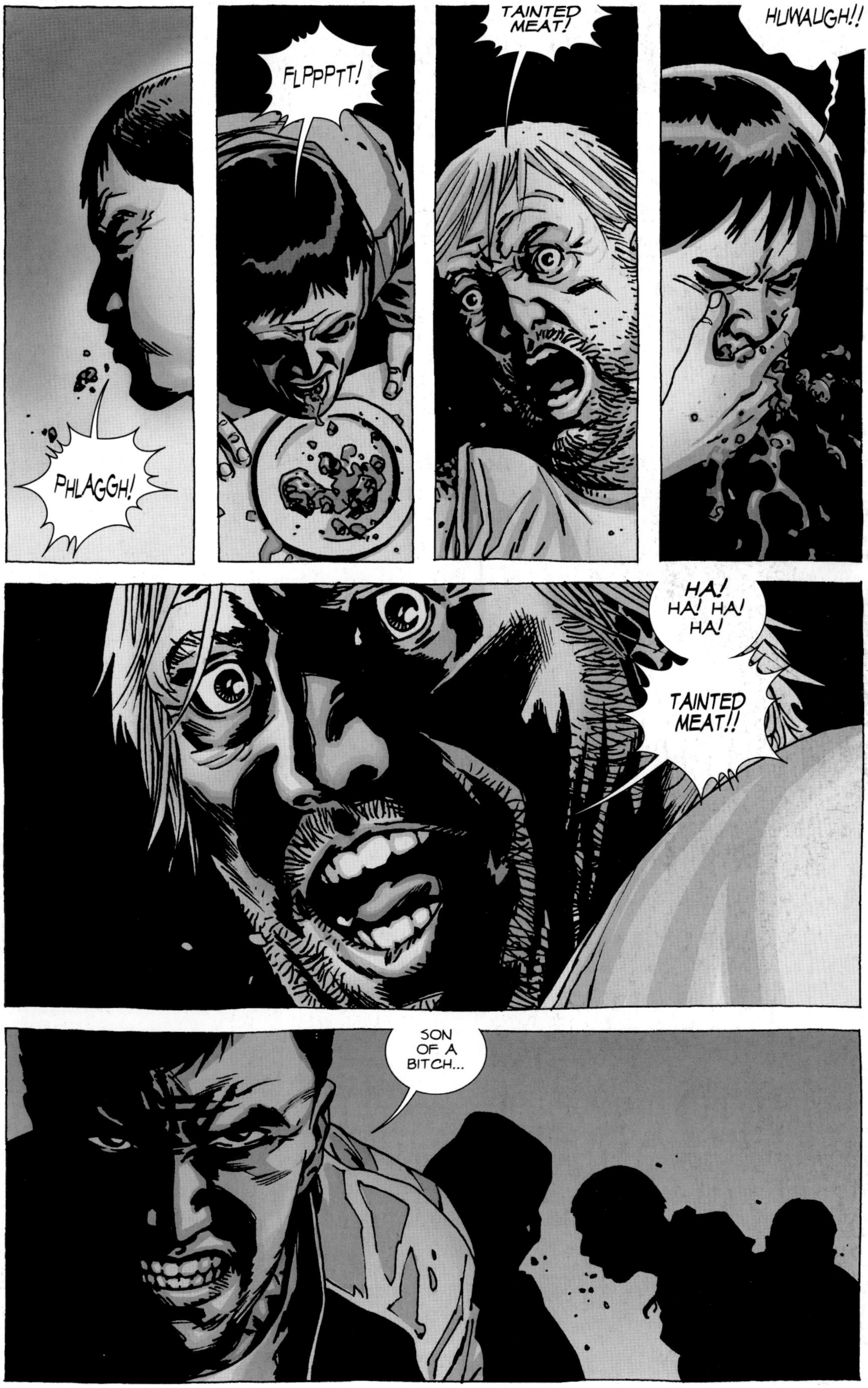
PHLAGGH!
FLPPPTT!
TAINTED MEAT!
HUWAUGH!!
HA! HA! HA! HA!
TAINTED MEAT!!
SON OF A BITCH...

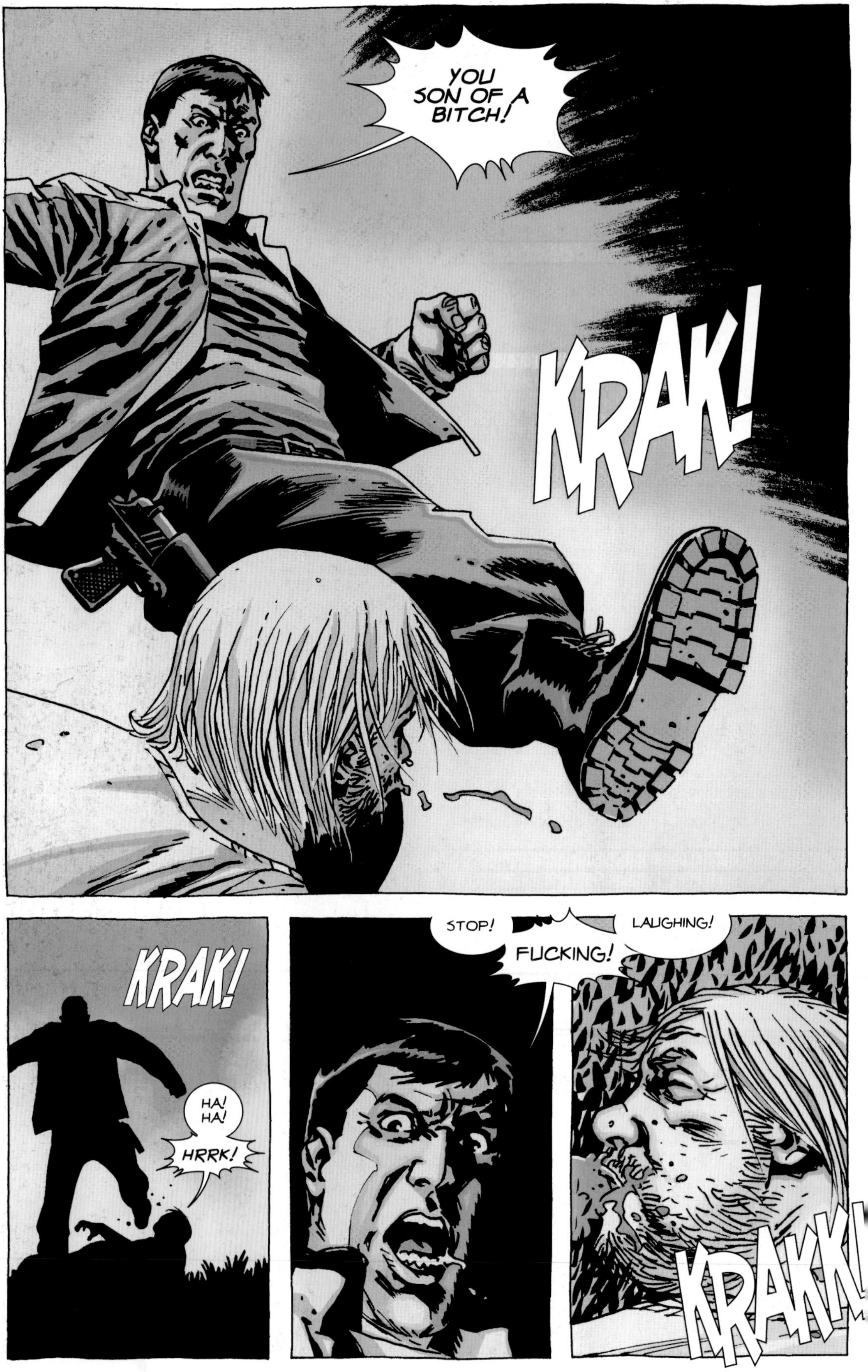
YOU SON OF A BITCH!
KRAK!
KRAK!
HA! HA!
HRRK!
STOP!
FUCKING!
LAUGHING!
KRAKK!

IS HE?

BLACKED OUT.

THAT'S IT--I'M CUTTING MY TONGUE OUT! I'M DOING IT!

I'M GONNA DO IT NOW BEFORE IT SPREADS! I AIN'T GOING TO BE NO DEADIE!

ALBERT-- STOP!

YOU'RE GOING TO DO NO SUCH THING BECAUSE IT DOESN'T MAKE A DAMN BIT OF SENSE. YOU CAN'T CUT OUT YOUR STOMACH, CAN YOU?

WE HAVE NO IDEA WHAT EFFECT, IF ANY, THIS WILL HAVE ON US. HE'S NOT DEAD YET--AND THE MEAT WAS COOKED.

WE DON'T HAVE REASON TO WORRY, YET.

I THINK DAVID'S RIGHT. WE ALL NEED TO CALM DOWN.

NOW, CHRIS-- WHAT ARE WE GOING TO DO WITH HIM?

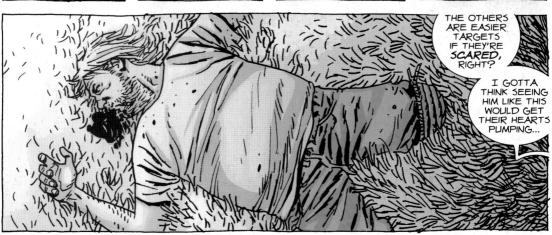

THE OTHERS ARE EASIER TARGETS IF THEY'RE SCARED, RIGHT?

I GOTTA THINK SEEING HIM LIKE THIS WOULD GET THEIR HEARTS PUMPING...

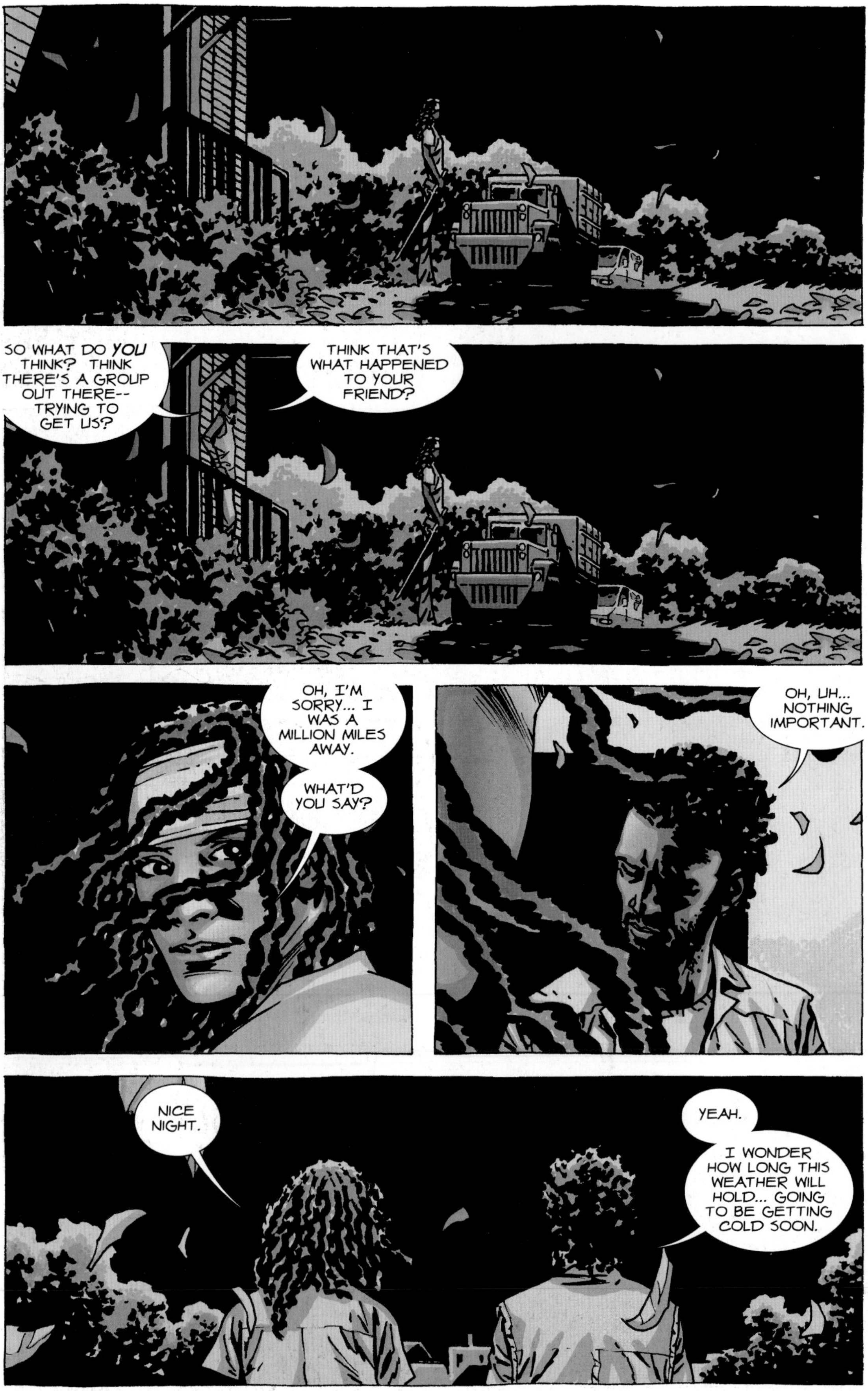

SO WHAT DO YOU THINK? THINK THERE'S A GROUP OUT THERE-- TRYING TO GET US?
THINK THAT'S WHAT HAPPENED TO YOUR FRIEND?
OH, I'M SORRY... I WAS A MILLION MILES AWAY.
WHAT'D YOU SAY?
OH, UH... NOTHING IMPORTANT.
NICE NIGHT.
YEAH.
I WONDER HOW LONG THIS WEATHER WILL HOLD... GOING TO BE GETTING COLD SOON.

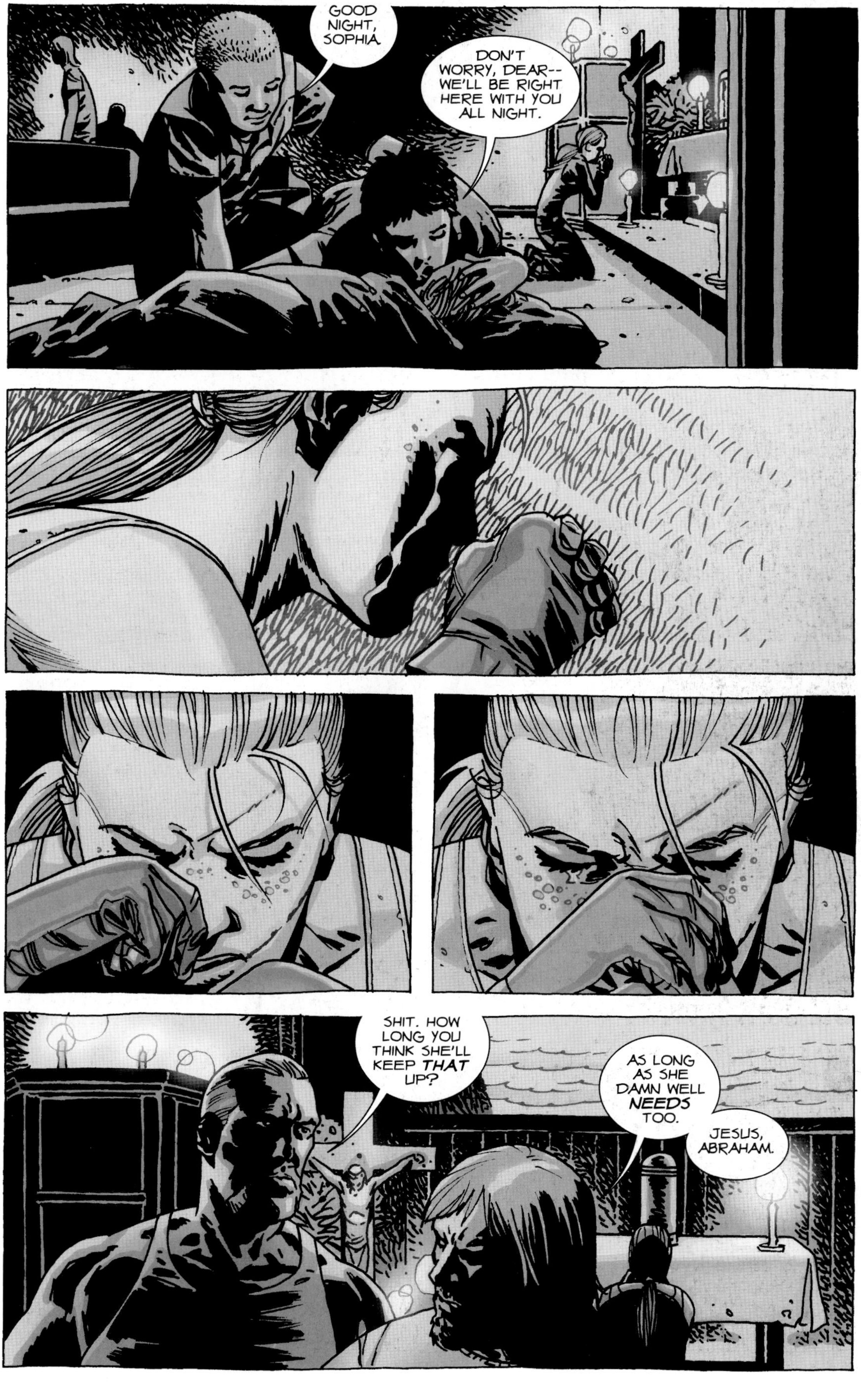
GOOD NIGHT, SOPHIA.
DON'T WORRY, DEAR-- WE'LL BE RIGHT HERE WITH YOU ALL NIGHT.
SHIT. HOW LONG YOU THINK SHE'LL KEEP *THAT* UP?
AS LONG AS SHE DAMN WELL *NEEDS* TOO.
JESUS, ABRAHAM.

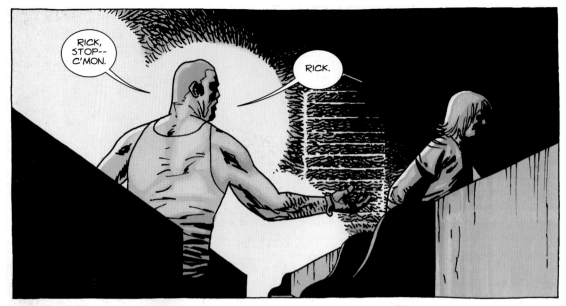

RICK, STOP-- C'MON.

RICK.

LISTEN, MAN... I KNOW SHE'S A FRIEND OF YOURS. I DIDN'T MEAN ANYTHING BY IT.

SORRY I SNAPPED AT YOU--IT'S JUST, SHE'S LOST THE MAN SHE LOVES. IF PRAYING MAKES HER FEEL BETTER-- I'M ALL FOR IT.

WHATEVER IT TAKES TO GET BY.

I KNOW HE WAS A GOOD PERSON AND EVERYONE LOVED DALE--BUT WE'RE NOT GOING TO FIND HIM.

MAN'S GOTTA BE LONG GONE OR LONG *DEAD* BY NOW.

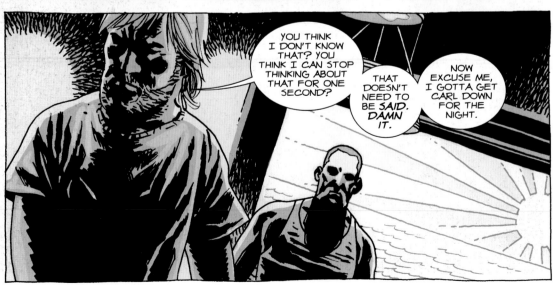

YOU THINK I DON'T KNOW THAT? YOU THINK I CAN STOP THINKING ABOUT THAT FOR ONE SECOND?

THAT DOESN'T NEED TO BE *SAID*. *DAMN* IT.

NOW EXCUSE ME, I GOTTA GET CARL DOWN FOR THE NIGHT.

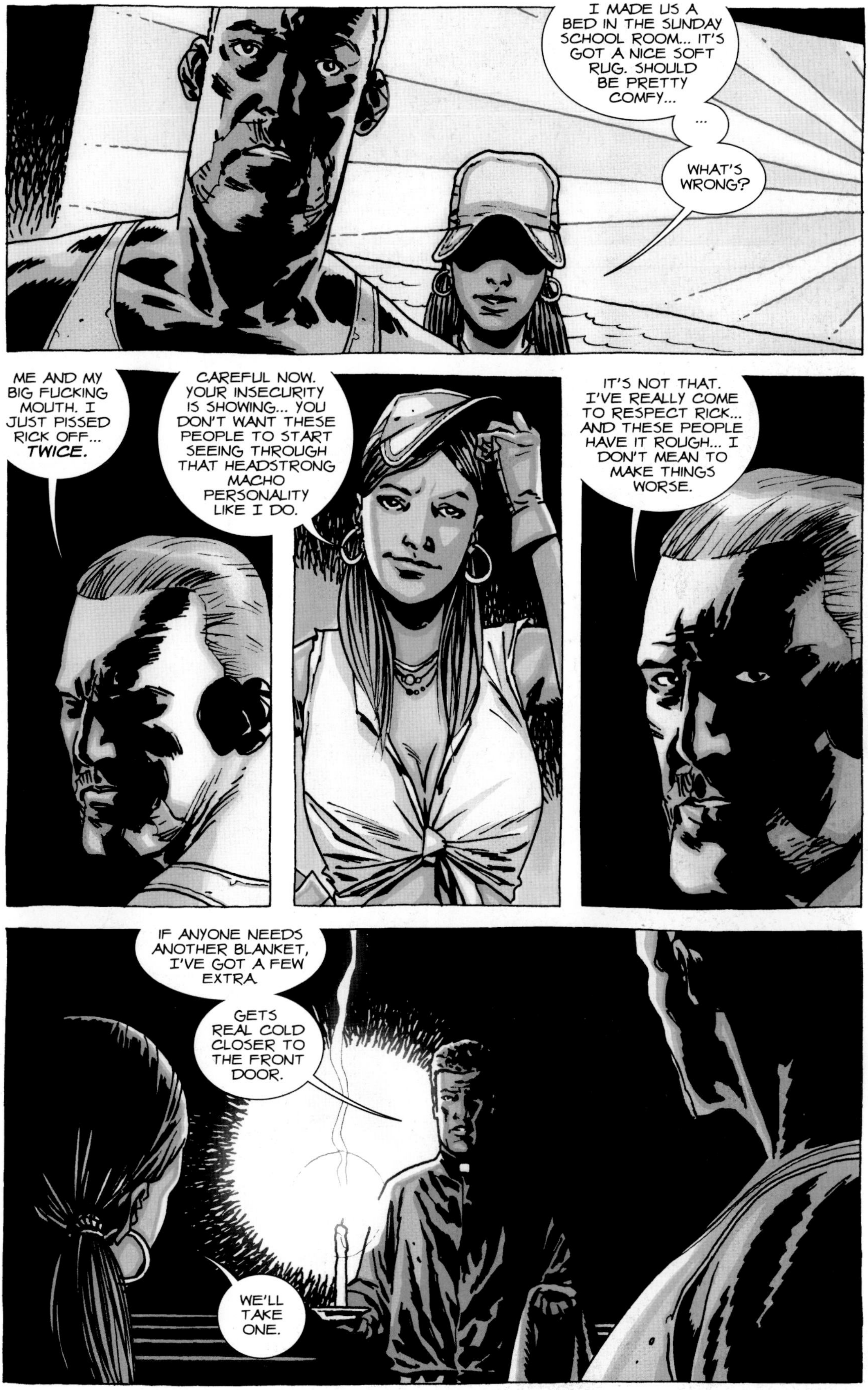

I MADE US A BED IN THE SUNDAY SCHOOL ROOM... IT'S GOT A NICE SOFT RUG. SHOULD BE PRETTY COMFY...
...
WHAT'S WRONG?
ME AND MY BIG FUCKING MOUTH. I JUST PISSED RICK OFF... *TWICE.*
CAREFUL NOW. YOUR INSECURITY IS SHOWING... YOU DON'T WANT THESE PEOPLE TO START SEEING THROUGH THAT HEADSTRONG MACHO PERSONALITY LIKE I DO.
IT'S NOT THAT. I'VE REALLY COME TO RESPECT RICK... AND THESE PEOPLE HAVE IT ROUGH... I DON'T MEAN TO MAKE THINGS WORSE.
IF ANYONE NEEDS ANOTHER BLANKET, I'VE GOT A FEW EXTRA.
GETS REAL COLD CLOSER TO THE FRONT DOOR.
WE'LL TAKE ONE.

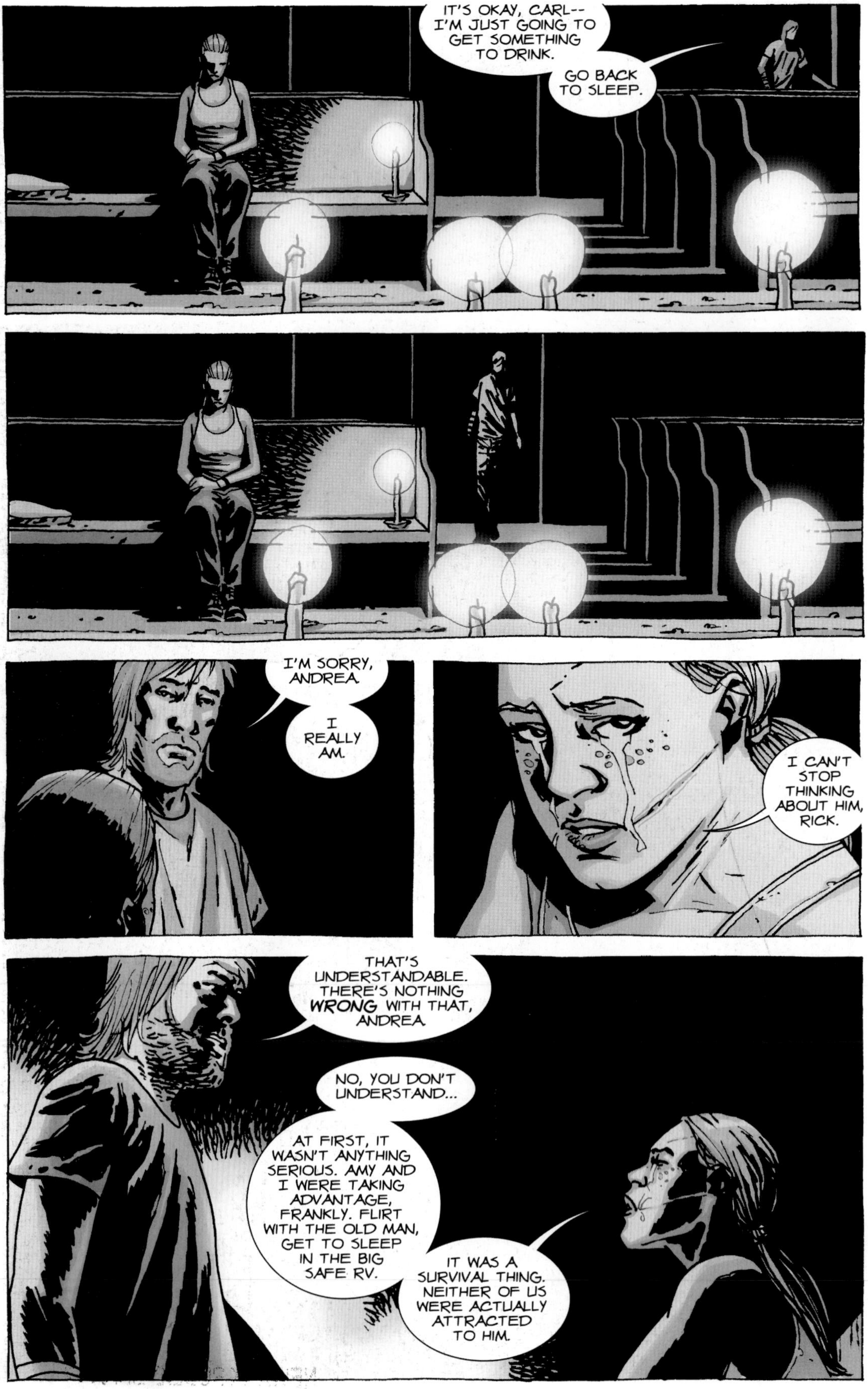
IT'S OKAY, CARL-- I'M JUST GOING TO GET SOMETHING TO DRINK.
GO BACK TO SLEEP.
I'M SORRY, ANDREA.
I REALLY AM.
I CAN'T STOP THINKING ABOUT HIM, RICK.
THAT'S UNDERSTANDABLE. THERE'S NOTHING WRONG WITH THAT, ANDREA.
NO, YOU DON'T UNDERSTAND...
AT FIRST, IT WASN'T ANYTHING SERIOUS. AMY AND I WERE TAKING ADVANTAGE, FRANKLY. FLIRT WITH THE OLD MAN, GET TO SLEEP IN THE BIG SAFE RV.
IT WAS A SURVIVAL THING. NEITHER OF US WERE ACTUALLY ATTRACTED TO HIM.

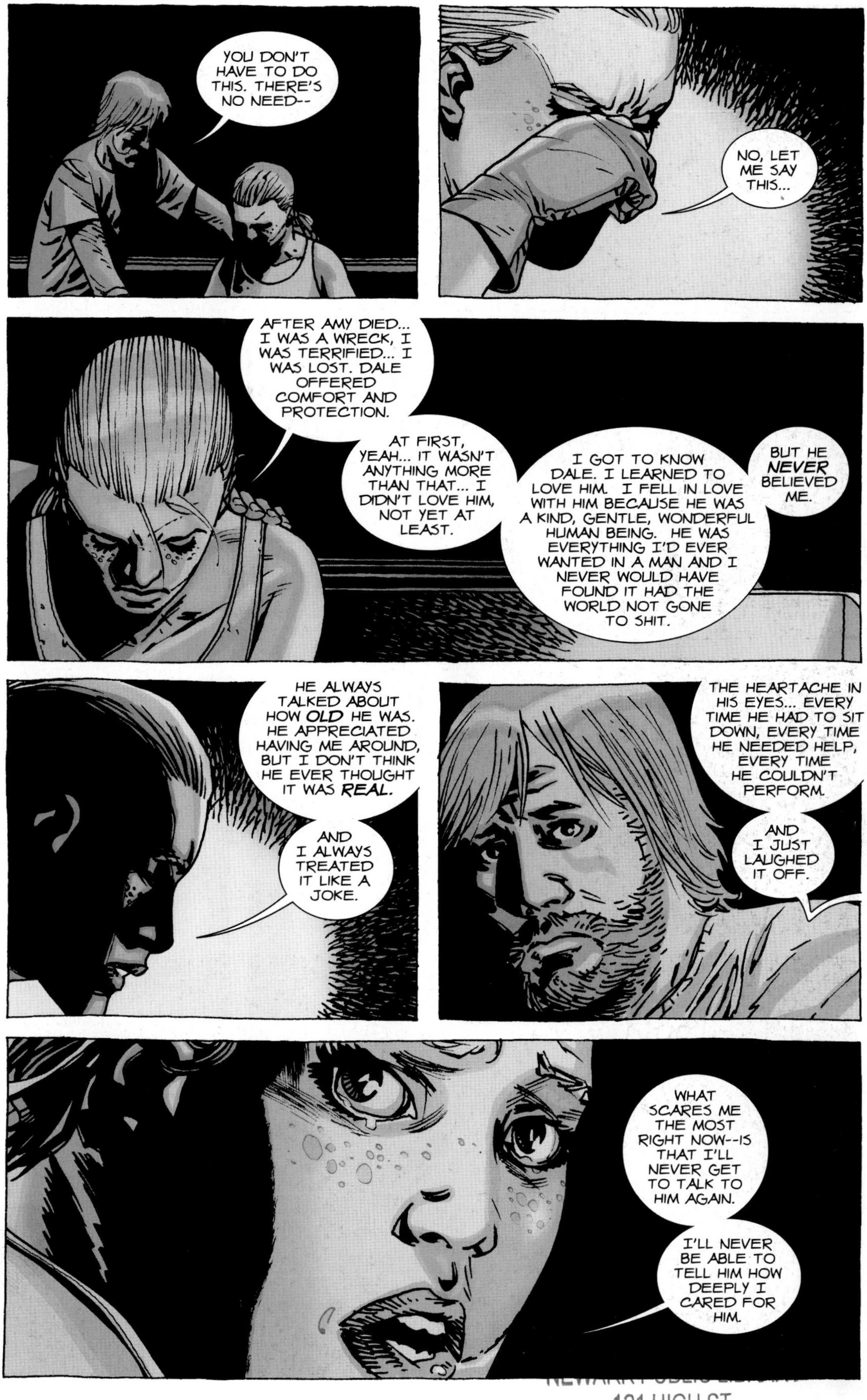
YOU DON'T HAVE TO DO THIS. THERE'S NO NEED--
NO, LET ME SAY THIS...
AFTER AMY DIED... I WAS A WRECK, I WAS TERRIFIED... I WAS LOST. DALE OFFERED COMFORT AND PROTECTION.
AT FIRST, YEAH... IT WASN'T ANYTHING MORE THAN THAT... I DIDN'T LOVE HIM, NOT YET AT LEAST.
I GOT TO KNOW DALE. I LEARNED TO LOVE HIM. I FELL IN LOVE WITH HIM BECAUSE HE WAS A KIND, GENTLE, WONDERFUL HUMAN BEING. HE WAS EVERYTHING I'D EVER WANTED IN A MAN AND I NEVER WOULD HAVE FOUND IT HAD THE WORLD NOT GONE TO SHIT.
BUT HE NEVER BELIEVED ME.
HE ALWAYS TALKED ABOUT HOW OLD HE WAS. HE APPRECIATED HAVING ME AROUND, BUT I DON'T THINK HE EVER THOUGHT IT WAS REAL.
AND I ALWAYS TREATED IT LIKE A JOKE.
THE HEARTACHE IN HIS EYES... EVERY TIME HE HAD TO SIT DOWN, EVERY TIME HE NEEDED HELP, EVERY TIME HE COULDN'T PERFORM.
AND I JUST LAUGHED IT OFF.
WHAT SCARES ME THE MOST RIGHT NOW--IS THAT I'LL NEVER GET TO TALK TO HIM AGAIN.
I'LL NEVER BE ABLE TO TELL HIM HOW DEEPLY I CARED FOR HIM.

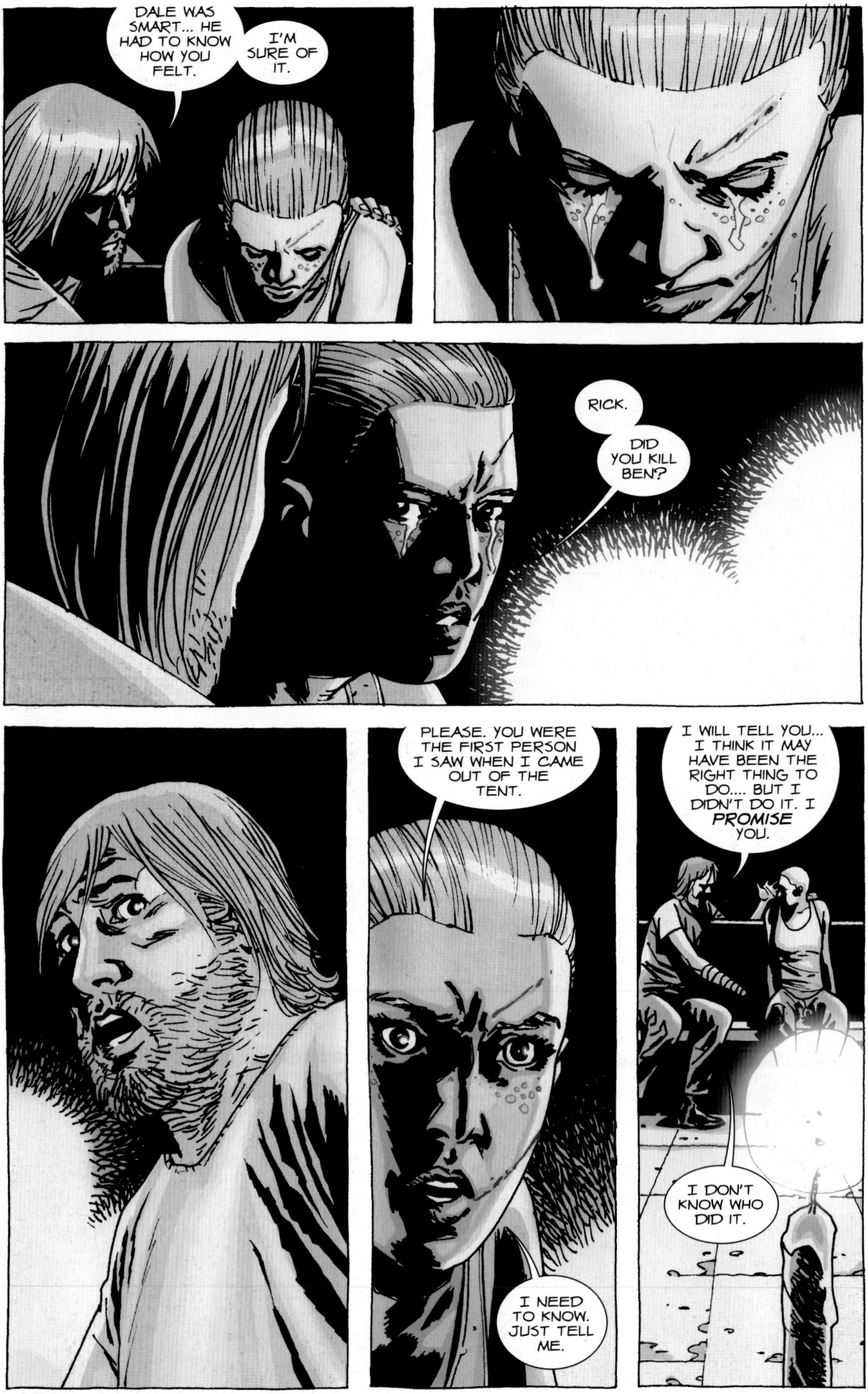
DALE WAS SMART... HE HAD TO KNOW HOW YOU FELT.
I'M SURE OF IT.
RICK.
DID YOU KILL BEN?
PLEASE. YOU WERE THE FIRST PERSON I SAW WHEN I CAME OUT OF THE TENT.
I NEED TO KNOW. JUST TELL ME.
I WILL TELL YOU... I THINK IT MAY HAVE BEEN THE RIGHT THING TO DO.... BUT I DIDN'T DO IT. I PROMISE YOU.
I DON'T KNOW WHO DID IT.

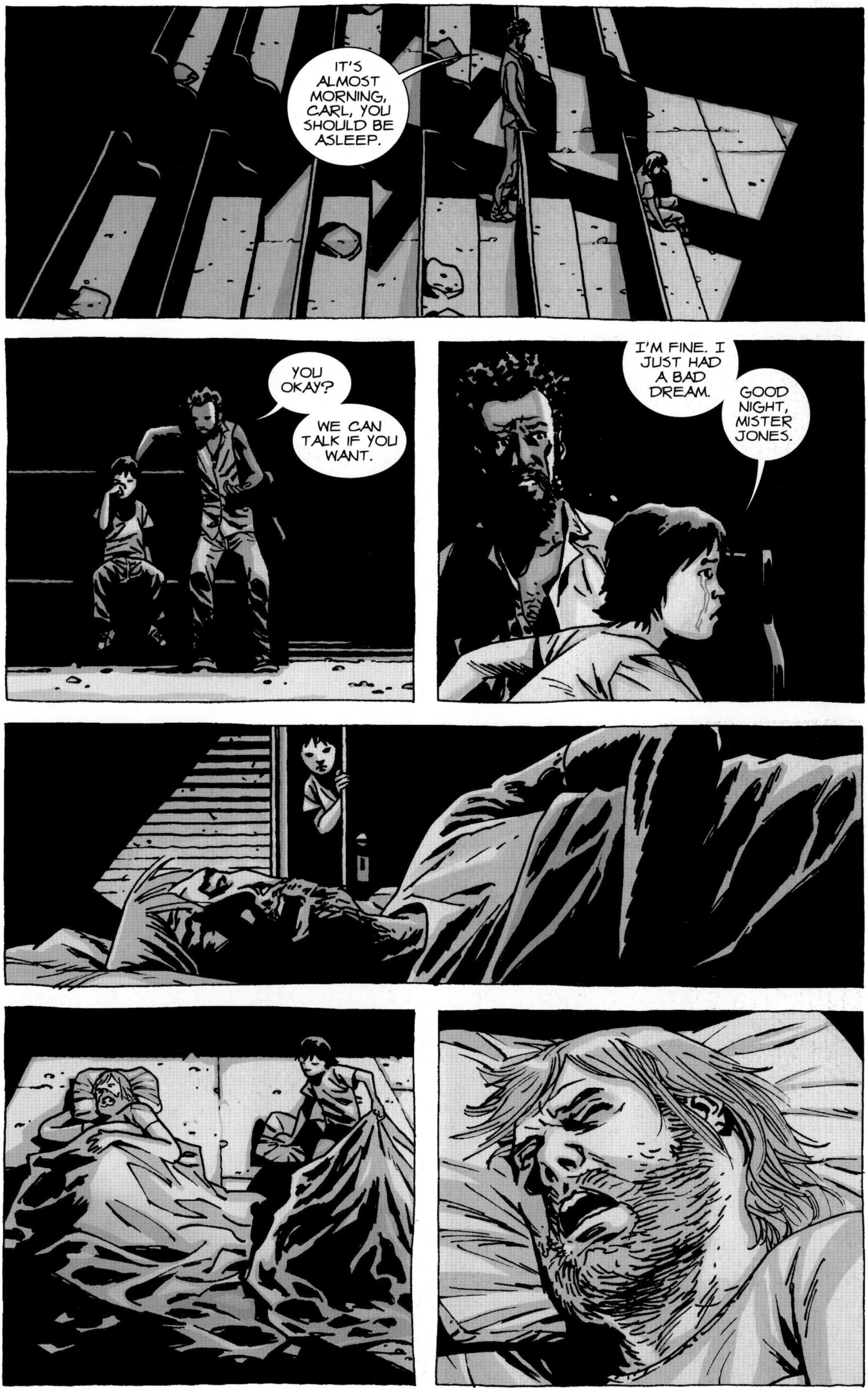
IT'S ALMOST MORNING, CARL, YOU SHOULD BE ASLEEP.
YOU OKAY?
WE CAN TALK IF YOU WANT.
I'M FINE. I JUST HAD A BAD DREAM.
GOOD NIGHT, MISTER JONES.

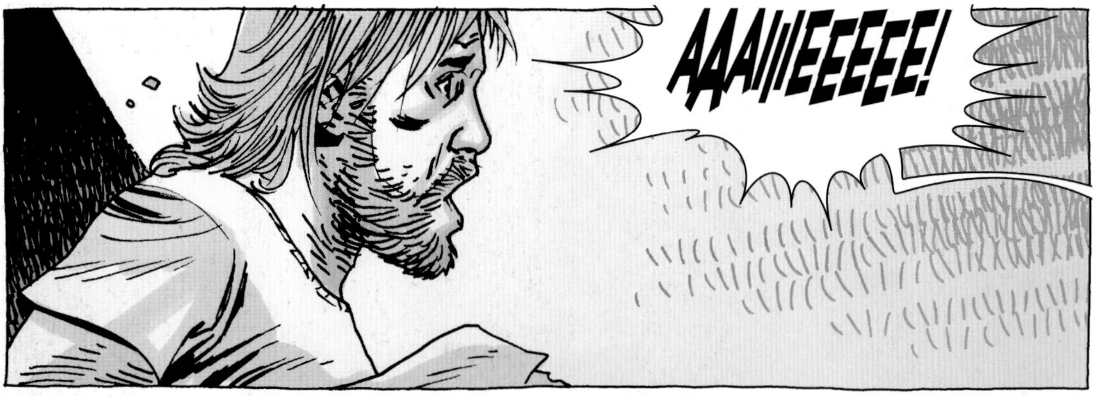
AAAIIIEEEEE!

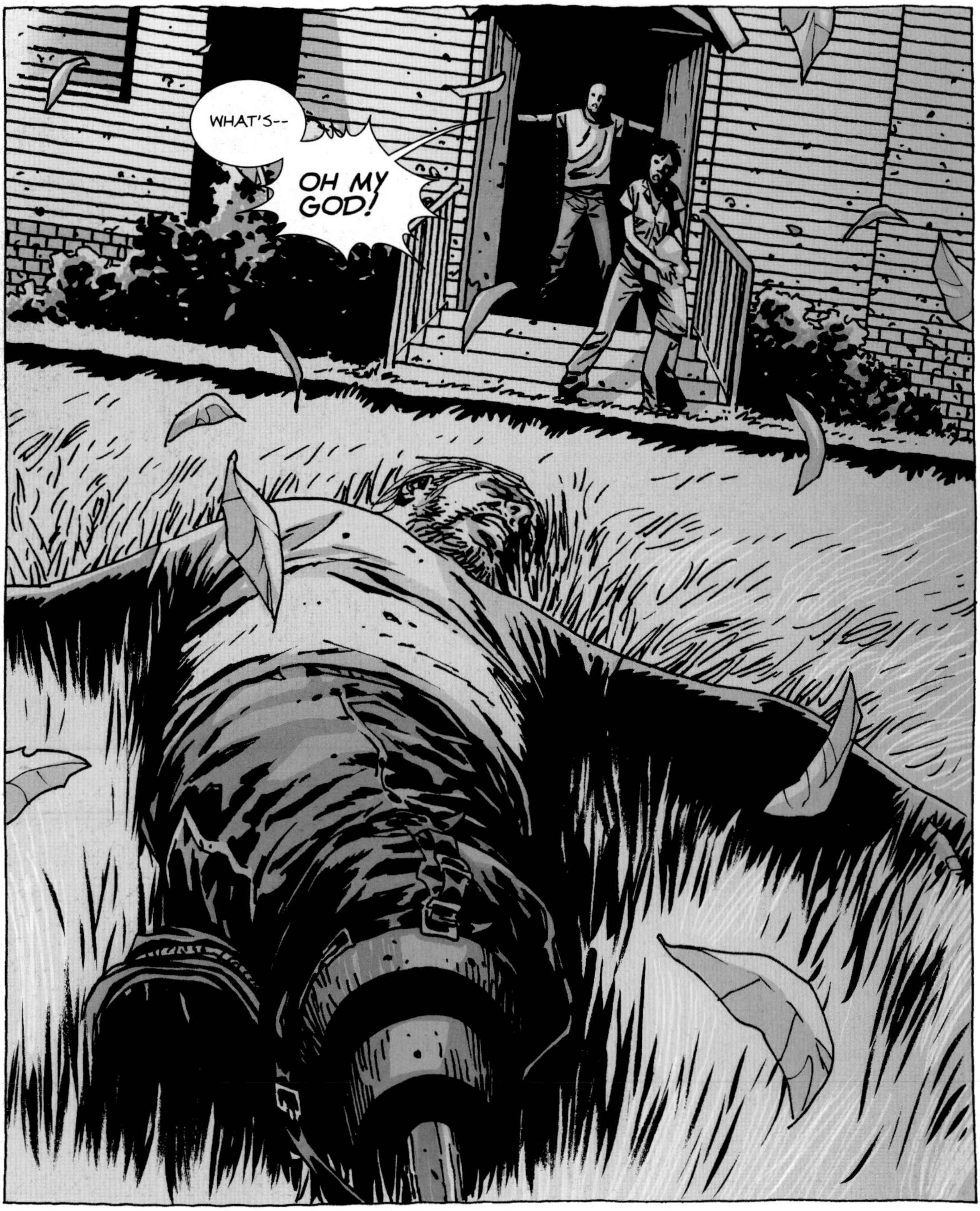
WHAT'S--
OH MY GOD!

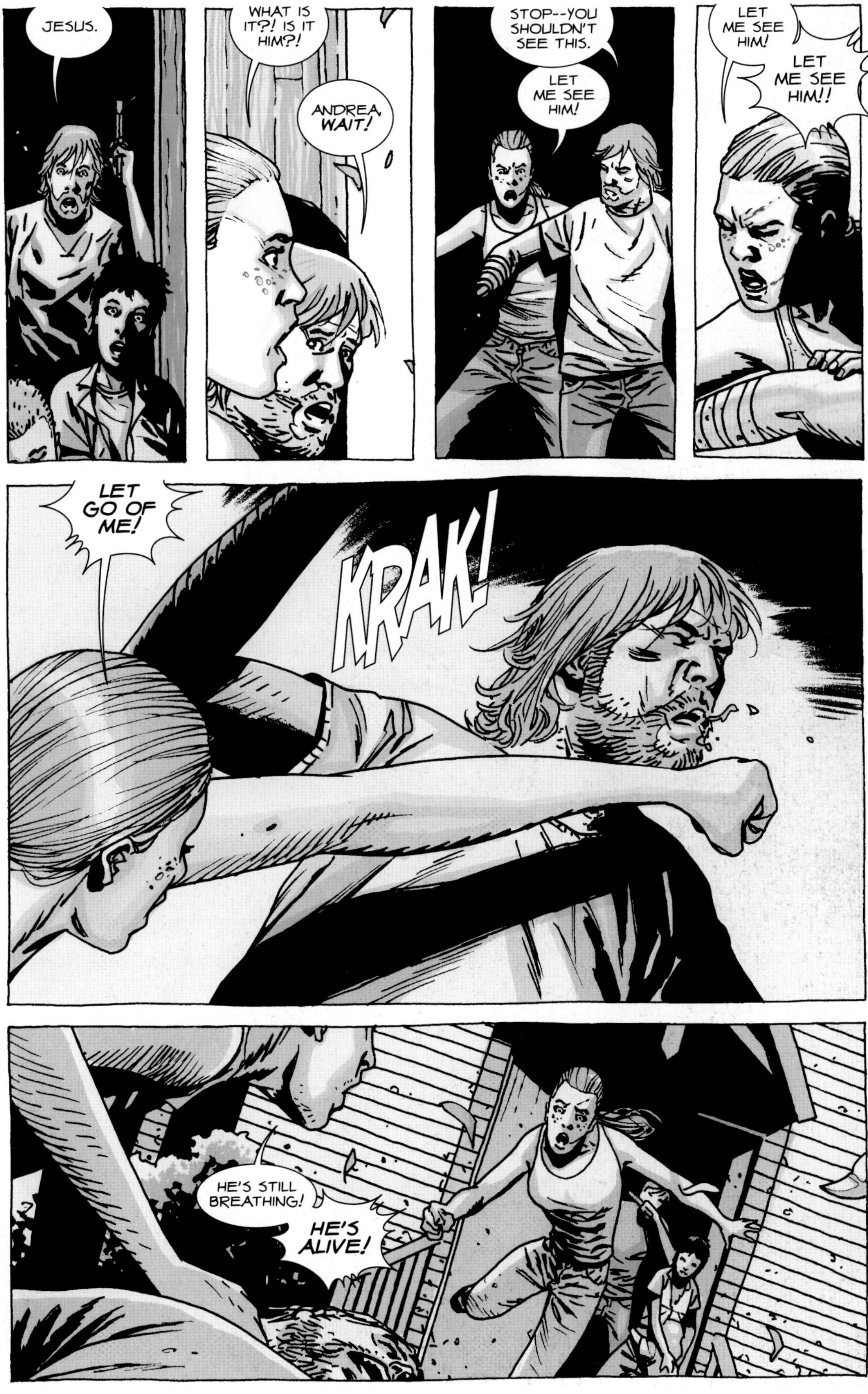
JESUS.
WHAT IS IT?! IS IT HIM?!
ANDREA, WAIT!
STOP--YOU SHOULDN'T SEE THIS.
LET ME SEE HIM!
LET ME SEE HIM!
LET ME SEE HIM!!
LET GO OF ME!
KRAK!
HE'S STILL BREATHING!
HE'S ALIVE!

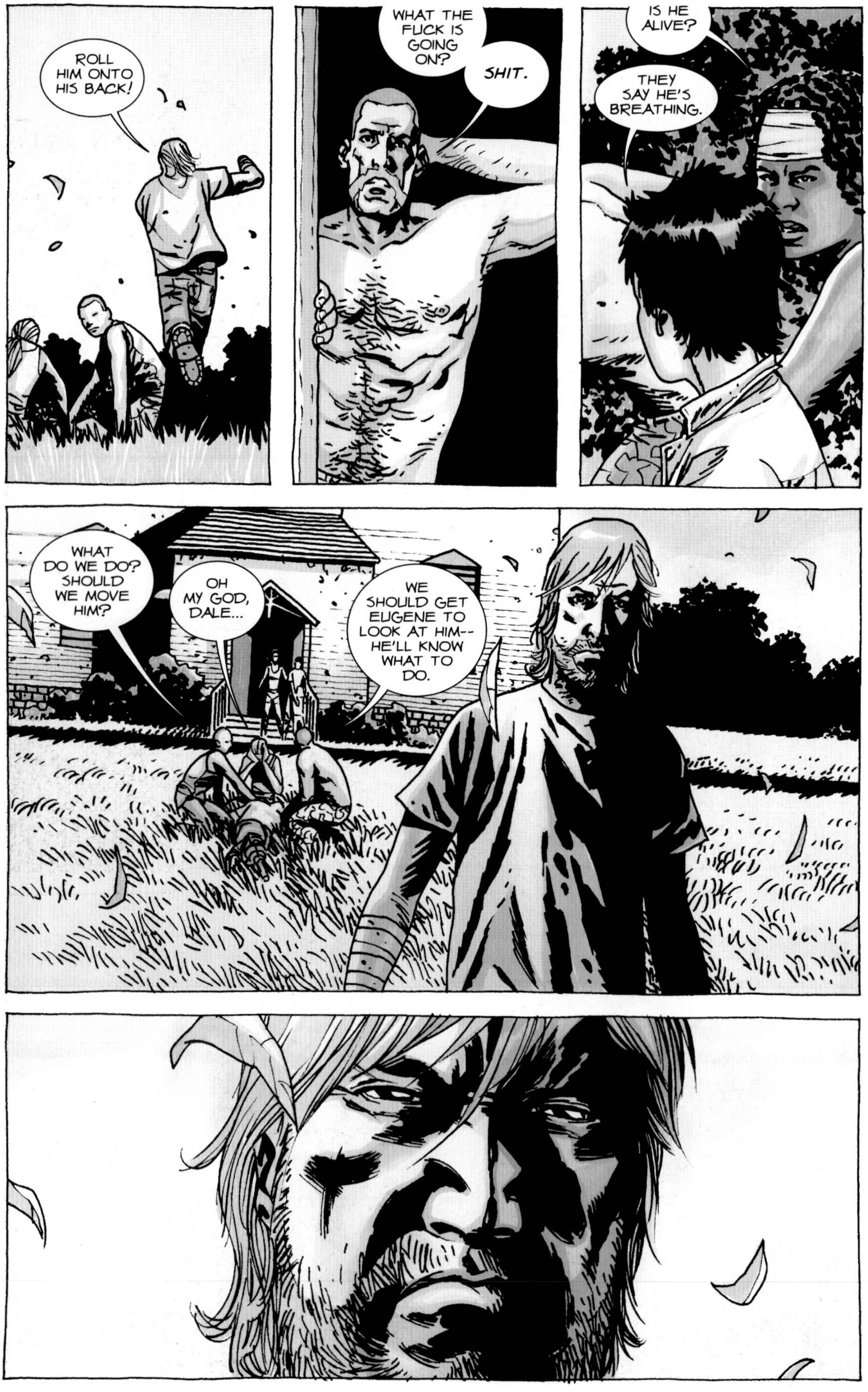
ROLL HIM ONTO HIS BACK!
WHAT THE FUCK IS GOING ON?
SHIT.
IS HE ALIVE?
THEY SAY HE'S BREATHING.
WHAT DO WE DO? SHOULD WE MOVE HIM?
OH MY GOD, DALE...
WE SHOULD GET EUGENE TO LOOK AT HIM-- HE'LL KNOW WHAT TO DO.

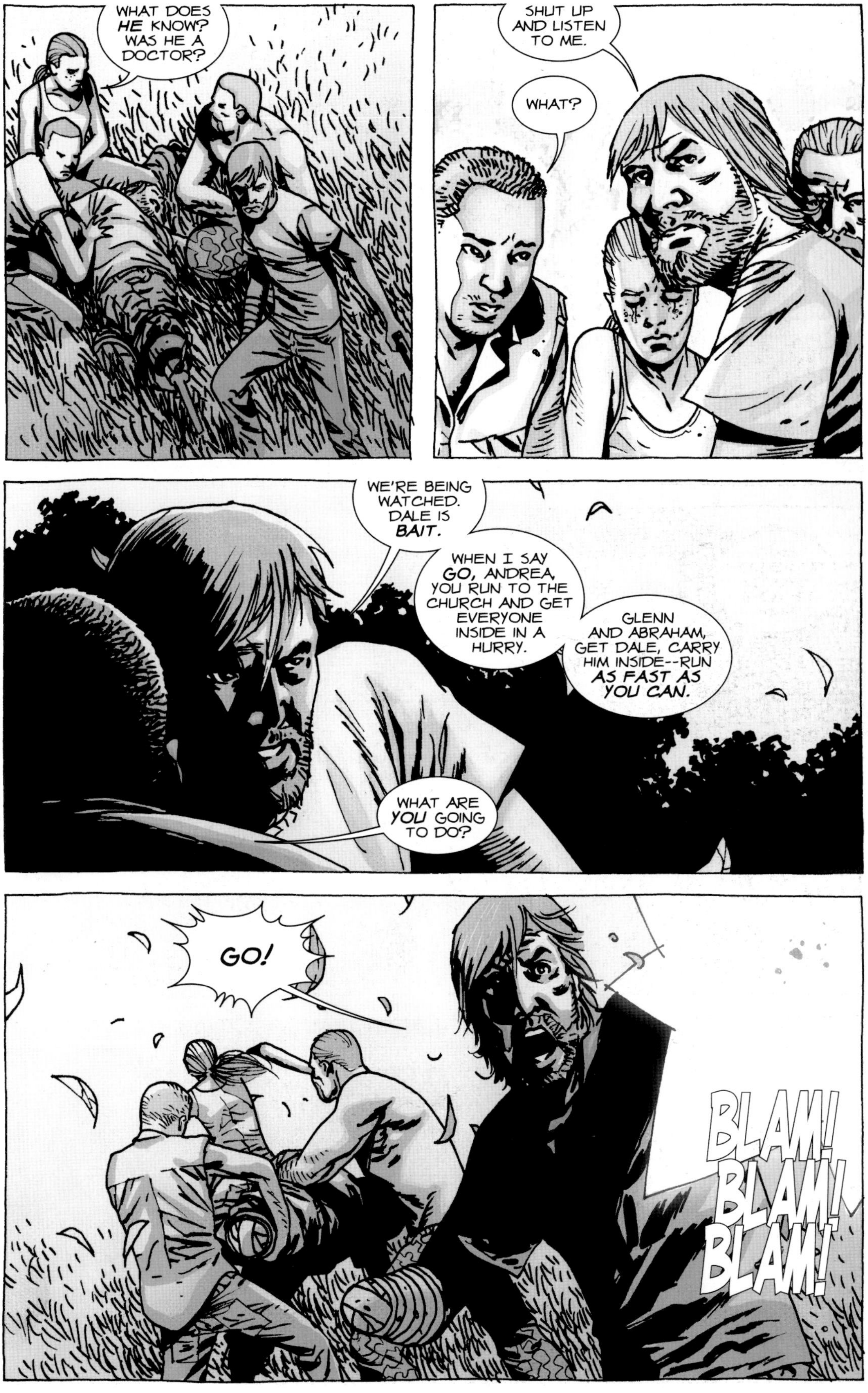
WHAT DOES HE KNOW? WAS HE A DOCTOR?
SHUT UP AND LISTEN TO ME.
WHAT?
WE'RE BEING WATCHED. DALE IS BAIT.
WHEN I SAY GO, ANDREA, YOU RUN TO THE CHURCH AND GET EVERYONE INSIDE IN A HURRY.
GLENN AND ABRAHAM, GET DALE, CARRY HIM INSIDE--RUN AS FAST AS YOU CAN.
WHAT ARE YOU GOING TO DO?
GO!
BLAM! BLAM! BLAM!

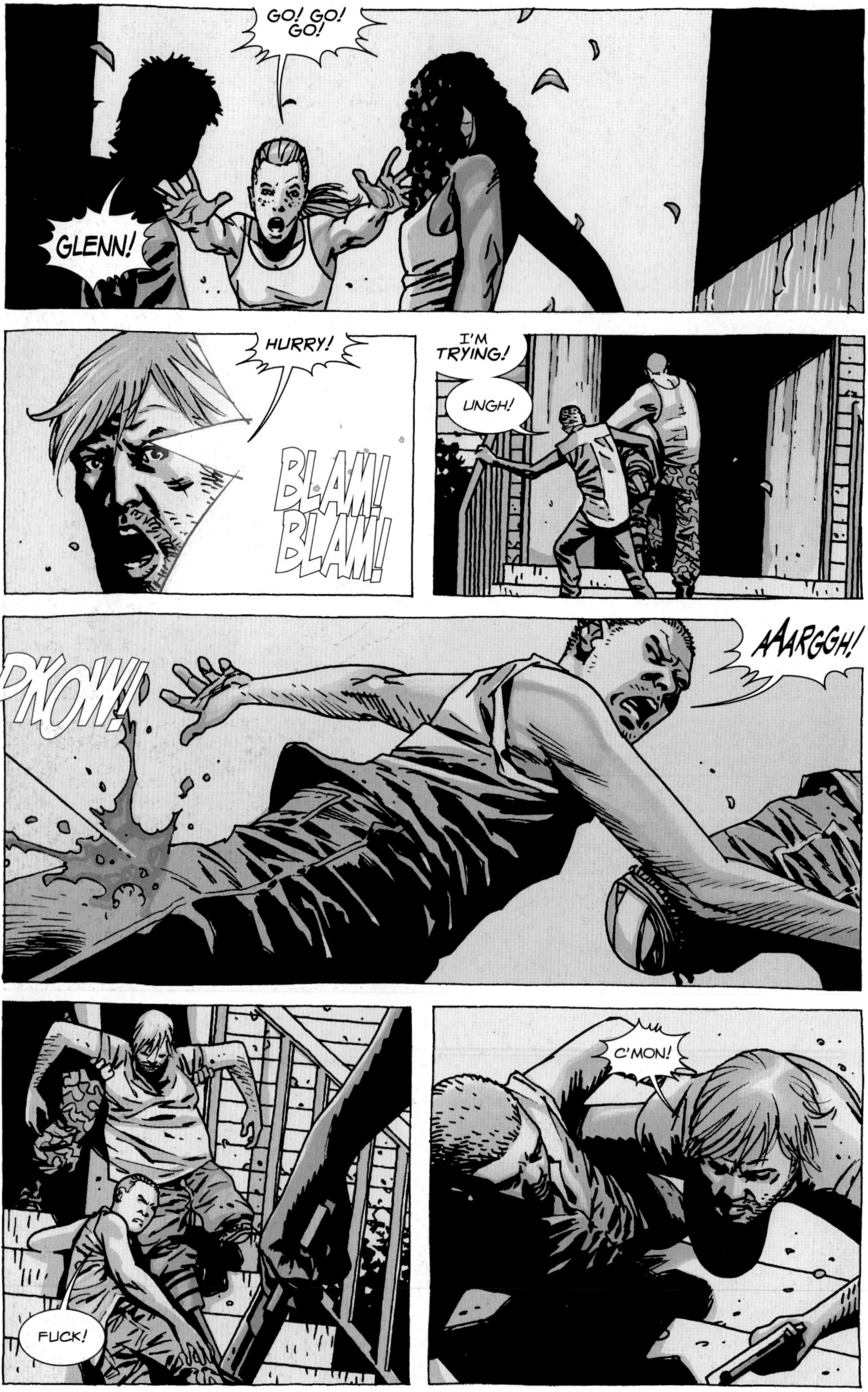
GO! GO! GO!
GLENN!
HURRY!
BLAM! BLAM!
I'M TRYING!
UNGH!
PKOW!
AAARGGH!
FUCK!
C'MON!

SHUT THE DOORS! LOCK THEM!

UNG.

EVERYONE GET DOWN. STAY AWAY FROM THE WINDOWS.

THEY'RE STILL OUT THERE!

EUGENE--CLEAN UP GLENN'S LEG AND THEN CHECK OUT DALE. EVERYONE--CLOSE THE WINDOWS AND STAY AWAY--BUT WE DON'T NEED TO BE HUGGING THE FLOOR.

ABRAHAM-- WHAT ARE YOU DOING?!

THEY ONLY FIRED ONE SHOT, RICK.

WHAT DO YOU MEAN?

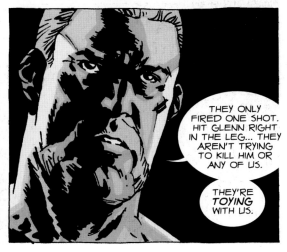

THEY ONLY FIRED ONE SHOT. HIT GLENN RIGHT IN THE LEG... THEY AREN'T TRYING TO KILL HIM OR ANY OF US.

THEY'RE TOYING WITH US.

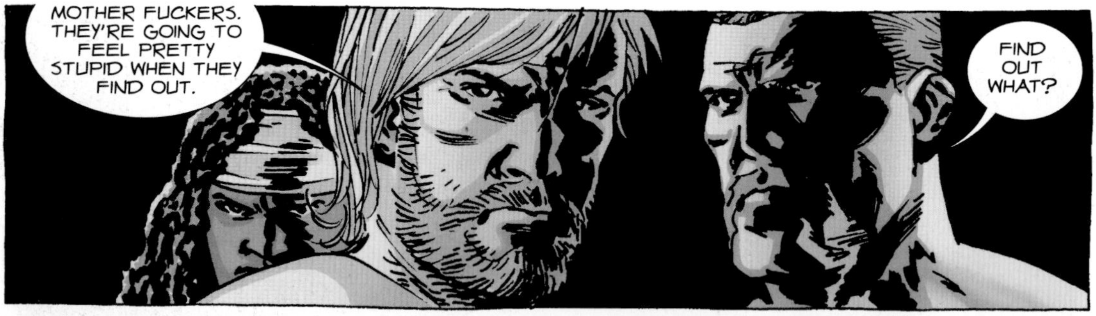
MOTHER FUCKERS. THEY'RE GOING TO FEEL PRETTY STUPID WHEN THEY FIND OUT.
FIND OUT WHAT?

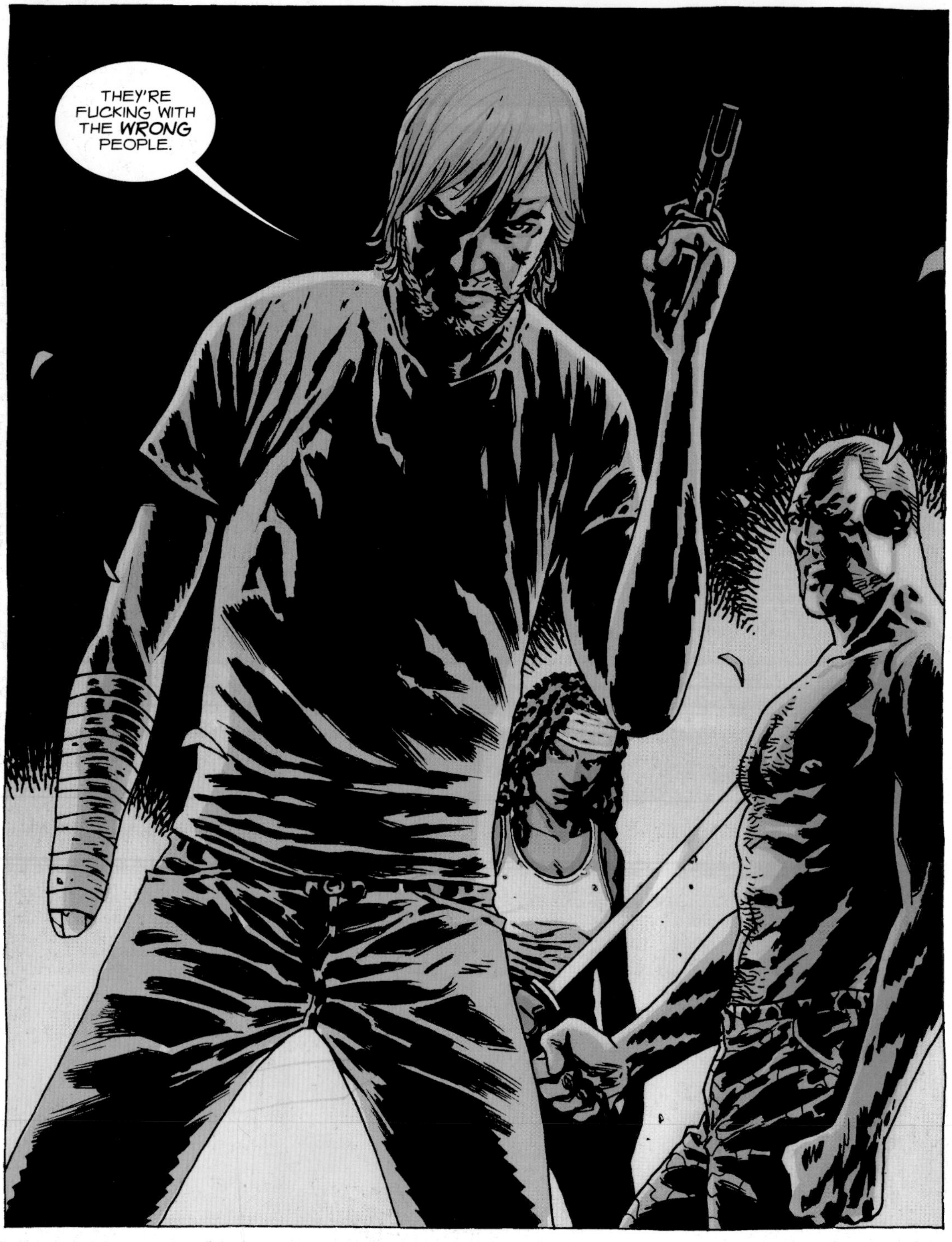
THEY'RE FUCKING WITH THE **WRONG** PEOPLE.

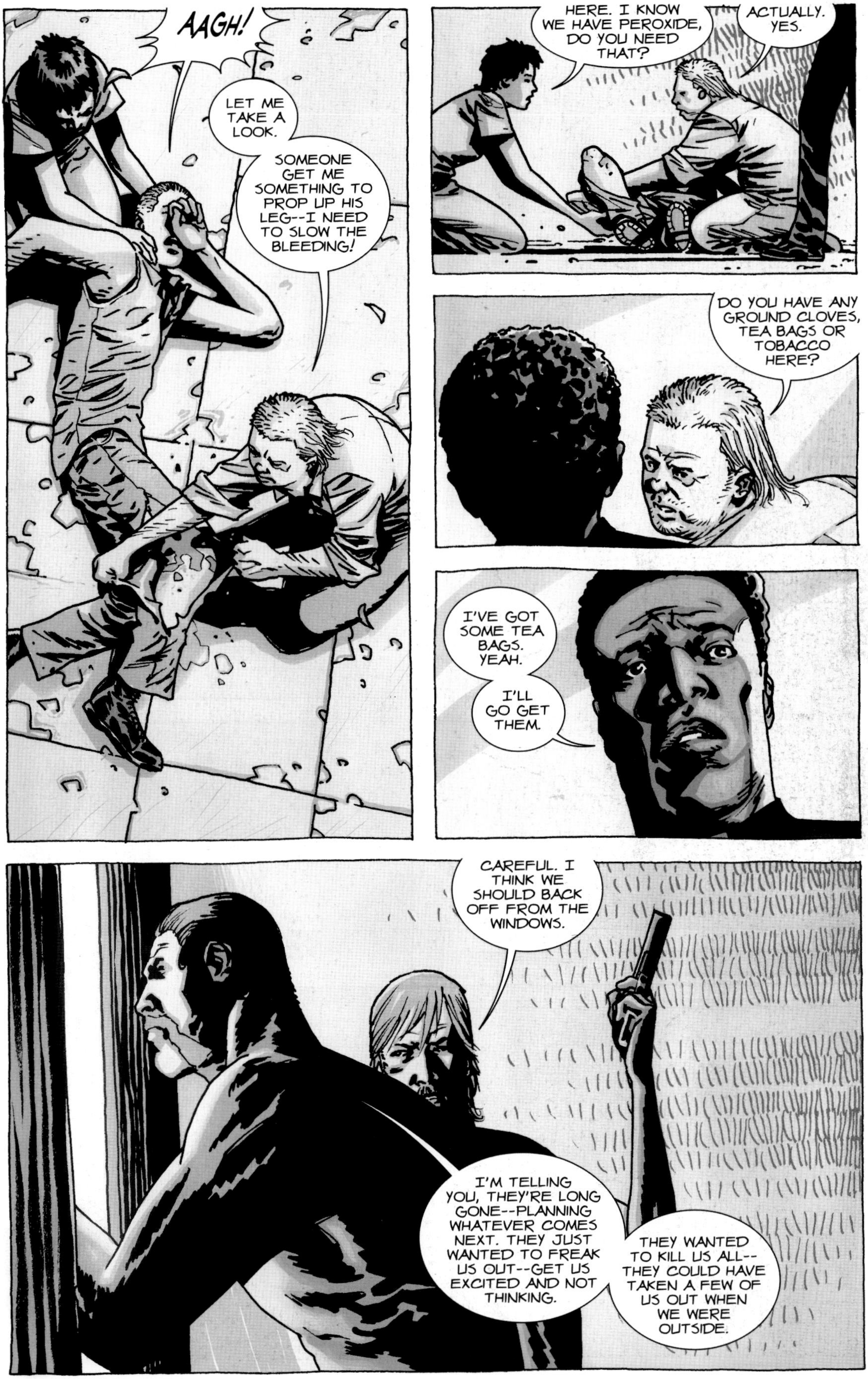
AAGH!
LET ME TAKE A LOOK.
SOMEONE GET ME SOMETHING TO PROP UP HIS LEG--I NEED TO SLOW THE BLEEDING!
HERE. I KNOW WE HAVE PEROXIDE, DO YOU NEED THAT?
ACTUALLY. YES.
DO YOU HAVE ANY GROUND CLOVES, TEA BAGS OR TOBACCO HERE?
I'VE GOT SOME TEA BAGS. YEAH.
I'LL GO GET THEM.
CAREFUL. I THINK WE SHOULD BACK OFF FROM THE WINDOWS.
I'M TELLING YOU, THEY'RE LONG GONE--PLANNING WHATEVER COMES NEXT. THEY JUST WANTED TO FREAK US OUT--GET US EXCITED AND NOT THINKING.
THEY WANTED TO KILL US ALL-- THEY COULD HAVE TAKEN A FEW OF US OUT WHEN WE WERE OUTSIDE.

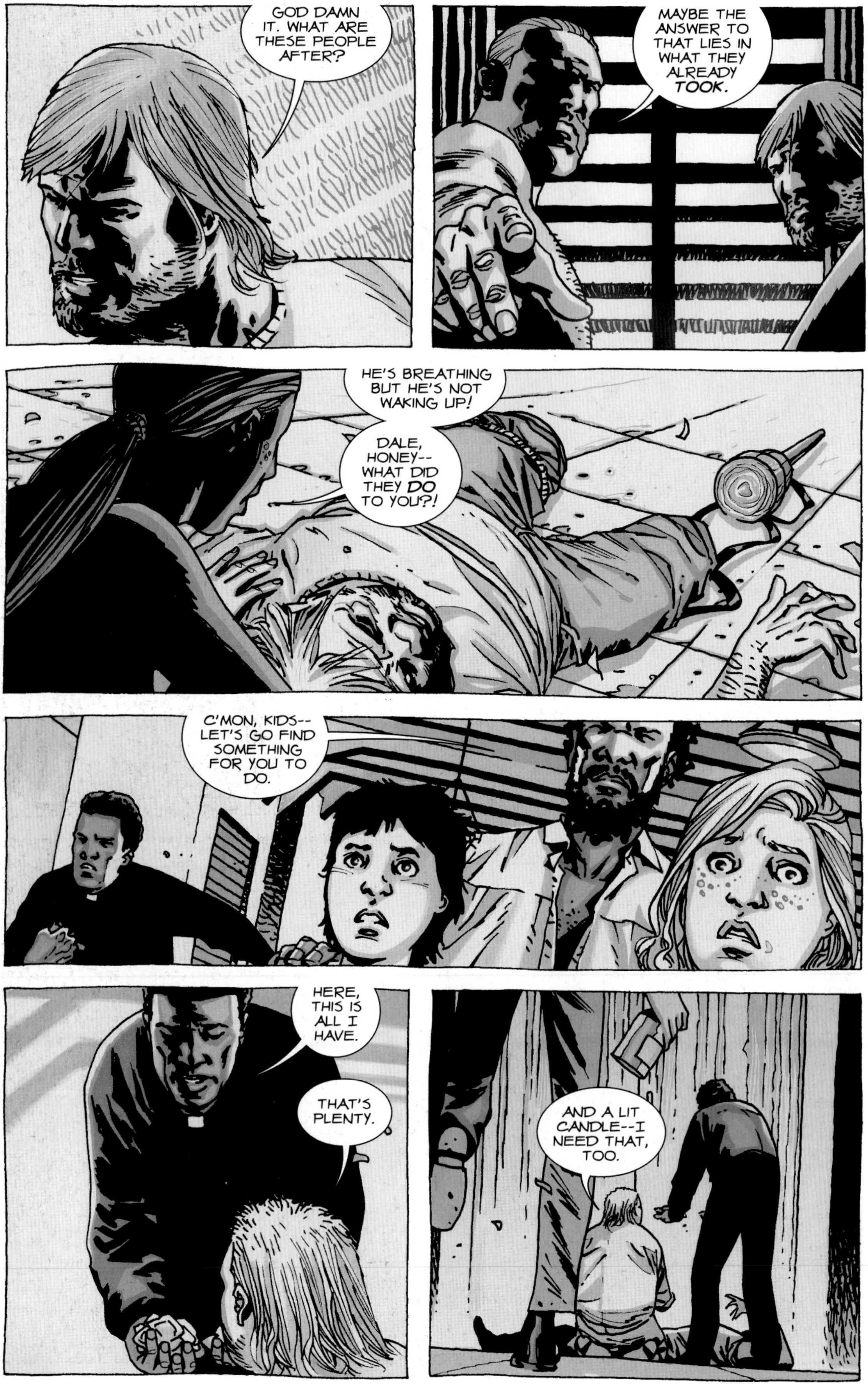
GOD DAMN IT. WHAT ARE THESE PEOPLE AFTER?
MAYBE THE ANSWER TO THAT LIES IN WHAT THEY ALREADY *TOOK*.
HE'S BREATHING BUT HE'S NOT WAKING UP!
DALE, HONEY-- WHAT DID THEY *DO* TO YOU?!
C'MON, KIDS-- LET'S GO FIND SOMETHING FOR YOU TO DO.
HERE, THIS IS ALL I HAVE.
THAT'S PLENTY.
AND A LIT CANDLE--I NEED THAT, TOO.

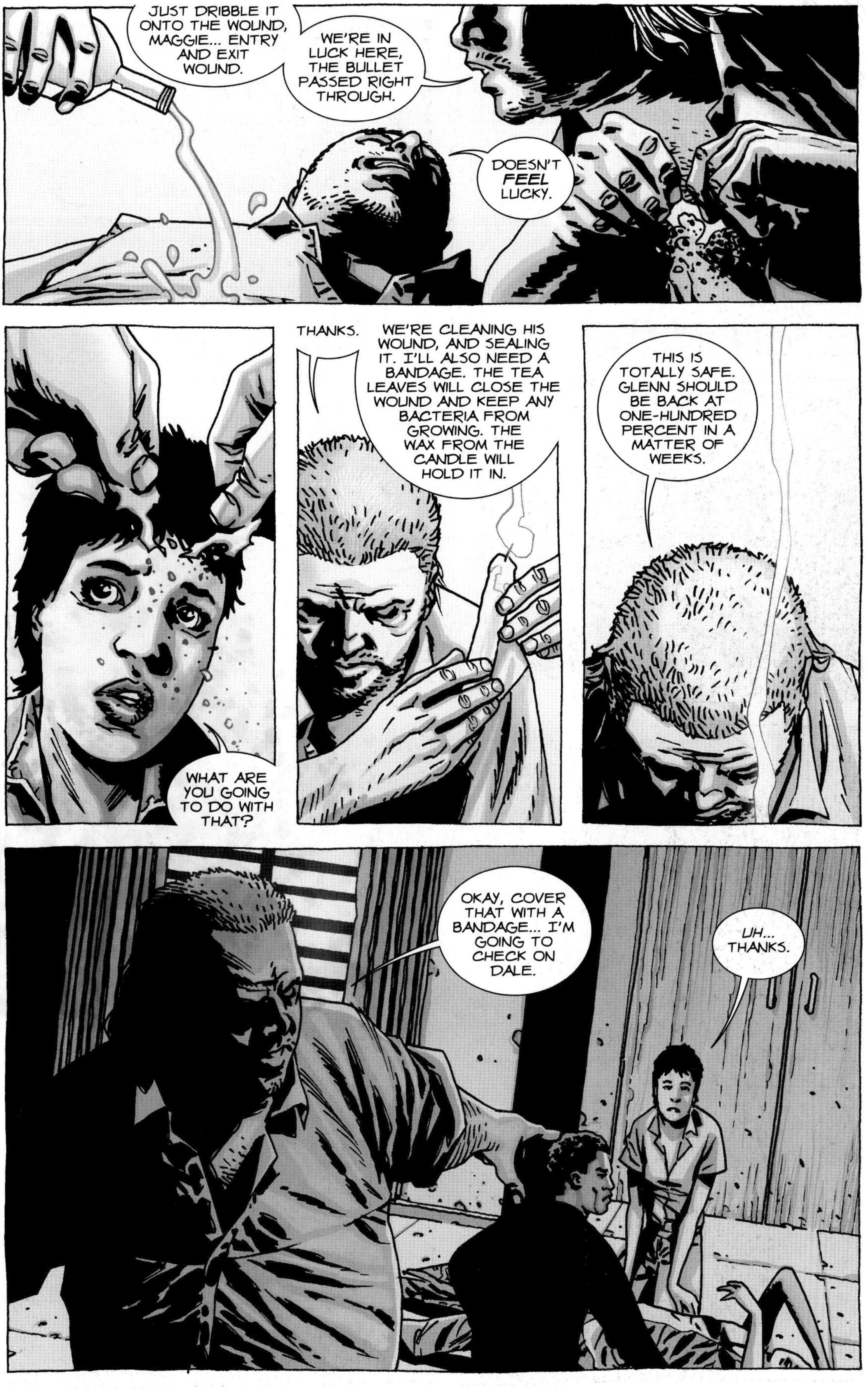
JUST DRIBBLE IT ONTO THE WOUND, MAGGIE... ENTRY AND EXIT WOUND.
WE'RE IN LUCK HERE, THE BULLET PASSED RIGHT THROUGH.
DOESN'T FEEL LUCKY.
WHAT ARE YOU GOING TO DO WITH THAT?
THANKS.
WE'RE CLEANING HIS WOUND, AND SEALING IT. I'LL ALSO NEED A BANDAGE. THE TEA LEAVES WILL CLOSE THE WOUND AND KEEP ANY BACTERIA FROM GROWING. THE WAX FROM THE CANDLE WILL HOLD IT IN.
THIS IS TOTALLY SAFE. GLENN SHOULD BE BACK AT ONE-HUNDRED PERCENT IN A MATTER OF WEEKS.
OKAY, COVER THAT WITH A BANDAGE... I'M GOING TO CHECK ON DALE.
UH... THANKS.

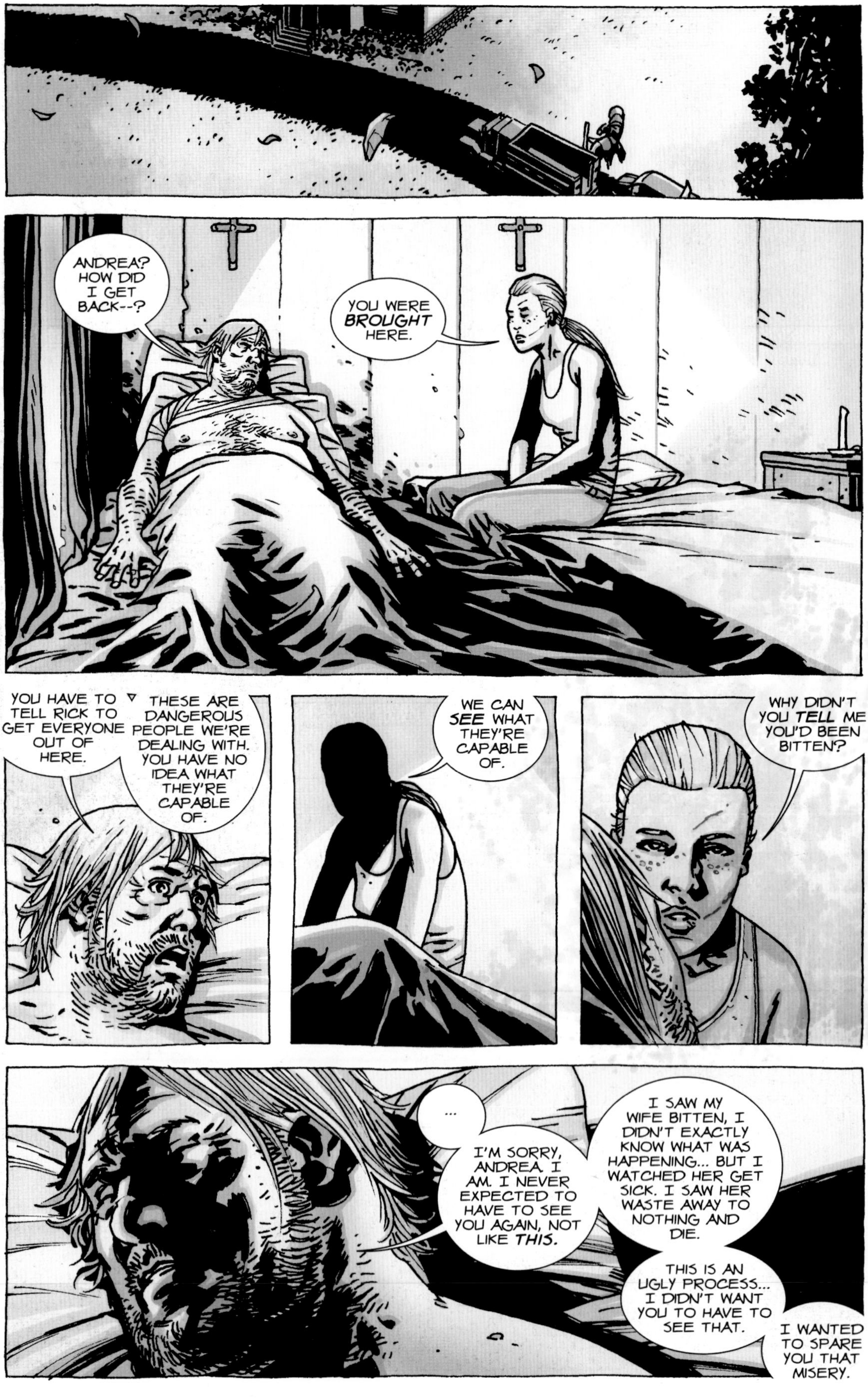
ANDREA? HOW DID I GET BACK--?
YOU WERE BROUGHT HERE.
YOU HAVE TO TELL RICK TO GET EVERYONE OUT OF HERE.
THESE ARE DANGEROUS PEOPLE WE'RE DEALING WITH. YOU HAVE NO IDEA WHAT THEY'RE CAPABLE OF.
WE CAN SEE WHAT THEY'RE CAPABLE OF.
WHY DIDN'T YOU TELL ME YOU'D BEEN BITTEN?
...
I'M SORRY, ANDREA. I AM. I NEVER EXPECTED TO HAVE TO SEE YOU AGAIN, NOT LIKE THIS.
I SAW MY WIFE BITTEN, I DIDN'T EXACTLY KNOW WHAT WAS HAPPENING... BUT I WATCHED HER GET SICK. I SAW HER WASTE AWAY TO NOTHING AND DIE.
THIS IS AN UGLY PROCESS... I DIDN'T WANT YOU TO HAVE TO SEE THAT.
I WANTED TO SPARE YOU THAT MISERY.

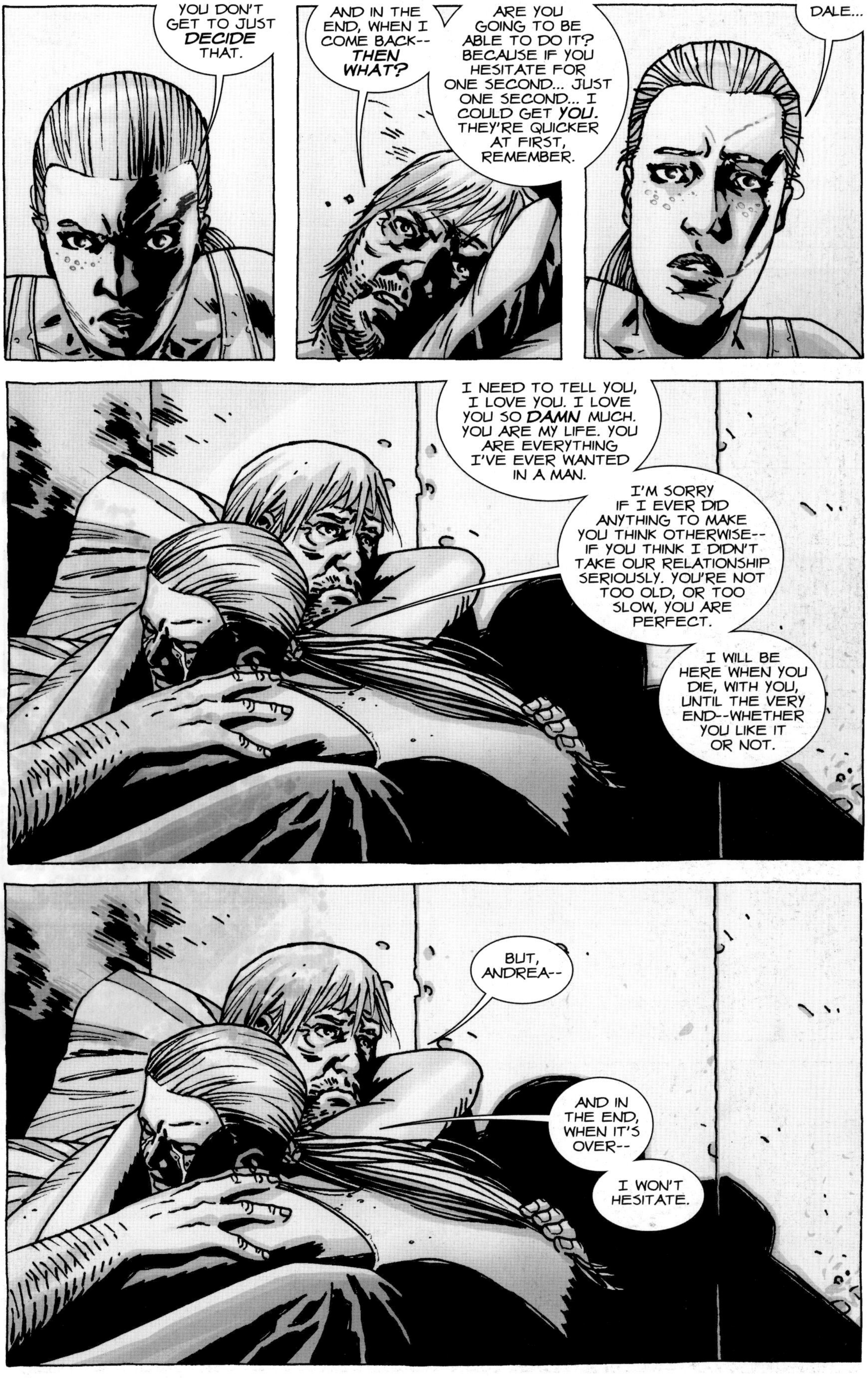
YOU DON'T GET TO JUST DECIDE THAT.
AND IN THE END, WHEN I COME BACK-- THEN WHAT?
ARE YOU GOING TO BE ABLE TO DO IT? BECAUSE IF YOU HESITATE FOR ONE SECOND... JUST ONE SECOND... I COULD GET YOU. THEY'RE QUICKER AT FIRST, REMEMBER.
DALE...
I NEED TO TELL YOU, I LOVE YOU. I LOVE YOU SO DAMN MUCH. YOU ARE MY LIFE. YOU ARE EVERYTHING I'VE EVER WANTED IN A MAN.
I'M SORRY IF I EVER DID ANYTHING TO MAKE YOU THINK OTHERWISE-- IF YOU THINK I DIDN'T TAKE OUR RELATIONSHIP SERIOUSLY. YOU'RE NOT TOO OLD, OR TOO SLOW, YOU ARE PERFECT.
I WILL BE HERE WHEN YOU DIE, WITH YOU, UNTIL THE VERY END--WHETHER YOU LIKE IT OR NOT.
BUT, ANDREA--
AND IN THE END, WHEN IT'S OVER--
I WON'T HESITATE.

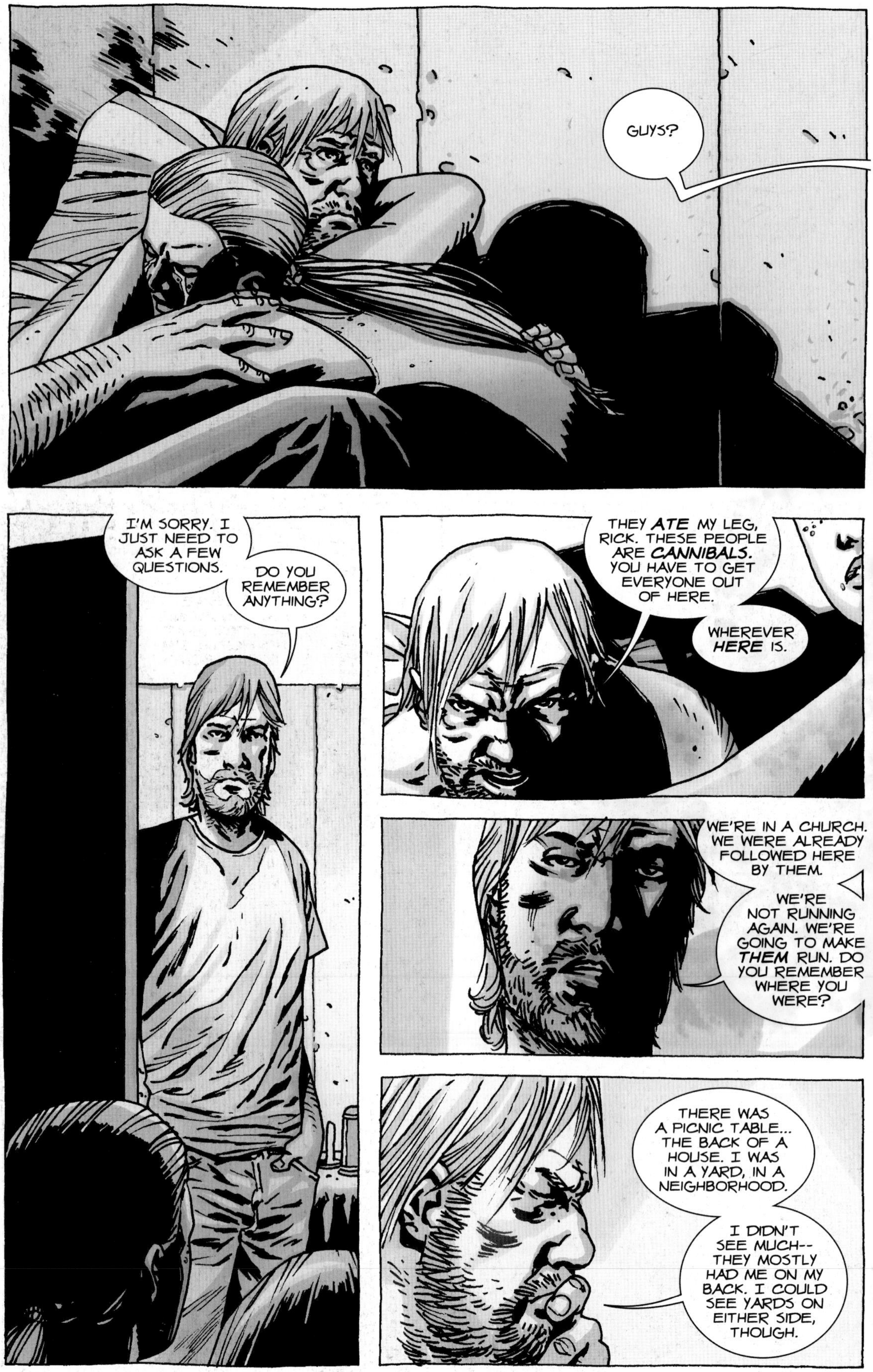
GUYS?
I'M SORRY. I JUST NEED TO ASK A FEW QUESTIONS.
DO YOU REMEMBER ANYTHING?
THEY ATE MY LEG, RICK. THESE PEOPLE ARE CANNIBALS. YOU HAVE TO GET EVERYONE OUT OF HERE.
WHEREVER HERE IS.
WE'RE IN A CHURCH. WE WERE ALREADY FOLLOWED HERE BY THEM.
WE'RE NOT RUNNING AGAIN. WE'RE GOING TO MAKE THEM RUN. DO YOU REMEMBER WHERE YOU WERE?
THERE WAS A PICNIC TABLE... THE BACK OF A HOUSE. I WAS IN A YARD, IN A NEIGHBORHOOD.
I DIDN'T SEE MUCH-- THEY MOSTLY HAD ME ON MY BACK. I COULD SEE YARDS ON EITHER SIDE, THOUGH.

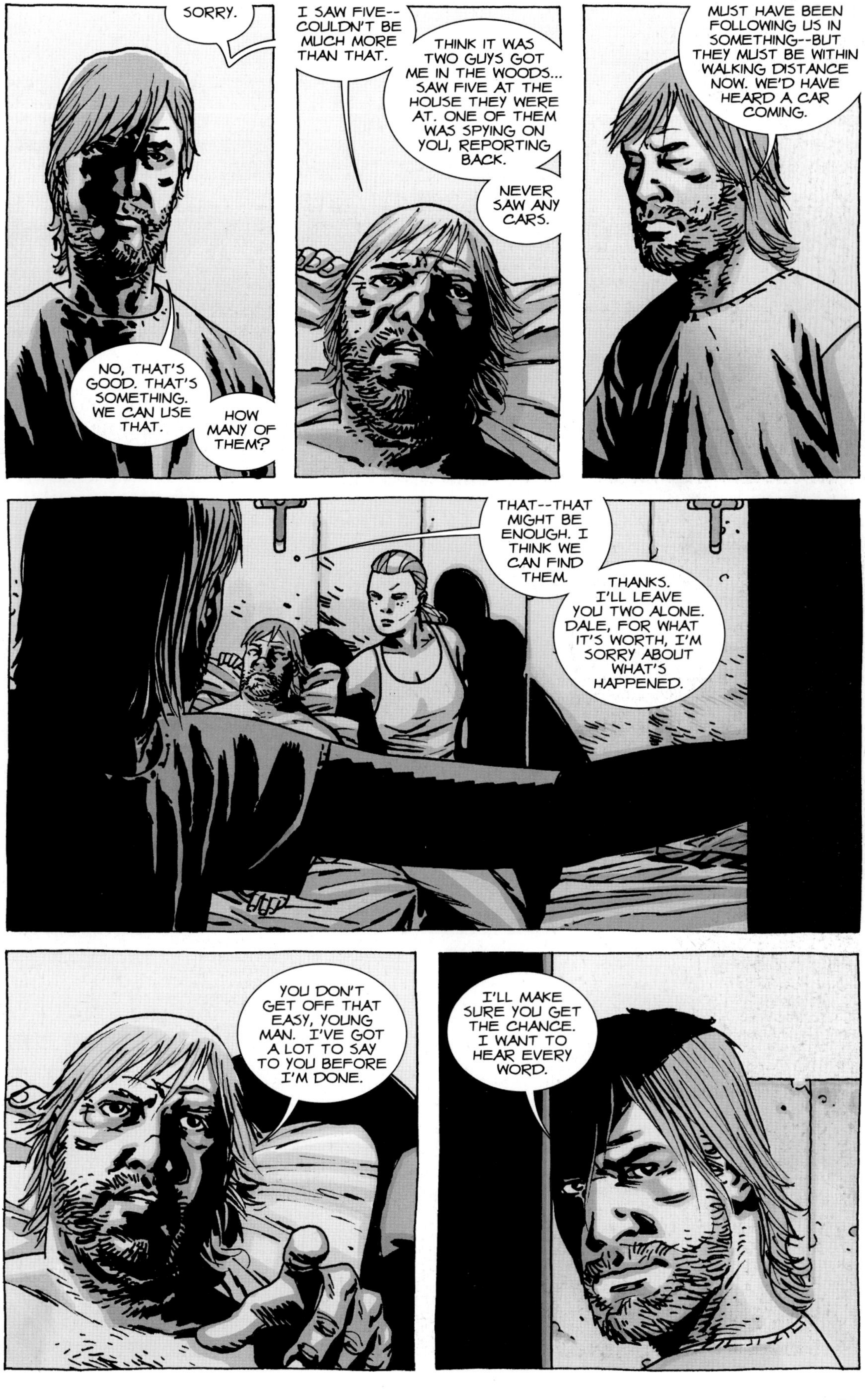
SORRY.
NO, THAT'S GOOD. THAT'S SOMETHING. WE CAN USE THAT.
HOW MANY OF THEM?
I SAW FIVE-- COULDN'T BE MUCH MORE THAN THAT.
THINK IT WAS TWO GUYS GOT ME IN THE WOODS... SAW FIVE AT THE HOUSE THEY WERE AT. ONE OF THEM WAS SPYING ON YOU, REPORTING BACK.
NEVER SAW ANY CARS.
MUST HAVE BEEN FOLLOWING US IN SOMETHING--BUT THEY MUST BE WITHIN WALKING DISTANCE NOW. WE'D HAVE HEARD A CAR COMING.
THAT--THAT MIGHT BE ENOUGH. I THINK WE CAN FIND THEM.
THANKS. I'LL LEAVE YOU TWO ALONE. DALE, FOR WHAT IT'S WORTH, I'M SORRY ABOUT WHAT'S HAPPENED.
YOU DON'T GET OFF THAT EASY, YOUNG MAN. I'VE GOT A LOT TO SAY TO YOU BEFORE I'M DONE.
I'LL MAKE SURE YOU GET THE CHANCE. I WANT TO HEAR EVERY WORD.

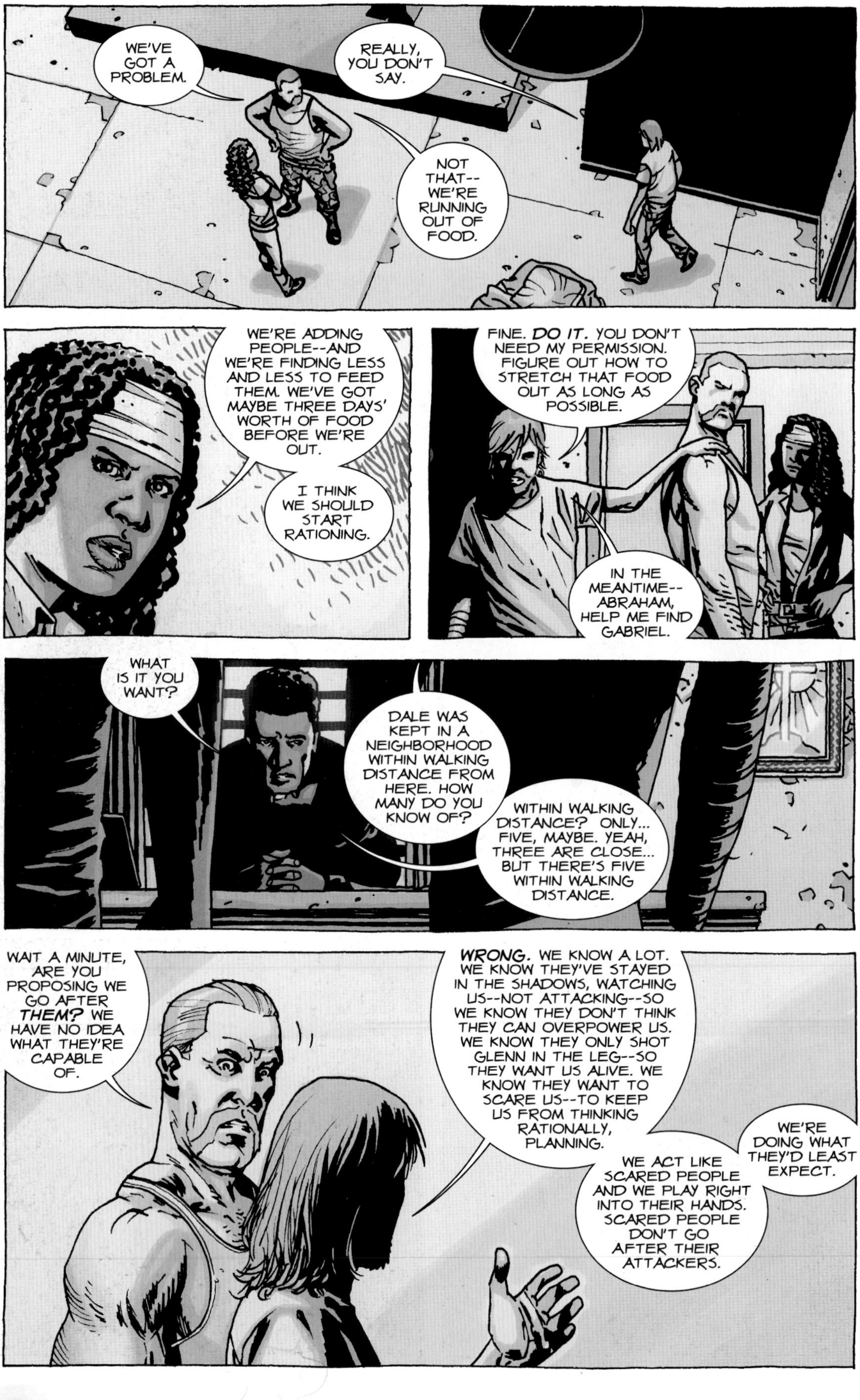
WE'VE GOT A PROBLEM.
REALLY, YOU DON'T SAY.
NOT THAT--WE'RE RUNNING OUT OF FOOD.
WE'RE ADDING PEOPLE--AND WE'RE FINDING LESS AND LESS TO FEED THEM. WE'VE GOT MAYBE THREE DAYS' WORTH OF FOOD BEFORE WE'RE OUT.
I THINK WE SHOULD START RATIONING.
FINE. DO IT. YOU DON'T NEED MY PERMISSION. FIGURE OUT HOW TO STRETCH THAT FOOD OUT AS LONG AS POSSIBLE.
IN THE MEANTIME--ABRAHAM, HELP ME FIND GABRIEL.
WHAT IS IT YOU WANT?
DALE WAS KEPT IN A NEIGHBORHOOD WITHIN WALKING DISTANCE FROM HERE. HOW MANY DO YOU KNOW OF?
WITHIN WALKING DISTANCE? ONLY... FIVE, MAYBE. YEAH, THREE ARE CLOSE... BUT THERE'S FIVE WITHIN WALKING DISTANCE.
WAIT A MINUTE, ARE YOU PROPOSING WE GO AFTER THEM? WE HAVE NO IDEA WHAT THEY'RE CAPABLE OF.
WRONG. WE KNOW A LOT. WE KNOW THEY'VE STAYED IN THE SHADOWS, WATCHING US--NOT ATTACKING--SO WE KNOW THEY DON'T THINK THEY CAN OVERPOWER US. WE KNOW THEY ONLY SHOT GLENN IN THE LEG--SO THEY WANT US ALIVE. WE KNOW THEY WANT TO SCARE US--TO KEEP US FROM THINKING RATIONALLY, PLANNING.
WE ACT LIKE SCARED PEOPLE AND WE PLAY RIGHT INTO THEIR HANDS. SCARED PEOPLE DON'T GO AFTER THEIR ATTACKERS.
WE'RE DOING WHAT THEY'D LEAST EXPECT.

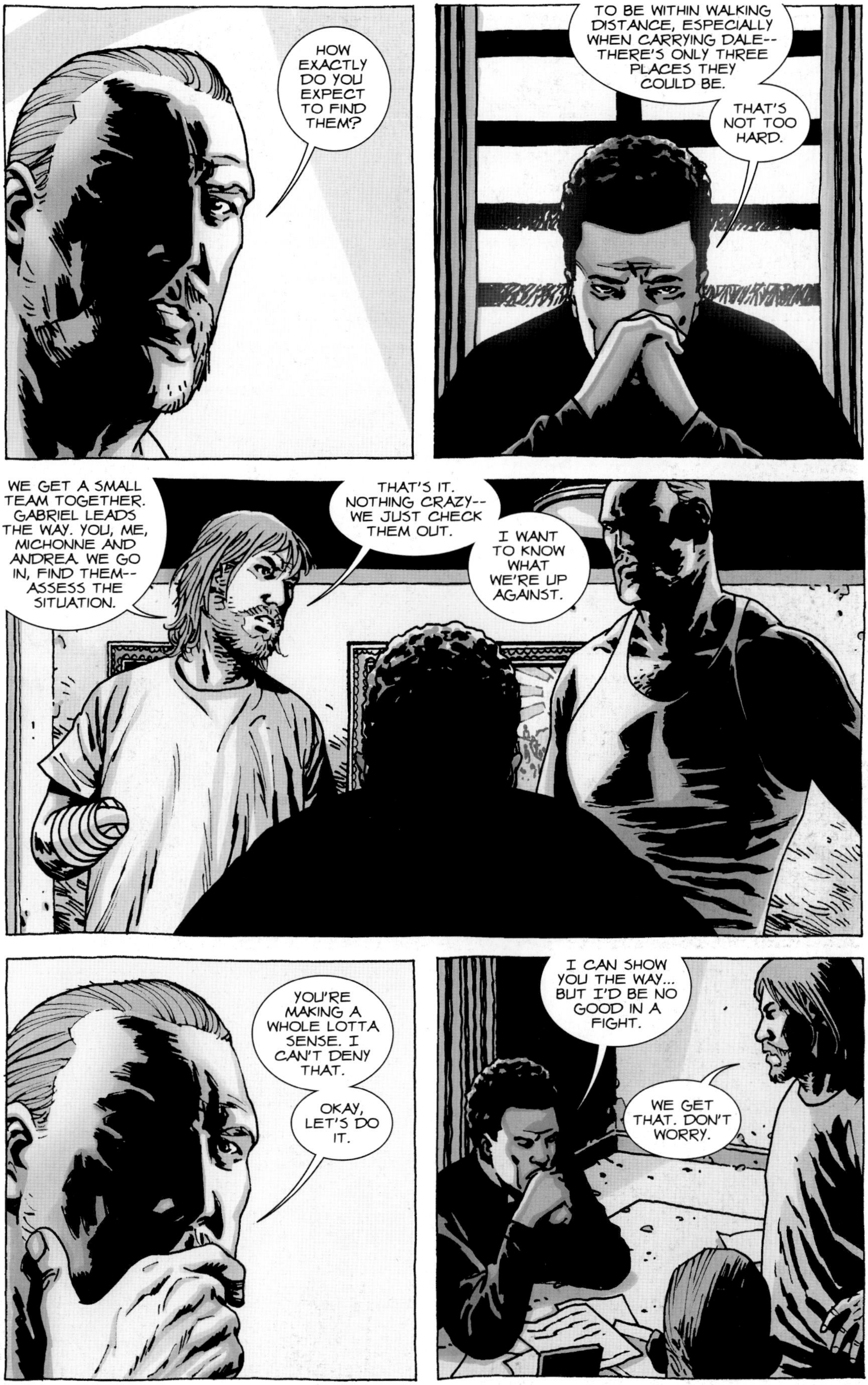
HOW EXACTLY DO YOU EXPECT TO FIND THEM?
TO BE WITHIN WALKING DISTANCE, ESPECIALLY WHEN CARRYING DALE-- THERE'S ONLY THREE PLACES THEY COULD BE.
THAT'S NOT TOO HARD.
WE GET A SMALL TEAM TOGETHER. GABRIEL LEADS THE WAY. YOU, ME, MICHONNE AND ANDREA. WE GO IN, FIND THEM-- ASSESS THE SITUATION.
THAT'S IT. NOTHING CRAZY-- WE JUST CHECK THEM OUT.
I WANT TO KNOW WHAT WE'RE UP AGAINST.
YOU'RE MAKING A WHOLE LOTTA SENSE. I CAN'T DENY THAT.
OKAY, LET'S DO IT.
I CAN SHOW YOU THE WAY... BUT I'D BE NO GOOD IN A FIGHT.
WE GET THAT. DON'T WORRY.

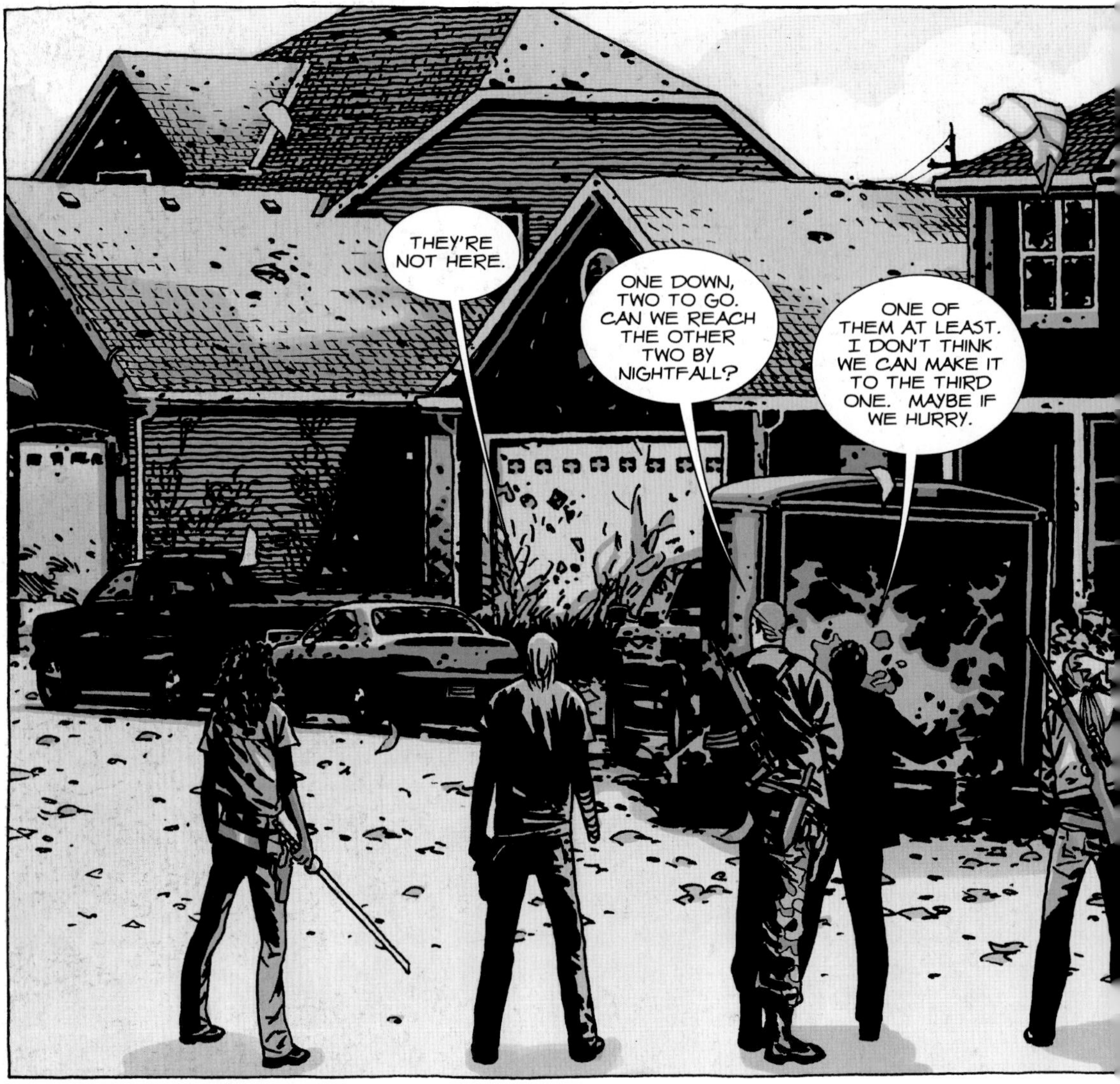
THEY'RE NOT HERE.
ONE DOWN, TWO TO GO. CAN WE REACH THE OTHER TWO BY NIGHTFALL?
ONE OF THEM AT LEAST. I DON'T THINK WE CAN MAKE IT TO THE THIRD ONE. MAYBE IF WE HURRY.
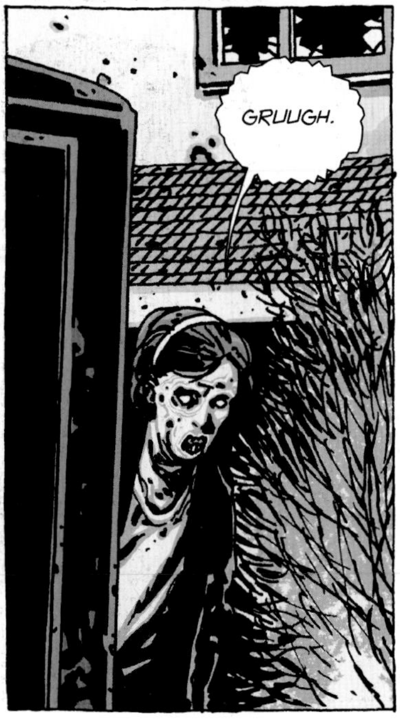
GRUUGH.
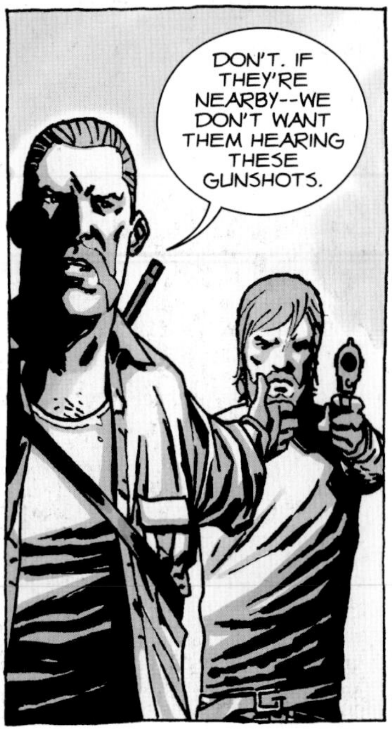
DON'T. IF THEY'RE NEARBY--WE DON'T WANT THEM HEARING THESE GUNSHOTS.
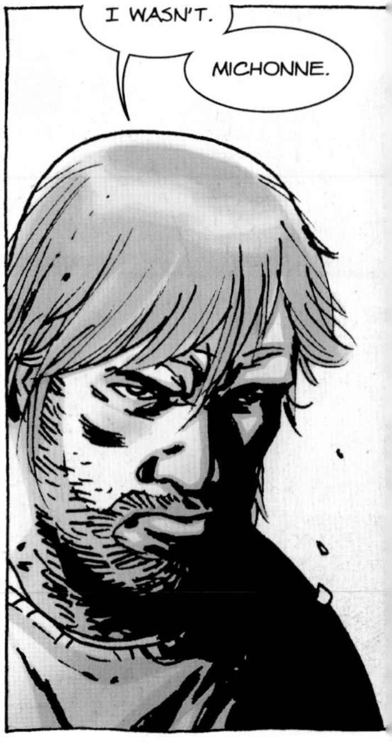
I WASN'T.
MICHONNE.

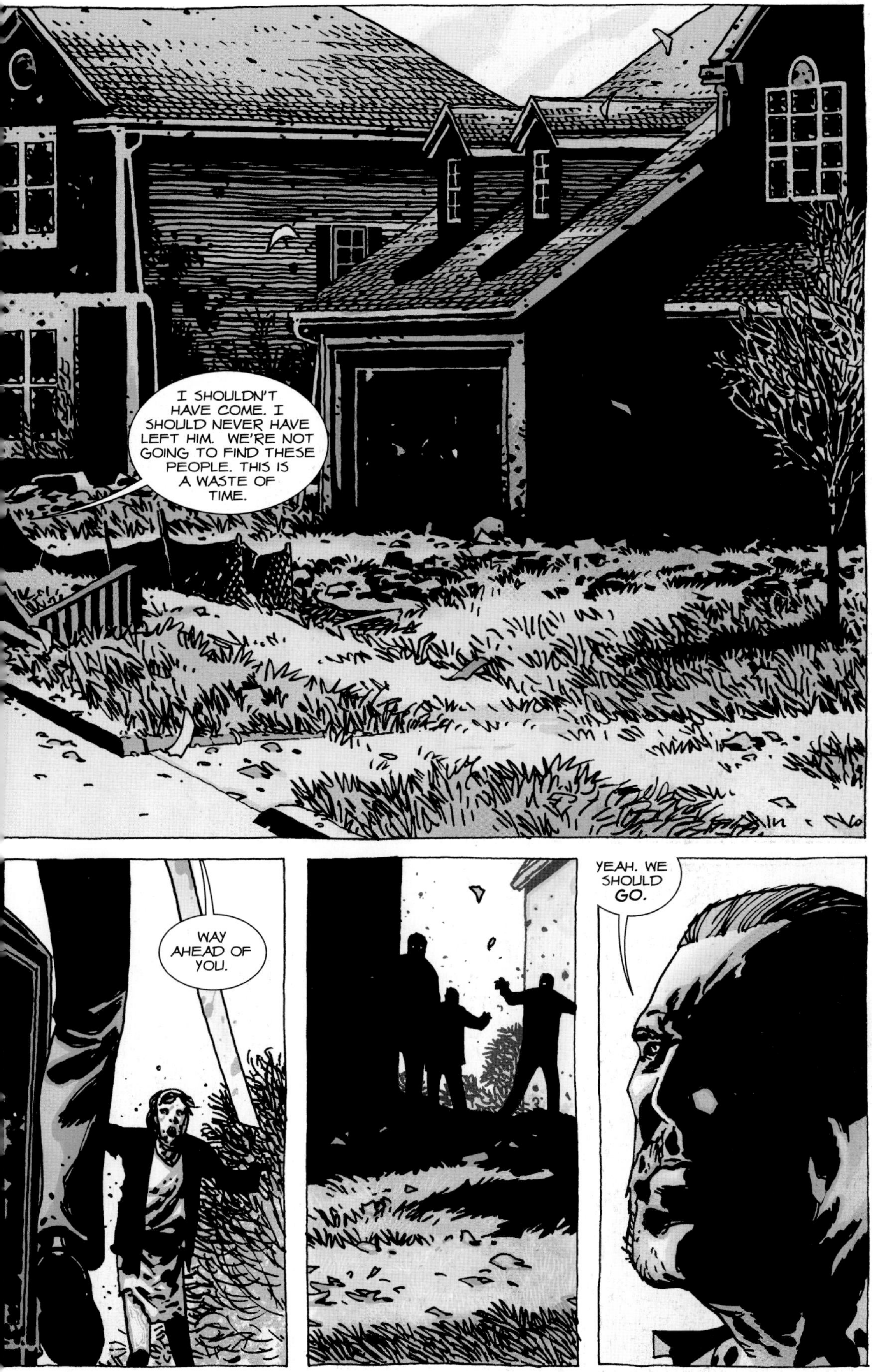
I SHOULDN'T HAVE COME. I SHOULD NEVER HAVE LEFT HIM. WE'RE NOT GOING TO FIND THESE PEOPLE. THIS IS A WASTE OF TIME.
WAY AHEAD OF YOU.
YEAH. WE SHOULD GO.

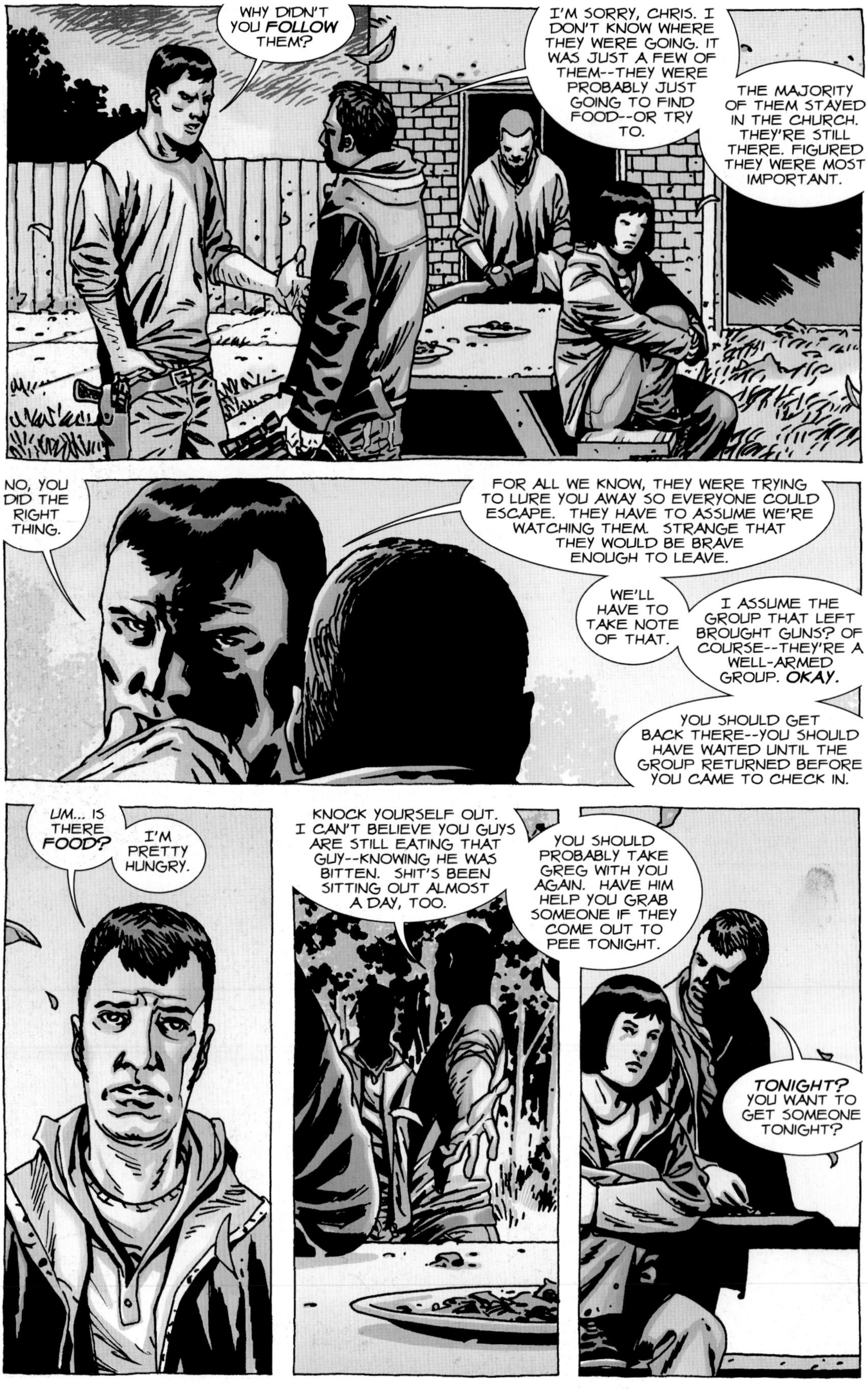
WHY DIDN'T YOU *FOLLOW* THEM?
I'M SORRY, CHRIS. I DON'T KNOW WHERE THEY WERE GOING. IT WAS JUST A FEW OF THEM--THEY WERE PROBABLY JUST GOING TO FIND FOOD--OR TRY TO.
THE MAJORITY OF THEM STAYED IN THE CHURCH. THEY'RE STILL THERE. FIGURED THEY WERE MOST IMPORTANT.
NO, YOU DID THE RIGHT THING.
FOR ALL WE KNOW, THEY WERE TRYING TO LURE YOU AWAY SO EVERYONE COULD ESCAPE. THEY HAVE TO ASSUME WE'RE WATCHING THEM. STRANGE THAT THEY WOULD BE BRAVE ENOUGH TO LEAVE.
WE'LL HAVE TO TAKE NOTE OF THAT.
I ASSUME THE GROUP THAT LEFT BROUGHT GUNS? OF COURSE--THEY'RE A WELL-ARMED GROUP. *OKAY.*
YOU SHOULD GET BACK THERE--YOU SHOULD HAVE WAITED UNTIL THE GROUP RETURNED BEFORE YOU CAME TO CHECK IN.
UM... IS THERE *FOOD?*
I'M PRETTY HUNGRY.
KNOCK YOURSELF OUT. I CAN'T BELIEVE YOU GUYS ARE STILL EATING THAT GUY--KNOWING HE WAS BITTEN. SHIT'S BEEN SITTING OUT ALMOST A DAY, TOO.
YOU SHOULD PROBABLY TAKE GREG WITH YOU AGAIN. HAVE HIM HELP YOU GRAB SOMEONE IF THEY COME OUT TO PEE TONIGHT.
TONIGHT? YOU WANT TO GET SOMEONE TONIGHT?

YOU KNOW THE DRILL--WE'VE GOT TO KEEP THESE PEOPLE SCARED SHITLESS. I KNOW WE'VE NEVER DONE A GROUP THIS LARGE BEFORE, BUT IT'S THE SAME DEAL.

WE SHOULD ACTUALLY PICK THEM OFF SOONER, THIN THEIR NUMBERS OUT AND MAKE THEM FEAR FOR THEIR LIVES.

WISH THEY HADN'T FOUND THAT CHURCH. IT'D BE EASIER IF THEY WERE ON THE MOVE. WE'D HAVE MORE OPPORTUNITIES TO SNAG SOMEONE.

WHAT IF THEY STAY IN THAT CHURCH ALL NIGHT? MIGHT NOT HAVE TO GO OUTSIDE TO USE THE JOHN. WHAT DO I DO THEN?

JUST WAIT. SOMEONE WILL GET STUPID SOONER OR LATER. THEY ALWAYS DO.

WE'VE BOUGHT OURSELVES A LITTLE TIME BY DROPPING OFF THE OLD MAN. HE'LL BE A CONSTANT REMINDER OF THE DEEP SHIT THEY'RE IN.

SEEING THEIR MAN LIKE THAT... THAT SHOULD DRIVE THEM CRAZY.

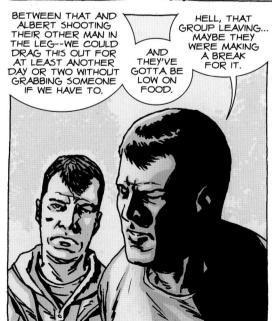

BETWEEN THAT AND ALBERT SHOOTING THEIR OTHER MAN IN THE LEG--WE COULD DRAG THIS OUT FOR AT LEAST ANOTHER DAY OR TWO WITHOUT GRABBING SOMEONE IF WE HAVE TO.

AND THEY'VE GOTTA BE LOW ON FOOD.

HELL, THAT GROUP LEAVING... MAYBE THEY WERE MAKING A BREAK FOR IT.

THEY'RE ALL PROBABLY SHITTING THEMSELVES RIGHT NOW.

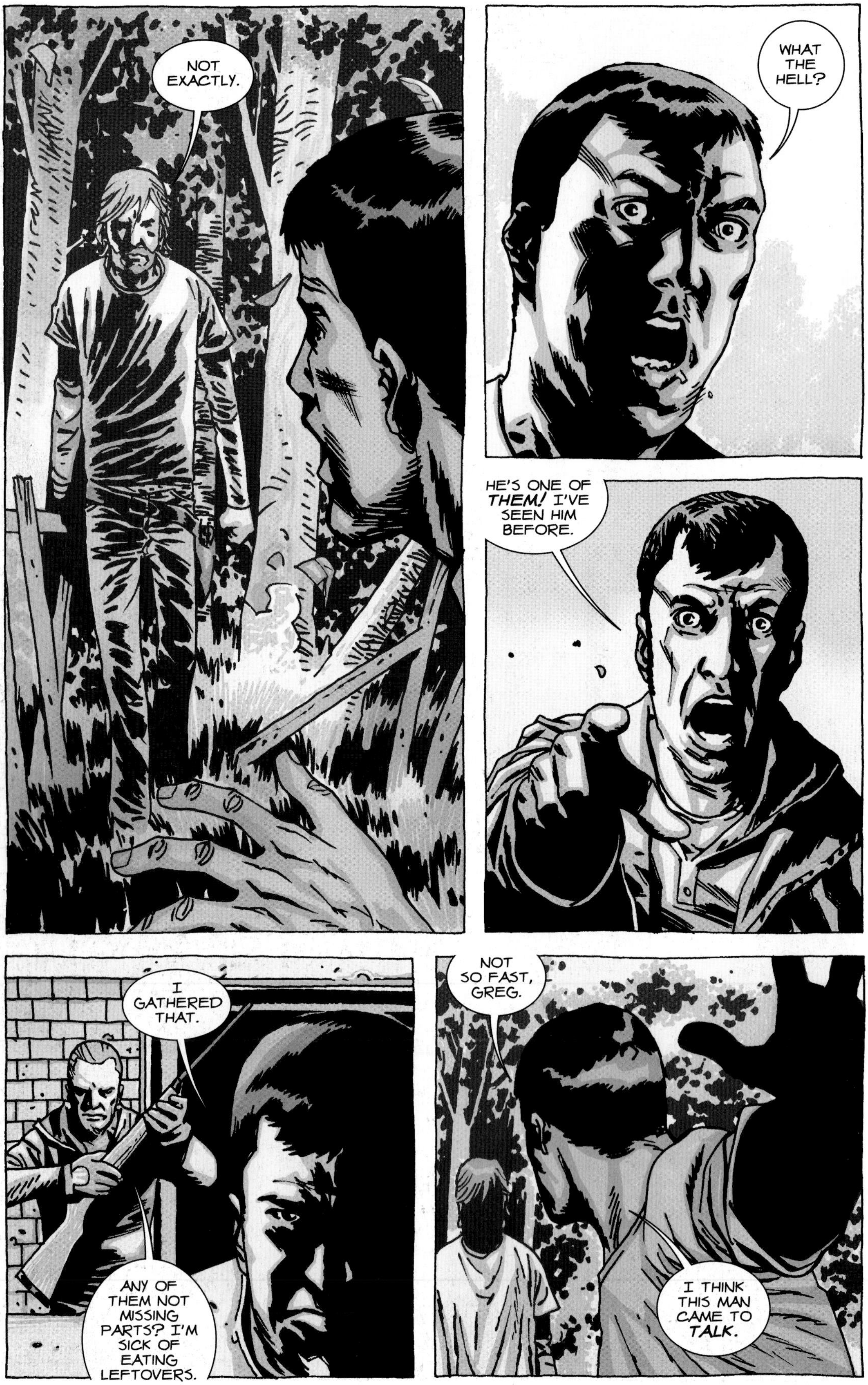
NOT EXACTLY.
WHAT THE HELL?
HE'S ONE OF *THEM!* I'VE SEEN HIM BEFORE.
I GATHERED THAT.
ANY OF THEM NOT MISSING PARTS? I'M SICK OF EATING LEFTOVERS.
NOT SO FAST, GREG.
I THINK THIS MAN CAME TO *TALK*.

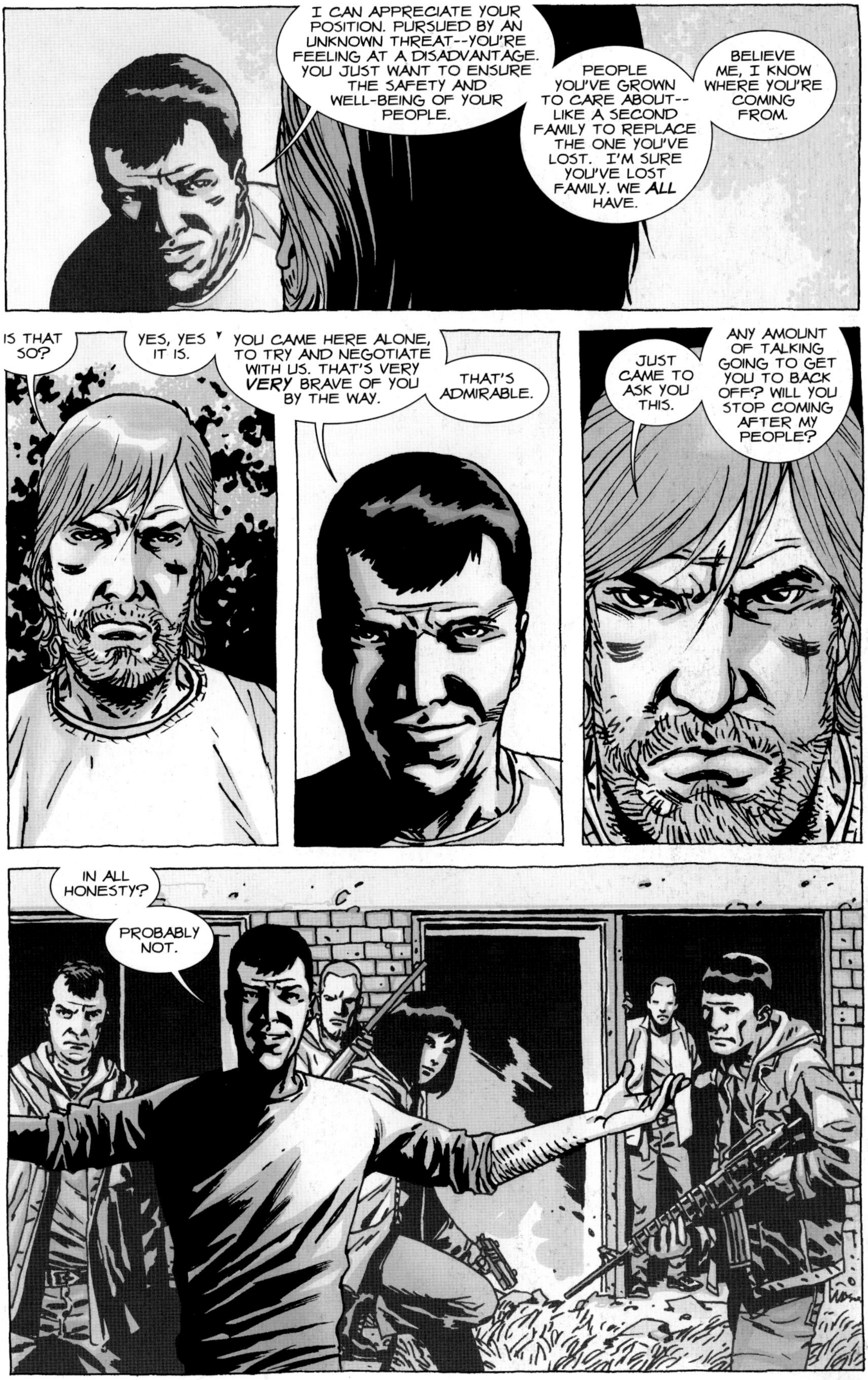

I CAN APPRECIATE YOUR POSITION. PURSUED BY AN UNKNOWN THREAT--YOU'RE FEELING AT A DISADVANTAGE. YOU JUST WANT TO ENSURE THE SAFETY AND WELL-BEING OF YOUR PEOPLE.
PEOPLE YOU'VE GROWN TO CARE ABOUT--LIKE A SECOND FAMILY TO REPLACE THE ONE YOU'VE LOST. I'M SURE YOU'VE LOST FAMILY. WE ALL HAVE.
BELIEVE ME, I KNOW WHERE YOU'RE COMING FROM.
IS THAT SO?
YES, YES IT IS.
YOU CAME HERE ALONE, TO TRY AND NEGOTIATE WITH US. THAT'S VERY VERY BRAVE OF YOU BY THE WAY.
THAT'S ADMIRABLE.
JUST CAME TO ASK YOU THIS.
ANY AMOUNT OF TALKING GOING TO GET YOU TO BACK OFF? WILL YOU STOP COMING AFTER MY PEOPLE?
IN ALL HONESTY?
PROBABLY NOT.

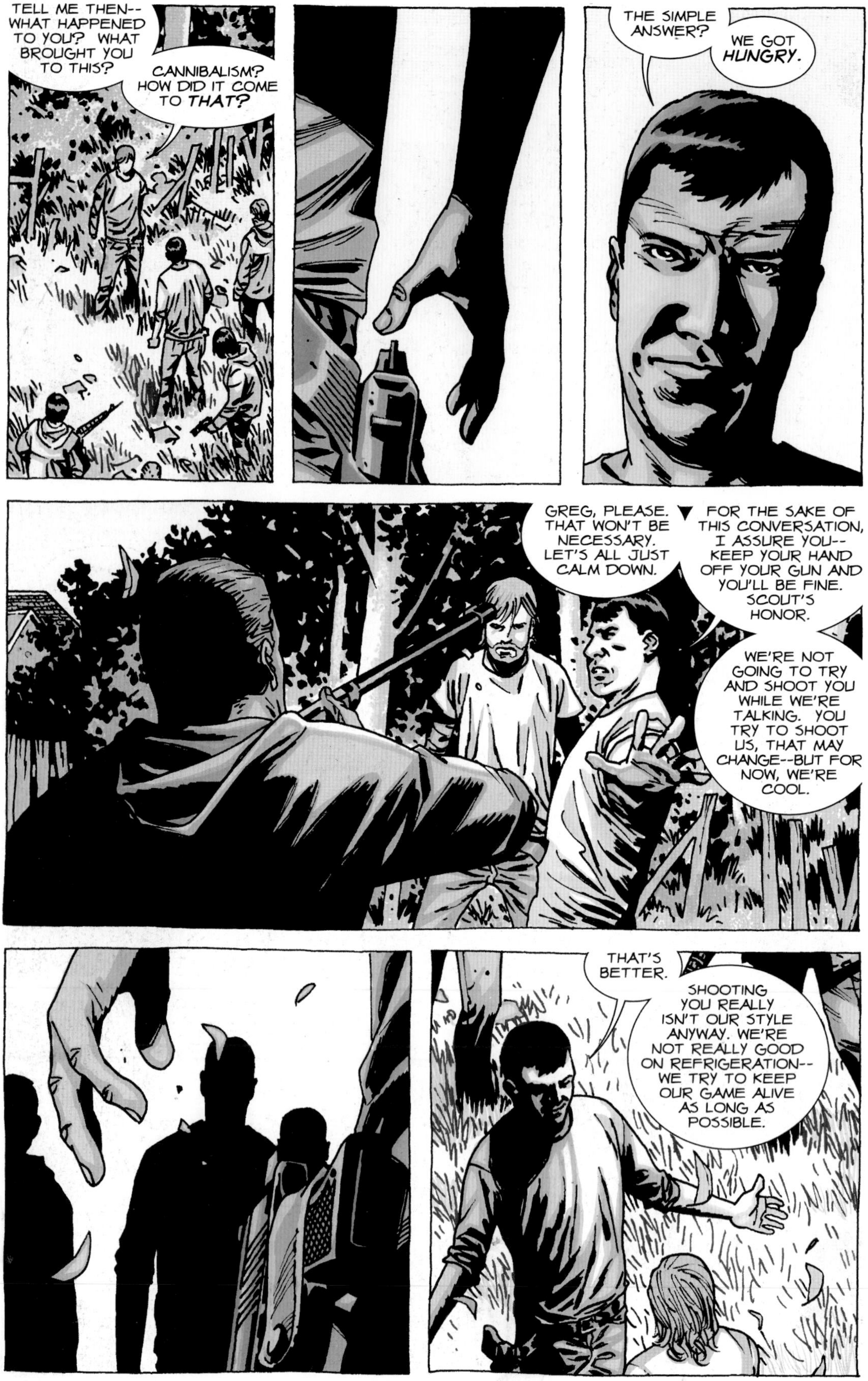
TELL ME THEN-- WHAT HAPPENED TO YOU? WHAT BROUGHT YOU TO THIS?
CANNIBALISM? HOW DID IT COME TO *THAT?*
THE SIMPLE ANSWER?
WE GOT *HUNGRY.*
GREG, PLEASE. THAT WON'T BE NECESSARY. LET'S ALL JUST CALM DOWN.
FOR THE SAKE OF THIS CONVERSATION, I ASSURE YOU-- KEEP YOUR HAND OFF YOUR GUN AND YOU'LL BE FINE. SCOUT'S HONOR.
WE'RE NOT GOING TO TRY AND SHOOT YOU WHILE WE'RE TALKING. YOU TRY TO SHOOT US, THAT MAY CHANGE--BUT FOR NOW, WE'RE COOL.
THAT'S BETTER.
SHOOTING YOU REALLY ISN'T OUR STYLE ANYWAY. WE'RE NOT REALLY GOOD ON REFRIGERATION-- WE TRY TO KEEP OUR GAME ALIVE AS LONG AS POSSIBLE.

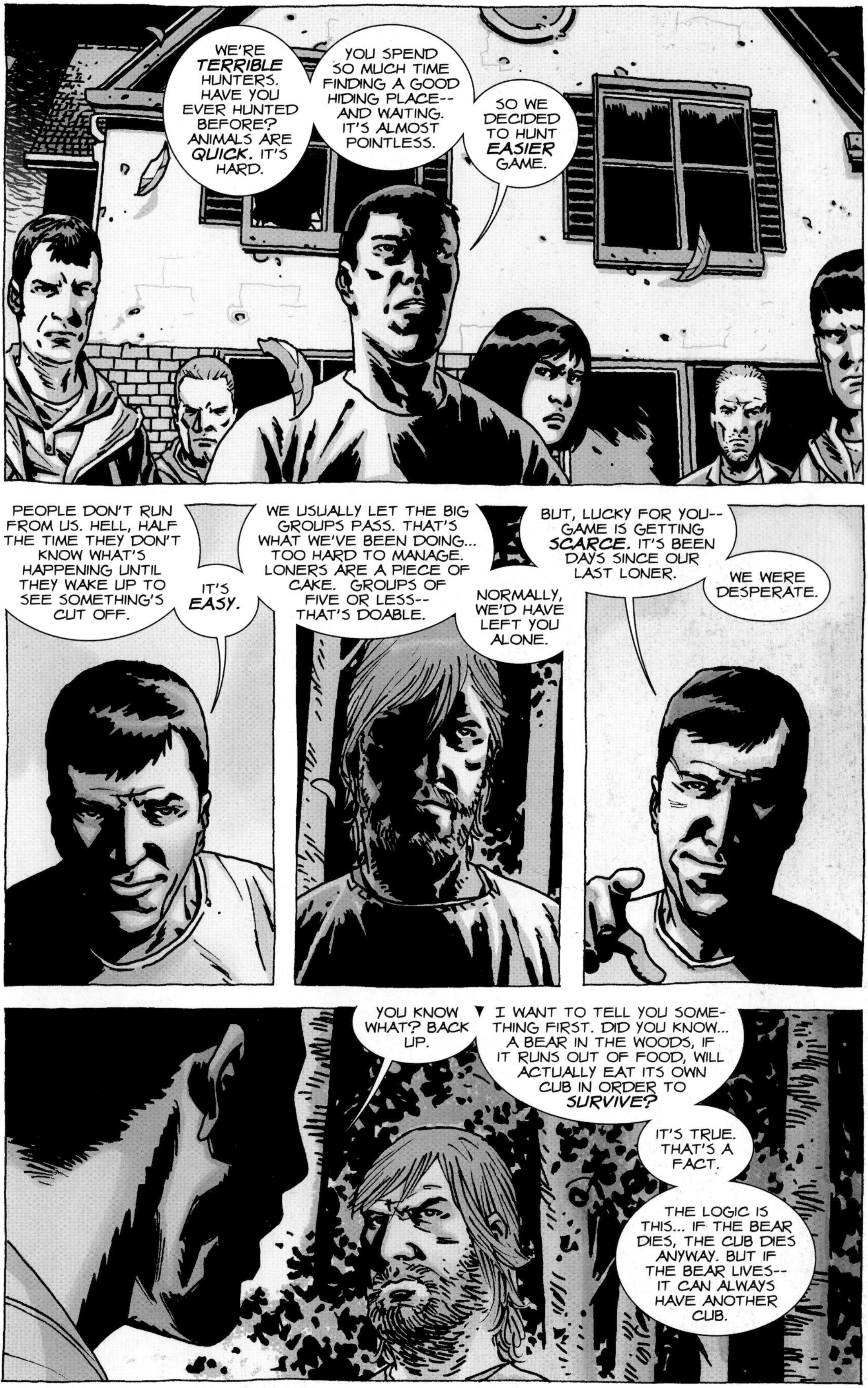
WE'RE TERRIBLE HUNTERS. HAVE YOU EVER HUNTED BEFORE? ANIMALS ARE QUICK. IT'S HARD.
YOU SPEND SO MUCH TIME FINDING A GOOD HIDING PLACE-- AND WAITING. IT'S ALMOST POINTLESS.
SO WE DECIDED TO HUNT EASIER GAME.
PEOPLE DON'T RUN FROM US. HELL, HALF THE TIME THEY DON'T KNOW WHAT'S HAPPENING UNTIL THEY WAKE UP TO SEE SOMETHING'S CUT OFF.
IT'S EASY.
WE USUALLY LET THE BIG GROUPS PASS. THAT'S WHAT WE'VE BEEN DOING... TOO HARD TO MANAGE. LONERS ARE A PIECE OF CAKE. GROUPS OF FIVE OR LESS-- THAT'S DOABLE.
NORMALLY, WE'D HAVE LEFT YOU ALONE.
BUT, LUCKY FOR YOU-- GAME IS GETTING SCARCE. IT'S BEEN DAYS SINCE OUR LAST LONER.
WE WERE DESPERATE.
YOU KNOW WHAT? BACK UP.
I WANT TO TELL YOU SOMETHING FIRST. DID YOU KNOW... A BEAR IN THE WOODS, IF IT RUNS OUT OF FOOD, WILL ACTUALLY EAT ITS OWN CUB IN ORDER TO SURVIVE?
IT'S TRUE. THAT'S A FACT.
THE LOGIC IS THIS... IF THE BEAR DIES, THE CUB DIES ANYWAY. BUT IF THE BEAR LIVES-- IT CAN ALWAYS HAVE ANOTHER CUB.

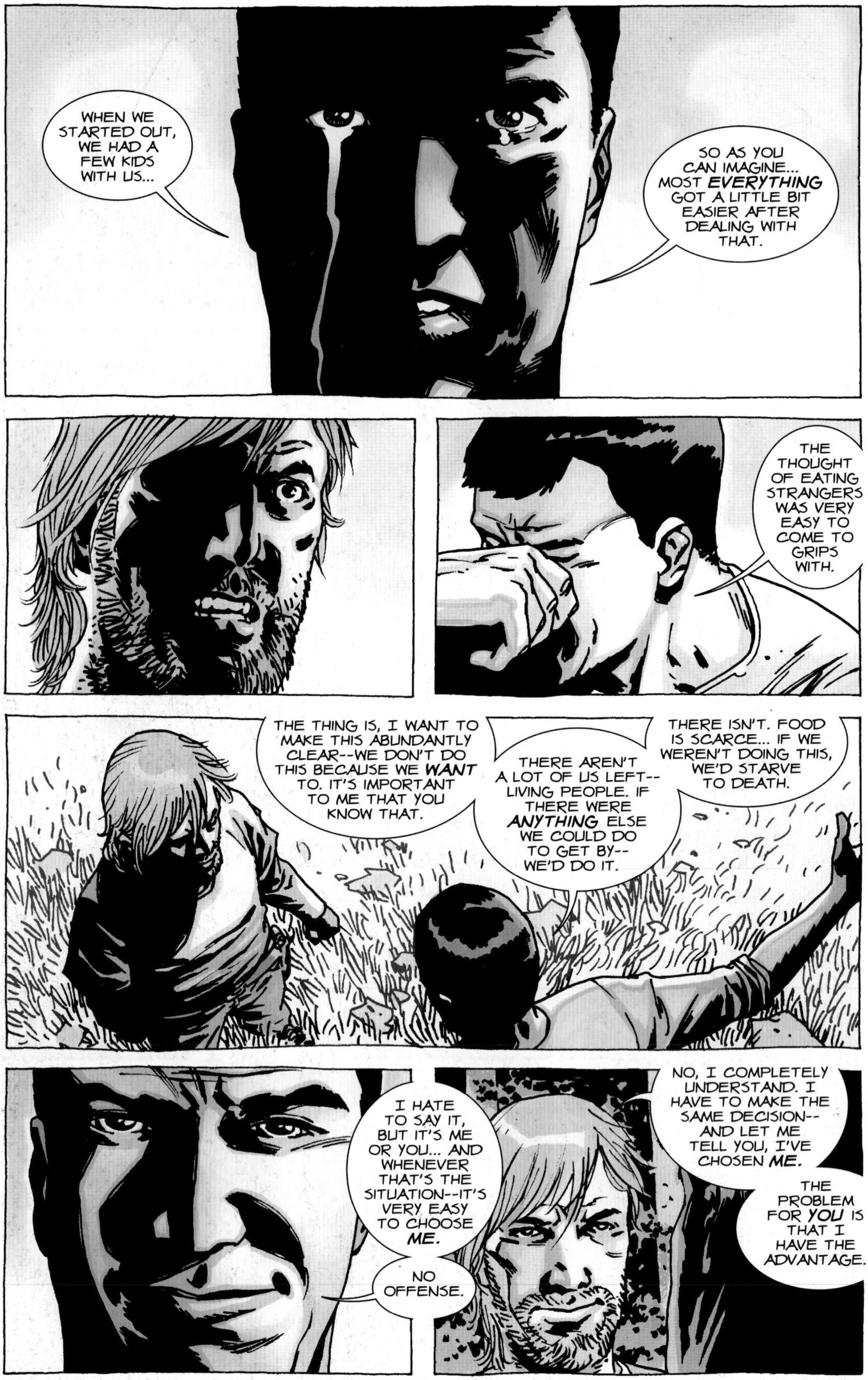
WHEN WE STARTED OUT, WE HAD A FEW KIDS WITH US...
SO AS YOU CAN IMAGINE... MOST EVERYTHING GOT A LITTLE BIT EASIER AFTER DEALING WITH THAT.
THE THOUGHT OF EATING STRANGERS WAS VERY EASY TO COME TO GRIPS WITH.
THE THING IS, I WANT TO MAKE THIS ABUNDANTLY CLEAR--WE DON'T DO THIS BECAUSE WE WANT TO. IT'S IMPORTANT TO ME THAT YOU KNOW THAT.
THERE AREN'T A LOT OF US LEFT--LIVING PEOPLE. IF THERE WERE ANYTHING ELSE WE COULD DO TO GET BY--WE'D DO IT.
THERE ISN'T. FOOD IS SCARCE... IF WE WEREN'T DOING THIS, WE'D STARVE TO DEATH.
I HATE TO SAY IT, BUT IT'S ME OR YOU... AND WHENEVER THAT'S THE SITUATION--IT'S VERY EASY TO CHOOSE ME.
NO OFFENSE.
NO, I COMPLETELY UNDERSTAND. I HAVE TO MAKE THE SAME DECISION--AND LET ME TELL YOU, I'VE CHOSEN ME.
THE PROBLEM FOR YOU IS THAT I HAVE THE ADVANTAGE.

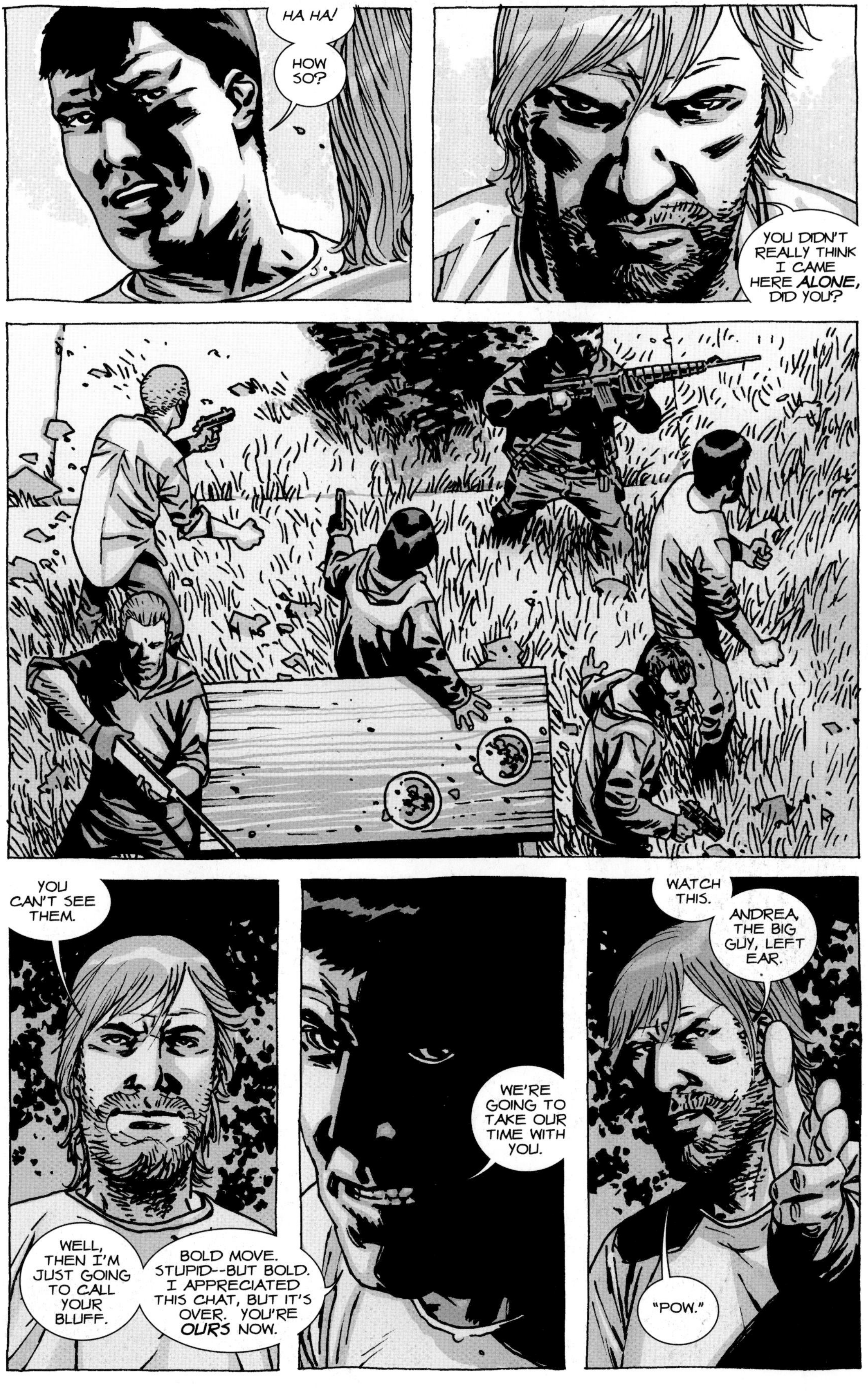
HA HA!
HOW SO?
YOU DIDN'T REALLY THINK I CAME HERE ALONE, DID YOU?
YOU CAN'T SEE THEM.
WELL, THEN I'M JUST GOING TO CALL YOUR BLUFF.
BOLD MOVE. STUPID--BUT BOLD. I APPRECIATED THIS CHAT, BUT IT'S OVER. YOU'RE OURS NOW.
WE'RE GOING TO TAKE OUR TIME WITH YOU.
WATCH THIS.
ANDREA, THE BIG GUY, LEFT EAR.
"POW."

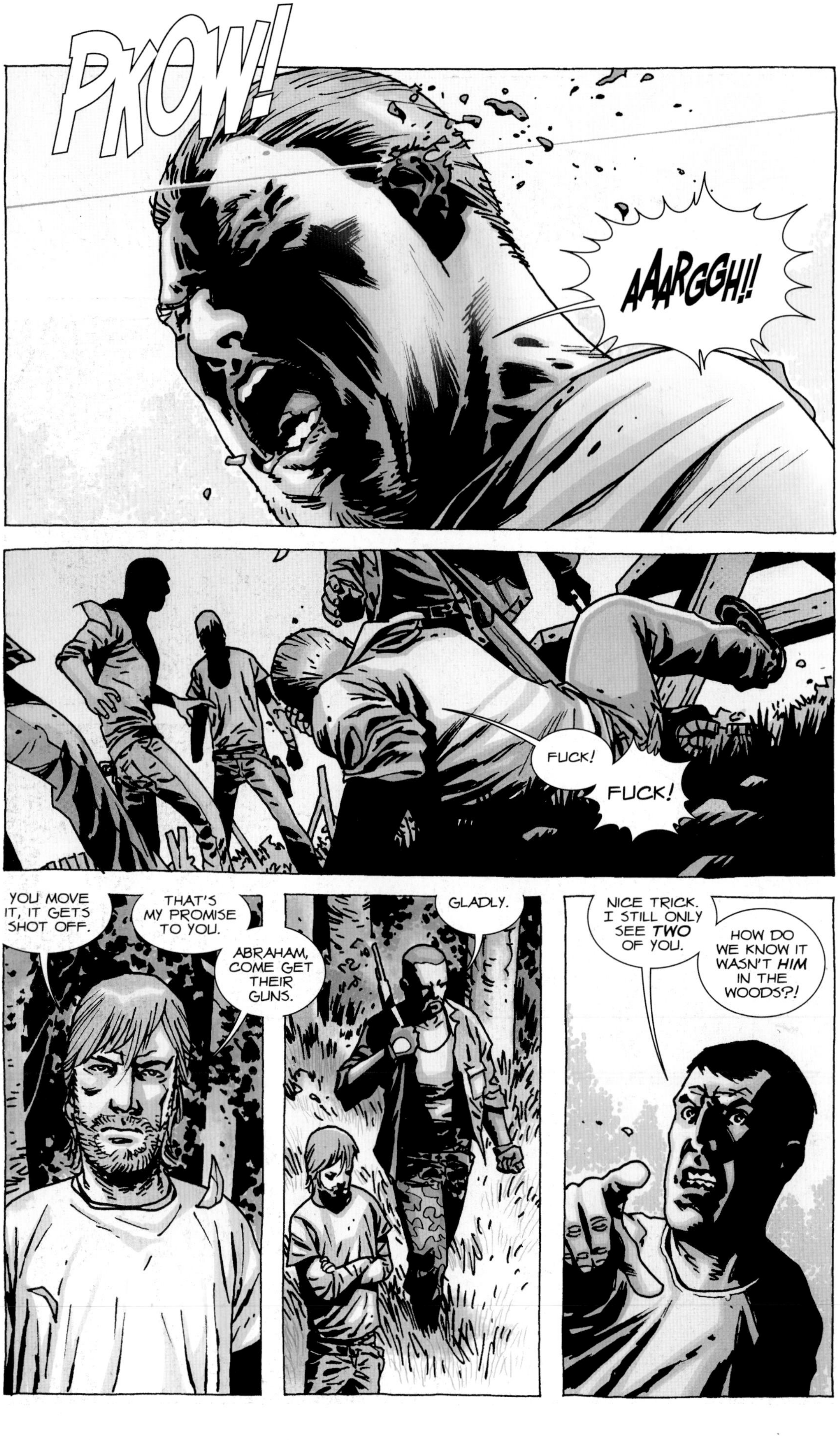
PKOW!
AAARGGH!!
FUCK!
FUCK!
YOU MOVE IT, IT GETS SHOT OFF.
THAT'S MY PROMISE TO YOU.
ABRAHAM, COME GET THEIR GUNS.
GLADLY.
NICE TRICK. I STILL ONLY SEE TWO OF YOU.
HOW DO WE KNOW IT WASN'T HIM IN THE WOODS?!

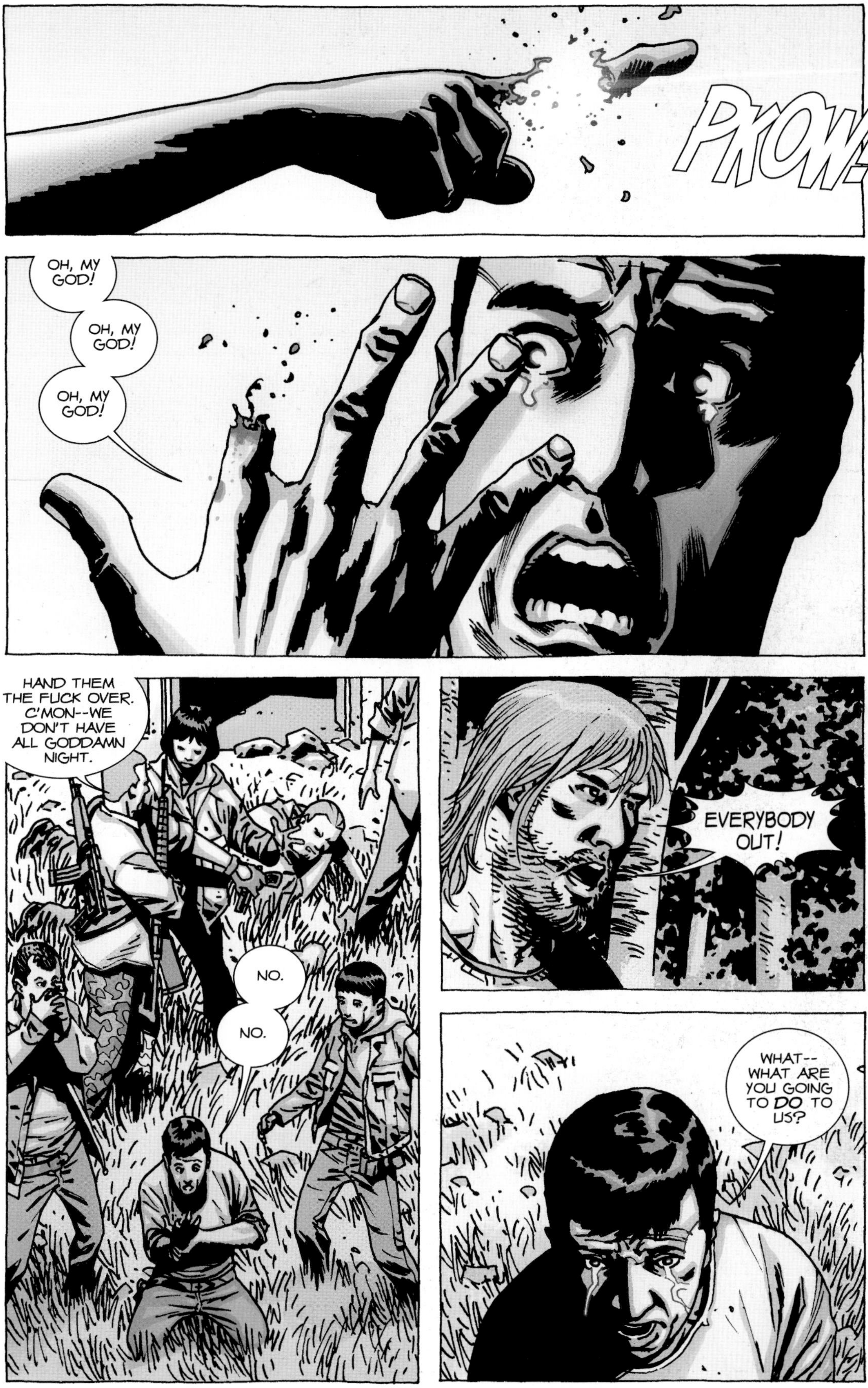
PKOW!
OH, MY GOD!
OH, MY GOD!
OH, MY GOD!
HAND THEM THE FUCK OVER. C'MON--WE DON'T HAVE ALL GODDAMN NIGHT.
NO.
NO.
EVERYBODY OUT!
WHAT-- WHAT ARE YOU GOING TO DO TO US?

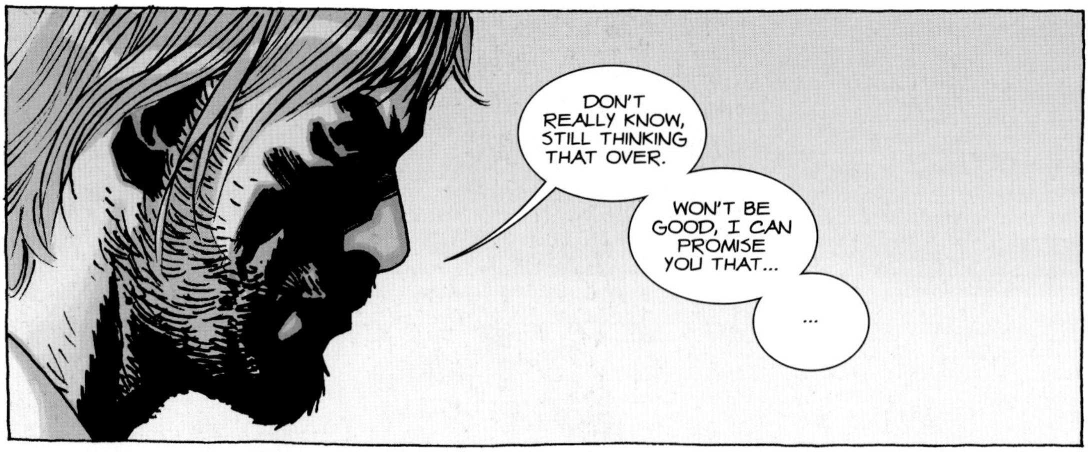
DON'T REALLY KNOW, STILL THINKING THAT OVER.
WON'T BE GOOD, I CAN PROMISE YOU THAT...
...

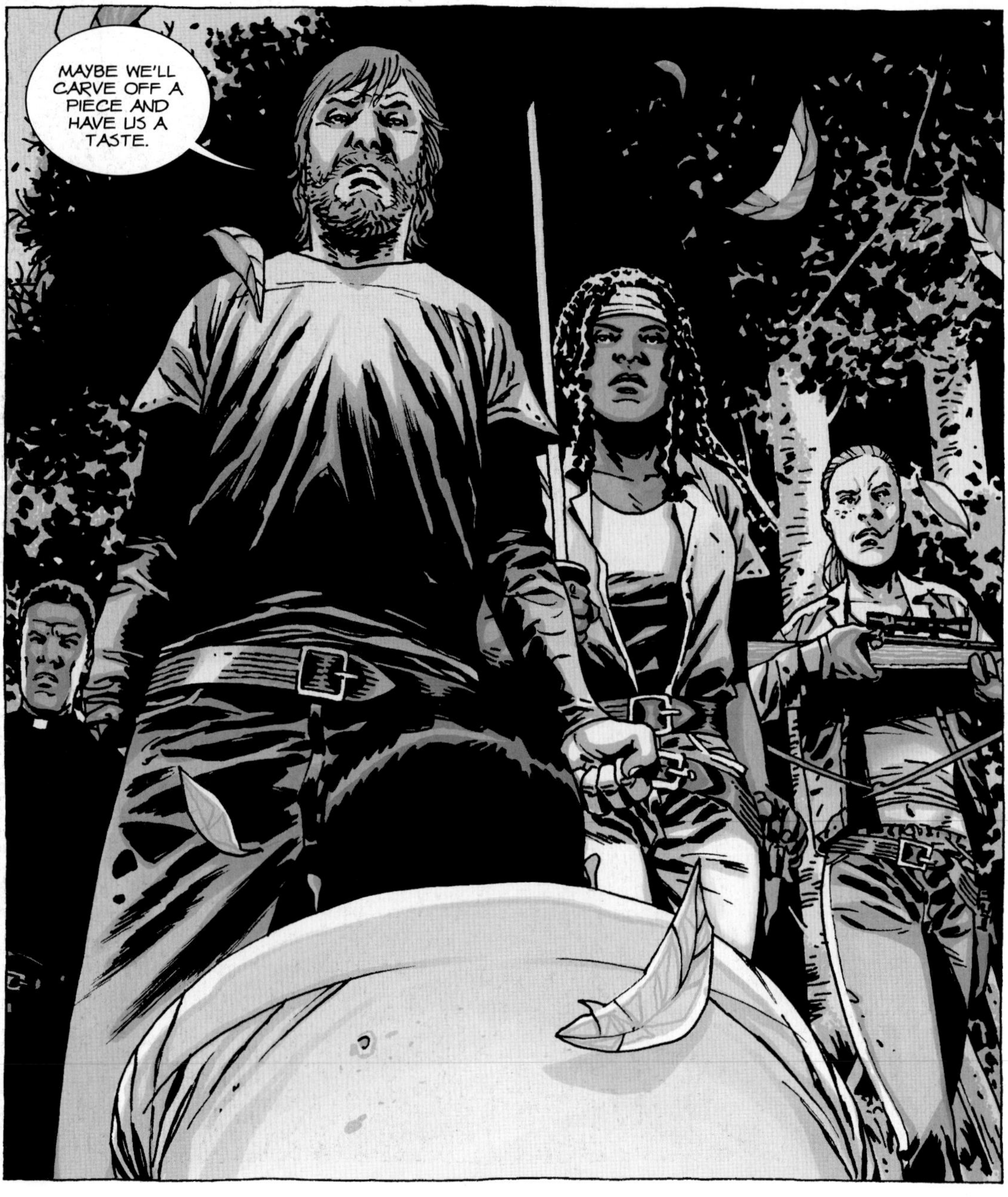
MAYBE WE'LL CARVE OFF A PIECE AND HAVE US A TASTE.

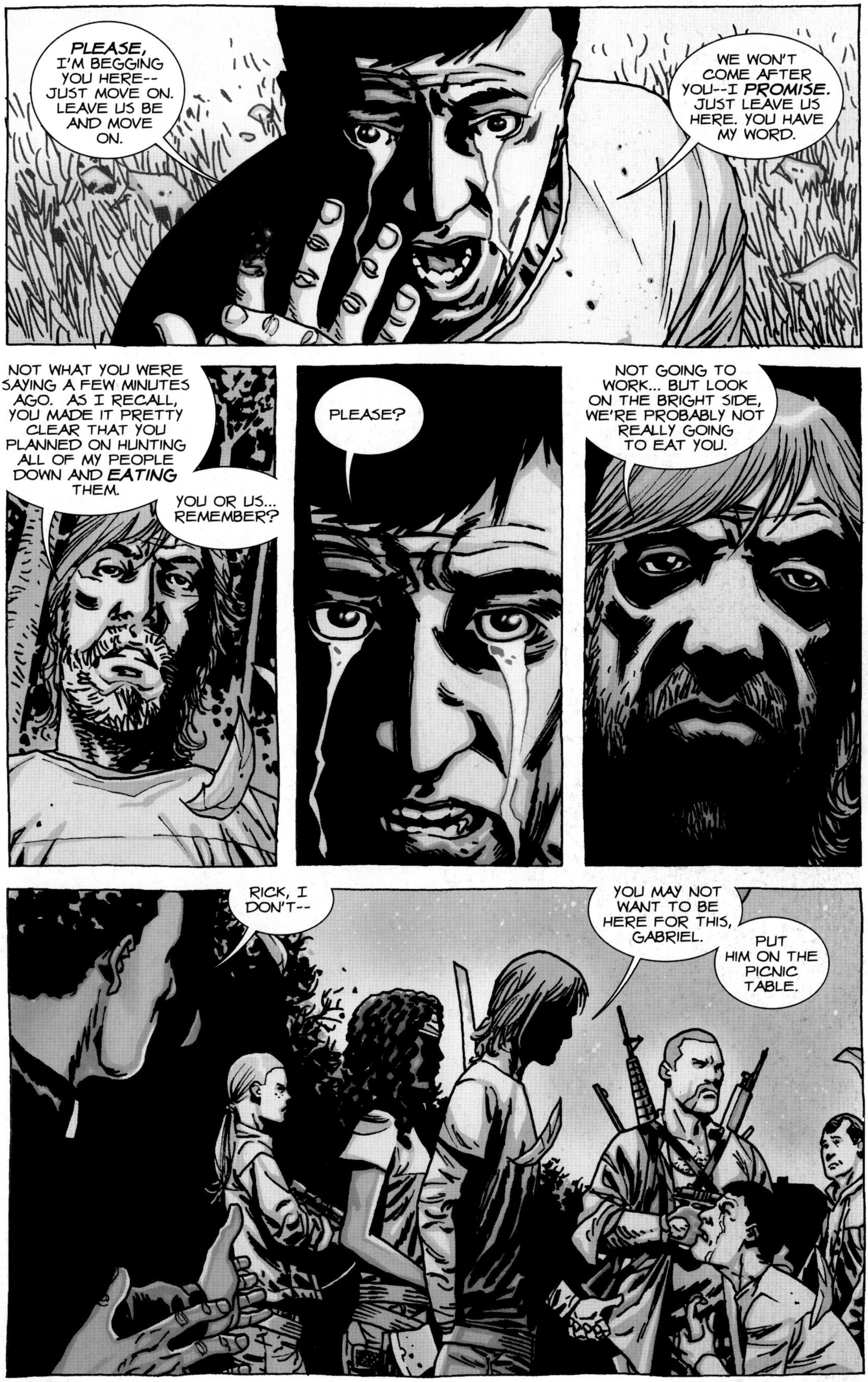
PLEASE, I'M BEGGING YOU HERE-- JUST MOVE ON. LEAVE US BE AND MOVE ON.
WE WON'T COME AFTER YOU--I PROMISE. JUST LEAVE US HERE. YOU HAVE MY WORD.
NOT WHAT YOU WERE SAYING A FEW MINUTES AGO. AS I RECALL, YOU MADE IT PRETTY CLEAR THAT YOU PLANNED ON HUNTING ALL OF MY PEOPLE DOWN AND EATING THEM.
YOU OR US... REMEMBER?
PLEASE?
NOT GOING TO WORK... BUT LOOK ON THE BRIGHT SIDE, WE'RE PROBABLY NOT REALLY GOING TO EAT YOU.
RICK, I DON'T--
YOU MAY NOT WANT TO BE HERE FOR THIS, GABRIEL.
PUT HIM ON THE PICNIC TABLE.

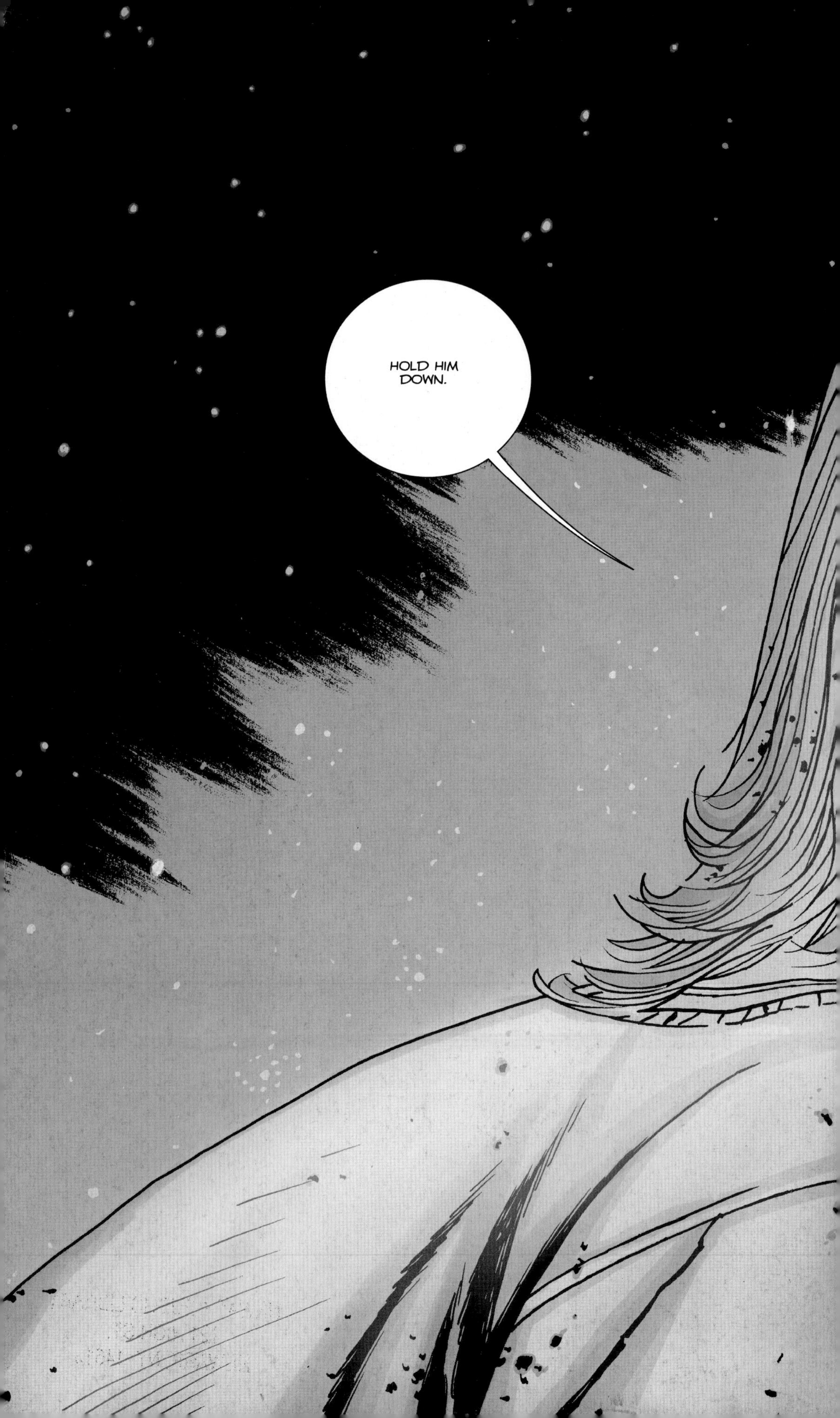
HOLD HIM DOWN.

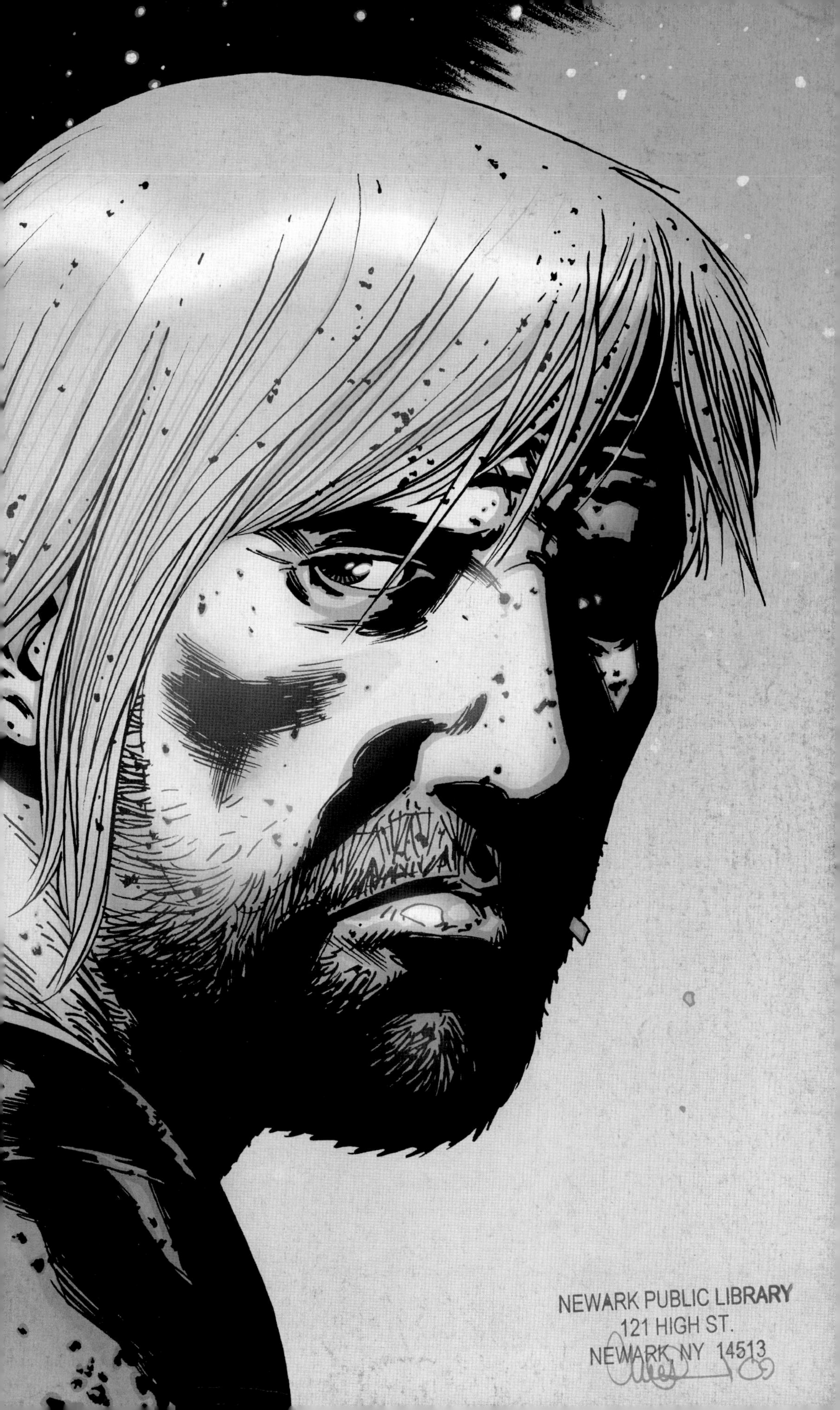

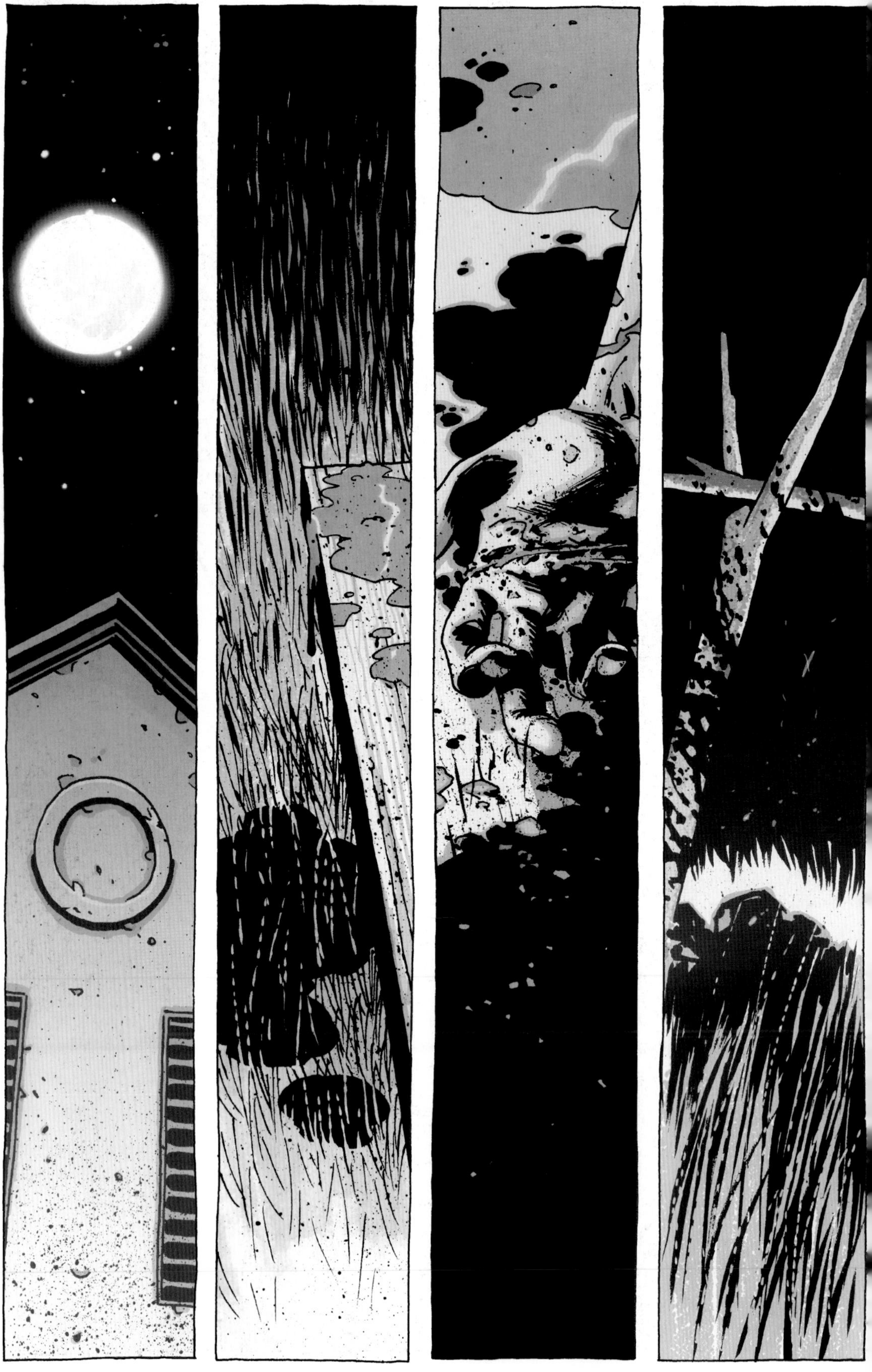

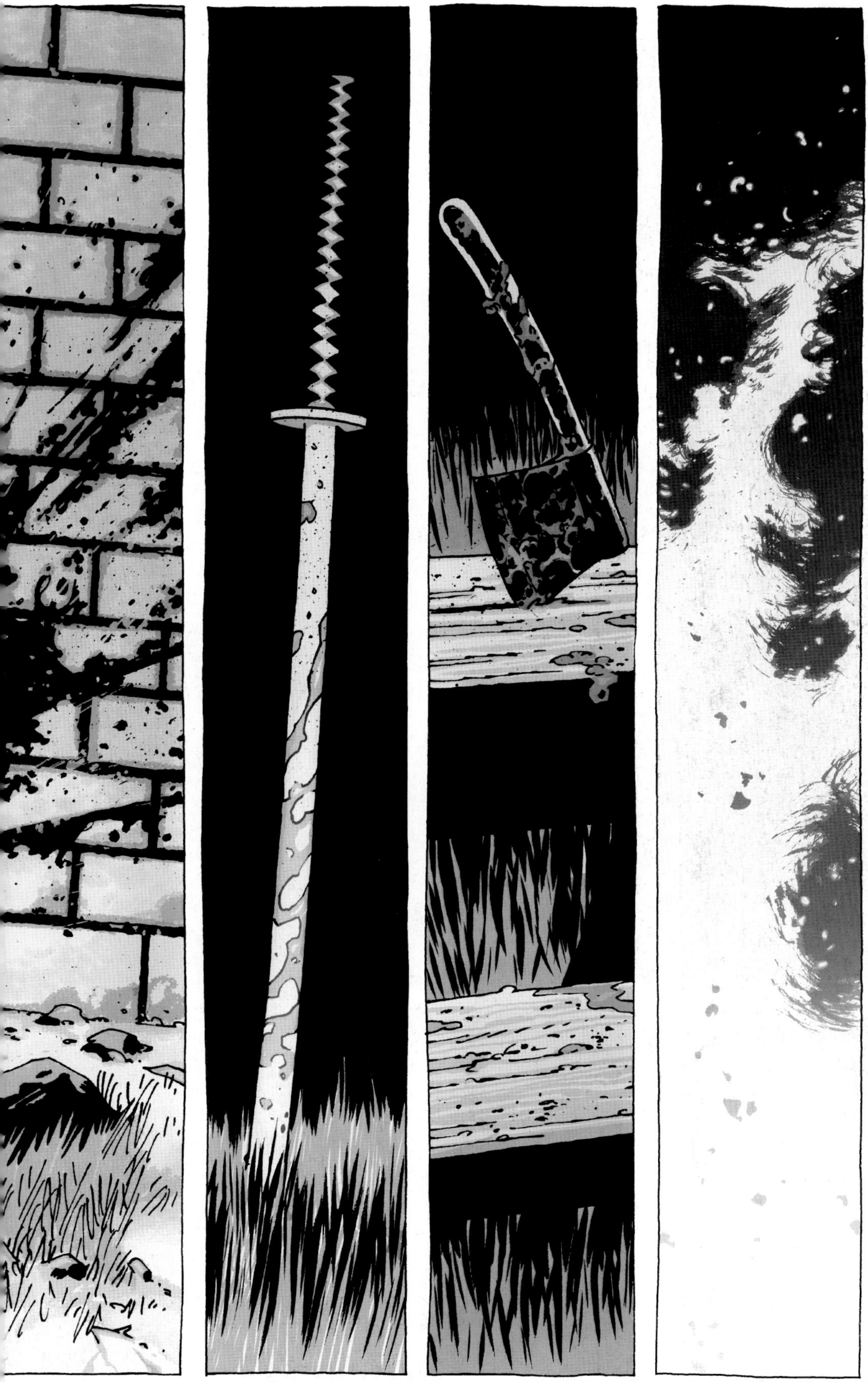

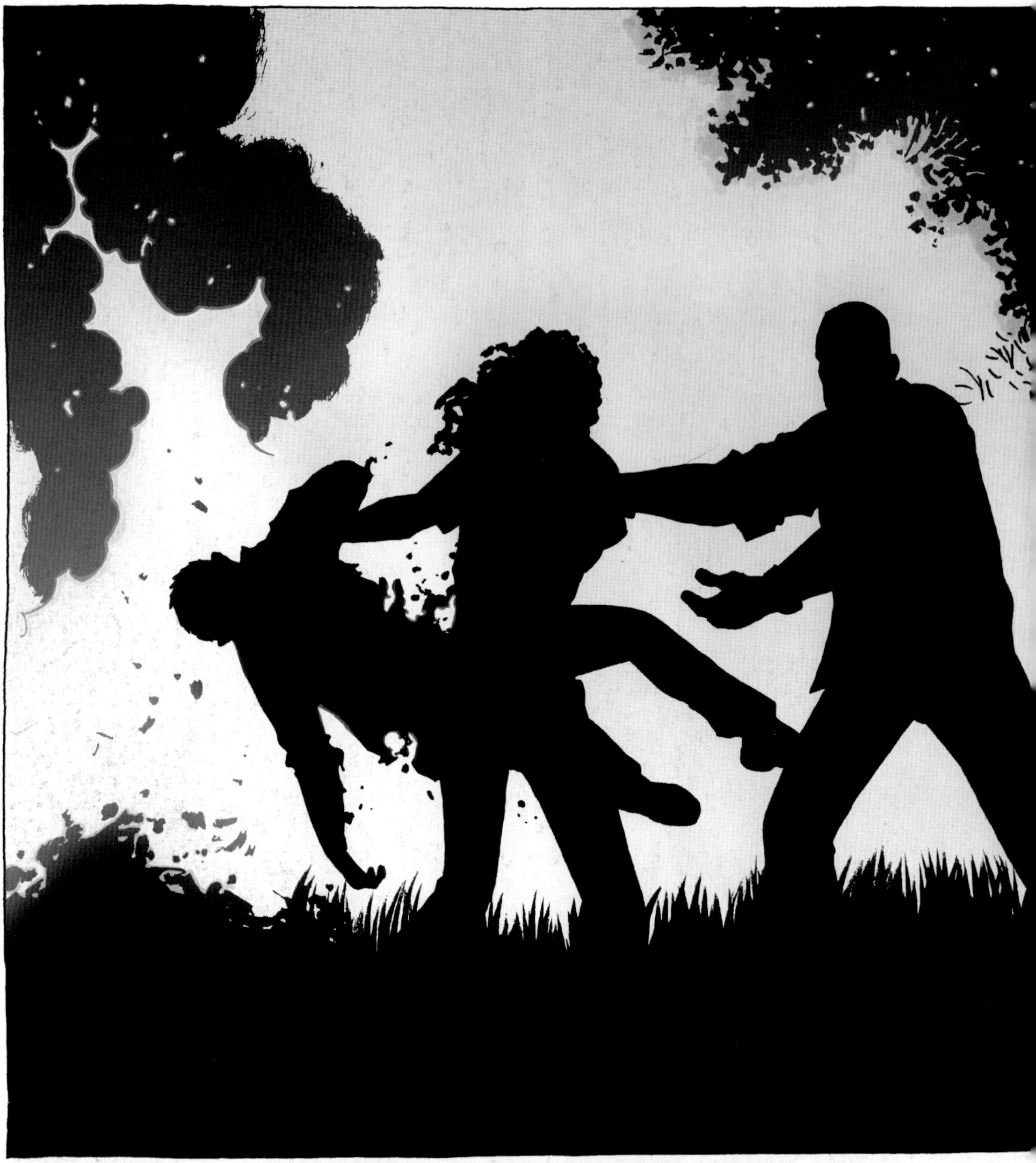

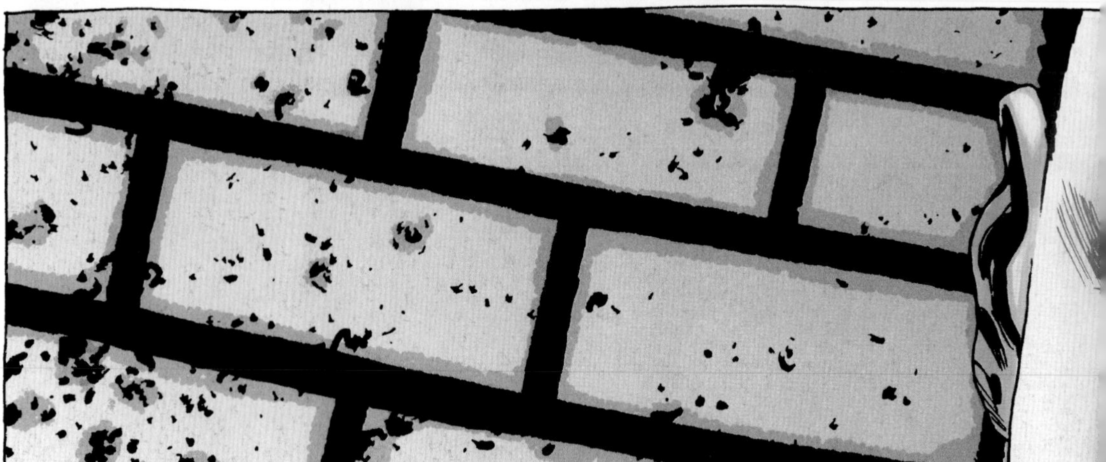

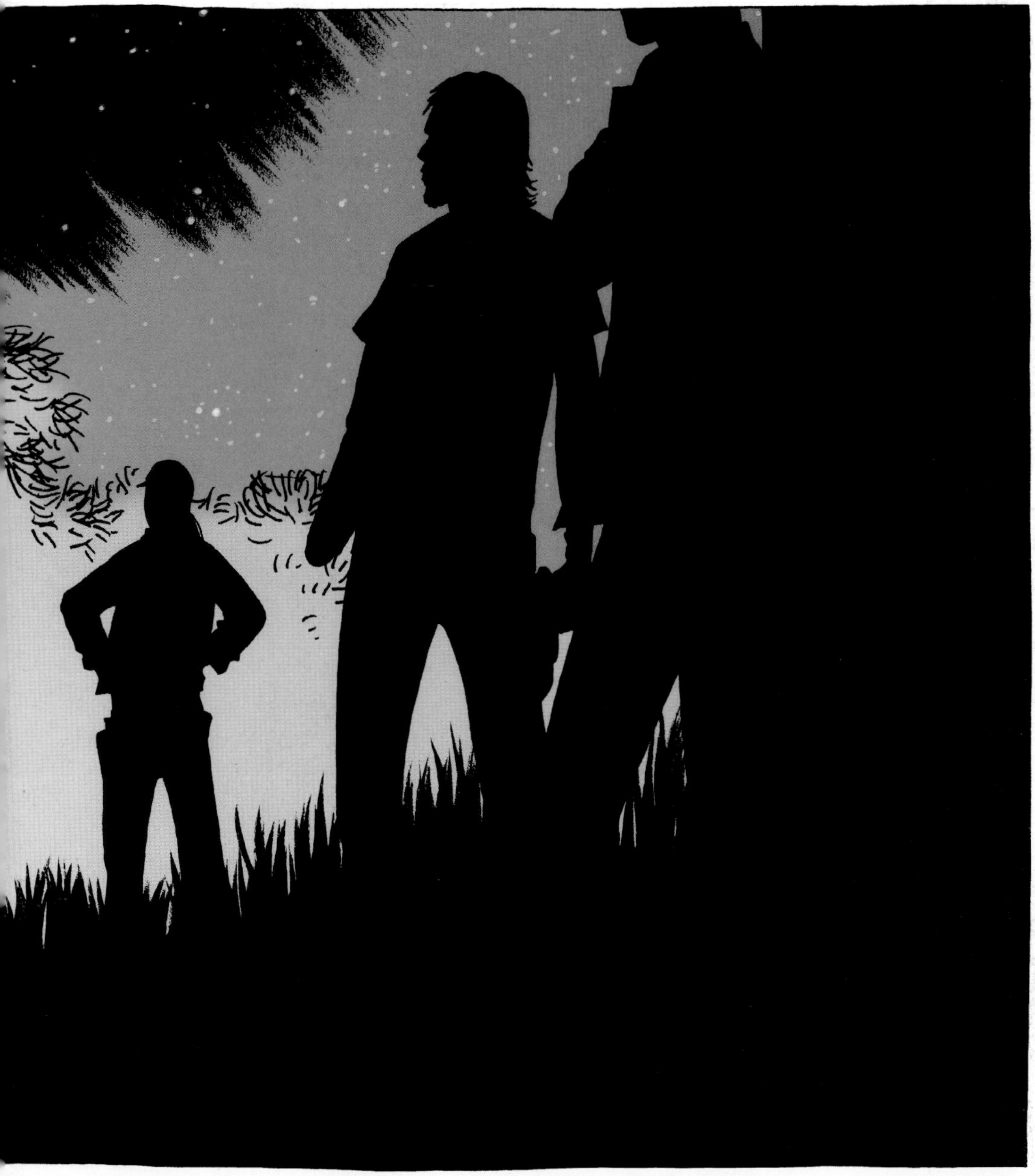

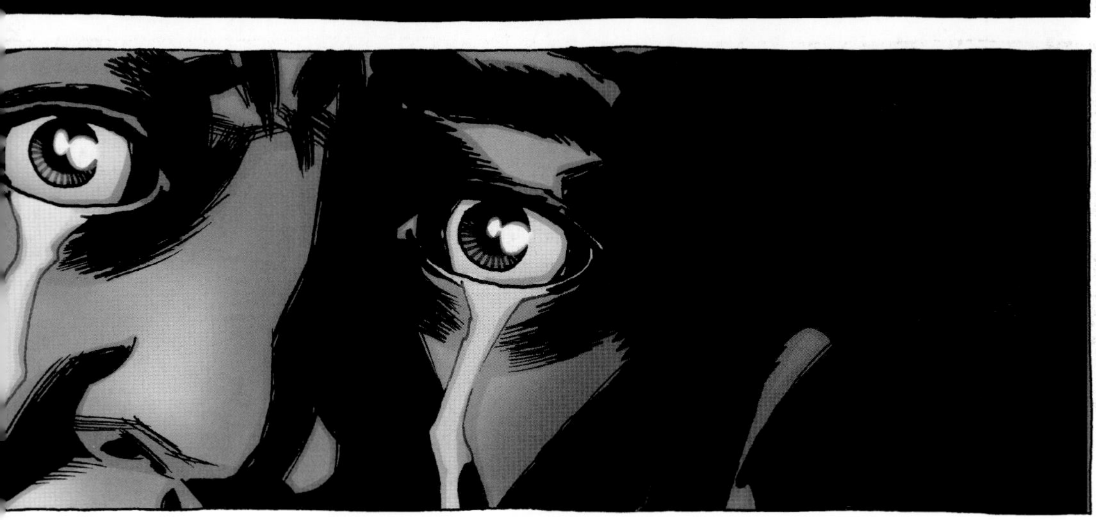

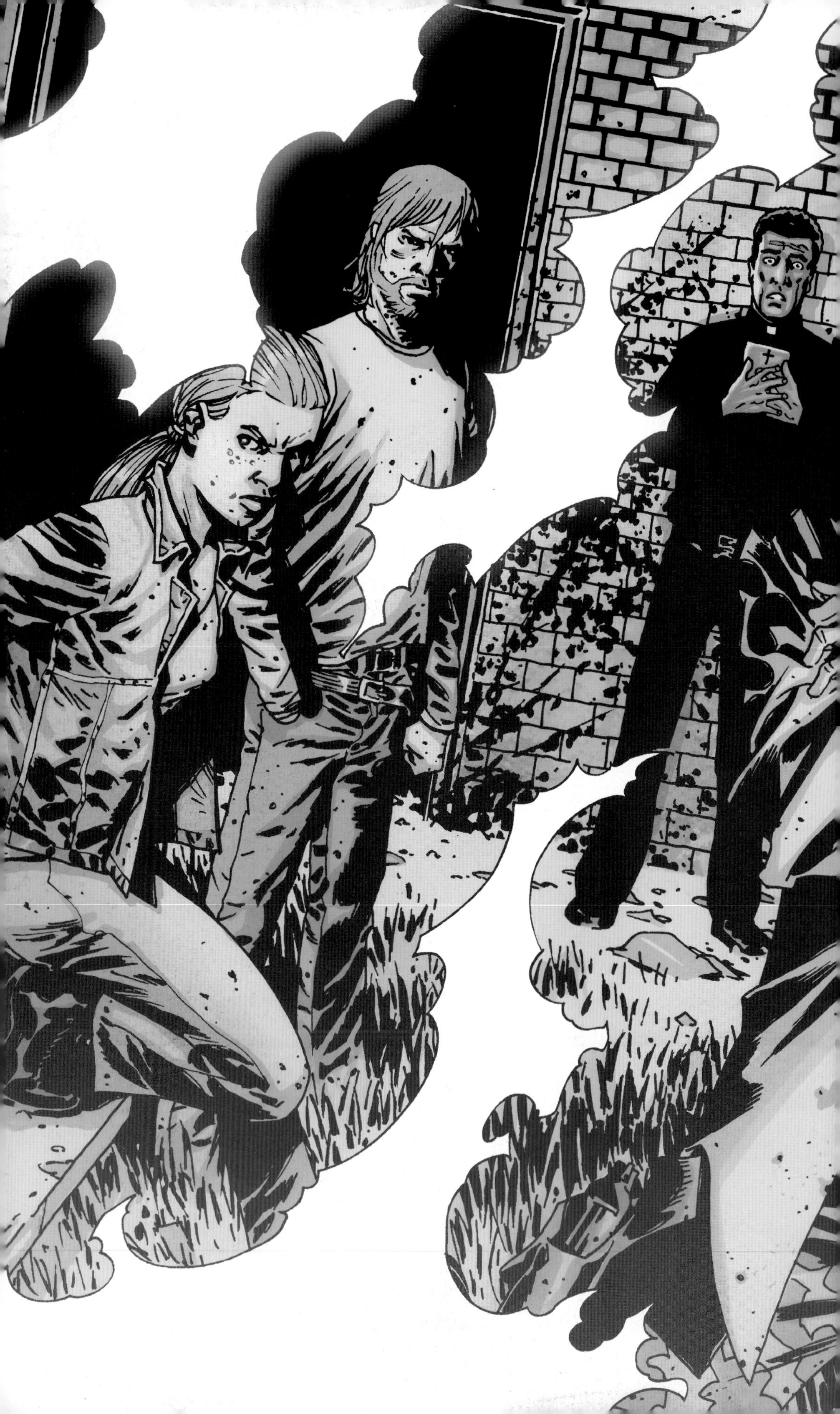

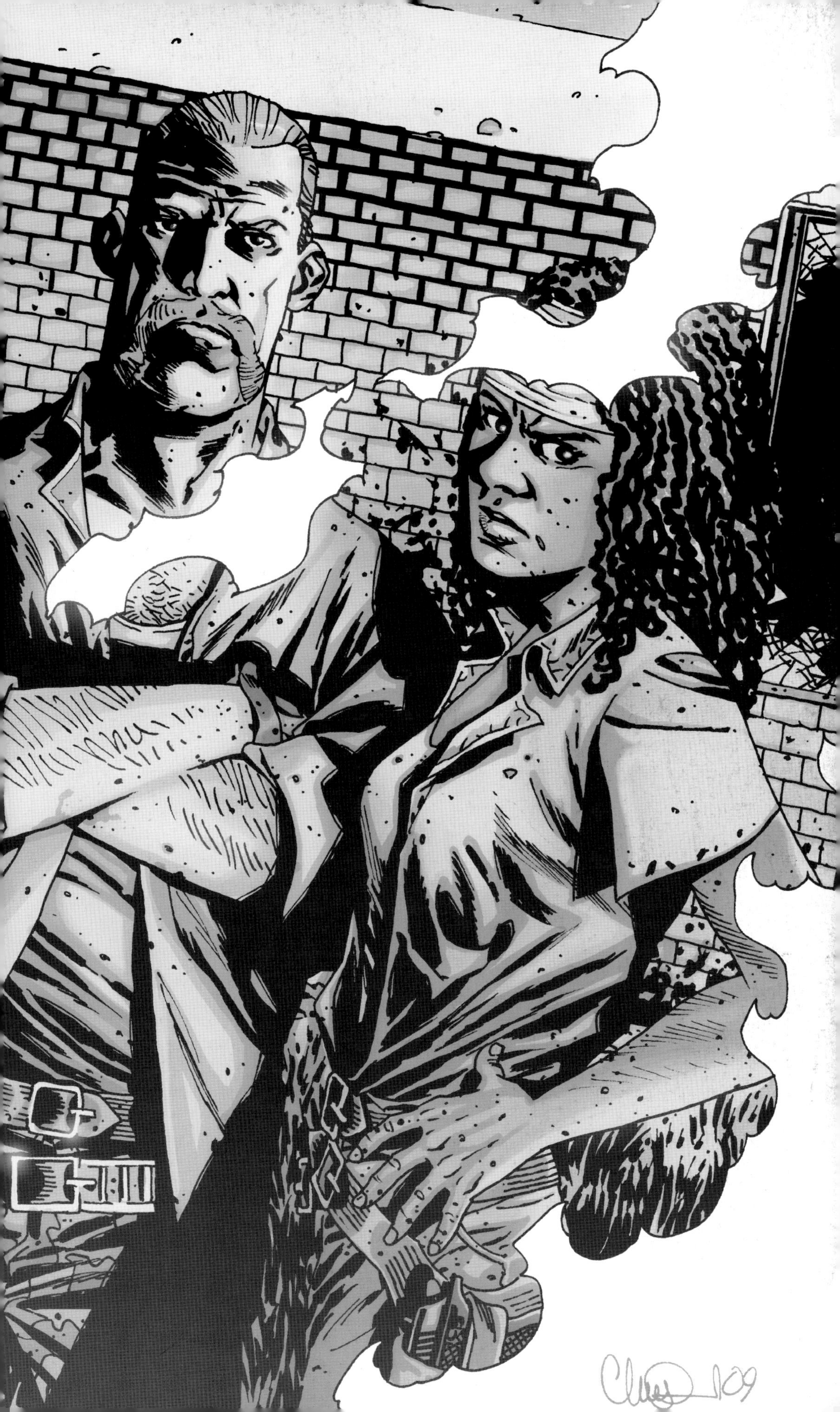

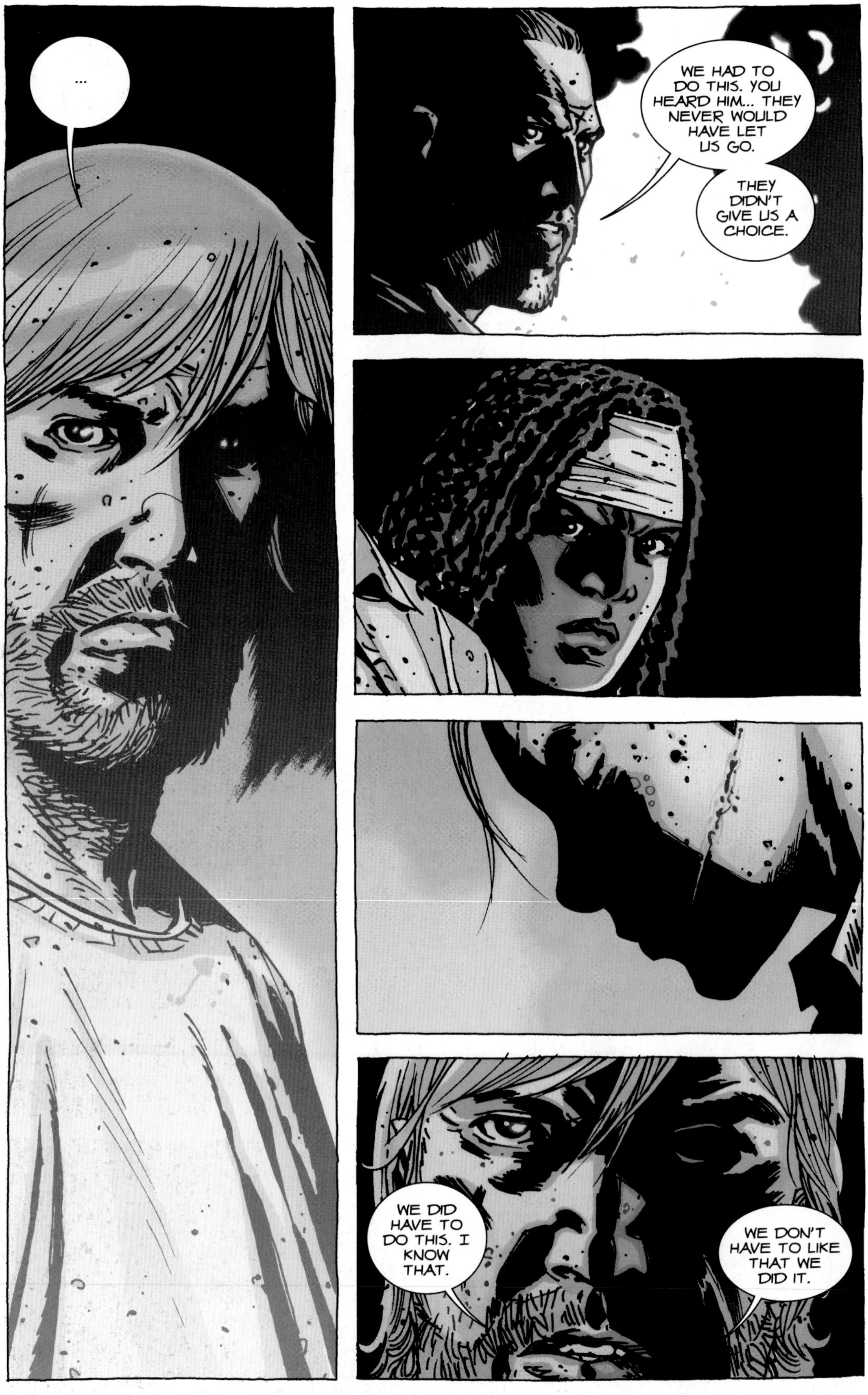
...
WE HAD TO DO THIS. YOU HEARD HIM... THEY NEVER WOULD HAVE LET US GO.
THEY DIDN'T GIVE US A CHOICE.
WE DID HAVE TO DO THIS. I KNOW THAT.
WE DON'T HAVE TO LIKE THAT WE DID IT.

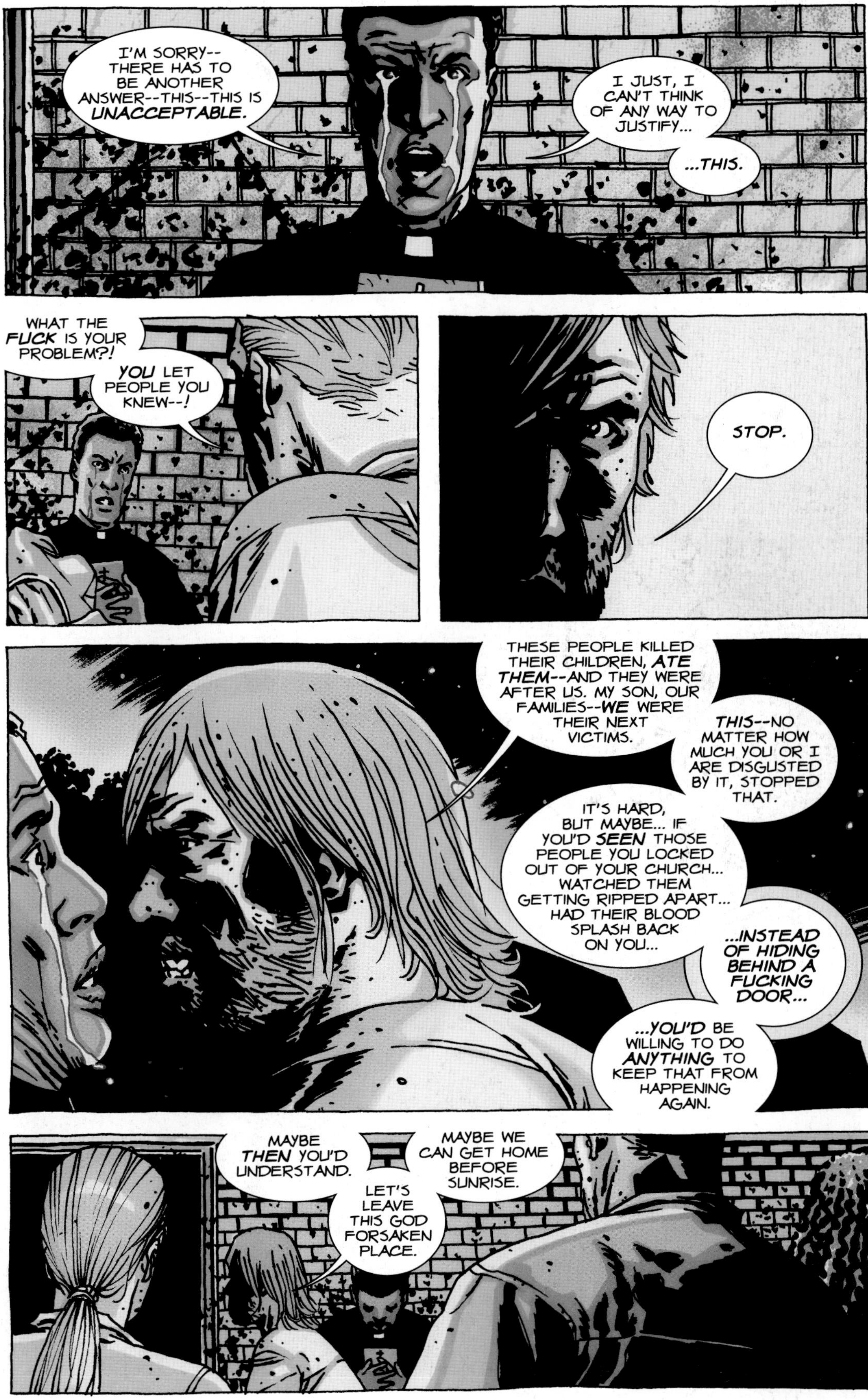
I'M SORRY-- THERE HAS TO BE ANOTHER ANSWER--THIS--THIS IS UNACCEPTABLE.
I JUST, I CAN'T THINK OF ANY WAY TO JUSTIFY...
...THIS.
WHAT THE FUCK IS YOUR PROBLEM?!
YOU LET PEOPLE YOU KNEW--!
STOP.
THESE PEOPLE KILLED THEIR CHILDREN, ATE THEM--AND THEY WERE AFTER US. MY SON, OUR FAMILIES--WE WERE THEIR NEXT VICTIMS.
THIS--NO MATTER HOW MUCH YOU OR I ARE DISGUSTED BY IT, STOPPED THAT.
IT'S HARD, BUT MAYBE... IF YOU'D SEEN THOSE PEOPLE YOU LOCKED OUT OF YOUR CHURCH... WATCHED THEM GETTING RIPPED APART... HAD THEIR BLOOD SPLASH BACK ON YOU...
...INSTEAD OF HIDING BEHIND A FUCKING DOOR...
...YOU'D BE WILLING TO DO ANYTHING TO KEEP THAT FROM HAPPENING AGAIN.
MAYBE THEN YOU'D UNDERSTAND.
MAYBE WE CAN GET HOME BEFORE SUNRISE.
LET'S LEAVE THIS GOD FORSAKEN PLACE.

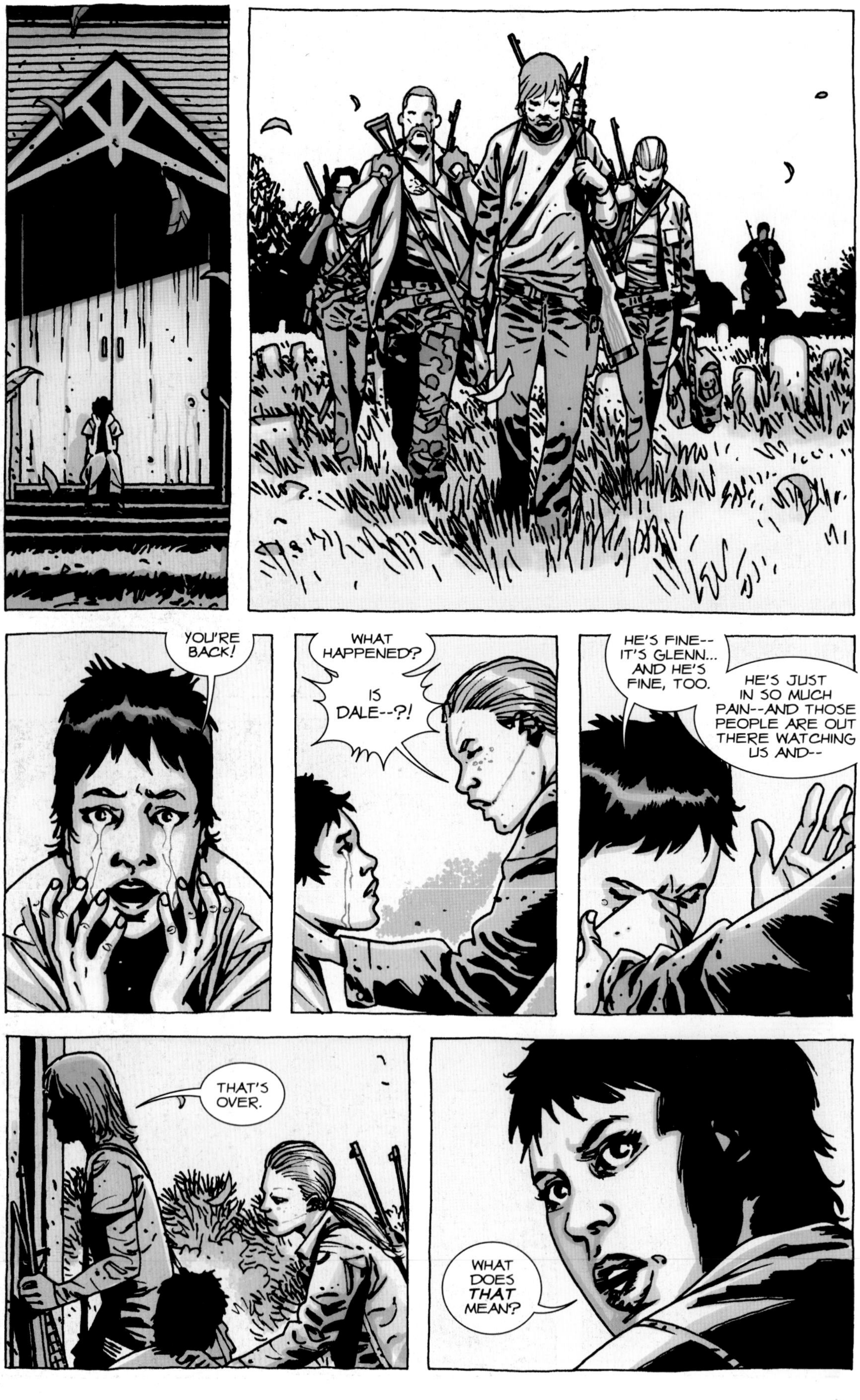
YOU'RE BACK!
WHAT HAPPENED?
IS DALE--?!
HE'S FINE-- IT'S GLENN... AND HE'S FINE, TOO.
HE'S JUST IN SO MUCH PAIN--AND THOSE PEOPLE ARE OUT THERE WATCHING US AND--
THAT'S OVER.
WHAT DOES THAT MEAN?

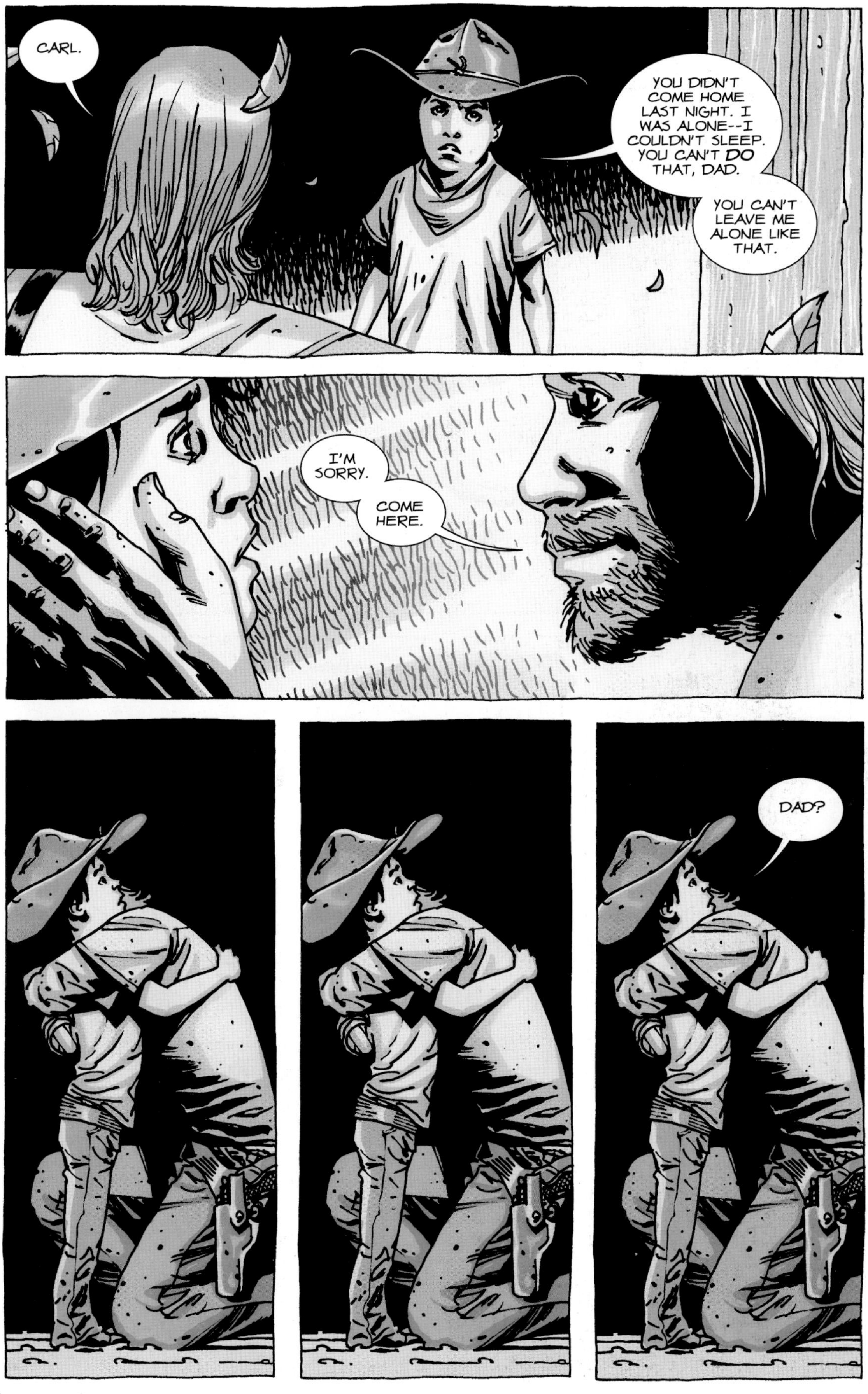
CARL.
YOU DIDN'T COME HOME LAST NIGHT. I WAS ALONE--I COULDN'T SLEEP. YOU CAN'T **DO** THAT, DAD.
YOU CAN'T LEAVE ME ALONE LIKE THAT.
I'M SORRY.
COME HERE.
DAD?

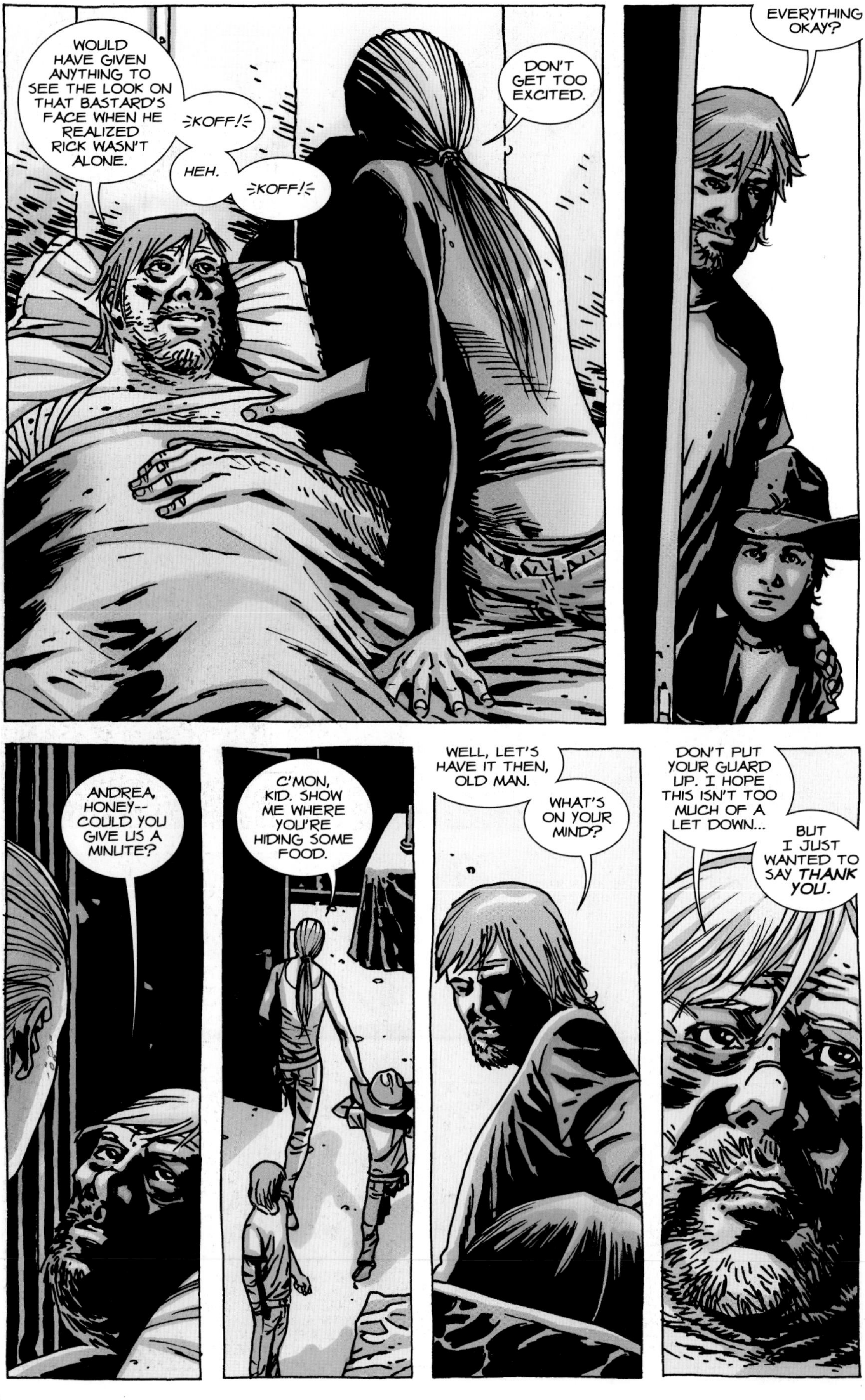
WOULD HAVE GIVEN ANYTHING TO SEE THE LOOK ON THAT BASTARD'S FACE WHEN HE REALIZED RICK WASN'T ALONE.
KOFF!
HEH.
KOFF!
DON'T GET TOO EXCITED.
EVERYTHING OKAY?
ANDREA, HONEY-- COULD YOU GIVE US A MINUTE?
C'MON, KID. SHOW ME WHERE YOU'RE HIDING SOME FOOD.
WELL, LET'S HAVE IT THEN, OLD MAN.
WHAT'S ON YOUR MIND?
DON'T PUT YOUR GUARD UP. I HOPE THIS ISN'T TOO MUCH OF A LET DOWN...
BUT I JUST WANTED TO SAY *THANK YOU.*

FOR WHAT?

FOR--

≈KOFF!≈

"FOR WHAT?," HE SAYS!

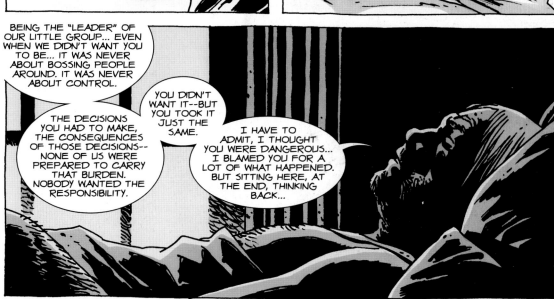

BEING THE "LEADER" OF OUR LITTLE GROUP... EVEN WHEN WE DIDN'T WANT YOU TO BE... IT WAS NEVER ABOUT BOSSING PEOPLE AROUND. IT WAS NEVER ABOUT CONTROL.

THE DECISIONS YOU HAD TO MAKE, THE CONSEQUENCES OF THOSE DECISIONS-- NONE OF US WERE PREPARED TO CARRY THAT BURDEN. NOBODY WANTED THE RESPONSIBILITY.

YOU DIDN'T WANT IT--BUT YOU TOOK IT JUST THE SAME.

I HAVE TO ADMIT, I THOUGHT YOU WERE DANGEROUS... I BLAMED YOU FOR A LOT OF WHAT HAPPENED. BUT SITTING HERE, AT THE END, THINKING BACK...

IT'S EASY TO BLAME YOU FOR WHAT HAPPENED AT TIMES--AND THAT'S YOUR BURDEN FOR TAKING CONTROL--FOR TAKING CARE OF STRANGERS-- TRYING TO PROTECT US.

IT'S NOT AS EASY TO GIVE YOU CREDIT FOR THINGS THAT DIDN'T HAPPEN.

A LOT OF PEOPLE ARE DEAD... BUT LOOK AT HOW LONG THIS GROUP HAS LASTED.

I THINK THAT'S YOUR FAULT, TOO.

YOU HELPED ME LAST THIS LONG, GAVE ME THE TIME I HAD WITH THE BOYS, WITH ANDREA... AND I APPRECIATE THAT VERY VERY MUCH...

SO THANK YOU.

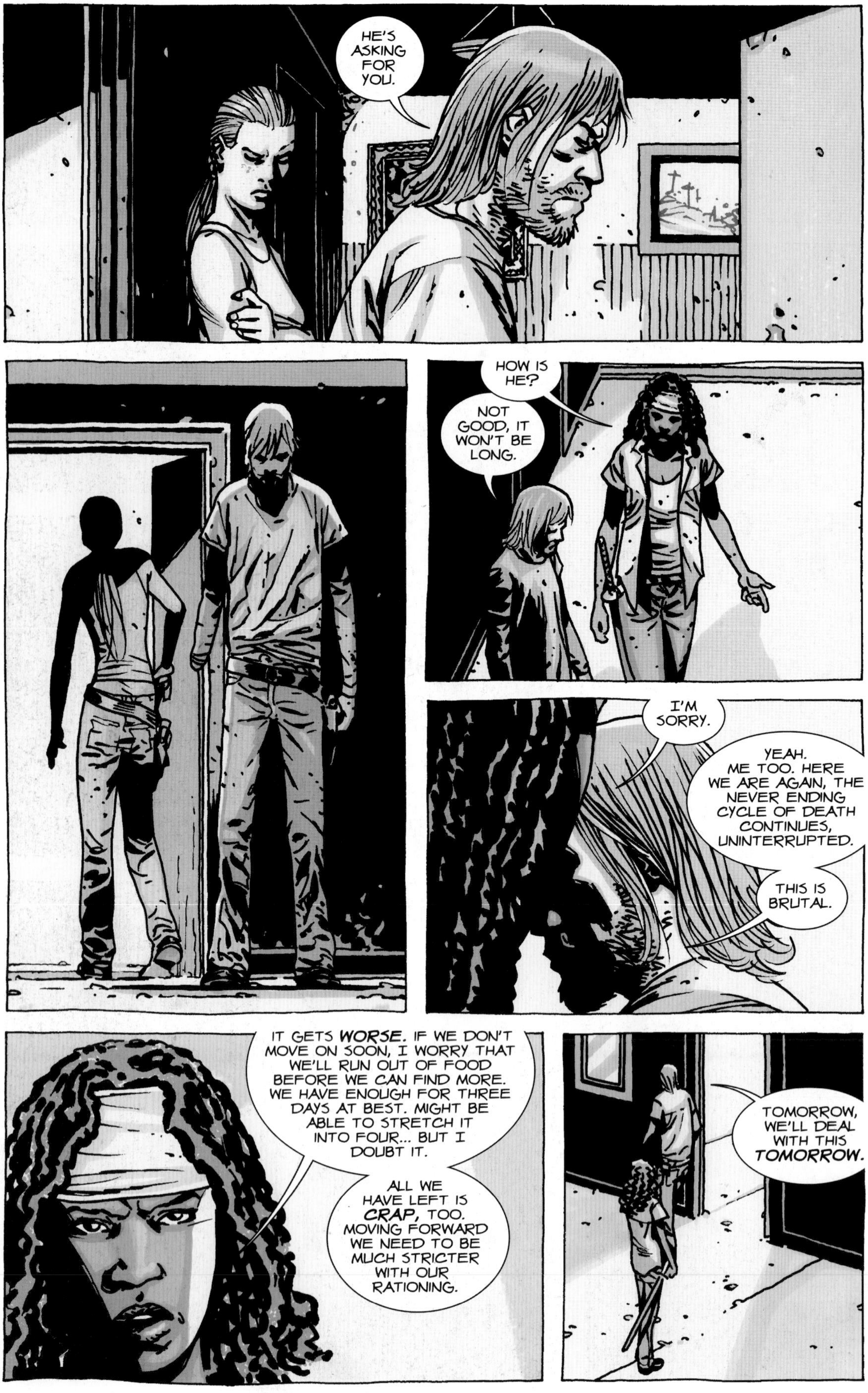
HE'S ASKING FOR YOU.
HOW IS HE?
NOT GOOD, IT WON'T BE LONG.
I'M SORRY.
YEAH. ME TOO. HERE WE ARE AGAIN, THE NEVER ENDING CYCLE OF DEATH CONTINUES, UNINTERRUPTED.
THIS IS BRUTAL.
IT GETS WORSE. IF WE DON'T MOVE ON SOON, I WORRY THAT WE'LL RUN OUT OF FOOD BEFORE WE CAN FIND MORE. WE HAVE ENOUGH FOR THREE DAYS AT BEST. MIGHT BE ABLE TO STRETCH IT INTO FOUR... BUT I DOUBT IT.
ALL WE HAVE LEFT IS CRAP, TOO. MOVING FORWARD WE NEED TO BE MUCH STRICTER WITH OUR RATIONING.
TOMORROW, WE'LL DEAL WITH THIS TOMORROW.

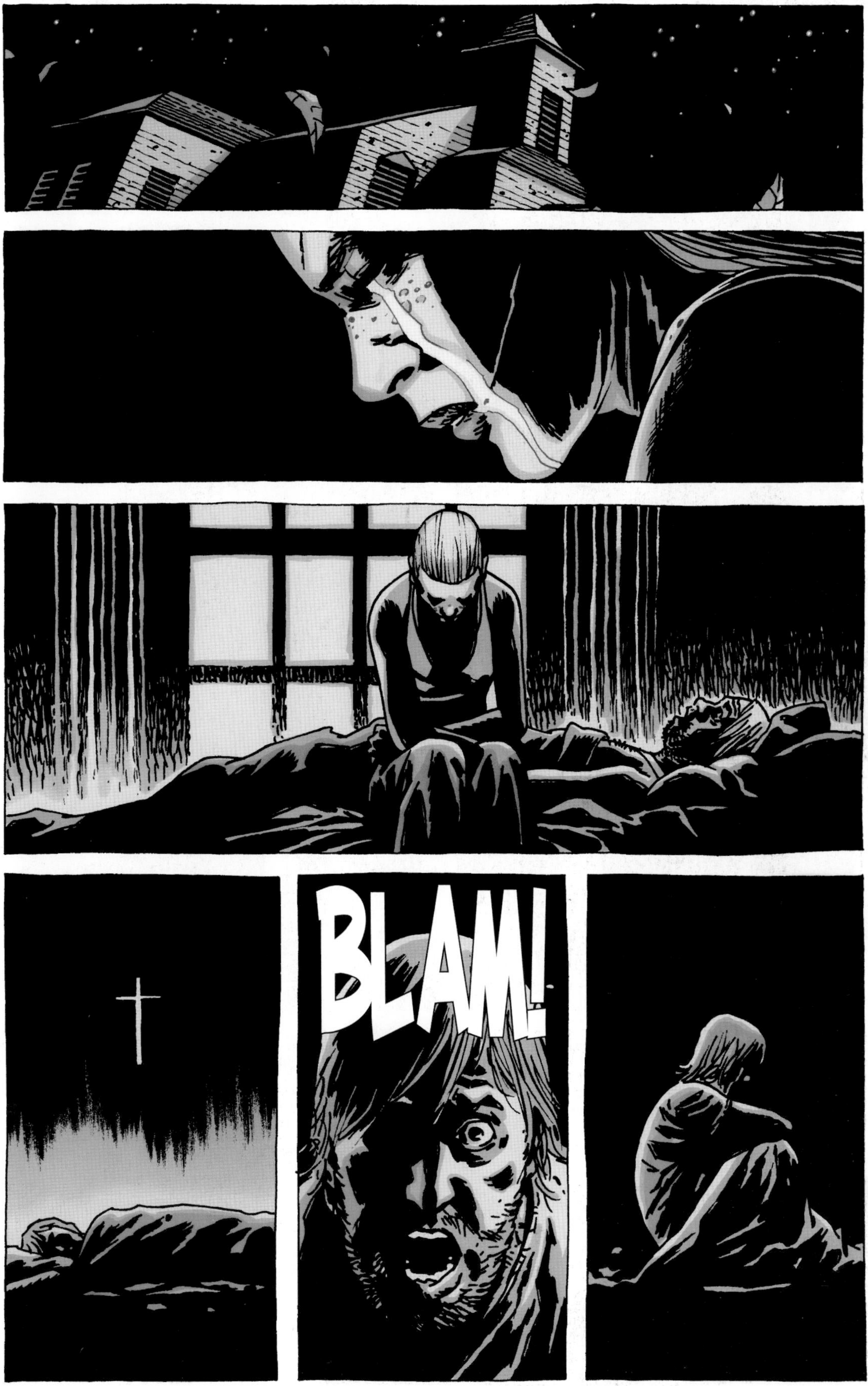
BLAM!

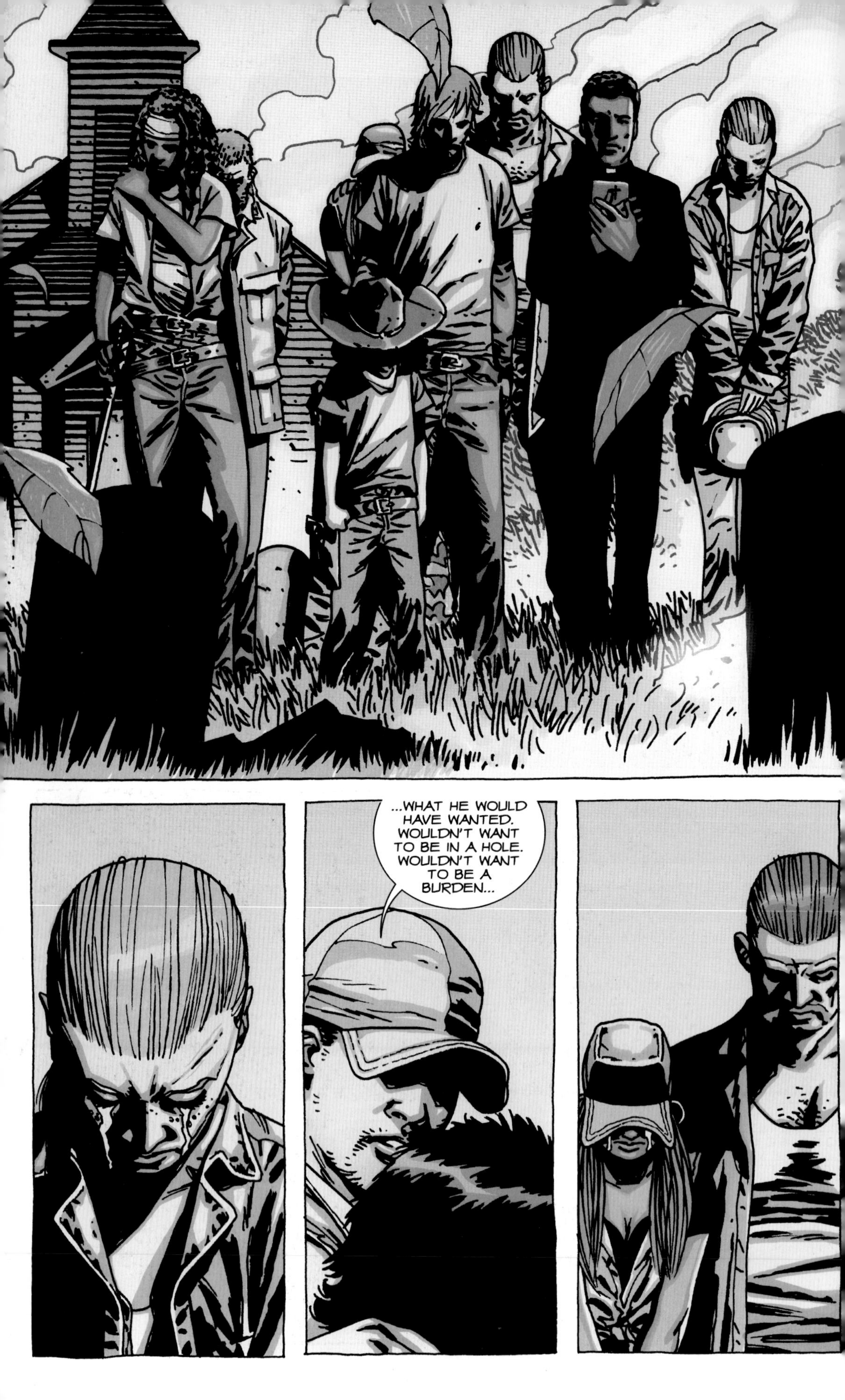
...WHAT HE WOULD HAVE WANTED. WOULDN'T WANT TO BE IN A HOLE. WOULDN'T WANT TO BE A BURDEN...

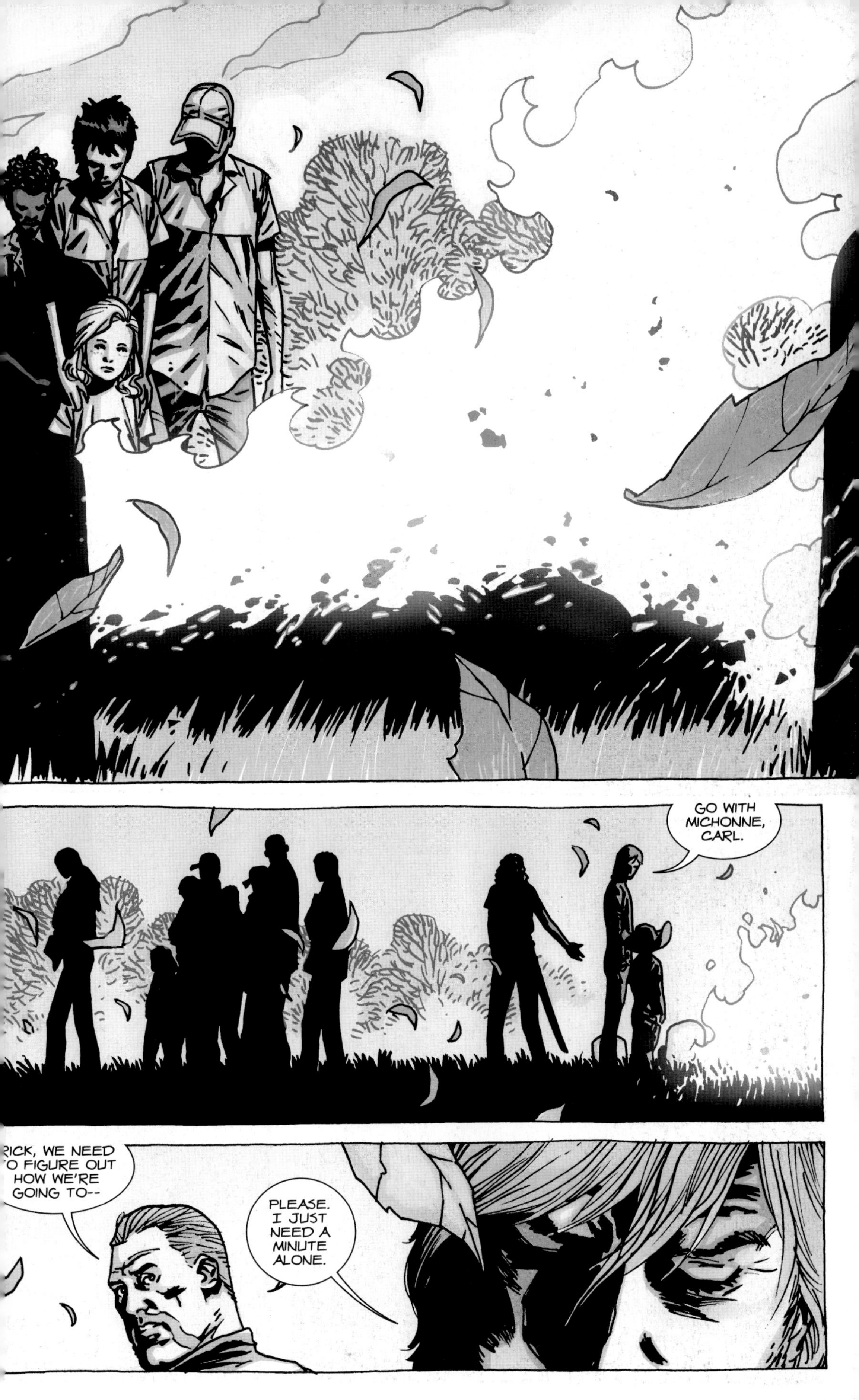
GO WITH MICHONNE, CARL.
RICK, WE NEED TO FIGURE OUT HOW WE'RE GOING TO--
PLEASE. I JUST NEED A MINUTE ALONE.

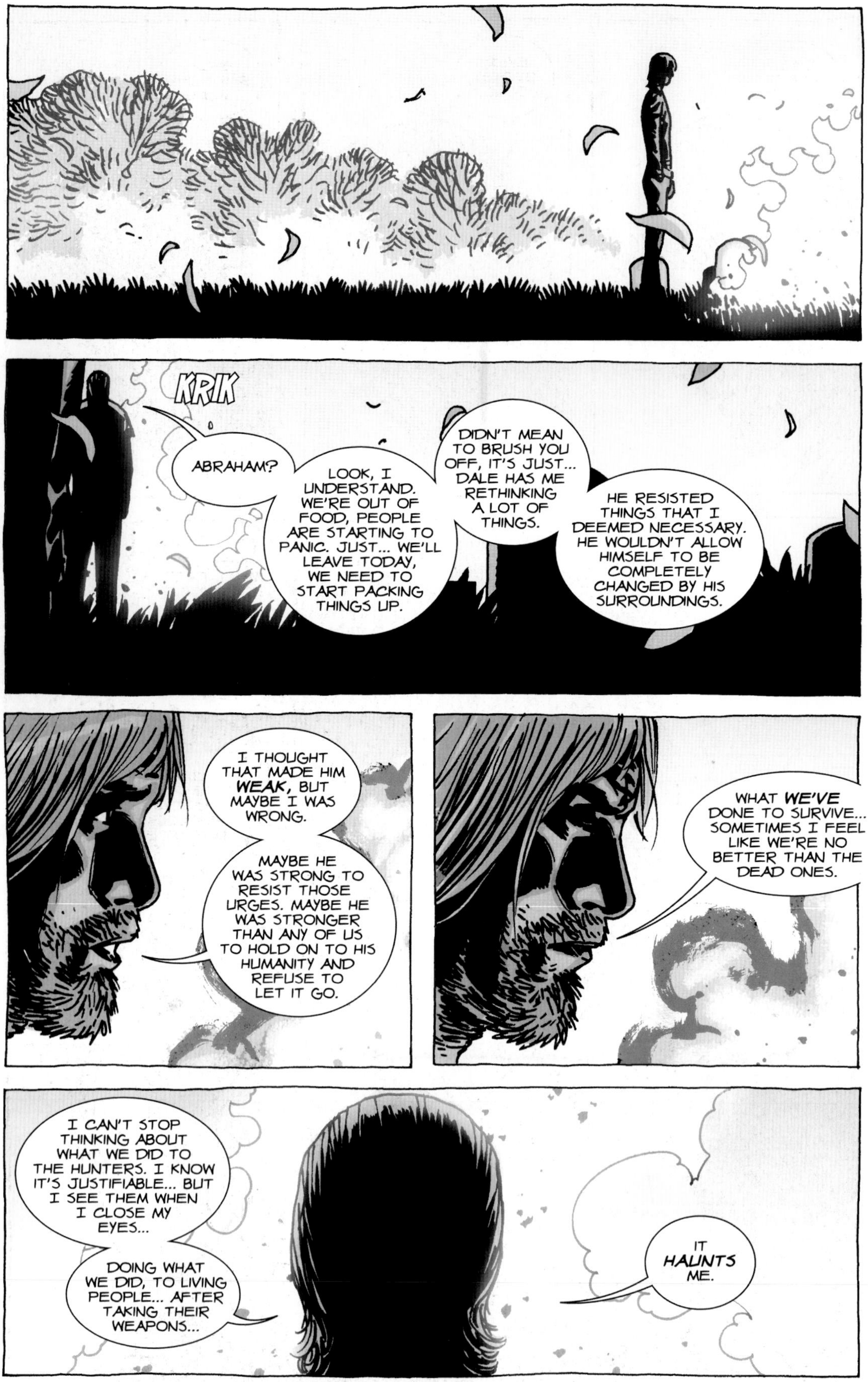
KRIK
ABRAHAM?
LOOK, I UNDERSTAND. WE'RE OUT OF FOOD, PEOPLE ARE STARTING TO PANIC. JUST... WE'LL LEAVE TODAY, WE NEED TO START PACKING THINGS UP.
DIDN'T MEAN TO BRUSH YOU OFF, IT'S JUST... DALE HAS ME RETHINKING A LOT OF THINGS.
HE RESISTED THINGS THAT I DEEMED NECESSARY. HE WOULDN'T ALLOW HIMSELF TO BE COMPLETELY CHANGED BY HIS SURROUNDINGS.
I THOUGHT THAT MADE HIM WEAK, BUT MAYBE I WAS WRONG.
MAYBE HE WAS STRONG TO RESIST THOSE URGES. MAYBE HE WAS STRONGER THAN ANY OF US TO HOLD ON TO HIS HUMANITY AND REFUSE TO LET IT GO.
WHAT WE'VE DONE TO SURVIVE... SOMETIMES I FEEL LIKE WE'RE NO BETTER THAN THE DEAD ONES.
I CAN'T STOP THINKING ABOUT WHAT WE DID TO THE HUNTERS. I KNOW IT'S JUSTIFIABLE... BUT I SEE THEM WHEN I CLOSE MY EYES...
DOING WHAT WE DID, TO LIVING PEOPLE... AFTER TAKING THEIR WEAPONS...
IT HAUNTS ME.

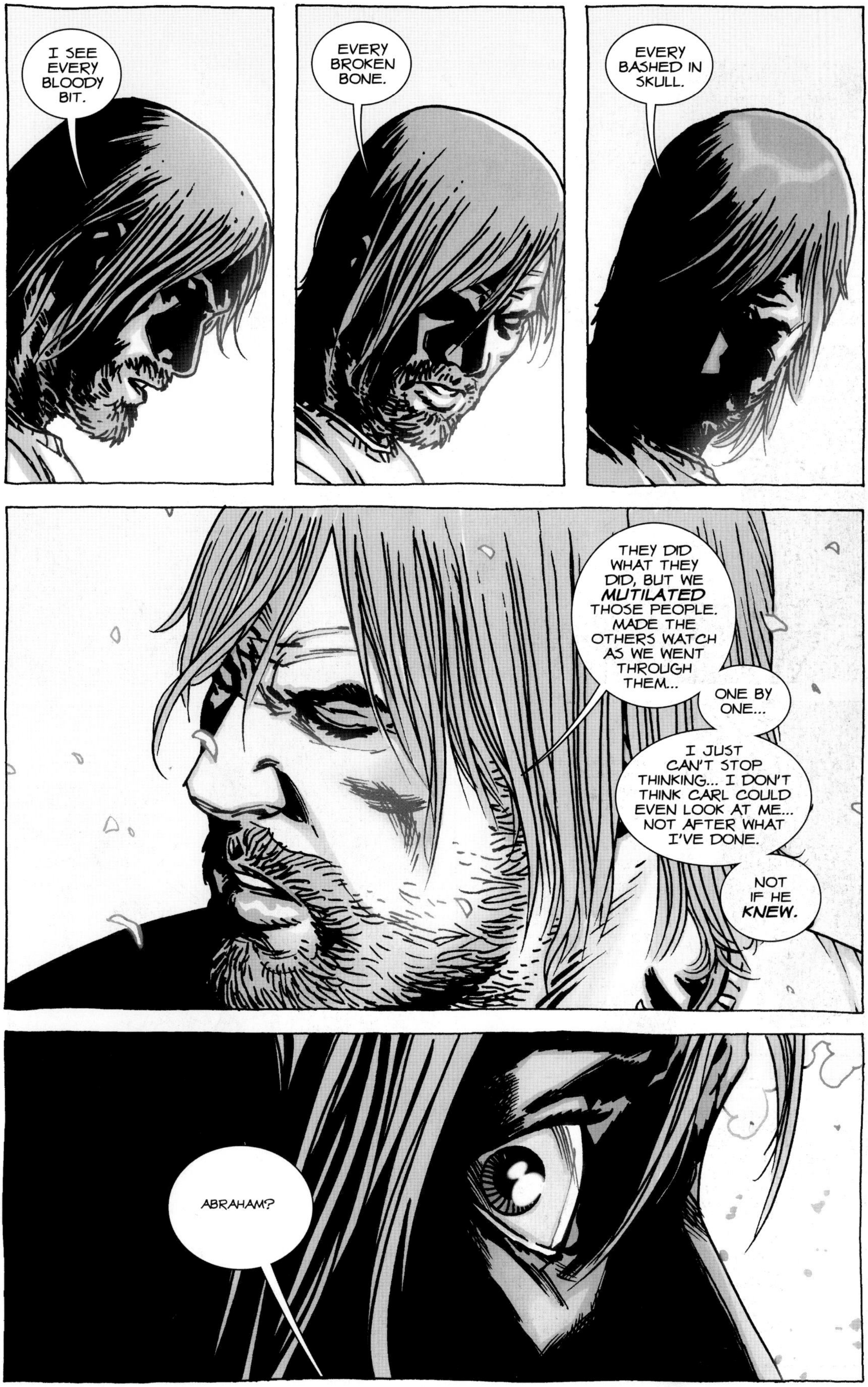

I SEE EVERY BLOODY BIT.
EVERY BROKEN BONE.
EVERY BASHED IN SKULL.
THEY DID WHAT THEY DID, BUT WE *MUTILATED* THOSE PEOPLE. MADE THE OTHERS WATCH AS WE WENT THROUGH THEM...
ONE BY ONE...
I JUST CAN'T STOP THINKING... I DON'T THINK CARL COULD EVEN LOOK AT ME... NOT AFTER WHAT I'VE DONE.
NOT IF HE ***KNEW.***
ABRAHAM?

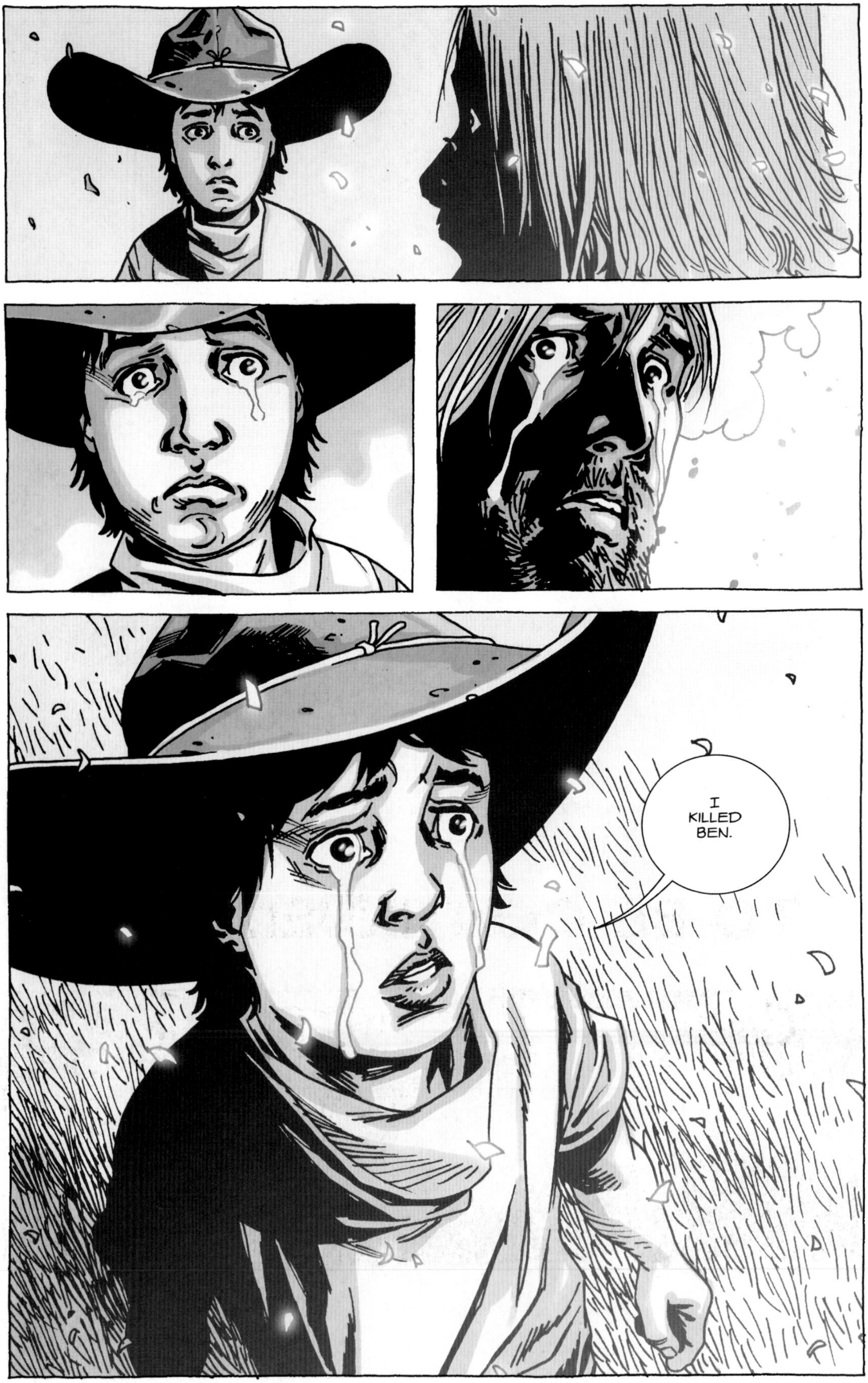
I KILLED BEN.

TO BE CONTINUED...

MORE GREAT BOOKS FROM ROBERT KIRKMAN & IMAGE COMICS!

TECH JACKET
THE BOY FROM EARTH
THE WALKING DEAD
BOOK ONE
BRIT
VOLUME THREE: FUBAR
THE WALKING DEAD
REAPER
BRIT
VOLUME ONE: OLD SOLDIER
PUNCHING

THE ASTOUNDING WOLF-MAN
VOL. 1 TP
ISBN: 978-1-58240-862-0
$14.99
VOL. 2 TP
ISBN: 978-1-60706-007-9
$14.99
VOL. 3 TP
ISBN: 978-1-60706-111-3
$16.99

BATTLE POPE
VOL. 1: GENESIS TP
ISBN: 978-1-58240-572-8
$14.99
VOL. 2: MAYHEM TP
ISBN: 978-1-58240-529-2
$12.99
VOL. 3: PILLOW TALK TP
ISBN: 978-1-58240-677-0
$12.99
VOL. 4: WRATH OF GOD TP
ISBN: 978-1-58240-751-7
$9.99

BRIT
VOL. 1: OLD SOLDIER TP
ISBN: 978-1-58240-678-7
$14.99
VOL. 2: AWOL
ISBN: 978-1-58240-864-4
$14.99
VOL. 3: FUBAR
ISBN: 978-1-60706-061-1
$16.99

CAPES
VOL. 1: PUNCHING THE CLOCK TP
ISBN: 978-1-58240-756-2
$17.99

CLOUDFALL
GRAPHIC NOVEL
$6.95

INVINCIBLE
VOL. 1: FAMILY MATTERS TP
ISBN: 978-1-58240-711-1
$12.99
VOL. 2: EIGHT IS ENOUGH TP
ISBN: 978-1-58240-347-2
$12.99
VOL. 3: PERFECT STRANGERS TP
ISBN: 978-1-58240-793-7
$12.99
VOL. 4: HEAD OF THE CLASS TP
ISBN: 978-1-58240-440-2
$14.95
VOL. 5: THE FACTS OF LIFE TP
ISBN: 978-1-58240-554-4
$14.99
VOL. 6: A DIFFERENT WORLD TP
ISBN: 978-1-58240-579-7
$14.99
VOL. 7: THREE'S COMPANY TP
ISBN: 978-1-58240-656-5
$14.99
VOL. 8: MY FAVORITE MARTIAN TP
ISBN: 978-1-58240-683-1
$14.99
VOL. 9: OUT OF THIS WORLD TP
ISBN: 978-1-58240-827-9
$14.99
VOL. 10: WHO'S THE BOSS TP
ISBN: 978-1-60706-013-0
$16.99
VOL. 11: HAPPY DAYS TP
ISBN: 978-1-60706-062-8
$16.99
ULTIMATE COLLECTION, VOL. 1 HC
ISBN 978-1-58240-500-1
$34.95
ULTIMATE COLLECTION, VOL. 2 HC
ISBN: 978-1-58240-594-0
$34.99
ULTIMATE COLLECTION, VOL. 3 HC
ISBN: 978-1-58240-763-0
$34.99
ULTIMATE COLLECTION, VOL. 4 HC
ISBN: 978-1-58240-989-4
$34.99
ULTIMATE COLLECTION, VOL. 5 HC
ISBN: 978-1-60706-116-8
$34.99
THE OFFICIAL HANDBOOK OF THE INVINCIBLE UNIVERSE TP
ISBN: 978-1-58240-831-6
$12.99
THE COMPLETE INVINCIBLE LIBRARY, VOL. 1 HC
ISBN: 978-1-58240-718-0
$125.00

THE WALKING DEAD
VOL. 1: DAYS GONE BYE TP
ISBN: 978-1-58240-672-5
$9.99
VOL. 2: MILES BEHIND US TP
ISBN: 978-1-58240-413-4
$14.99
VOL. 3: SAFETY BEHIND BARS TP
ISBN: 978-1-58240-487-5
$14.99
VOL. 4: THE HEART'S DESIRE TP
ISBN: 978-1-58240-530-8
$14.99
VOL. 5: THE BEST DEFENSE TP
ISBN: 978-1-58240-612-1
$14.99
VOL. 6: THIS SORROWFUL LIFE TP
ISBN: 978-1-58240-684-8
$14.99
VOL. 7: THE CALM BEFORE TP
ISBN: 978-1-58240-828-6
$14.99
VOL. 8: MADE TO SUFFER TP
ISBN: 978-1-58240-883-5
$14.99
VOL. 9: HERE WE REMAIN TP
ISBN: 978-1-60706-022-2
$14.99
VOL. 10: THE ROAD AHEAD TP
ISBN: 978-1-60706-075-8
$14.99
VOL. 11: FEAR THE HUNTERS TP
ISBN: 978-1-60706-181-6
$14.99
BOOK ONE HC
ISBN: 978-1-58240-619-0
$29.99
BOOK TWO HC
ISBN: 978-1-58240-698-5
$29.99
BOOK THREE HC
ISBN: 978-1-58240-825-5
$29.99
BOOK FOUR HC
ISBN: 978-1-60706-000-0
$29.99
THE WALKDING DEAD DELUXE HARDCOVER, VOL. 2
SBN: 978-1-60706-029-7
$100.00

REAPER
GRAPHIC NOVEL
$6.95

TECH JACKET
VOL. 1: THE BOY FROM EARTH TP
ISBN: 978-1-58240-771-5
$14.99

TALES OF THE REALM
HARDCOVER
ISBN: 978-1-58240-426-0
$34.95
TRADE PAPERBACK
ISBN: 978-1-58240-394-6
$14.95

OFFICIAL HANDBOOK OF THE
INVINCIBLE
UNIVERSE
INVINCIBLE
THREE'S COMPANY
THE ASTOUNDING
WOLF-MAN
VOLUME ONE
INVINCIBLE
HAPPY DAYS
THE WALKING DEAD
THE WALKING DEAD
BOOK THREE

TO FIND YOUR NEAREST COMIC BOOK STORE, CALL:
1-888-COMIC-BOOK